Under The Big Sky

What Heaven hath joined together... let no man cut asunder.

by

S. Bryan Gonzales

Bloomington, IN Milton Keynes, UK

authorHOUSE®

AuthorHouse™
1663 Liberty Drive, Suite 200
Bloomington, IN 47403
www.authorhouse.com
Phone: 1-800-839-8640

AuthorHouse™ UK Ltd.
500 Avebury Boulevard
Central Milton Keynes, MK9 2BE
www.authorhouse.co.uk
Phone: 08001974150

First published by AuthorHouse 11/15/2006

ISBN: 978-1-4259-6525-9 (e)
ISBN: 978-1-4259-6524-2 (sc)

Library of Congress Control Number: 2006909539

Printed in the United States of America
Bloomington, Indiana

This book is printed on acid-free paper.

Dedicated to Brown Bear, Golden Bear, and Diane

CHAPTER 1

The explosion was earsplitting. Thousand-pound hooves slammed into the dirt, reeling dust violently into the air. *Help me!*

The boy fell.

Then came the crushing—blood squirting and soaking the ground. It was the relentless crack of bones echoing throughout the stands that made Cash sick to his stomach. He wanted to retch.

Snarling deep within its throat, eyes rolled back, whites fully revealed—there was no stopping. The angry bull snorted—mouth foaming. Without warning, it reared-up and spun wildly—completely insane.

Where were these thoughts coming from?

Over and over, Cash could see it plain as day. He could hear the screams as if he was physically there. *But where was there? Who was this boy?* He certainly didn't look familiar—at least no one he knew.

Snap!

Abruptly, Cash was heralded back to reality with the crack of the ruler on the surface of his desk. "Mr. McCollum, rodeo daydreaming again?" Mr. Vincent, an old former Marine—stood looming over Cash's head as if he were still assuming DI duties at Paris Island. "Perhaps we should all buy a ticket?"

What a smartass, Cash sourly thought. *Treating me as if I'm one of his dumbfuck recruits. Hell!*

Several snickers erupted—rousing an impish, demonic stir throughout the room. Pushing himself back up in his seat, he felt defiance gnaw at his control. He hated shit like this. Bowing his head to the desk, he sucked in air and allowed an angry tooth to bite mercilessly into the flesh of his inner mouth. Be damned if he was going to allow anyone catch him in a full-freckled burn.

With the sound of the teacher's footsteps trailing back to the blackboard, Cash's eyes remained focused on the open textbook—avoiding everyone's stare. Feeling his heart return back into a normal beat, he allowed his mind to slip quietly back into a shadowy, secluded dream world.

Sniffing, inhaling the ever-present residue pine smoke embedded in the fuzzy flannel fabric of his shirt cuff, his thoughts, this time, escaped down an old meandering dirt road leading to a weather-weary house nestled deep in the river bottoms.

This was *his* home.

No, the McCollum's didn't have a lot of class… they didn't need to; it was their pride, determination, and fierce independence that ran as thick as Irish stew in their blood. It was what gave them solid grounding under their feet.

Since the cattle drives, his Texas ancestors had settled along the rocky banks and bluffs of the mighty Yellowstone—their lives protected from the never-ending winds blowing across the stark hide of an area known as the Great Open. Cowboys by nature, roughnecks at heart, five generations created a heritage coveted by many—beginning with the old ranch house they all called home. His great, great grand dad had started out with two bedrooms, large kitchen and a modest parlor area. Through the years, as the family had grown, additions had been added to where there were now four bedrooms—two added upstairs in a loft overlooking the living room, and a bathroom to replace the outhouse.

Cattle herding and the ever-lasting tug of the rodeo circuit seemed to weave into every nerve and fiber of each McCollum. In Cash's case, he seemed to be bit with a double portion of the bug, enticing him to spend many free hours in the corral getting dusty and collecting a fair share of manure on his pair of well-worn boots.

"Don't you think it's time to retire 'em?" His dad would occasionally chide him.

"Why?" Cash would always come back with a grin. "They feel like a glove."

With eyes scanning the room, he popped off a huff. *To hell with the open book on his desk.* For God's sake, he could barely concentrate—between the strange daydream and the incredible weather outside—it was torture to his soul. Math equations on the page seemed to jumble together in one massive, geometric heap—tempting him to impatiently bounce the end of his pencil repeatedly off a blank sheet of notebook paper.

And so it was, Cash shoved his frustration into a mental closet of indifference. He'd concern himself about it all later.

Glancing up toward the clock, his heart skipped a beat—five more minutes. All he could envision right now was Brownie, his feisty quarter kicking up heels with a heap of dust in the small corral located out behind the grain house.   He could hardly wait to harness him up—tossing an old wooly blanket and saddle on that gracefully curved back. It seemed to be what both of them lived for—afternoon rides along the river banks, then on up into the rugged crevices of the badlands. Impatiently, a tinge of excitement shot through his veins—he could already feel the fresh autumn air whip across his ruddy, chiseled face and strawberry blond hair.

Sure enough, at the stroke of three there began a hurried shuffle toward the door like a cattle stampede. Falling in line, Cash scuffed his boot heels over the newly waxed floor. He couldn't help but notice everyone else's desire to get out of the building as well.

You know, he told himself, *it's a damned sin to keep kids cooped up like a bunch of chickens on such a perfect autumn day.*

Afternoons such as this one certainly didn't come often… especially in Montana.

Fumbling his long, slender fingers with the combination lock, he heard a somewhat familiar voice from over his shoulder.

"Thought today would never end."

"Yeah", chuckled Cash, tossing his books on the shelf, "…felt like I was gonna blow in Vincent's class."

He slammed his locker door shut and turned to find himself gazing face-front into a black t-shirt. *Geez!* He told himself. Talk about being engulfed. Cocking his head upwards, his eyes became welded to the bluest blue he'd ever seen. Shit, he never knew the varsity football's tight-end was so big, nor his eyes so blue.

"Yeah, we all thought you were going to do just that after he whacked your desk." Instantly, a full, broad smile flooded Travis' rugged, Val Kilmer-handsome face. "…especially when you turned beet red."

Resembling a brick wall, or an invincible Roman guard—every tough, curved muscle in this giant's chest, arms, and back seemed to swell and explode through the skin-tight shirt fabric. Moreover, from his heavy dark-lined forehead and brow, to that finely sculpted squared-off jaw, the boy standing before Cash resembled a robot or machine than a mere mortal.

Travis Hunter was an enigma… a true riddle. Cash knew little about him except that he had come from California with his mother one year ago. Why they had moved up here, he wasn't sure. Mrs. Hunter was the director at one of the banks in town. Local gossip was that she had just left her husband and had moved back with her only child to be near family in Miles City.

From Cash's perspective, Travis appeared to be the conceited type—stuck on himself. Smart, good-looking and very athletic, he obviously had what it took to quickly move up the social ranks, into the inner-circle of the 'SNOBS' crowd—cynically dubbed by the others in school. And while he was friendly and quite audacious, yet his mannerisms were very arrogant towards those seeping from lower ranks.

What the hell did he want? Never making a special point to talk with him before, Cash wondered to himself, why now? There was no reason to have their paths cross; although something inside made him feel good to have this big jock approach him. Something even stranger, he liked looking at Travis. He couldn't take his gaze off those piercing eyes of his. A funny, prickly feeling shot up his spine and throughout the rest of his body. Suddenly, he felt fully awake—his senses charged to explosion.

"What's up?" he lowered his voice, struggling to remain cool, but all the while his hands trembling. Thank God he was holding on to his jacket. His fingers quietly forged a death grip around the supple leather.

"I heard you're selling a paint."

Well, that was odd, Cash went on to think. Travis' words sailed through the air light and smooth—something that didn't correlate with that body of his.

"It's my brother's." Cash squinted, studying him closely. *Humph*, he thought. Off the cuff, Travis didn't seem like the horseman type. Glued to that sleek, red Viper of his, he appeared more like a 'material boy' than a 'back to nature' kind of guy. No offense, but there was no way he could picture this guy tending to anything running around with four legs and a tail—especially a horse.

"How old is it?" Travis asked, slowly shifting his position from one leg to the other, his arms crossed.

"About two years." Feeling braver, Cash began to step away from the wall. "She's a good mare—lots of life." A smile snuck across his face as he could not help envisioning her skip and buck around in the field, avoiding Clayton and that annoying saddle of his at all cost.

"I'd like to see it." Travis said, apparently noticing the grin. Uncrossing his arms, he allowed his eyes to mechanically rove over Cash as if he were the bull's eye on a target.

"Give Clayton a call. He'll be glad to show 'er off."

At that point, Cash locked. He couldn't talk. He couldn't move—he didn't want to. Somewhere deep inside, a thought whisked his mind—sending a swell of wetness throughout his throat and mouth. *What would those lips of Travis' be like to kiss? Would they be soft or hard?*

For God's sake! He quickly snapped out of it—instantly shifting his gaze into all directions—but Travis'. *What was the matter with him?* Suddenly, he needed air… *lots* of air.

"Right," responded Travis with a continued stare. "I'll give him a ring." Then with a pause, he purposefully extended his hand toward the awkward cowboy, and said, "Thanks."

He probably wouldn't have given their little chat a second thought, but then came the handshake. If there was ever a moment of truth… slipping his fingers into Travis' palm, Cash expected an immediate release. How wrong he was. To his surprise, he was caught in a hold that seemed to last forever. In fact, Travis appeared to be in no hurry of letting go.

Not sure where all these wild feelings were coming from, Cash nervously shuffled his legs to manage a situation that was unbelievably growing out of hand. *What the hell?!*

Eventually, the undaunted jock relented, releasing Cash's hand and allowing a hint of a grin to slide slowly over his mouth. He looked pleased… *very pleased*. "See ya later."

"Yeah, no problem." Overwrought with a shock of hormones, Cash could barely squeak out his words.

Pushing the school doors open, he grabbed for the pack of crumpled smokes from his pocket, and with jittery fingers, he fired one up. *God*, he asked himself. *What was up with that?* In one way, it was flattering to have someone like Travis Hunter approach him since he never seemed to cross social boundaries—the football team being his *total* life. On the other hand, it was unnerving. Something was up. Maybe he was reading too much into this, but it seemed Travis wanted more. Something like… *oh, come on, don't be stupid!* He swore at himself. *That's impossible!* He didn't seem like that type of guy. But yet, there had been that look and the linger in the hand shake. Taking the smoke deeply into his lungs, he felt a dizzy-crazy buzz settle in. Why was he shaking like this? His lanky, jean-torn legs carried him quickly across the broken pavement. He couldn't get to his pick-up fast enough.

The memory of the encounter with Travis still lingered in Cash's mind when he arrived at the ranch. An unsettled sense remained as he shut the engine off and crawled out of the cab. What was it that he sensed back there? Why the arousal? Was he attracted to Travis? Was he attracted to men? Even though it bothered him, there was something inside he found deeply exciting. And while he had always been told attraction to other men was wrong, somehow, within his conscience, it seemed right. Natural. Maybe he was reading more into it than what it actually was. His mom always said he had a wild imagination, like the time he had insisted a ghost was hanging around in the upstairs loft. He could have sworn he had seen his great grandma dusting off the book shelf at the end of the hallway. She had looked so real, hunched over, meticulously moving her duster across the top in a manner done many times before when he was a small boy.

Perhaps that was it—his usual tendency to overreact... and, *of course,* he wasn't gay.

Making his way towards the house, he bounded up the steps and forced open the heavy oak door. The faint hint of livestock musk, fireplace ashes, and an enticing aroma of baking biscuits filled his nostrils. He loved it. It made him feel safe and warm—a feeling he would never verbally admit to anyone else in the family lest he be ridiculed to death. The McCollum's were a tough breed, hard to understand, and difficult to communicate with. But there was a certain stability that seem to bring their peculiar tendencies into perspective. And in spite of all the irregularity, there was a place where it all made sense... plain and simple, with open honesty, and no complications... the type of set-up a guy could be comfortable with.

"Cash, is that you?" A voice called from upstairs.

"Yeah, Mom. I'm goin' out and spend some time with Brownie," he replied, making his way out to the kitchen. He heard her footsteps come down the stairs.

A slight, graceful, red-headed woman dressed in jeans, sneakers and old work shirt, Janice McCollum stood at the entryway to the kitchen with a small package in her hands. "I'm runnin' over to see Dad for a minute, then to the post office to get this off to Clint."

"Okay," Cash smiled as he reached over the counter, lifting the lid from the cookie jar. He was in the mood for something sweet. Something chocolate—one of his strange cravings—something else he'd never dare admit.

Soon, with bit and bridle, blanket and saddle, Brownie was gracefully adorned. Cash always loved fittin' his horse out. The two of them made their way up the long driveway, anticipating the afternoon venture. His horse's clip-clopping gait echoed on the rocky gravel with ecstasy.

"Hey boy," Cash leaned forward and whispered in the old quarter's ears. "You're havin' fun aren't you?"

Understanding the words, Brownie nodded. Cocking his silky brown head to the right, his wispy mane was caught by the breeze. With a small snort, and a turn of the hooves, they left the road and wandered up the hillside beyond a patch of thorn bushes and cottonwoods. Around the small creek bed, at the other end of the ravine, Brownie increased his speed. Bounding past the property fence and on toward the highway, they continued to the large grassy field. Cash knew where they were heading. The gentle quarter loved spending time skulking about in the sage brush edging the badlands. There were usually lots of critters in that neck of the woods—rabbits, ground squirrels, and countless birds hanging about, feasting on goodies such as wild berries. "I know where you're goin'." Cash chuckled. "You wanna go stir some nests, huh?" This time Brownie ignored Cash. There was mischievous anticipation in his trot, as if he had more important things on his mind.

9

Cash simply went along for the ride. He knew he was not in control of this one. The best thing he could do was sit back and go with the flow.

Looking into the cloudless, deep-blue sky, he took a long breath. The hassles of school seemed a world away. With the faint, sweet aroma of sage nearby, the gnawing stress that marinated his muscles from the day seemed to fade out with the last rays of sunlight stretching across the unending expanse. Every now and then, a whispering breeze would blow around his hat and past his ears. Pulling the collar around his neck, he buttoned up as a chill buried itself in his bones—a gentle reminder that winter was just around the corner.

As they headed back to the corral, the last hues of blue sky began to deepen into violet with the hint of stars in the eastern horizon. What time was it? He didn't realize it had gotten so late. A growl from his stomach told him he was hungry. Instantly, he recalled the earlier smell of stew in the house.

The winds started blowing, howling later that evening—seeming to kick up anything that wasn't bolted or nailed down in the yard. By bedtime, gusts pounded at the panes and under the eaves. Strange, Cash didn't recall hearing a storm heading their way in the forecast. As he crawled into the sack—sliding his legs between the soft fuzz of the flannel sheets, warmth soon crept back into his body. The heavy wool blanket sure felt good tonight, he told himself. Pulling the covers up around his shoulders, he snuggled in for a good night's sleep.

As he lay still, the hazy memory of the locker scene with Travis kept creeping back into his mind—bringing on its own whirlwind of raging squalls between his legs. The bottom line, why was he thinking about Travis in this way? How could he get to sleep—being all charged up like this? Closing his eyes, he could see him—again and again. There was no doubt; Cash loved looking deep into that big jock's grin, his ice-blue eyes, and those cherry-red, full lips. Vividly, he could still recall the hint of sweet cologne—well-mixed with a batch of musky sweat. Even now, his mouth salivated.

The question was now, what did he want to do with all those good-looking things? A picture can only go so far. This thought perplexed him greatly. Was there a drive inside coaxing him to go further? Was he... truth be said, was he *gay*?

Well, up to now, he'd never really thought of it before—it had never been an issue. Shit, he'd always considered himself attracted to girls, women. He loved looking at cute ones, small and petite. He even thought about asking a few of them out from time to time. But somehow, situations never really worked out right. Lying in his bed, this particular evening, thinking about all this stuff, he had to be honest with himself. Never once, could he recall a time of truly fantasying in gettin' it on with a gal—bonin' the livin' shit outta her.

Eventually a funny feeling settled over him. Should he be alarmed? Concerned? Worried that something might be wrong? It made him become somewhat anxious, but there was something stronger that tantalized him—tickling his fancy and kicking his heart into high gear. Picturing him and Travis together—why, it looked fuckin' great.

It must have been past midnight when sleep finally overtook him. The last time he had glanced at the clock was just before twelve. Somewhere, in the midst of his dream state, and the nagging need to take a leak, various people and events floated in and out of his sub-conscious—including the one and only...Travis Hunter.

When the bull ring transformed into a football grid iron, Cash could not tell. Between Brownie, Black Lightning, a mix of cousins, and cinching up Hell in the chute, a tall, extremely well-built man walked out of a cloud of swirling dust wearing shoulder pads, sleek-tight football pants, and cleats. In his hand, he held a helmet. From a distance, he looked like a Greek god—perhaps Achilles marching valiantly into Troy. The closer he walked toward Cash, the more evident it became who it was. Travis wore the same sly grin he had bore in the school hallway.

Suddenly, he found himself alone in a dark locker room—only the faint glow of light radiating from a nearby room. Before realizing what was going on, or where Travis had disappeared, he felt a soft touch of fingers slide underneath his shirt and across his chest. Tenderly, they brushed across his nipples. Travis' big hands felt so good! Somewhere in his mind, he knew he wanted to pull away, but something stronger made him stay. Not moving a muscle, he allowed those smooth, gentle fingers to float effortlessly over his body.

The shrill ringing woke him up. Reaching out, he slammed the alarm clock with his fist. *Damn it! What a time to wake up!* Instantly, his mood went crabby. Just when things were getting interesting.

Pushing himself out from the warmth of the bed, he plopped his feet on the cold, hardwood floor. For Christ's sake, was he simply conjuring all this shit up… indeed, making a damn mountain out of a mole hill! Even though he admitted being attracted to Travis, how could he be sure the feeling was mutual? Being such a hot-shot jock, Travis could have *anyone* he wanted—at the drop of a hat. Why would he want such an ordinary, run-of-the-mill, kind of cowboy? Entertaining that idea bore a mean and ruthless hole into his waking brain.

By the time he got dressed, he had wholeheartedly decided he didn't want to go to school. There was no way he could face Travis. This whole scene, he concluded, was nothing more than a sick, hopeless desire for something that would never be. In spite of it all, he still collected himself—grabbing his jacket and trudging heavy-heartedly down the stairs. And like the sand blowing vigorously against his face, he tackled the day with a gravelly disposition—reluctantly making his way to the pick-up.

All of this could be rightfully blamed upon one reason…

…that shit-assed conversation by the lockers. Since that moment, everything in his life seemed tossed and stirred—jumbled up.

Going back to yesterday afternoon for the millionth time, Cash honestly wondered if all of this was just completely blown out of proportion because of his own stupid, wild imagination. More realistically, Travis was only trying to play with his mind by throwing him that mysterious grin and holding onto his hand too long. If that was the case, then the encounter which had occurred the day before was probably nothing more than a manipulative, condescending expression from a cocky asshole.

If yesterday had been a bear trying to concentrate on studies, today was virtually impossible. In the hallways between classes, at lunch—two tables away, and finally, the algebra class across the aisle, Cash continuously found himself situated in direct eye-shot of Travis.

There's the old saying, "Curiosity kills the cat." Well, Cash was one who could never keep his fingers off a hot stove. Unable to refrain stealing several clandestine glances, he discovered each time his gaze was locked with Travis'. In fact, there wasn't a time he didn't catch Travis watching him—closely spying his every move with prey-like calculation. *Didn't he care that others could be watching them?* This was more than an over-active imagination; something was definitely up, he finally determined. Cat-n-mouse, he figured. He hated to admit what role *he* was playing. The entire scenario made his heart pound wildly in his chest. Why couldn't he just blow this whole thing off and ignore him?

Their little game continued throughout the day until Cash walked down the steps of the school and out to his truck.

"Hey, I've been trying to touch base with you all day."

Recognizing the voice, Cash's heart nearly jumped through his throat. "Well, I've been here." He could hardly believe such a sharp retort could escape from his mouth. Actually, it wasn't the words, but the tone in his voice that made it so cutting.

With an unexpected softness in that tough, masculine face of his, Travis gave a whispered chuckle. "And that you have." Scanning the area nearby, he appeared to be ensuring their privacy was intact before continuing. "You're sort of a hard one to nail down."

Coming to a complete stop, Cash turned on his heals and looked square into Travis' eyes. "Yeah, why's that?" He felt cockiness overtake his innards.

"I don't know," Travis replied. Suddenly, he himself looked a little uncomfortable. "You tell me."

Cash could sense his fingers slightly tremble; the adrenaline was really getting pumped. At any moment, he believed he was going to crawl out of his skin. "Tell you what?" With an ornery spirit, he whapped the ball back across the net. "I thought you were gonna call Clayton last night."

Shifting his weight from left to right, Travis barricaded himself by crossing his arms.

This looked familiar; Cash wryly thought—remembering his stance during their conversation the day before.

"I had practice, besides I couldn't find your number."

"We're in the book." Cash fumbled for a cigarette from his shirt pocket.

"Yeah?" Travis scanned the parking lot one more time and then focused back onto Cash who was lighting up a smoke. "Well, it was getting pretty late."

"I see." Cash leaned up against his pick-up and propped one boot back on the foot rail. Slowly, he blew smoke from his nostrils. Suddenly, a certain gutsiness swept over him. He could no longer hold back his curiosity. "Tell me, Travis, what is it you're lookin' for?"

Cash was never known for pulling punches, and on this occasion it was no exception. The powerful magnetic force caught Travis off guard; his eyes nervously shot into several directions. Cash found it interesting to see such a rugged giant squirm. Fighting off a grin that wanted to surface across his face, he told himself, *Travis sure looks cute standing there trying to weasel his way through this conversation.*

Suddenly, there was an overpowering urge to step forward, reach out and draw him in with cowboy-rough hands. He wanted to feel Travis' flesh. So with the burning, sizzling desire deep in his guts, he continued to eye him down—realizing there was no turning back now. God, he could not believe this was happening.

"Uh," Travis stammered for words. "We need to go someplace to talk."

Taking a long, hard hit from his cigarette, Cash flipped the butt with his fingers and asked, "Where do you wanna go?"

"I dunno." Urgent frustration rode in Travis' voice as he nervously glanced down at his wristwatch. "Fuck, I have to be at practice right now."

"You set the time and place." Cash purposely ignored the impatience.

Looking intently at Cash, Travis quaked out his words. "Let's talk tomorrow."

They both studied each other closely in an effort to determine mutual sincerity. Cash finally nodded and turned back to the pick-up. Jumping up into the cab, he started the heavy-thundering engine. He knew the cops would eventually pull him over, ordering him to put a lid on the noise. Until that time, however, his truck, the 'Pound Puppy,' would rock the world.

Travis rested a hand on the door. "This is just between us. I mean, no one needs to know—okay?" There was pleading in his voice.

Shifting the gear stick, Cash pulled his dirty old Stetson down tightly over his forehead. "I only sing loud as I'm told to," and having said that, he throttled down and drove away. As he glanced back into the rear view mirror, he could not help noticing Travis. Like a lost lamb, the big football star remained motionless from the spot where the truck had been. With slumped shoulders and heavy brow furled as dark as a thunderstorm in June, it took Cash by surprise. Was he seeing things? Travis was always so rough and tough in school; was this a side nobody knew? Quickly steering the monster-wheeled mudder around the lot—back where he'd been, he leaned out the window and threw a quick snip, *"What?"* Edginess carried in his voice as if dozens of ants were crawling up his ass. By nature, Cash was not a cool-headed guy. He knew it all too well. Attributing his feistiness to the blood line—using the excuse that it was only an Irish temper, his mother would never buy in. "You're just like a jackrabbit," she would always say, "…can't wait for anything. Some day, you're gonna learn to simmer down."

The sound of a whistle blew from the football field.

"You need to get to practice."

"I know," Travis replied, looking down at the ground. "I'm already late."

An awkward silence fell between them.

Cash wasn't sure where this was going to end up, but he knew something had to be done. Cocking his head toward the passenger's side of the cab, he finally said, "Get in." Without protest, Travis bounded around the truck, hopping in.

Gunning the engine, a deep-throated roar echoed against the school front and back across the parking lot. As the 'Puppy' rolled onto the street, both remained silent—seeming to know what would happen next.

As they drove through town and out to the levee the charge between them became explosive. Cash knew of several secluded areas where they could park. By the time they got to the sandy river banks, boiling blood pounded throughout his body. He could barely hold the steering wheel. Shutting down the engine, he slid back in the seat and let out a slow, deep sigh. *Now what?* They both remained at a loss for words. Who was going to break the ice? Thoughts in his mind kept telling him he was nuts for doing this—simply jack-assed insane. But something else deeper seemed to take over his will... something much more powerful and demanding than he ever dreamed.

Lighting up another cigarette, Cash sucked in the thick tobacco smoke as deep as his lungs could take. Slowly exhaling, he sensed a pair of eager, hungry eyes fixed on him. A spell enveloped—hot as lightening, blazing throughout his body. And like iron dust attracted to a magnet, he yearned to bring his hands—every one of his fingers—to a place they had never been before. Forbidden flesh. Hungry for what he saw, his mouth watered for what he deliciously smelled. Travis' unique body scent, laced with that musky sweat and the woodsy cologne—it all drove him crazy. He knew he could ride any goddamn bull put in front of him!

Facing Travis, he closely studied each feature—one by one. That extreme high 'n tight flat top contrasted nicely with a thick, gallant neck and broad shoulders. His skin—smooth and deep-tanned, respectfully earned from all those summer days lifeguarding at the city pool, created a magnificent backdrop to a perfect set of ivory white teeth. And lastly, every curve of his face—cheeks, dimples, forehead and chin seemed to form a symphony of beauty that was absolutely breathtaking.

Instantly, Cash's memory dug back to the first day when Travis had walked through the school doors. It was the beginning of his junior year...

"There's a new guy startin' here today."

The news had started as a trickle. By third period, it had spread throughout the school.

"Yeah?"

...Cash had picked up on the conversation in the hallway while making his way to his next class.

"What's he like?"

"I dunno. I guess he seems alright."

"Where's he from?"

"Someplace in California."

"*Great*," a sarcastic laugh had quickly followed. "He'll fit in *real* good here."

"I heard he's pretty good-lookin' and really big."

Now there was no way that Cash was prepared, in the slightest, for what his eyes would soon behold. Upon settling into his desk with a long sigh, his eyes suddenly caught sight of the most unbelievably handsome, sharp-dressed boy—definitely *not* countrified, and *no* hillbilly. Suave, nonchalant, Travis entered the room—his eyes smoothly roving, searching for a vacant desk.

It was the silence that followed which Cash would never forget. Seized by the power of his presence, the entire room had fallen into a hush. Cassie Johnston, one of the varsity cheerleaders, seemingly broke the spell by letting out a long, hoarse gasp. *"Oh... my... God..."*

Continuing to search the room, the new student's gaze unexpectedly landed on Cash—locking, penetrating. Blazing eyes of cool ice pierced the still air of the classroom and drilled a crater deep into Cash's conscience.

What the…? He could only freeze.

At that moment, time had stopped. With their glances quickly welding into a stare, the space between them became lightening bolts—Cash feeling something mysteriously scorch, seducing his spirit. But just as he had been caught under the trance, he was rudely yanked back to reality by his rodeo buddy, Josh Parker.

"Like he's never seen a real live cowboy before? God, this guy's a trip." Kicking the back of Cash's seat, his friend had leaned over and whispered into his ear, "Better watch out, he's got the hots for you."

"Shut up!" was Cash's quick reply—feeling his face scald…

Bringing himself back to the present, Cash realized what it all meant, plain as day. He knew why they were here.

In their concrete world of hesitation, Travis eventually reached for the door handle. Twisting it with a tight fist, he slid out of the cab—slamming the door with an angry thrust. Slowly, he walked to the river's edge. With hands thrust deeply into his front pockets, he allowed a small chuckle to escape from his hidden face.

Quickly, Cash opened his door. Something needed to happen. A first move needed to be made. They certainly had not come this far for nothing. Extending his leg out on the rocky sand, he pushed himself out. Boot heels sliding over the stones, he made his way to Travis who remained motionless. Defying all fear, he finally reached out and softly touched Travis' shoulder.

Chapter 2

How is a line defined between two raging storms becoming one? Energy unleashed, wielding fierce power against uncontrolled passion, Travis and Cash had collided like a raging frenzy. Nothing... absolutely nothing else had ever etched so deeply—permanently into their lives as what that warm, sunny afternoon had done on the stony banks of the muddy Yellowstone.

Cash could still smell Travis on his skin as he drove back to the ranch in the moon-bathed darkness. The cologne, his sweat, mixed with the sweetness of the prairie air permeated his nostrils and senses like catnip. It made him feel loopy.

The question that repeated in his mind was—why him? What would make such a handsome boy as Travis go after him? Not that he wasn't good-looking, he knew he had rugged features that were 'easy on the eyes'. Each time he walked down the hallway at school, or strolled around the aisles at the local Shop Mart, he was fully aware of the lingered glances at his face and lean muscular frame. Mostly, it was gals who seemed to spot him; but from time to time, a guy could be caught stealing a glimpse as well—which made him wonder about something else… was he obvious? Did he act gay? He certainly didn't think he carried himself like that. What was it then? What made Travis comfortable enough to approach him? Looks? Actions? Who knows? To be honest, he really didn't care. The fact was—he was mighty pleased it had happened and that something was igniting between them.

Suddenly, he realized the time… his stomach knotted.

What was the family going to say? A tightness gripped at his guts. For God's sake, he had missed supper hours ago. Quickly, he needed to come up with a good-sounding alibi. His dad would be upset and it would undeniably be an issue. A McCollum never missed supper unless they were out of town on special business. With a snort, Cash cynically told himself, well, this had definitely been 'special business'.

"Damn right!" Bellowed Mr. McCollum, taking off his glasses and tossing them on the end table. "You better have a good reason for draggin' your tail in here so goddamn late!"

"I'm sorry sir," Cash repeated, just in case his father hadn't heard the first time. Slipping his cowboy hat off, he went on to say, "I guess I should've called." Deep inside, he knew nothing said at this point would calm the thundering, angry man who had risen to his feet from the large recliner.

"Where the hell have you been? You missed supper two hours ago!"

Continuing to look down at the worn-weary hardwood floor, Cash struggled with his conscience about delivering the lie. McCollum's were always known for their honesty. Passed down from generation to generation, integrity had been a quality woven into each family member. Until now, Cash had faithfully followed that tradition. In fact, he had prided himself greatly on possessing the ability to shoot straight with others in all matters. Tonight, however, standing face to face with the rugged, hard working cattleman who had brought him into the world, he would lie. Never in the good Lord's green earth, would the man ever be able to deal with the raw truth of this situation. "I was at a buddy's helping him with his truck."

Studying him closely with a scrutinizing eye, Eugene McCollum remained motionless. "And you didn't realize how late it was getting?" There was an incredulous tone in his voice. Slowly, he shook his head and let out a long, tired sigh.

Cash repositioned his stance by the doorway, his head remaining down. "I'm sorry."

It didn't matter that the food was cold, and the bread a bit dry as Cash ravaged everything on his plate. He had not realized how hungry he was until he sat down at the big, empty table and began to eat by himself. His mother quietly placed a large wedge of apple pie on his plate, her gesture that everyone had gotten past the tenseness of the moment.

As Cash's mouth slowly savored the dessert, his mind kept running back to that incredible groove at the river bank. Something had happened out there—much more than simply two people coming together and getting off. He knew it.

Fixing his gaze on the delicately-decorated china and crystal resting inside the old cabinet of the dining room, he visualized Travis' reflection—those eyes, carrying a soft, droopy, sleepy appearance. At one time, he had heard the term—bedroom eyes. Now he knew what it meant. The way he moved those eyelids, and spoke with his lips, it drove him wild. *Everything* about Travis drove him wild.

Remembering the words Travis had spoken before they exchanged their first kiss, Cash knew they had to be protected—stored in a safe place inside his heart—where they'd never be stolen or forgotten…

"Cash, you've gotta know something. I've wanted to have you for a long time, and I know you've had feelings for me as well. Ever since mom and I moved here, I've longed to touch you, hold you, and make you mine."

With a sight tremble in his lips, he looked at the ground, and continued in a still, soft voice, "You probably think this is sick, and I-I wouldn't blame you if you did."

Taking Travis' strong, burly hand, Cash was surprised to find it so smooth. Funny, he hadn't noticed it the day before. His warmth felt comfortable. Desperately fighting back a strange tear, Cash quickly rubbed it away with his shirt sleeve and muttered under his breath, "Sand or somethin' musta' blown in my eye." Suddenly, he felt himself shake—like a leaf on a cottonwood in October. "I don't think it's sick. I feel the same way about you, Travis."

Raising his head and looking into the hard-headed cowboy's freckled, wind-burned face, Travis continued. "I want you in my life."

And that, was that—it left no room for disagreement.

At first, Cash believed his knees were giving out. Quickly, Travis grabbed his shoulders to steady him. A fiery jolt seized his trembling body while big, steady arms quickly slid around the small of his back, drawing him in.

"Christ, are you all right?" Travis looked frightened.

Regaining composure, Cash nodded. "Yeah."

Travis continued to hold him with a powerful, but yet gentle grip. And like a piston to a hot-oiled shaft, their mouths came together—smooth 'n tight. From there, they shared kisses that slid smoother than the creamiest chocolate.

"You're a wiry little shit," Travis said admiringly, backing up—allowing his arms to draw Cash into his hard, muscular chest. "I like that." A broad grin covered his face from ear to ear.

With Cash's beat-up Stetson falling to the ground, they continued to kiss-hard, beard stubble grinding deeply on their lips and cheeks as tongues freely dripped of warm, wet saliva in each other's hungry mouths. They just couldn't get enough….

"I'm foldin' up," Cash said with a yawn. In spite of his frisky mood, he felt extremely torn down. The sacred solitude of his room and bed seemed unbelievably inviting. All he could think of was curling up naked under the covers with a pillow and conjuring dreams of a particular football jock.

"Good night," his father called out from his recliner.

Since the accident, each evening was the same old scene. Buried in the newspaper or a nameless television show, Mr. McCollum seemed to find his life stalled on a runway of broken aspirations. An event that was resistant to any degree of mellowing from the passing of time seemed to birth a relentless grip crippling the very spirit his dad had been famed for.

Who would have anticipated the freak ice storm so late in June? Fog settling in the valleys, and a freezing rain followed by a thick buildup of ice on the roads, had created a driving nightmare for many truckers along the Divide. And losing his air breaks on the highway had been the last straw. Steering frantically through the heavy darkness, Cash's father had endeavored to stay on the pavement. He had successfully managed to keep the truck on the steeply graded pass most of the way down, but coming to a sharp bend, he had lost control. Feeling the cab veer off the embankment, Mr. McCollum remembered clinging to the wheel as the truck spun mercilessly into a wild, careening tumble down the face of the mountainside. A miracle that anyone had survived, the first responders all stated they were amazed that he was alive when they finally pulled him from the gnarled wreck.

It wasn't long after the recovery from broken legs, a shattered collarbone and countless internal injuries, that Eugene formally announced his retirement from truck driving—and the rodeo circuit. Selling his equipment, and most of the horses, he eventually cashed in the remainder of his cards for a modest herd of Black Angus cattle. He knew it would never bring in the amount of money which he had earned from bull riding, but the career switch had been inevitable. Regardless of the two-bit advice of well-meaning family members, Cash's dad never appeared overly receptive to the fact that "cattle herdin'" was—for a lack of better words—the old family standby. And even though Cash couldn't prove it, there seemed to be a certain degree of resentment harbored within his father concerning the outcome of that fateful night which would be carried to his grave.

Making his way up the stairs, Cash entered the private confines of his bedroom and slowly closed the door. The house seemed unusually quiet tonight as he undressed and crawled into bed. Clayton must be out with some of his buddies, he reasoned. That was all right, he was not in a visiting sort of mood—especially with his brother. With a deep sigh, he rested his head on the soft, goose down pillow and closed his weary eyes. Nothing personal against anyone… he just wanted to be alone with his thoughts about Travis.

It was another windy morning. The clouds were dark and thick—a peculiar heaviness seemed to emanate from them giving Cash a chill to the bone. Forecasters had predicted a Pacific front to blow in from the mountains later that day—bringing with it a cold, hard rain. "Bet it snows," Mr. McCollum griped, hobbling with his cane around the kitchen. "I feel like shit. …never have pain like this unless it snows." Finally sitting down at the table with a fresh cup of coffee, he looked at Cash and asked, "What time did Clayton get in?"

"Dunno," replied Cash with a mouthful of cereal. "I went to sleep right away."

Running a hand across his weather-wrinkled forehead, Cash's dad sighed and took a sip of the fresh aromatic brew. "Gotta go into town this afternoon and pick up feed for the horses. You wanna help me?"

"'Bout what time?"

"Four thirty?"

"Yeah." Cash etched it in his mind. No sense in repeating the same taboo two times in a week. Just like him, his dad hated to be held up by others running late.

"Damn rude when you've gotta wait up on people." Mr. McCollum would always complain when someone was late for an appointment.

A gust of wind blew wildly against the house with a roaring vibration; sand and gravel scratched at the windows. If his dad was right, this was going to be one hell of a storm.

Something unheard of… the football game was postponed to the impending weather. School administration made the final decision to delay the game until the following Wednesday.

"That never happens," Travis quipped to Cash during lunch.

By mid-afternoon, the mountains had been issued a winter storm warning. Snow was already piling up in the passes, and was expected to move out to the plains that evening.

With the plans changed, Travis threw out an invitation. "What do you wanna do tonight?" There was a sparkle in his baby-blues.

"Git naked with you." *Had those words come from his mouth?* Cash could not believe what he had just said. Instantly, his mouth became wet—his rose-colored cheeks quickly revealing a set of hidden dimples.

With a short gasp, Travis leaned closer to his cowboy friend, his lips slightly opened. Resting a hand against the wall behind Cash's shoulder, he softly whispered, "I'll bet you say that to all the hot guys."

Looking squarely into Travis' eyes, Cash replied, "I've never said it to no one… *never*."

"Yeah?" replied Travis, continuing to lock his gaze deep into Cash.

"Uh huh." Once again, Cash felt himself caught under the black magic. He couldn't move a muscle.

"You know what I wanna do with you?" Travis leaned in closer. The warmth of his breath brushed against Cash's ear and neck like a wispy feather.

Chill bumps quickly covered Cash as wind walloped the building—slamming a hard, unrelenting rain against the window panes. The glass trembled and shook from the force. *God's sake, was this a hurricane?*

"What?"

"Everything you want."

"And what might that be?" Cash became coy.

"For starters," Travis drew in closer, "…me kissin' you." Slowly, deliberately—his warm sensitive lips brushed up against Cash's mouth.

Exploring every sensuous ridge and curve of his smooth lips, seduced deeper by an entangling tongue, Cash slid into Travis with a raging hunger. Tasting faint sweetness, a flame within his flesh was irretrievably stoked, boiling hot, seething with passion throughout his veins. Bound and locked, he found himself webbed into insatiable desires—drinking the other boy's warmth and touch, succumbing to the inevitable intoxication of his potion.

"Jesus!" Travis gasped under his breath, his arms drawn tightly around the small of Cash's waist. "You *are* an addiction."

Bringing a finger to his lips, Cash whispered, "Shhh! Someone's downstairs."

From one of the floors below, a door opened and footsteps scuffed on the stairway. Together, Cash and Travis stood frozen as the shuffle finally stopped—the door closing with an echoing bang. Intently listening for any more movement, they remained still. Apart from the crazy storm—its assault on the window, silence, once again, overtook the stairwell.

As if reading Cash's mind, Travis warned, "We're gettin' in too deep here." No sooner had he finished when his cell phone shrieked out its chime.

The two boys nervously jumped.

"Hello."

"Travis?" A woman's voice carried out from the small speaker.

"Yeah, mom?"

"I'm stuck here in Billings. The roads are a sheet of ice."

"So what are you going to do?" Travis asked.

"I've decided to stay one more night here at the hotel, are you going to be all right?"

"Sure," he replied. "The game's been cancelled tonight."

"Not surprised." She laughed.

"How were the meetings?"

"They were okay," she said. "I'm glad they're done."

"That's good."

"I'll let you know when I'm coming back."

"Okay," Travis said, "...be careful."

"You too." Her voice was beginning to break up. "I've gotta go... love you!"

"Love you too." Travis shut the phone down and slipped it back into his pocket. "Wow, this is one heck of a storm."

"That's what my dad said this mornin'."

Scoping the situation, Travis finally said, "Let's get outta here—go to my house."

"I've gotta meet my dad at four-thirty." Cash remembered his promise made early that morning.

With a sly grin, Travis slid out his words. "You know, a lot can be done before then... let's go to my house."

Cash bit his lip. The offer was too inviting.

Following the little sports car with the thundering 'Puppy', thoughts gnawed at Cash's mind. Complete opposites... the two of them. They couldn't get more different. What was it that was bringing them together?

As they made their way through the slushy streets to a newly developed neighborhood, Cash became increasingly uncomfortable. This was out of his league. Warily, he watched Travis turn into a long driveway. He caught his breath. *Oh, God...* he hopelessly thought. There, situated against a hillside overlooking the entire valley, was an elegant, two-story home with large bay windows. The house was magnificent.

All he could think—Travis is rich.

Steering the mud-caked truck against the curb, he pounded his foot on the break. He couldn't go on with this.

One of the three garage doors attached to the house automatically opened, allowing Travis to zip in. Cash remained parked in the street, frozen in the cab, engine idling. Keeping his hand on the stick shift, he told himself, *no way*. No way would this ever work. It was obvious Travis needed to move on—find another guy that would match this lifestyle.

Making his way down the driveway, slipping and sliding, Travis' face was buried with bewilderment. "What's wrong?" Frustration floated from his voice as he opened the passenger's door and stuck his head in.

"I can't do this," Cash flatly stated, looking straight ahead—fingers tightly gripping the steering wheel.

"What do you mean?" The big boy's eyes became as round as saucers.

"Travis," Cash surrendered—a tear threatened to escape, "we're from two separate worlds. This ain't ever gonna work."

As if the wind had been knocked out of him, Travis stood halfway in the rain, halfway in the cab, speechless—his eyes fixed on the young cowboy slumped behind the wheel.

"What's scaring you?" Travis scrambled to regain composure.

"Nothin's scarin' me!" Cash quickly came back in a defiant manner.

Shaking his head in disbelief, Travis went on to ask, "Then what's going on?"

"It's not right." Cash allowed his emotions to spill out. "We're comin' from two different cultures—can't you see that?"

"Yeah, I know…" Travis nodded, groping to understand where Cash was taking this.

"You obviously come from money…I don't." Cash wiped away the tear that had been welling in his eye. "I never will." Sliding down in his seat, he took a deep sigh.

"You can't be serious," Travis rolled his head—letting out an incredulous laugh. "We can work through this, Cash. I know we can!"

"I dunno," Cash was not convinced.

"I want you to get to know me…my world. I wanna get to know you…and your world. Cash, you need to know that I've wanted our lives to come together since the day I first saw you…in that classroom." His voice trailed off.

"What?" A puzzled look came over Cash, staring intently at the half-soaked boy leaning into the truck.

"Remember when I walked into Hanson's English class?"

"Your first day?" Funny that he would mention it, Cash mused—once again resurrecting that familiar scene back into his mind.

"Yup."

"Yeah, I remember it."

"Do you recall me staring at you?"

Remaining quiet, Cash nodded.

"It was then I knew I had to get to know you. Regardless of how complicated it would be, I swore at that moment I would do anything to bring our worlds together."

Suddenly, anger flared up in Cash. "Why the hell has it taken you 'till now to tell me this?!"

"You're not the easiest one to approach, you know!" Travis instantly snapped back. "I can't tell you how many times I've hedged my bets about bringing this up with you. In case you're not aware, there's a lot of mixed signals you send out."

As if his mind was swimming with enough stuff, Travis' words made no absolute sense. "Huh?"

"You're difficult to read. Most of the time, I can't tell what's going on in that mind of yours. I know you cruise me up and down when it looks like I'm not paying attention... then there are times you completely ignore me. *What's that all about?*"

Cash's face began to redden as silence fell between them.

Travis finally chuckled, allowing a smile to sweep across his shivering face. "You know, Cash McCollum, I think you're the hottest cowboy around, but you can be one hell of a little badger." He paused. "All I want is to have you right smack-dab in the center of my life."

Staring at Travis, Cash remained quiet. What could he say? Finally, a smile cracked the stoniness of doubts carved in his face. "You're crazy."

"No, I'm soaking wet!" exclaimed Travis, gesturing toward the house. "Come on!"

Travis ran up to the front entry and waited for Cash.

Nearly slipping over the smooth, polished marble, Cash took a deep breath. "Oh my God!" he softly exclaimed. He had never seen anything like this before. Within the foyer, there was a large grand staircase leading upstairs. Each step was solid marble. Above him, he noticed an elaborate crystal chandelier that sent reflections of light into virtually every corner of the room.

"What time were we to meet your dad?" Travis asked, looking at his watch.

"Four thirty."

"It's twenty after right now." Travis said, taking his jacket off and resting it on the staircase banister. "I don't think we're gonna meet up with your dad on time. Think you should call him and tell him we're running late?"

'Yeah, I better," replied Cash thoughtfully. "Where's your phone?" He reached down, yanking his boots off.

"Down at the end of that hallway," Travis pointed. "I've got to get out of these," gesturing to his wet clothes. "Make yourself at home—I'll be up in my room changing."

Cash slid across the cold marble in his sweaty socks. This house was unbelievable. He could not help curling his toes into the thick, white carpet that spanned the hallway. Every room was immaculately furnished with elegant virgin-white upholstery. Pieces such as end tables, dressers, and vanities were meticulously constructed of solid white oak. Nothing... not even the small table at the end of the hall, where the phone rested, was out of synch. Everything blended together—like in one of those *House Beautiful* magazines.

Picking up the receiver, he dialed his home number. Ringing several times, his father eventually answered.

"Hello."

"Dad?"

"Where you at?" There was a tone of concern in his voice.

"At a buddy's," Cash replied. "Hey, I'm runnin' late. The roads are really bad."

"I know, the radio station's been tellin' everyone to stay indoors. Tree limbs are fallin' all over town."

Cash could tell his dad was all worked up.

"It's too early for this shit."

"I know, "Cash agreed.

"I think we're gonna pass on getting' feed today," Mr. McCollum finally conceded. "It's not worth riskin' our lives."

Cash felt relieved. He wasn't in any mood haulin' huge bags of grain about. "Good, we have enough for several more days, anyway."

"When you comin' home?"

"In a little bit." A tinge of irritation swept over Cash—realizing how tired he was of having to continually account for every minute of his life. *For crying' out loud—all guys need a little space of privacy now and then.*

There was a pause on the other end of the line, as if his dad knew what was going on in his youngest son's mind. Cash could tell he was struggling whether or not to push the issue of ordering him to come home on the double. Finally, with a sigh, the man spoke in a tired, sandpaper tone, "All right…be careful."

"Thanks." Cash took a deep breath. "I will."

Hearing a click from his dad hanging up, Cash slowly rested the hand piece back on the cradle. *Well, that went well*, he told himself sarcastically. Truth be told, he hadn't meant to be disrespectful, but sometimes, his father could be so difficult. Pushing the regret from his mind, he decided to go upstairs and find Travis.

There was an uneasy, sterile quietness that pervaded through this house. It made him feel uncomfortable.

As he reached the landing, his eyes searched down the darkened hall. Spotting a glow from a room at the end, Cash picked up his pace. It was so quiet; he wondered what Travis was up to. Peeking in, he let out a tiny gasp—his eyes riveting on the scene before him.

Stretched and sprawled out, secure in his physical beauty with rows of bulging muscles carefully defined by years of hard work and play, was a naked dream come true. Travis lay easily across the top of the turned-down bed. With arms resting behind his head, he revealed two perfect mattes of pit hair, a smooth, rounded chest, and a pair of nipples that glistened invitingly against the glow of a bedside lamp. His legs casually straddled—exhibiting an unbelievable endowment that stood straight up like an exclamation point. Tossing an inviting nod, Travis gently said with a devilish grin, "Come here." His eyes gleamed.

Unsnapping the pearl buttons from his shirt, and throwing it on the dresser, Cash became hungry—mouth watering hungry. With cowboy hat pushed back, he unfastened the big belt buckle and unzipped his jeans. Slipping off his boots and tossing them in a corner with a thud, he went over toward the bed side—knee softly touching the tip of Travis' toes. The sensation was electric.

"Careful for what you request," Travis seductively smiled, moistening his lips with a sliding tongue. He went on to whisper, "I'll always deliver."

...Where the time had slipped away, Cash would never know. While they quietly lay together in each other's arms, the room resounded with rank odors of cum, cologne, Marlboros, man-sweat, and the ever-faint hint of pine smoke. As Cash took a hit from his cigarette, Travis watched silently with an intent eye.

"I love to watch you smoke," he finally said.

Blowing the smoke from his lips in a straight line out into the room, Cash replied, "Yeah?"

"Uh huh." Travis smiled. "It's hot."

Cash returned by giving him a big grin.

"I love being with you." Travis finally stated, brushing his fingers softly against the back of Cash's neck.

"Hmmmm." Cash didn't know what to say. It made him feel good—special, but somewhat awkward. Having a boyfriend... being a boyfriend. This was all new to him.

 Looking about the room, he noticed several certificates and awards achieved from various sports. Football, wrestling, and baseball...there was even one for placing first in a tennis tournament. Hell, was there any sport he wasn't good at? On his desk was a computer, globe, and a nicely framed picture of a man wearing a suit and tie.

"Who's that?" Cash asked, pointing to the picture.

"That's my dad." Travis' voice suddenly changed—the muscles in his flesh tightened.

Instantly, Cash sensed the tension. Had he said something wrong? "I'm sorry. I didn't mean to be nosey," he quickly apologized, sitting up—propping an elbow against a pillow.

"No," Travis' words were gentle—non-condemning. His eyes avoided Cash's quizzical gaze. "That's okay."

An awkward quiet fell on them.

He went on to say, "I think you would have liked him."

"Yeah?" Cash asked, crushing the remainder of his smoke out.

"Uh huh, he was a great guy."

"Where's he at?" It was an innocent question, Cash considered.

"He's dead." Travis' voice trailed off.

At first, Cash wasn't sure he had heard correctly. He simply stared at the boy lying next to him—trying to determine if this was a joke. "What?"

"My dad died in a plane crash."

"I—I thought..." Cash fumbled for words; a prickly feeling shot through his body. He could see Travis was serious.

"I know," Travis cut him off, saving him the pain of going on. "Everybody thinks mom and him split up. She's wanted it that way so everyone will leave the subject alone."

Cash was now fully aroused, his eyes fixed on the one who was repositioning himself in the bed.

Taking a deep breath, Travis continued to speak—his voice was shaky, "Dad was killed on nine-eleven."

Cash was taken back even further. He couldn't move.

"He was on the jet that had left Newark to head back to San Francisco— where we lived. It was the plane that had crashed near Pittsburgh... flight ninety-three."

Instantly, Cash's memory went back to that fateful day. He recalled the sad, gruesome reports about the ill-fated United flight. Coldness swept over him. "I'm sorry." Cash whispered, putting his head down.

"He had called me from the cell phone just before they went down...to tell me he would always love me." Travis' voice drifted away, like a puff of smoke—his eyes staring blankly off into space.

Slowly, deliberately, Cash drew his arms around big, hunky boy—embracing him tightly. He couldn't believe what had just been shared. He wouldn't have guessed.

The pain. The shock. It was something he simply couldn't fathom.

CHAPTER 3

It was difficult to make the phone call. Not because he dreaded getting his ass chewed, but because it just didn't seem right—considering the tender time between him and Travis. A sense of relief filled his heart when he heard his mother's voice come over the other end.

"Mom?"

"I had a feeling it was you." Her voice was reassuring.

"I'm running late." Looking at the clock on the dresser, he knew his dad was probably furious.

"So I figured."

Usually, no matter what was going on, she possessed a gracefulness that could soften the toughest of moments among the male members of their family. Grandma would always say it was her gift to the McCollum clan. No one else had the ability to smooth over the rough edges that could surface from time to time. "Are you okay?"

"Yeah, I'm fine," Cash sighed. "I'm sorry about…"

"Don't worry," she interrupted, sparing herself any long, detailed explanation. "I'll take care of your father. He's been a little difficult with everyone this week. I think it's the weather."

"I'll be home in a little bit," he promised.

"There's plenty of supper left. I suppose you're hungry."

"Starved," Cash explained, feeling the emptiness in his stomach.

"Drive safely," she cautioned. "The roads are a mess from what I hear."

"I will," he said reassuringly. "Love you."

"Love you, too."

Walking over to the window, Cash watched the large snow flakes gently flutter down to the white-covered ground. The wind had finally stopped; everything outside looked so peaceful. It was the season's first snow, the earliest he could remember.

The view from Travis' room was beautiful. Overlooking the large river valley, the city lights below, and the looming bluffs on the other side—it was a totally different sight than that at the ranch.

Suddenly, he felt something touch his leg. A cold, wet nose and a friendly tongue lapped against the hairs of his calf and thigh. Looking down, he spotted a golden bundle of furry energy playfully pull at his feet. "Well, who are you?" Cash let out a laugh. Reaching down, he ran his fingers through the dog's soft fur. "You're a little cutie…you know that?"

"Meet Casper," Travis introduced, returning from the bathroom.

Cash let out a few more chuckles. "An interestin' name…"

"Mom named him that because he tends to sneak up on everybody," Travis went on to explain.

The little dog let out all stops, obviously attracted to Cash.

"Casper, behave," Travis firmly spoke. "He gets a little wigged out when new people visit."

"I think he's excited the wind has stopped." Cash said observantly, casting a smile towards Travis.

"We *all* are." Travis ran a brush through his flat-top—leaning in front of the vanity mirror for a last-minute inspection. Putting on a grey flannel shirt, black jeans and a pair of motorcycle boots, he stole one more glance.

Cash could not help but stare. He looked tough.

"Travis, I'd like you to come over," he invited. "You 'n I can grab a bite, 'n I'll show you 'round."

Smiling at Cash, excitement flooded his face. "Sure."

Ushering Travis into the old rustic living room for introductions and left-over supper was like dragging him into a television sitcom. Unlike the pristine stillness back at the Hunter house, a powerful electric charge seemed to flow strongly through every room at the McCollum ranch, with Clayton, Cash's older brother, supplying most of the energy as the main generator.

"Hey, Bucky, whacha doin'—brinin' your *boyfriend* home to introduce him t'allus?" Leaning back in the couch, face held high, Clayton let out a perfect yowl. "Yee haw!"

Where had that grizzly come from? Freezing square in their tracks, Cash and Travis found themselves completely taken back. Instantly, Cash's mind recalled an old proverb that his grandma used to say, "Things spoken in jest are often the closest to the truth." *For God's sake*, he frantically thought, *shut up, Clayton*. He honestly assumed he could stop himself from turning his head away, or shifting his eyes down. He struggled to keep the cough out of his throat. Frantically, he steadied himself enough so not to appear ready to stumble, but for his damned red head complexion, betraying him with a full-on flush, the game got called.

Clayton stared, smiling only half-way, because at that moment, his mouth wouldn't close—even on command. It was at that instant, he *knew*.

"Clayton…" Mrs. McCollum had said, in an effort to rope in her renegade middle boy. With a flash, she tossed him a wary eye.

This wasn't the first time he had blurted out something outrageously crass in front of others, especially house guests. Cash reckoned it to something like a nervous twitch. Winding himself up like a mechanical monkey, Clayton had the distinct character of saying things completely out of line for mixed company.

Trying to ignore Clayton's comments, Cash pushed forward in a non-affected manner by saying "I'd like ya'll to meet my friend, Travis Hunter."

"Nice to meet you," Mrs. McCollum courteously replied—her sharp, green eyes studying her son's newly announced companion closely. It wasn't every day he brought friends home to meet the family.

"Hi," Mr. McCollum, on the other hand, greeted reservedly, pushing himself out of his chair and extending a cordial hand.

"Pleasure to meet you, sir." Travis initiated a quick, hearty handshake, then glancing over to his mother, he respectfully said with a nod, "Ma'am."

…And thus, was Travis' baptism into the holy waters of the McCollum clan. Drowning was more like it, thought Cash, as silence engulfed the room with only the sound of a snap and crackle from the logs burning in the huge stone fireplace. Fumbling for something to say—anything to break the ice, he went on to explain, "His mom's stranded in Billings, so I asked him if he wanted to come over 'n have some supper 'n spend the night."

"He can sleep in Clint's room," Cash's mother quickly offered, refocusing her full attention back to her son. It was obvious from the expression on her face; she was trying to piece it all together.

A sick feeling overtook Cash's senses as the realization of the situation began to sink in—his mother was hot on the trail. She, too, had been quick to see the coloring of his face along with the catch of his gait. At that moment, he knew it would only be a matter of time until she figured the whole thing out...but, why did it have to be so soon? On the other hand, what else did he expect? Rarely, did he bring anyone to the house. In fact, he couldn't even remember the last time. The real clincher to all of this—Travis was not the typical dumb-assed country-boy type which he was known to hang out with. From an outsider's point of view, they both seemed to be the most unlikely matched pair of playing cards in the deck. Of course, his mother would have questions—not to mention his dad. And then, there was Clayton. Always itching to stir a pot, he would probably jump in there and stoke up the fire to a scalding blaze. He usually saw any controversy in the family as humorous, and given the nature of this topic, he would probably find this particular one a true rip-roarin' riot.

Cash determined to dig in. "That's alright; he'll be in my room. He can use the sleeping bag." The words shot forth from his mouth firm and defiant. He was not going to budge one inch.

Taking his entire family by surprise, they all remained motionless—their eyes riveted on him—waiting for the next move.

Travis must have sensed the depth of awkwardness present in the room. Taking several steps back, he quietly lowered his head—as if sending up a pleading prayer of intervention from Heaven....

His mother was not one for hanging dirty laundry out for others to see. She would mill this over in her brain and later address the issue in a logical, matter-of-fact fashion. It was no surprise, then, that after several exceedingly long moments, she calmly, and graciously, said, "You boys must be hungry. There's plenty of leftover food in the fridge." Rising to her feet, she made her way to the kitchen. "Come on, let's get you two situated."

With that, Cash's father once again buried himself in the newspaper, and Clayton, intending to come off as the family skeptic, grunted a mumbling noise from his throat, "Auh, auh, auh." Springing off the couch, he bounded like a bunny across the room, up the staircase, and into his room.

How would he have known about Travis' father? All this time, everyone had been told his folks had divorced. Who would have guessed he had lost his dad from the attacks on nine-eleven? The more Cash had an opportunity to kick it around in his mind, the more he realized how profound of an impact it had on himself. He couldn't imagine how Travis could have lived through all the effects of that and yet continue to press on with his studies and sports activities.

"...this is between you and me," Travis confided, his voice drawn down to a whisper. He lay closely cuddled against Cash on the bed. "You're the only one I've shared it with."

"Why?" asked Cash, unable to put any of it together.

"Because I believe you should know the truth. When mom decided to move here, she wanted a fresh start. She said she was tired of all the attention... and the pity."

"So do you have family here?"

"This is mom's home, although most of the relatives have moved away, or are dead," Travis replied. "There's a great aunt and she's pretty close to us. Mom had to put her in the nursing home several months ago. She used to live with us at the house." Pausing, as if reflecting upon a particular memory, he went on to say with a warm smile, "She's a sweetie."

"My granddad's in the nursing home too." Cash added—fixing his gaze on the opaque glow which was cast against the wall from the yard light that brightly shined through the curtainless window by his bed. He felt eerie, as if the entire world he had grown accustomed to quietly vanished—like the green trees and grass of summer from the shortening of days.

"I really like your family." Travis stated thoughtfully. He softly ran his fingers over the cowboy's silky chest hair.

Not moving a muscle, Cash slowly breathed in the cool air from the room. There was something more to Travis' touch...more than sex. Somewhere in the midst of all this chaos, he felt stability within this young, muscular man. Something which he needed—desired—much like a deer panting for cool, fresh water in a mountain stream. Telling himself their lives had to come together, he could not deny what his spirit sensed. Yes, things were changing. The key was to learn how to groove with it—like ridin' a buckin' bronc or a fire-snortin' bull—get into the rhythm and channel it to your own benefit.

Looking into Travis' shadowy face, his eyes glistened in the room's dark-woven void. The words that flowed from his lips bore a peculiar prophetic tone as every line and curve of his handsome face radiated an undeniable determination towards its fulfillment. "They *will* grow to love you."

Pondering the statement for a moment, Travis suddenly pushed himself up and leaned over—kissing Cash. The words he eventually whispered into his ear were soft and tender—blended with his special brand of hot, masculine passion..."*I love you.*"

After what seemed to be forever, Travis finally drifted to sleep. Now, peacefully snoring away in the old sleeping bag that Cash used on hunting trips, he had look of perfect contentment—all bundled up, on the floor, close beside the tiny bed. And as the entire house eventually settled down into a quiet stillness, Cash debated whether or not to slide into that bag with him. The truth was, he wanted to in the worst way. Instead, he stared up at the ceiling, allowing his mind to review all the events of the past several days.

The morning was cloudy and cold. A heavy blanket seemed to hang closely to the river valley and the bluffs beyond, creating a dark, misty, almost-depressing world. There was no wind, but a certain bite in the air, bringing a paralyzing chill deep to the bone.

"Shit," exclaimed Cash, blowing his breath into his hands and fingers. Vigorously, he rubbed them together in an effort to get them warm. "It's too early in the season for this stuff."

"Yeah," agreed Travis, as he turned his jacket collar up and pulled the zipper as far as it would go. "Goin' on my second year, and I'm still not used to this."

Tossing a glance toward Travis, Cash noticed him shivering.

"Christ's sake," he chuckled, taking a hit from his smoke, "you're gonna have to get a heavier jacket."

Together they walked across the white-frosted yard toward the stables and corral. Their feet made a crunching sound on the snow and pockets of ice from each step that they took.

Looking around, Travis asked, "You've lived here all your life?"

"Yup," Cash proudly replied. "Five generations on this very spot."

"No shit?" There was a tone of astonishment in Travis' voice. "That's incredible."

"The family originally came up from Texas," explained Cash.

They reached the stables, and Cash forced open one of the doors. It wasn't much warmer inside, but between the straw and heat from the animals, the combination took the chill off.

"Texas," Travis thoughtfully said, trying to piece it all together.

"My great, great granddad used to work the cattle drives from Abilene to here after the Civil War. He eventually decided to stay in Montana 'n start a ranch by the river." With a quick sweep of his arm he concluded, "This is it."

"Wow," Travis exclaimed under his breath, fixing his eyes on Cash. He seemed to do a lot of that.

At first, Cash had felt rather uncomfortable about all the close attention—as if he needed to do something in return. But over the last couple of days, he was beginning to really enjoy it. It made him feel good that someone else found so much interest in him—as a person.

"What was his name?" he asked curiously—taking Cash's hand.

Pausing for a moment, Cash took one last drag from his cigarette and then dropped it to the ground. Slowly, he ground the butt out with his boot. "John... John McCollum. He used to ride bulls 'n bust broncs... a real rodeo man."

"Does everyone in your family do the rodeos?" Travis stepped behind Cash; slowly, he slipped his arms around his man's tight waist—hitching his thumbs into the loose belt loops.

Cash loved it. Travis' body felt so warm against his.

"My dad used to. He worked the professional circuit 'till he had a truckin' accident over by the Idaho border several years ago. Clayton does a little every now n' then—whenever he gets the urge. Clint, my oldest brother, has been busy at college. He hasn't ridden in ages." His voice trailed off like the steam from his breath.

"Where's he attending?"

"Billings…wants to be a teacher."

"That's great." There was a tone of enthusiasm in Travis' voice.

A moment of silence fell between them. Cash felt Travis draw his body in closer against his.

"And you?" Travis went on to ask. "I see your name and picture in the rodeo columns all the time."

Cash became embarrassed. He really hated talking about himself. "What's there t'know? I ride bull 'n bust bronc—not much to that."

"Shit," Travis instantly came back with a sharp reply. "Like hell there's not much to that…you're good, and you know it."

Pulling away from Travis' grip, Cash turned and stared with wide eyes. "Whatcha talkin' about? How do you know?"

"I have my ways." Travis cast him a sly grin. "I know you're up for state high school championship—All-Around Cowboy."

Cash was shocked. He would have never dreamed anyone kept track of that stuff—especially Travis.

"In fact, cowboy," Travis went on to say, "I believe you need to try your hand at the professionals this spring."

"Yeah?" Cash asked, throwing him a side-glance beam.

"Yessir," Travis flatly stated. "Your name's written on that title—I know it."

Cash was truly amazed. Fixing his eyes on Travis, he felt himself completely overtaken. He'd never had feelings for anyone like this before.

Leaning over, Cash took advantage of their private moment—stealing a frosty kiss. Yup, Travis tasted good. Sweet. Without hesitation, he dove back in for a second helping.

"I'm sorry about last night." Cash eventually pulled away, shifting his eyes toward the horses that were busy chewing hay.

"Actually," Travis said thoughtfully, "I think it went a lot better than what it could have."

"Clayton's such a prick." Cash allowed the enmity to appear.

"He's your brother."

"Yeah?" Cash let out a long sigh. "Well, right now, he's not on my favorite person list."

"I can understand that." Travis seemed careful to choose his words. Allowing is eyes to rove, he aimlessly scanned the stables. "Your mom's tough—in a good way."

"She's the one who keeps us all together." Cash had to agree. "We're all so damn stubborn 'n independent, this place wouldn't exist if it wasn't for her."

"She's gonna be our biggest support. You know that."

Stated as fact, Cash knew Travis was right. Once the word got out about them, it would be her thoughtful determination that would keep everyone in line.

After taking Travis back to his house, the remainder of the weekend seemed rather mundane—slipping by rather quietly. Sunday afternoon, the sun had peeked through the gloomy clouds—melting snow and ice on the ranch house shingles and the front walkway. By evening, the winds had set in from the northwest bringing with them an arctic chill from Canada.

Cash's father had stoked up a big fire which radiated its heat throughout the living room. The flicker of flames wildly danced across the stucco-vaulted ceiling creating an illusion that the room itself was alive.

Not caring where the inspiration had come, Cash had retreated to his room to study. Rarely, did he ever take time to do homework, figuring if it couldn't be done in seven hours at school; it didn't need to be done. Algebra, however, was becoming a concern to him as he had failed to hand in the last three assignments. He knew he had better get caught up with the work, or it would 'catch up' with him.

Sitting at his desk with a small lamp hovering over the textbook, Cash busily worked over equations with a dull, erasure-less pencil.

There was a knock on his door.

"Cash?" His mother's voice called from the hallway.

"Come in." Cash pushed his chair from the desk and sheepishly smiled. He knew what was coming down the trail. He had been expecting it all weekend.

"Can we talk?" she asked, walking over toward his bed. Sitting on the edge, her hands rested easily on her lap.

Janice McCollum was not an abrupt lady. Everything she did was usually thoughtfully considered. And even though she was one who could keep her temper in check, everyone acquainted with her knew she never beat around the bush.

This evening, Cash could tell from the appearance on her face, she had to talk about something very important. The lines in her soft, yet aged face bore the hint of a considerable amount of concern and pain. Suddenly, he felt his stomach tie up in knots. He hated seeing her look this way. "Sure," he softly replied, his fingers nervously fidgeting with the pencil.

Taking a deep breath, she cleared her throat and said, "You know, when I was seventeen I thought I knew what I wanted to be—where I was going to live and who I was going to marry... until I met your dad."

Cash's eyes were fixed on the woman dressed in blue jeans, an old Montana State Bobcat sweatshirt, and her favorite sneakers. She looked comfortable sitting on the edge of his bed. With her hair pulled back in a ponytail, she looked like a young girl.

"Everything changed for me when he came into my life. My dream of going to college and getting a degree seemed to fly out the window when he told me he loved me." She paused for a second, and then with a sigh, went on to say, "I truly thought before then I would leave this area and start out on my own—making a life for myself. Cash, all that disappeared. I guess you would say... I fell in love." A smile crossed her face. Looking deeply into her son's eyes, she finally stated, "I don't regret those unexpected changes, even though I wonder at times what life would have been if I would have continued with my plans."

"What are you trying to say?" Cash could feel his impatience overtake. He wished she would get to the bottom line.

Giving a little laugh, she replied, "I guess I'm not really sure except that life continually brings us surprises—things we never expect. It's during those times we're forced to make decisions...life choices."

"Yeah," Cash agreed, still not fully understanding where she was taking this.

Refusing to take her gaze off Cash, her words lowered to a near whisper. "What's up with you and Travis?"

Cash's heart skipped a beat as he could feel his body begin to tremble. Wanting to speak, yet unable to get any words out, he squirmed in the chair.

"Are you in love with him?" His mom threw the question out and waited. There was no harshness in her inflection.

Struggling to reply, Cash froze. He didn't know what to do… what to say. Finally, nodding his head, he stared blankly down to the floor. For God's sake, he couldn't bring himself to look at her.

Silence fell between them for some time as they both tried to absorb what was happening. And within the dimly lit room, only the ticking from the alarm clock on the bed stand made a sound.

It was eventually Cash's mother who broke the stillness by speaking in a warm, reaffirming way, "I want the best for you, Cash. I brought you into this world and I love you so very much. I can't fight what's going on in your life right now. I can only stand back and support you in the way you believe destiny is directing you. You're a smart young man and I believe you know what you're doing."

She paused, as if struggling not to cry.

With regained composure, she concluded with a sincere, honest warning. "Be careful. You don't need to sell yourself short, because you're still young, and there's plenty of time to sort things out. You don't need to rush into anything."

"I know," Cash replied, fighting back the tears in his eyes as well.

"As for the family—I think it will be best for you to keep this relationship at a low key until everyone has had time to work through it all. It's been a shock to all of us, and we're gonna need some time to—as you would say—get into the groove." A grin snuck across her lips as she leaned forward, and hugged her boy. Softly, she kissed him on the forehead.

Rising to her feet, she slowly walked toward the door.

"Mom," Cash looked up. "Thanks."

As she turned back, Cash could see a tear run down her cheek. She placed her hand on the doorknob and said, "Travis seems like a very nice guy. I just can't believe how *good-looking* he is." Shaking her head—as if in disbelief—she softly laughed. "One thing I'll say about you, Cash. You certainly don't settle for anything less than top-grade."

Only from the mouth of a rancher woman, thought Cash, as he allowed a broad smile to flood his face. He loved her with all his heart.

CHAPTER 4

Getting back into the world of school was like pulling teeth. Cash found it nearly impossible to lock in on anything demanding concentration. Thinking about Travis. Dreaming about Travis. Being with Travis. It was his obsession. Travis was becoming his entire world. Thank God this wasn't mid-terms or he'd be sunk.

The football game Wednesday afternoon came and went with Travis pulling off several great plays. He assisted the team in breaking a tie between the Cowboys and the Sidney Eagles. Unfamiliar with most of the plays and calls, Cash sat in the bleachers feeling a little out of place, somewhat dumb, and greatly cold—shivering like a frozen goat in his thermal Carharts and cowboy hat. Actually, it was the feet, in those pointy-toed boots, that was the most frozen of all. Football… he grimly thought to himself. He would have never dreamed of attending one of these games. Until now, it had never been an interest to him. As his mother had stated, his life was going to change—*and that it was*—quite dramatically. In spite of the weather and all the newness to everything, he could not help feeling pride swell up as he watched his other half work hard on the field. He looked excellent—very natural. Indeed, Travis was definitely in his niche…

"Hang onto your hats, folks." The announcer's voice blasted over the stadium's PA system. "The Cowboys are out of the huddle. It's down to one play, and fifteen yards to go…"

The ball was at the Cowboy's thirty-five yard line.

"Hagan at the center, he snaps it to Jovanovich."

Looking at the clock, Cash felt a surge of adrenaline shoot through his body… seven seconds remaining in the fourth quarter. The scoreboard read a tie at twenty-one points each. By now everyone was standing.

"Jovanovich, out of the pocket, looks for an open. He passes to number eighty-nine, Hunter on the right. Hunter gets completion for a five-yard reception… he turns and it's an option play. Let's see, he makes a rush from the line—and Kendall, twenty-five, comes from behind and blocks Sidney player, number sixteen. Hunter has it clear to the end and he carries the ball right into home! Touchdown for number eighty-nine, Travis Hunter, and the Cowboys!"

Instantly, the horn blew. Time was out. The crowd went nuts.

"And that's the game!" The announcer's voice boomed over the roar of hoots and hollers of excited fans. "The final score… Miles City Cowboys—twenty-seven, and the Sidney Eagles—twenty-one."

"That was one hell of a good job you did out there on the field tonight," Cash said grinning with great admiration as Travis strutted out of the locker room clutching his gym bag and jacket.

"Hey!" Travis' face quickly lit up when he saw Cash. "You were there?" Surprise was in his voice.

"Yup," Cash nodded. "Wouldn't have missed for the world."

Travis stopped and turned toward Cash; his eyes were shining. "I'm so glad. I wondered if you would be."

"Remember, I'm curious by nature," Cash gave a snort. "I had to find out what this game of yours is all about."

"That means a lot, Cash, it really does." Travis barely got his words out when a voice sounded from down the hall.

"Hey, Hunt! You goin' over to Welker's?"

"I wasn't plannin' to," replied Travis, pulling his attention away from Cash—directing it down the hall to a big-bellied senior named Harlan Jens.

Cash felt the hair on the back of his neck bristle upward as he watched Harlan waddle his way toward them. Considered one of the good 'ol boys, Harlan had a mouth that didn't stop at any form of vulgarity. *What a tub of lard*, thought Cash... *simply disgusting*.

"What's goin' on?" Travis asked.

"We're havin' a little celebration at his place tonight." Shifting his gaze toward Cash, the bodacious crew-cut blond cocked his head back and said, "Hey, Cash, how's it goin'?"

"All right," Cash mustered, "'n you?"

"Super," said Harlan, checking out Cash's hat, Carharts, and pointy-toed boots.

"Coach up on this?" There was hesitation in Travis' voice. "You know we've got a road game this Friday."

"Aw, he ain't gonna know 'bout it. Besides, we're only gonna have a couple of brews 'n that's it." Harlan had a way of making it all sound so small, sweet 'n innocent—a perfect blow-off.

"I don't know…" Travis was not convinced. Quickly, he glanced down at his watch. "I'll see."

"That's cool," Harlan nodded, shifting his attention back to Cash. With a smooth, roving eye, he let out a deep, gravelly laugh. "Surprised to see *you* out of the river bottoms."

"I get out every now 'n then." A hot streak of defensiveness shot through Cash's flesh.

"I see…" Harlan dragged his words, fixing his gaze squarely into Cash's eyes. With a cocky grin plastered to his face, the ape-shaped jock continued his expose`. "You git them boots any more pointy, cowboy, 'n you'll be hired by the bug man!" With that, he let out a loud, boisterous guffaw that echoed throughout the hallway.

Him and Clayton, Cash hotly thought. They could easily be thrown into the same damned barrel since they seemed cut from identical molds. Deciding Harlan's dumb-assed comment wasn't worth a sack of shit at a feed store, he refrained from emitting the cutting remark that was pursed at his lips. Remaining silent, he allowed a sarcastic grimace to cross his face. After a tense, passing moment, he finally gagged out a half-baked response, "Good to see you too, Harlan." *What a fat-ass*, he cynically told himself.

In an effort to break the stare-down between Harlan and Cash, Travis interjected with a brisk tone, "Well, I suppose we better be moving on. It's getting pretty late." And with one swivel of the heel of his motorcycle boot, he started for the stairwell.

Travis' abruptness in squelching the conversation caught Cash off guard. And like a newborn calf caught in its first thunderstorm, the revered football star was already halfway up the staircase by the time Cash realized he had actually left. *"What the hell?"* Breaking away from Harlan, he tried to catch up.

As he bounded up the stairs, Cash breathlessly asked, "Travis, what's up?"

Travis stopped at the top landing and without turning or facing Cash, he let out a sigh. He looked frustrated.

"What?"

Fixing his gaze on an emergency-fire sign posted on the wall, Travis remained quiet. "I knew this was going to happen." He put his head down.

"*What?*" Cash felt himself coming apart at the seams.

"That the guys on the team would give you shit."

Feeling like a bucket of concrete had just been dumped on him, Cash froze. "What are you saying?" Pursuing the issue, he wanted to hear Travis say the words he sorely dreaded.

"You're right," spoke Travis with despondent resolve. "We come from different worlds."

With an angry ball of fire exploding inside, Cash tried to regain his ricocheting senses. "In other words, you're ashamed to be seen with me in front of your friends?"

"I didn't say that!" Travis hotly retorted in behalf of his own defense.

"In so many words you have!" An angry sneer etched over Cash's face. His blood boiled. "Just admit it!"

"No!" Travis pleaded—trying to redeem himself against Cash's relentless rage.

"I don't need this!" Cash turned, pounding his fists onto the stairway door handle bar and shoving the door so hard it slammed fiercely against the wall.

"Cash, wait!" Travis fruitlessly tried to gain control of him.

Bolting out of the doors like a mad dog, Cash hotly marched toward his pick-up, angrily stomping his boot heels into the gravel with each step.

"Stop and listen to me!" Travis demanded, running after him—his voice forcefully deep. His voice boomed throughout the parking lot.

Instantly, Cash froze. Travis' heavy tone was seizing like a death grip.

"WHAT?"

"You misunderstood me." A breathless Travis slowed himself. "I am *not* ashamed of you. If anything, I'm extremely proud of you. You're a high achiever; and at times, I don't think you even realize it."

Several calming moments crept in between them…

"It's just like you said the other day… we *do* come from different worlds. Our friends are probably gonna start to wonder, and we'll have to work through all that." Noticing he had captured Cash's full attention, he went on to say in a hushed manner, "It's gonna take time… and a lot of patience. For Christ's sake, look at how your family reacted when I walked through the front door Friday."

"Harlan's an ass," Cash couldn't get his mind off of what had just happened.

"He needs to get to know you." Travis quickly came back. "Like your family with me—*it's going to take time.*"

"Why d'you take off from Jens 'n me so fast?" Cash was demanding. He wanted an explanation for that one.

Shifting his weight from one foot to the other, Travis quickly glanced away as if making sure they were alone in the parking lot. Refocusing, back on Cash, he finally said, "*I'm sorry.* I had to get away from that scene. If I would have stayed any longer, I would have grabbed him by the fuckin' throat and tossed him down the hall. How do you think I felt watching him pick at you?"

"I can take care of myself." Defiance swelled inside Cash. He didn't need anyone to watch out after him. His family was bad enough.

"I know that." A hint of a grin slid across Travis' lips. "It's just that I wanted to jump in too—raise a little hell." Pausing, he took a deep breath and went on to say, "You're one feisty little shit, you know that?"

"I've been told that a time or two." Flashbacks of constant scraps between him and his brothers quickly resurrected within his memory. Countless times, he recalled being sat down by either his dad or mom and given the sound warning that he needed to put a lid on his temper.

"Cash, you've gotta know I won't do anything to deliberately hurt you." The look on Travis' face was serious—as if making a vow before the God Himself. "*...Ever.*"

Cash remained quiet, looking down at the ground. Slowly, he shuffled a boot across the frozen dirt. His feet were ice. It would be the last time he'd wear cowboy boots to a damn football game.

Indian summer had its own brand of beauty as it finally settled across the vast, enveloping sky of the high northern plains, and upon the blazing ravines of the endless river valley. What made it more special was the rare absence of that ever-present wind. No one could have asked for a more beautiful Saturday; and Cash knew it was the perfect time to saddle up Brownie and head for the hills.

As they made their way out of the stables and into the ranch yard, Cash could hardly believe that only a week before all hell had been breaking loose from the unusually early snow storm. Going down into the records as one of the strongest Pacific systems this time of year, Cash knew he would not forget it—especially what had happened during that time in the school stairwell... and up in Travis' bedroom. The hurricane-force gusts, and unrelenting rain and sleet, had seemed to ditto what was occurring in his world.

It was as if he didn't know the young man looking at him each morning in the bathroom mirror. Oh, of course, he recognized the sun-bleached, strawberry-blond hair with the square-off, chiseled jaw and prominent dimple resting in the middle of his chin. Same too, with his deep-set, hazel eyes—accented by high cheek bones, rugged, heavy eyebrows, and a short, narrow nose that tended to curl up at the tip near the nostrils. As far as his physical features were concerned, everything was familiar...the usual and ordinary. But apart from that, it was all different.

He didn't feel like the same person—even his thoughts seemed new and strange. It was funny—in an odd sense—that no one ever crossed his mind as much as Travis did now. It wasn't the fact that he never thought of people, it was just that there was something about that Hunter boy which seemed to sneak into every corner of his conscience. There was nothing more in Cash's longings and desires than to be with Travis—talking to him, looking at him, doing virtually *anything* with him without feeling obligated, smothered or manipulated. In short, he found it simply fun just to be with him—whatever the activity. *Was this love... or an obsession?* He couldn't tell. Really, he didn't care.

Brownie's shuddering snort, the rhythmic grinding of his hooves on gravel, and an energetic nod with his shiny-mane quickly brought Cash back to the present.

Sections of the driveway were still muddy from melting snow. Earlier in the week, it had become a real mess with gumbo caking almost to the truck rims. Cash, Clayton, and his dad had planned to lay a coat of coarse stone over the entire length that previous spring, but the timing had never seemed to work out.

Reaching a trail head that led alongside the river bank, they left the drive at a sloppy dip to cut across a grassy level through a patch of brittle dry-wood. The afternoon sun baked warmly against Cash's back and neck as he looked up into the deep ocean of sapphire blue. It gave a feeling he could drown if he kept his head up. Cirrus clouds feathered across the endless expanse with a silence demanding reverence for the moment. The air inhaled through his nostrils was unusually sweet and fresh from the drying of flaming leaves and snow-washed earth.

Thinking of the football game that had been held up on the high-line in Havre the evening before, he could not help but feel an immense level of pride and excitement as Travis had remained focused on the plays, ultimately assisting the team to another victory... the tenth in a row.

Recalling a quote from the radio announcer...

"What an outstanding offensive aerial play! Number twelve, Jovanovich scrambles and sets up a forty-five yard screen pass to number eighty-nine, Hunter. And listen to this, folks, Hunter leaps into what looks like to me as the greatest body-stretched-out-full-finger-extension-catch of all time! Let's see, what's he going to do? He's taking the ball in for a touchdown from the fifteen!"

Later, in a brief interview with Travis, the announcer asked him, "What was going through your mind when you saw the ball shooting at you?"

"Well, I really didn't have much time to think," Travis' voice sounded really good over the radio waves. "We were waiting for the play, and I saw the screen right away—I knew I was in the open." Pausing for a moment, he eventually went on to say, "I just fell in line and did the dance." Cash could hear that familiar chuckle and picture the glowing look on his face. "Once I got the ball, I didn't look back—I just put my head down and ran as fast as I could..."

So far, the Cowboys were undefeated and ranked number one in the division. It had been a long time since the team was so tight like this. Cash truly believed it was because of Travis' unwavering spirit... not only because he was extremely dedicated in winning, but because he was so supportive to each of his teammates. From Cash's viewpoint, Travis was the main solder that bound the team together as a unified fighting machine. He knew how to work with everyone and they all loved and respected him for that.

Travis' call had come through right after the game. He was on his way back to Miles City and the excitement rode high in his voice.

"We won!"

"I knew you guys would do it," Cash assuredly stated. He had felt it all afternoon. It seemed like Travis and the rest of the team was extremely honed into each game. Nothing like this had ever existed before, and the attention of the entire state was beginning to focus on them with breathless anticipation. Would they take the state title this year? "I'm really proud of you."

"Yeah?" Travis asked as if he wanted to hear it from Cash's lips one more time.

"Hell, yeah!" exclaimed Cash. "I think you're the reason the team's been doing so good this year! You have a way of bringin' everyone together."

Travis laughed, "Hah!" But then pausing—as if allowing Cash's words to sink into his heart and soul, he quietly said, "I love you, Cash."

"I love you, too..." Cash reaffirmed, casting a wary glance over his shoulder from the phone in the hallway. He hoped his dad and brother were not overhearing their honest words of affection. But then again, he didn't give a good goddamn if they had.

With the playoffs starting the following week, everyone in the county was pumped with anticipation as the team blazed a trail to the state championship game. Scheduled to fight Butte Central in the first round, it would be a tight match. But the odds, however, seemed to be in Miles City's favor as the game was scheduled to be a home one. Even though the Saints from the Mining City were mean as devils, they tended to have a week spot in their defensive lineup. No doubt, the locals would show their support in droves.

That was more, however, than what could be said at the ranch. Clayton and his father continued to struggle with the stark reality of having Travis eventually become part of the family. Cash wondered how Clint would react. Having inherited a generous portion of their mother's personality, Cash surmised that he would probably be open to the matter.

Working their way along a margin of the trail, Cash heard the familiar song of a Western meadowlark announcing its presence from a lone cottonwood that stood like a guarding sentinel at the end of the next bend. They paused, Cash putting his mind in reverse—back to the previous Saturday after he had taken Travis back to his house. The dinner scene was still unnervingly fresh...

"Was Travis' mother back from Billings when you dropped him off?" Janice had innocently asked—passing the salad bowl to Cash.

Reading the stony visages that surrounded the table, it was apparent the others didn't want to hear that name. As if entombed in sound-proof vaults, Clayton and his dad remained silent and quite reposed.

"Yup," Cash hesitantly replied. "She said the roads were clear most of the way."

"I guess Forsyth had no electricity until this morning." In spite of the thick, heavy air hanging throughout the room, Mrs. McCollum seemed very determined to carry on the conversation.

"There's still no electricity out toward Colstrip," Cash added, thinking it was ironic since the huge power plant was based there.

"Well, I'm sure they'll get everyone back on line as soon as possible." Cash's mother stated with a twinkle in her eye. It had been hard not to pick up on the implication of her comment—as if she had purposely gone out of her way to make that point.

Cash could not prove it, but he honestly believed that it had been one of the quietest suppers the family had ever had in his life. Not a word, not even a grunt was uttered from either his dad—who busily positioned himself directly over his plate—not looking up except to drink his water, and Clayton who, with a surly countenance, kept shuffling his food from one side of the plate to the other with his fork. Talk about one hell of an awkward situation.

Cash's attention was suddenly drawn back by Brownie who shied and reared without warning. "Wo!..Wo!" he called out to the startled horse—trying to control his spooked behavior. About twenty yards down the trail's straight way, a timid coyote bounded from the brush with a light spring in its feet. Sleek and graceful, it suddenly stopped and closely watched the unexpected intruders with a wary eye. There must have been a tinge of curiosity hidden within the heavily grey-coated animal as it continued to stand perfectly still. Except for the rotation of its large ears, seeking to pick up the slightest sound of aggressive movement, every muscle remained taut in case of the need for a fast escape.

"That ain't no wildcat," Cash softly reassured.

Brownie, however, just wasn't convinced as he continued to nervously dance from side to side.

"He ain't gonna hurt you. He's just curious…wants to see what we're all about."

Cash's calm explanation seemed to finally soak in as the horse eventually relaxed his taut muscles.

With a snort, Brownie cocked his head sideways, giving Cash a critical eye. He seemed disgusted that nothing was being done to scare their silent observer away.

The coyote remained motionless for another brief moment, then without a sound, jumped off the trail into a thicket of willows and on toward the riverbank's marshy edge.

Cash leaned forward and gently stroked Brownie's long, glistening neck with slow-moving fingers. Softly whispering into the horse's right ear, he said, "Well, what'd ya think 'a that one? Pretty excitin'… huh?"

As if slipping off into a little trance, Brownie's long lashes began to slide down over his eyes—head drooping lower at every breath.

Cash gave a small chuckle. "Hey you…don't you fall asleep on me." He began to scratch the whiskers of his warm, soft muzzle.

In a way, the young, handsome cowboy found himself completely satisfied hangin' out with Brownie and the other animals on the ranch. He knew where each of them were comin' from, and he believed they understood him as well. Rarely, was there ever the crazy misunderstandings he so often experienced with humans. People tended to be a lot more complicated— with a ton of prejudgments and expectations. Oftentimes, it was downright exhausting—even with Travis.

What was it that attracted him to that guy? His body? His easygoing personality? The fact that he was interested in him? Perhaps it was a combination of all these things—and then some. The bottom line was,

Travis was truly an exception to the norm. He knew he wanted Travis in his life, and he would do nothing to ever change that.

Resuming their afternoon trek, Cash and Brownie continued along the trail until the river met up with a series of bluffs that led to a desolate area. Beyond that, they worked their way to a grassy plateau where the view of the plains was endless. For miles, all one could see was sky and prairie. It was so…big.

As they cut across the barren land, Cash's thoughts were redirected to the rodeo arena. The district's last qualifier for the season was scheduled in Glendive the next weekend. He knew it would be a fairly big show with a good number of contestants for both the rough stock and timed events. Having registered for three, he knew it would be a busy, challenging two days. And as Travis had stated—so far, he was doing unbelievably well in the standings for the year—earning top scores in saddle bronc and bareback, and placing second in bull riding. His overall scores currently had him tied for number one in the state for the High School Rodeo Association's All-Around Cowboy title. It had always been his dream to work the circuit and now all that hard work and dedication throughout his younger years seemed to be paying off with the possibility of a generous scholarship. Now, if he could just remain focused for this last competition until spring, he'd be set for the state championship title, a hefty scholarship, and the prized gold buckle.

Reaching for a pack of smokes from his jean jacket, he lit a cigarette and inhaled a slow, deep drag. As the thick tobacco smoke filled his chest, his thoughts went back to the last rodeo he had worked before Travis entered the picture—changing all the scenery…

It had been a big weekend at the town of Red Lodge. Huddled against the flanks of the Beartooths, the drive had been over a couple hundred miles each way. Cash, Clayton, and their father each took turns in driving and taking care of the animals throughout the trip. Since Mr. McCollum was a certified stock contractor for the organization. It meant a lot of work not only for Cash, but for his brother as well. He didn't mind helping out, though, because it was fun having his family present to support him for each event.

Cash's first round, saddle bronc, had gone very well as he had excited the sold-out crowd with a ninety-two point ride aboard an arm-jerker, double-kicker, stallion named Bad Blood.

Even in the beginning, he knew he was going in for one heck of a ride as the horse refused to stand still—vigorously fighting Cash before leaving the chute. Marking out with his spurs and gripping the rein with locked strength, he quickly determined the motion and rhythm of the frenzied animal, although, it was not easy to maintain the control. Bucking, double-kicking with the force of a cyclone, the momentum of the horse placed an excruciating pull on Cash's arm. From how far the horse dropped its head, he instantly adjusted the length of the rein and continued to ride into the bucking pattern. Before he knew it, the buzzer went off, and there were loud cheers from the stands. Dismounting in one giant leap, Cash noticed a number of people standing and waving as he made his way back to the ring.

"You're good, Cash." Mr. McCollum said very proudly, patting him on the back. "Damn good."

That had made Cash feel so fine. Rarely did his father extend himself with a compliment. He knew he would need to tuck that one away in a safe place forever.

Both days at the rodeo had proved equally good for him, as he walked away with eighty-eight points in bareback and a double-header score of seventy-nine points in both rounds of the bull-riding—placing first in each event. Clearly, he was recognized as the top scoring cowboy at Red Lodge, sliding him into the state's most coveted title with another stockman from Great Falls. On top of that, the crowd loved him—giving him a strut to his step and a kick in his spirit. His mom said he was always a good showman...

The chatter from a duo of indignant prairie dogs taking stance near a patch of prickly pear demanded Cash and Brownie's full attention from their separate daydreams. The two little fellers were obviously upset by the unannounced intrusion upon their territory.

"You both just settle down there." Cash spoke, finding himself rather amused by their cantankerous attitudes. "We ain't meanin' no trouble."

Flaunting several aggravated twitches with their bushy tails, and one last round of spunky bark, they quickly retreated into their burrowed ground holes.

"I guess they told us off, huh, Brownie?" Cash laughed quietly under his breath.

Looking at the dimming daylight stretch its rays across the gaping horizon, the pungent odor of sage and juniper, along with the musty smell of earth began to fragrantly rise up into Cash's nostrils, tantalizing his senses. As the sun dropped and the first twinkle of stars began to peek out from the bottomless sea of violet and midnight blue, a deafening stillness fell over the limitless landscape. The chill of night began to bite at his nose and cheeks. Turning around, satisfied in their souls, they eventually made their way back home.

CHAPTER 5

Secrecy, by nature, was simply not part of Cash's personality. It wasn't the fact he couldn't keep a confidence, it was just that he rarely meddled in other people's lives or caught himself in situations that required such behavior. In an odd way, he felt like he was sneaking around in an effort to keep everything at a low profile, per his mother's advice. Putting a hush concerning his relationship with Travis, on one hand, seemed fun and tantalizing; on the other, it bugged him—making him feel a little guilty and paranoid about his actions.

Aside from all the strangeness, he laboriously strove to keep everything under cover publicly, even around his family. His belief was that as long as they didn't flaunt it, things would be okay. The fact about him and Travis would remain a secret.

Clayton, however, shared a different viewpoint. Cash learned of the cracks in their cover immediately after first period that following Wednesday. Weaving through the mayhem of students in the crowded hallway, Cash mechanically made his way to his next class. Feeling rather tired from a long night of twisting and turning, he earnestly wished he could find a quiet spot to sack out, for an hour or so, in an effort to regroup.

His first clue that things were amiss came from a very interesting and unexpected source—his second cousin. From his back, without turning around, he heard her familiar voice. This was not a good morning to have a conversation with her, he told himself—quickly looking for an out. Jennifer Evers, oldest daughter from a first cousin on his mother's side, was a slightly pudgy, overly-friendly girl, who was a year behind Cash in school. And even though they were considered blood, and so close in age, Cash felt there really wasn't anything else they had in common. Most of the time, he never even thought about her.

"Hey, Cash!"

Turning slowly, he felt ripples flow over his skull and down the back of his neck.

Methodically, she trotted down the hallway in thick-heeled shoes, her light brown hair pulled back pony-tail fashion, reminding him at once of his mother. When she caught up to him, her bright blue eyes were wide—full of secrets and wild stories.

"Hey, Jen… watcha up to?" Cash felt like he had to force the words from his throat.

Standing just inches from him, her breath assailed at his face with a vengeance. At first she said nothing and then with a blink of her eyes, she smiled slowly. "What do you know about algebra?"

This is damned strange, thought Cash shaking his head. "You're asking me about somethin' I'm not particularly adept at, Jen. Why?"

"Well, I'm having the darnedest time with these equations we're having to do. I can't understand much of anything that's going on in that class. I know you've taken it, so I thought…" At that, her voice trailed off. Her eyes strayed around the hallway—surveying. "I tried to ask Clayton when I saw him at the Co-op last night, but he just blew me off."

"What was Clayton doing at the Co-op?" Cash idly asked, knowing that his brother spent a good chunk of time hanging out there after work from the Livestock Research Station. *Moreover, what was Jennifer doing there?* But he didn't say that.

"Well, he was looking for my father, number one. You know he goes down there on Tuesday evenings to hang with the guys. He always has, it's one of his strange habits."

What was strange about that? A spark ignited within Cash. At least the McCollums were somewhat predictable. Living up to their Bohemian reputation, the Evers clan was regarded as less than routine. Gypsies, was what his dad had labeled them. Having the tendency to drop in unannounced, and hang out for hours—they all seemed oblivious to the chores everyone else was committed to do at various times of the day— usually bringing the blood vessels straight to the surface of Mr. McCollum's neck. In short, planning ahead simply wasn't part of their vocabulary.

Moreover, it was rare for any of them to bring a project to some form of completion. Their house was a true example of this. Consisting of a hodge-podge of various styles of architecture, bearing no semblance of reason, it looked more like a by-product of random after-thoughts and clutter than a conscious break from tradition. To Cash, it never looked finished. There were always rooms not completely dry-walled or painted, floors not fully tiled, and a yard usually half-mowed or dug up for one reason or another. A refugee camp was what he always called it.

She definitely had no room to speak regarding 'strange habits'. *What a bunny*, he cynically thought to himself.

"Anyway," she crossed to stand more squarely before Cash, placing herself between him and his locker. "I couldn't get anything out of Clay, so when I saw you, I thought…"

Cash interrupted her, his impatience beginning to surface. "I'm not the best one to ask. Isn't your friend, Tiffany Jo or whatever her name is, pretty smart when it comes to stuff like that? I know she has the reputation…"

Jennifer snorted a laugh, raising a hand over her mouth. "Yep, you can say that about her!"

The direction of this conversation was troublesome. Cash had the urgency to be away from her like the need to piss after awakening in the middle of the night.

"Anyway, Jen, what I mean is, I'm not really good at math. Never have been. It's not what you'd call my strong suit."

Hoping that would redirect her away from his locker, he tried to take a step forward, but she still blocked him.

"Well, at least you're nice about it." Again, she took a searching look around. "Unlike your brother, Clayton."

At that, Cash had to smile. "I take it you're givin' me a compliment."

She reached behind her head and tugged at her hair—it looked like she was trying to yank it out. The hallway eventually cleared and suddenly the bell rang. Still, she remained like a linebacker on Travis' team.

"Naturally. I hope you don't mind." She started to turn, and then hesitated. Obviously something else was on her mind that wasn't algebra.

"You know," she continued, now facing away, "at the Co-op last night he was kinda drunk."

Cash couldn't pretend surprise. Clayton was always the one to get rowdy. But this had been a Tuesday night, not exactly characteristic of his brother. The sounds of several kids racing for their next class passed by the pair huddled close to the lockers. Cash waited with tightened jaw for Jennifer to continue the story she was obviously just beginning.

"I'm so glad you're not like your brother, really glad. Otherwise I couldn't tell you this. But he said some really terrible things about you last night. Really bad, *you* know?" Her tone was expectant.

Cash felt the floor tile begin to pull away from his feet. And in this nightmare there was no one—absolutely no one close enough to catch him in his fall. He already knew what she was going to say.

Standing too close to him now, he felt his oxygen being stolen. "Things about you and that new guy, Travis whatshisname." Her voice was coy.

Hell, everyone in school knows his name, thought Cash. *What the fuck was she playing?*

"Hunter," she went on to say. "Yeah, Hunter, right? From Cal-i-forn-ea." Her sudden laugh recalled the prairie dog's bark, only less honest. "You and Travis Hunter."

He resisted the urge to grab her by the shoulders and slam her against the wall. Instead, he shifted the books in his arms, restraining the hiss rising within him. "Said things, like what?"

The coyness came full to the front, along with a sly grin, "Things that really shouldn't be repeated," she offered. "But nothing nice, I can tell you that."

There was now a long silence, the waiting.

Get it over with, his head screamed. Instead, he remained perfectly still.

She was obviously becoming nervous, or maybe just impatient. Her voice lowered. "About how people in the town shouldn't be all excited about that Hunter kid, that's what Clay called him. Except not with the kid part—another name I won't say. But people shouldn't have expectations about him, because as far as he could tell—Clayton, I mean—as far as Clayton could tell, he was nothing more than a miserable faggot."

There it was, out in the open. Cash kept the silence like a vigil, knowing it would work to get her to tell the remainder of her rotten tale.

"And the worst thing he said, not that *that* wasn't bad enough. The worst thing he said was that you were hanging around him too much, and it would make *you* look like a faggot, too."

He couldn't get it out of his mind. It kept repeating over and over like an old, worn out record—something his grandma always used to say when Cash's mom would stand up to his dad concerning certain issues. This time, however, Cash conveniently reworded it to fit the current situation— "Hell hath no fury than that of a *brother* scorned." Cash felt himself swell with titanic rage as he drove home that afternoon. Yes sir, the line had been crossed. A price would have to be paid. There was no doubt that he would be able to customize his vengeance regarding what Clayton had done at the Co-op. He'd make it fit like a goddamn glove...

"You just couldn't keep your fuckin' mouth shut, could you?" The words shot forth from Cash's angry lips like speeding bullets from a sniper's rifle, piercing the still air of the horse barn, and taking his brother by complete surprise.

As if ambushed by a guerrilla commando, Clayton turned with a start and stumbled over several sacks of feed stacked on the floor, his eyes wide with terror. "W-what?" Quickly, he tried to play dumb, as if he didn't have a clue why Cash would be enraged. To the young man fumbling his way to some point of safety, it was evident on his face—he knew Cash wasn't playing games.

Like a rattlesnake coiling to strike its prey, Cash moved in closer, his fists tightly clenched. Nervously, Clayton took several steps back in a fruitless effort to avoid the line of fire.

There was no way his brother was going to smooth-talk his way out of this one, Cash resolved. The price of breaking precious family trust was simply too high—and today was the day he intended to drive that point home. "You know damn well what."

"Aw shit, Cash," Clayton coughed up a half-baked excuse, "I was only joking around."

"Yeah? Well, other people didn't take it like that." The fire inside Cash's chest was beginning to bring his blood to a scalding boil.

"Yeah?" mimicked Clayton, a sarcastic sneer swept across his heavy-browed, dark-eyed face. "Well, it's not my fault that what I said was the truth!"

That was it. All stops pulled, it was time to move in and teach this boy a lesson. "You son-of-a-bitch!" Cash threw himself over the sacks of horse feed and onto his brother who met the onslaught with flying fists. There was no question of who was more fit for this match. Cash balanced a slender, well-defined six-pack torso on two muscular, agile legs giving him a body made for ridin' and fightin'. With remarkably fast reflexes and an uncommon edge for depth perception, he had an undeniable ability to take the best-of-the-best down for the count.

Clayton, on the other hand, was extremely muscular, but he held a good share of extra weight around the waist and thighs—giving him the resemblance of a small yearling bear cub. It was this extra weight that seemed to hold not only his power, but speed back as a competitive fighter.

With the force and direct precision of a guided missile, Cash pinned his brother mercilessly against the wall inside the tiny feed room. And with the speed of lightening, he thrust a fiery fist into a powerful right-handed hook—slamming his knuckles squarely against the ridge of Clayton's nose. Instantly, he felt the break and heard the snap. Excreting a yelp of pain, Clayton frantically brought his hands to his face while streams of crimson blood began to flow down his chin and neck. As if anticipating what would happen, Cash, without a word, quickly scooped up his elder sibling and assisted him to the pick-up. Dashing into the house, he grabbed several towels from the linen pantry—nearly mowing his mother down along the way.

"I didn't know you were here!" she exclaimed, a high-pitched tone emitting from her voice. Suddenly, a look of horror flooded in her face. "My God, what's happened?" Fixing her gaze at the blood covering Cash and his shirt, she automatically followed Cash outside.

"Clayton 'n I got into a scrap; 'n I think I busted his nose." Cash could hardly get the words out for lack of breath. It felt like his heart was going to explode.

"You what?!" Janice snapped at Cash.

"You heard me!" Cash hollered back as he reached the truck and began to wrap towels around Clayton's face. "Put your head back!" Cash bellowed out as though he were a sergeant.

Clayton moaned, but remained relatively motionless. From the glassiness within his eyes, it looked like he was going into shock.

"I knew you two were going to get into it sooner or later." Exasperation settled into his mother's voice as the fear subsided to disgust.

"Look, I don't have time to be lectured right now. I need to get him to the hospital."

Shaking her head in disbelief, her words came out in somewhat of a detached manner—as if resolving to stay out of the entire mess and let them work it out on their own. "He's all yours."

As Cash ran around to the other side of the truck and hopped into the cab, he replied, "Thanks a lot."

Throwing out one last comment before Cash shifted down and drove off, Mrs. McCollum shoved her hands into her jean pockets, "Hope you both get this ironed out before you kill each other!"

Cash drove him to the hospital. The ride was quiet except for a few groans from Clayton. Never, in all their days had a conflict precipitated into something like this. Usually things could be settled in a day or two, having it culminate with a batch of choice words and a whole lot of hollerin'. Black eyes, bruises, and perhaps a busted lip would occur, but never a broken nose—or spirit. Cash knew this would settle inside his brother as molasses on a frigid morning. Clayton would nurse the hurt, find a good reason to hold onto the grudge, and bury the resentment deep into his bones. What little closeness they had exchanged before would be snuffed—like a votive candle being blown out by an indifferent priest.

As they sat together in the icy silence of the emergency room, stone bricks were set with fresh mortar, layer by layer. By the time Clayton came out of the examining room, face all bandaged up, Cash felt as if someone was yanking his guts out hand over fist a yard at a time. He wanted to puke.

Damn it! He thought to himself as they rode back home. *What was happening to this family?* Was it all because of him? Somehow, he knew he couldn't blame himself for the reactions of his brother and dad. He wouldn't! They would just have to get over it, or else there'd be a division... one hell of a rift.

CHAPTER 6

Saturday was quickly approaching—and with it—a mix of emotions. What of Clayton? What of his father? Ever since his apparent "coming out" episode on that fateful Friday, Cash had felt repercussions strong enough to slice and dice a coconut. Perhaps the most difficult part was being shoved into the company with two of the most tight-lipped creatures on Earth. And even though he was eager to get back out into the arena, he dreaded the moment his father would pull the damned truck and trailer out of the yard. As far as he was concerned, nothing seemed to be getting resolved and it was driving him nuts.

"...I feel like tellin' them don't bother takin' me to Glendive. I'll get there just fine on my own." Cash had complained to Travis over cold, dried-out grilled cheese sandwiches in the school cafeteria the day after his infamous encounter with Clayton. Seemingly, his mouth had lost its ability to taste.

Giving him a heartfelt smile, Travis had spoken earnestly—with that soft, soothing voice of his. "Things can change before Saturday. And even though you might not feel it right now, your family still loves you very much. Besides, it's gonna take time for them to get used to the idea you're gay. Shit, *you're* still working through it. You can't expect them to turn around over night. You know, it took some time for my mom to adjust after she found out. I think she had assumed that eventually there would be a daughter-in-law and some grandchildren coming down the line." Pausing for a brief moment, reflecting on what he had just said, he went on to say with a chuckle, "I guess I've blown that one sky high."

Cash remained quiet—hiding deep in a sea of inner thoughts. He knew Travis was right. Everyone simply needed time…

Despite his frustration, Cash was excited to get in there and ride. He loved rodeos and that was a joy no one would ever take from him. Even Travis was all caught up with Cash's excitement. Later that day after the tasteless lunch, Cash had felt a tap on his shoulder as he threw his books into his locker and grabbed for his sheepskin jacket.

"Hey Bucky," Travis interjected, leaning over, a sparkle in his eyes.

It had seemed that Travis was taking possession of Clayton's nickname for Cash. That was alright—in fact, it sort of made him feel good… kind of special.

"How would you like *me* to come along with you to Glendive?"

"You've got a game Saturday afternoon." Cash couldn't conceive in his mind how Travis would fit everything in. He knew the game would probably not be over until pretty late, and it would be a heavy haul to Glendive after that. Besides, his father and Clayton would be there. What would they say? How would they react having Travis trail around with them after a long, hard day at the arena? Covering his dry-lipped mouth with a fist, he coughed up a guilty excuse. "Clayton will be there—you know how he gets at times and Dad's one of the main stock contractors. We're all gonna be pretty busy getting' the animals tucked in for the night—I think you'll find yourself really tired, if not kinda bored."

"Are you sure?" Travis was not quick to have his offer turned down.

"You know I'd love to have you come along… I really want you to, but I know how tense it'll be with those two. I think it would be best for all concerned if you stayed."

Travis did not stop insisting. "I just wanna be with you."

A ripple quickly flowed across the dark lines on Cash's wrinkled brow, allowing a smile to be exposed over his face. Lately, a particular surliness had seemed to settle into Cash's spirit, encouraging the already brooding expression indigenous to his physical features to show even further.

Travis' eyes lit up at the arrival of the illusive grin. He stood back in silence—taking in the sight with a long admiring look. "There we go! That's the smile I've come to love with all my heart."

"You always know how to say the right things."

"Not always," Travis admitted, "but I usually speak what I feel." Not taking his gaze off Cash for one second, Travis stood broad shouldered, hands down at his waist, and thumbs hooked easily into the belt loops of his pants.

Never in all his days did anyone go out of their way to treat him so damn special. This boy sure did know how to make him feel good.

For a moment, Cash's brain went into high gear, working out the ways in his mind Travis might come along. But as quickly as the possibilities came to thought, so did the stark world of reality. Taking a deep breath, Cash painfully forced the words from his reluctant lips. "I'll be back on Sunday. We'll get together then."

"You drive a hard bargain, Mister McCollum." There was disappointment in the tone of Travis' voice. "…but I understand…"

Saturday morning, as Cash packed some last minute stuff into his gear bag, his fingers ran across something strange nestled against one of the sides of the main compartment. It was soft and furry. Already knowing what it was before he pulled the object out of the bag, the thought crossed his mind— *how did this get in here?*

Drawing it up to his cheek, he brushed the smooth white fur of the rabbit's foot against the rough beard stubble and skin. Someone had surreptitiously placed it in the bag. *Who?* Quickly, Cash's hand returned to the bag where he had discovered the charm. Scanning the space between the bag and his protection vest, he felt a folded piece of paper tucked into one of the pockets on the vest. As he pulled it out and unfolded it, he instantly recognized Travis' handwriting. In the dim light of the tiny bed stand lamp, he read the note...

"Hey, Bucky! Your mom let me slip this in your bag when you were out feeding the horses—hope you don't mind. I wish I could be with you today, although I understand why you did not want me to come along. Please know I will be thinking of you every minute. You will do a great job out there on the arena—I feel it in my bones. Don't forget how much I love you. I will always be by your side—even if it is only in my thoughts and prayers. Love, Travis. P.S. Stuff it deep in your pants!"

Cash caught himself laughing at the last line. Only his boyfriend would think of something like that. And since when were he and his mother in cahoots? That really took him by surprise. What he couldn't figure out—how did they do it right under his nose? He thought for sure he would have heard the Viper rolling into the yard... the whole thing seemed sort of mysterious, but overwhelmingly intriguing.

Cash flicked off the bedside light, making his way to the door. With a pause, he turned and looked into the dark room. This was his home, where he grew up. He would forever love this place. To him, it was his warmth and safety—a place where he could always be himself... with no pretenses.

Quietly, he made his way down the old, creaking stairs to the huge, shadowy living room. Each scuff of his boot heels on the hardwood floor fell into rhythmic syncopation with the steady ticking of the ancient clock—resting on the fireplace mantle.

Well, it looked like Clayton was going to pass on this one. In a way, he wasn't surprised. With his nose all bandaged up, he probably didn't want anyone to see him that way. At times, he wondered who was vainer… his brother, or himself. It was probably a toss up.

Shutting the heavy door behind him, he carried his saddle and gear to the pick-up where his dad was already waiting. The morning was brisk and still—stars twinkling brightly in the heavy, black sky. Today was going to be a great day. He could feel it in his spirit. Despite the fact that Clayton wasn't coming along, he sensed it would be a good time to regroup with his dad. So much had happened since the last competition.

Cash threw his saddle and bag in the back and crawled into the warm confines of the cab. His father was listening to an old country-western tune on the radio.

"All set?" Mr. McCollum asked, looking over his shoulder with a weary expression.

"Yup," Cash replied as he settled into the seat.

"Then let's get this show on the road." The gray-haired, slightly hunch-backed man shifted down and pulled slowly out of the yard. Looking back at the trailer in the rear view mirrors, his eyes cast one last inspection before they got to the highway. "The animals didn't fight me today. Hope they're not fixin' to be a bunch of hat-benders out in the arena." There was wariness in his voice.

"Maybe they're just wakin' up." Cash interjected earnestly.

"Yeah, well that's somethin' I damn well need to do as well."

Cash looked over at his dad. He really *did* look tired. "You want me to drive?" The offer was sincere.

"No," he said, grabbing for the coffee thermos between the seats. "I'll be good for awhile."

The trip to Glendive was long and mostly quiet with neither one really saying much except for a random comment here or there about the sunrise, empty highway, and foggy steam rising from the river into the frosty morning air. On the other side of Terry, Cash ordered his dad to pull over. After several sleepy nods from his father, he reckoned it was time to take over the wheel and let his dad catch up on a few winks.

By the time they arrived at the arena, the grounds were buzzing with activity. Stock contractors were unloading their animals while association officials quickly inspected each one. Throughout the morning, Cash assisted Mr. McCollum in getting the stock ready for the show. To his discovery, the bulls were already feisty and extremely agitated, thankfully putting his father's fear to rest. Brownie was once again in his element. Considered the Association's mascot, it was almost expected Cash and his dad bring him for each show. It seemed that horse got more attention then any of the McCollums put together. After getting the animals and his dad situated, he found an open space out behind the chute area where he could get ready. Checking his ropes, rigging, and saddle, he ensured everything was in good working condition. The sweet smells of aged leather and livestock, blending with the typical odors of straw, manure, and chewing tobacco all drifted easily into his nostrils. Cowboy catnip.

As he ran through several 'kicking out' routines on a bail of hay with his saddle, rein, and metal-bound wood stirrups, his mind kept going back to the tiny rabbit's foot and note safely tucked away in his jeans pocket. He could feel his focus sharpening on the task at hand. For the love of a hot, true-blue man, and the support of an understanding family, he would win this. There were no other options.

The freezing haze and fog of the morning eventually burned away to the warmth and brightness of a blazing strong afternoon sun. Before he knew it, the grandstands were starting to fill and the smell of vendor food wafted throughout the air. The time quickly arrived with the familiar booming-sound of the national anthem over the speakers followed by the rodeo announcer's hearty welcome and opening comments.

The timed events were first on the schedule. Historically, Cash never really got into team roping, or steer wrestling even though he had tried his hand at both on various occasions. His true love was rough stock. Saddle bronc was the first rough stock event of the show, and Cash's entry slot was fast approaching. The scores so far were somewhat less than desired—ranging from mid-fifties to upper-seventies; most of them, however, fell in the sixties. He *had* to do better than that, he dutifully told himself.

Leaning down and making some last minute adjustments to his spurs, chaps and vest, Cash drank in a long, calming breath before climbing into the chute. With a gentle pull from his forefinger on the brim of his hat, he drew it deeper across his brow. He needed some relief from the blinding rays of the cloudless autumn sun. Looking around, he finally decided to make his way toward the chute area. As his lanky legs fell into an easy stride, his spurs jingled against the heels of his boots. The special hand-designed chaps his dad had given him for his last birthday brushed leisurely over the powdery dirt and against a pair of well-worn Wranglers. He got his number and stock assignment from the officials. Chute number three. A mean-spirited stallion named Black Eye was his bronc. Suddenly, he felt a shudder flow through his legs. It would definitely be a challenge. He had heard about this horse's reputation and instantly he knew he was in for one hell of a ride.

Coming up to Cash, his father still appeared rather weathered by the early morning. But in spite of the dark shadows around his eyes, he carried a certain twinkle with a hint of an earnest grin. He reached over and patted him softly on the back. With heavy, rough-worn hands, he grabbed the back of Cash's pencil neck and in the spirit of their revered tradition, he whispered, "Cowboy up, son... go git 'em!"

Chills shot up Cash's spine. The gap was once again re-bridged... a relationship restored. *Hallelujah!*

He was ready to ride. "Let's go!" Cash sounded out as he hopped up on the railing. He and the assistants saddled up and cinched in Black Eye with the latigos. Sliding down into the narrow chute, he settled on the well-worn saddle sensing the wild kicks and stomps of the restless animal beneath him. With his boots sliding snugly into the stirrups, and his hands gripping the rein, he watched his bronc angrily nod—full, with hot, steamy snorts. The horse's eyes became wide with black animosity. He wanted a fight.

Inhaling its scalding breath deep into his yearning, thirsty lungs, Cash could taste the burning fire that blazed from deep within the breast and bowels of the twitchy, muscular creature. Into the stallion's ears, he hissed words of fire. *"Fight me, you bastard... give me all you've got!"* His tongue swelled thick with consuming hunger as he wanted to devour every morsel of this bronc's red-hot resistance.

Cash felt himself tighten—clenching his jaw with a force as if every tooth was welded together. As he leaned back with his legs pushed forward, he mercilessly dug the rowels of his spurs against the bronc's shoulders. With a commanding shout, the chute door thrust open; out they flew. Instantly, he marked out with a wide, clean sweep and began bicycling the flanks with his spurs. He could feel every joint—each nerve and fiber of his body jolted by unbelievable forces—as if he was slammed against a brick wall and then plunged deep into space like a rocket. Tightening his core, he fought from having his insides spew out from each thrust. The frenzied animal exploded with each expelling snort and low growl, starting with several high double-kicks and then sucking back from the right to an immediate buck for the left. Cash yanked the rein closer, gaining control before being set up with a fake turn. This animal was crazy, making it nearly impossible to determine its next move.

Overhead, the announcer's voice boomed across the PA, "Ladies and gentlemen, from chute number three, the cowboy we've all been waiting for—Cash McCollum, a senior from Miles City on top-challenge Black Eye!"

Somewhere in the mist of this mortal combat, Cash could hear the thunderous applause from the grandstands. The only thing he could concentrate on was the vicious struggle between him and the obstinate bronc bucking wildly between his legs. Keeping control was the name of this game; he was completely determined not to loose it.

No more had the thought entered Cash's head, and the frenzied animal reared up—lunging feverously. And like a gunshot, it broke in two— bucking and jumping as if it was a nervous frog on a scorching stove. Each pitch shot horse and cowboy higher and higher. Suddenly, Cash felt something unleash within his spirit. He could contain himself no more. *"Yee haw!"* he howled high into the air, his free hand wildly scratching into the deep-blue sky. Without a doubt, he knew he had himself a genuine honkin', high-roller. He loved animals like these. They were a freaking rush of high adrenalin!

Blending into its raw force and energy, Cash chose to give everyone *exactly* what they wanted… *a show.* With an arch in his back, head held high, and his free arm extended out behind like a lightening rod, he began to float each jump—pretending that he was being bucked—but all the while in full control. Suddenly, the buzzer blew, and Cash bailed out from the stirrups and saddle to land square with his boot heels in the soft, powdery surface of the arena ring.

The crowd was wild—many standing and cheering. Cash slipped his favorite black Resistol off and took a quick bow before turning back toward the chutes. *I did it!* He proudly told himself. He felt pumped. His heart pounded heavily.

"Well, there you have it, folks." The voice from the speakers flooded the arena. "One of Montana's top-ridin' cowboys—and a true showman at that… Cash McCollum! Let's give him a hand for a job well-done."

Looking up at the scoreboard, the tingly adrenalin swiftly sizzled and popped through his veins. He blinked as if to wake from a hazy dream. His eyes could not believe what he saw. It was obvious, he wasn't the only one taken by complete surprise. From the tone of the announcer's voice, Cash could tell he shared the same sentiment. *"Ninety-four!* Ladies and gentlemen, I believe that is a record breaker! This man is definitely blazin' a trail to the professionals!"

Each recovery step he took in his dusty, scuffed-out cowboy boots made him feel that much closer to passing out. His head was reeling. Closing his eyelids, he prayed his mind would clear. Still dizzy and appropriately dirty from the horrendous ride, he could only wonder what a mess he must look like as fellow cattlemen and spectators swooped in on him. Countless pats on the back and friendly grabs to his neck made him feel like a Shetland pony in a kiddie carnival. Inside his skull, a pain shot out with the explosive reverberation of a 30-30 caliber rifle.

"Way to go, Cash! Giddy-up-go! Great work out there! Ride'm cowboy! Your dad'll be mighty proud of you…"

It all continued to come at him like a barrage of artillery. People were everywhere, approaching Cash as though making a four-squared cage to enclose him. At first, he tried moving. Eventually, he just gave up and stopped in the middle of a footstep, acknowledging the arms extended, and hands pounding on his back. Somehow, his hat got knocked from his head, and after straightening back up from retrieving it, he found himself frantically looking for a quiet spot to sit and gather himself together.

Brushing at his shirt, he looked down at his boots. A strange, peculiar feeling quickly swept over him. All of these people around, yet he felt so alone. He should be proud—ecstatic even. It was the best rodeo ride of his career so far. Why didn't he feel better?

Damn it! Travis should have been there.

The last of the well-wishers finally wandered away, a few turning now and again to look back at him with a thumbs-up. *Yeah*, Cash thought, *everything is great...really.*

It was impossible to kid himself, however.

After retrieving his saddle and gear, he slowly... and painfully made his way back to the parking area. His knees, lower back, and shoulders burned with pain.

Somewhere between the arena and the family stock trailer, Cash heard a football game broadcasting from a portable radio. Breaking off the charted trail, he quietly meandered between the parked vehicles in an effort catch a better earshot. He knew it had to be the match between Butte Central and Miles City.

"...the ball's been taken by Central with Cowboys quarterback, number sixteen, Jovanovich, calling for a huddle."

What was the score? Cash impatiently asked himself as he stalled by the RV where the broadcast was coming from.

"Miles City comes out of the huddle. Forth down at the twenty-five. The ball is snapped to O'Brien who scrambles and finds Taylor, number twenty-three by the sideline. He throws him a forward pass at the fifteen. Reception is incomplete with Cowboy interception commanded by Travis Hunter, number eighty-nine! The clock is still running with one minute left in the third and Hunter finds a hole dug out by Harlan Jens, number eight, and Joel Hardy, number thirty-three. Taking it through, he hands it off to Nolan Hayes, number fourteen, who heads out—but gets tackled by Central's Eric Stolicowski, number twelve. Pile on by Central… and the clock is stopped."

Someone inside the trailer shut the radio off.

"Damn it!" Cash felt his temper flare.

Grabbing his gear, he hurried off to his father's pickup and trailer. He wanted to find out the score in the worse way. *They just had to be winning*, he told himself.

Perhaps it was the distraction of the game and wondering if the team was winning, or maybe it was the gnawing sensation he felt in his stomach over the fact he really missed Travis. The bottom line was—Cash was frustrated. Acidy fire was fueled even further when his good intentions of listening to rest of the broadcast were hastily cut off by his father's demanding for him to help with a sick horse in one of the stalls.

"Why that contractor brought the animal here in this condition is beyond me," griped Mr. McCollum as they made their way to the stall area. As his father slammed an antibiotic injection into its hip, he let out a string of swear words and continued with his complaint, "I told Jack this guy doesn't have half the brains of a common billy-goat."

"Hopefully none of the other stock 'll pick this shit up. *Hell!*" Another contractor spoke up—guardedly standing nearby watching the horse cough and wheeze.

"Cash, go get some water and have someone bring more straw to lay out so it can get some rest." Mr. McCollum ordered with a wave of his arm.

The rest of the afternoon, Cash found himself dedicated as the infirmary "gopher".

In spite of the fact that Cash didn't get to hear anymore of the broadcast, he did over-hear several individuals in the chute area commenting how well

Miles City played in regards to their victory over Butte Central. At one point, Travis' name was brought up—stating how he had taken the ball in for two touchdowns in the fourth quarter.

"...that tight-end for Miles City is one hell of a player."

"Yeah, Travis Hunter is collegiate material, you know. He's gonna stir things up next year if he gets on at the U."

A tingle of pride shot through Cash. He certainly needed to hear that.

The bareback ride later that afternoon lacked something. Mechanically, everything had been done right. He had been in control throughout the eight seconds and had colored up the time with a rather flamboyant ending. The horse, a two year old gelding named, Firecracker, had been full of spunk—turning out to be quite an honest bucker. Nothing in comparison to Black Eye, however.

Afterwards, the announcer broadcasted the current standings for all qualifying rough stock contestants and it was Cash who held the lead for both saddle bronc and bareback—by a large margin. "...In the state boy's standings as of today, we have Cash McCollum placing first in saddle bronc with sixty-nine, and bareback with sixty-four. And from his two outstanding rides here in Glendive, that gives him the year-end results of one-seven-seven in saddle bronc, and one-six-nine in bareback! Until today, ladies and gentlemen, Cash has been tied in first place for Boy's All-Around with Lee Biruni from Great Falls. That has been broken, however, by dethroning Biruni with a seven point lead at six-nine-six! Folks, let's give this man a great round of congratulations!"

As in the first go, the crowd had gone nuts after the announcement. The stampede of fans and fellow rodeo contestants seemed to take everything out of him. There was no denying it, the people loved him and he loved them. But enough was enough. He was already longing to be alone. After being swarmed upon and congratulated to death, Cash finally dragged a weary ass back to the stock trailer where his dad was working the last bull up the ramp. He felt so dirty, sore and tired.

In a translucent world of extended shadows, Cash found Brownie standing quietly by the stock trailer, just where he had left him earlier that morning. The contented quarter seemed completely unmoved by all the crazy activity of the day. For Brownie, it was more or less just another day. "In a way I envy you, boy," Cash whispered into the horse's ear. "You just do what you do best 'n don't worry about it. *Me*, I gotta work like hell; 'n then, I don't even know if *that's* good enough."

It was then, from the corner of his eye, he noticed Brownie's saddle bag had been disturbed. Always careful about his tack, Cash was usually fully aware—not even the smallest disruption could escape detection. He started to refasten the buckles when his fingers felt something small and hard in the bag. Pulling the flap up, he saw a folded piece of paper inside. Reaching in, he also came across a cold piece of metal. *What the hell?* Instantly, he knew what it was. There in his hand, gold, with a square-cut topaz stone—was a class ring. Cash opened the note, reading— *"You in chaps and nothing else."*

Quickly looking around to make sure no one was too close, Cash re-read the note then inspected the ring; peering at the initials engraved inside the band.

TJH. Of course, Cash realized. *Of course.*

Chills of excitement shot through his body.

He bobbed his head up and around, searching the best he could among those milling about. Instantly, the heaviness in his heart began to lift. With his eyes, he scanned the parking lot, stands and arena. But there was no Travis. *Where in the heck, was he?*

Refocusing back to the small shiny object clutched between his dusty fingers and the sweaty palm of his hand, Cash carefully placed it onto his ring finger. It was obviously too big for him as it slipped right off. A smile flooded his face. Did this mean they were 'going steady'? Maybe he'd have to wrap it in yarn. *"Oh God..."* he snickered under his breath. Jennifer would *love* this one. Hastily placing the note and ring in his shirt pocket, he fastened the snap and took a long, deep breath.

They finally got all the animals situated and the gear packed. With that, Mr. McCollum gave a long sigh. Heavy with fatigue he spoke, "I'm gettin' too old for this." Dark shadows hung unforgivingly beneath his eyes.

The sun was going down in that quick way it did that time of the year—shooting streaks of orange and red out across the deepening blue of the sky. If Cash turned his head a certain way, one of those rays would hit his forehead directly—forcing him to turn again in order to continue seeing. Shaking himself free of the glare, he saw his father giving a slight smile.

What? It caught him off guard.

They stood still for a moment, aware of something new about them. What was it? Nothing much, that Cash could understand. He had won rodeos before—lots of them. He had done well. Sometimes, it seemed it was the only thing he *did* do well.

"Dad," he murmured as they finished up, keeping his head respectfully bowed, "how'd ya like it?"

His father didn't say anything. Of course, he had seen. He had seen everything... but said nothing. That was his way.

"Maybe I could'a done better, but I don't think so." Cash smiled, coming close to the old man. Mr. McCollum reached out—pulling his arm up and across Cash's shoulder, slightly urging him close into an awkward hug.

Taken off balance, Cash returned the embrace—nervous and self-aware. Still, his father remained silent. It would be unnerving, he reasoned, if he wasn't already used to his father's ways. "We'll see about next time—what I can do."

His father's eyes met his—green on green.

Why haven't I ever seen it before, how much his eyes are like mine?

Cash glanced about; still wondering about Travis—knowing he was close by. The smell of damp dirt filled his nose in all its welcoming, mundane glory. He knew he was still in shock over everything—a zone of unreality.

"Cash, son, I'm so proud of you."

There were words people said with their mouths, and there were words they said with their hearts. Cash had no doubts which these were.

"Yeah, Dad?" He shook his head. Something unmovable began to swell and knot up in the heart of his throat. It made his eyes water.

"Damn right."

If he saw something else in the elder McCollum's face, he was unsure how to read it. He didn't care. It didn't matter. Just to be here with his dad—like this, was more than a thousand trophies or all the money in the world.

His father continued to stand… wordless. Within those grey weary eyes, there it was—wrapped up as a present and waiting to be seized.

Reach out and take it in, a voice commanded in Cash. *Just reach out—there it is.*

A light breeze stirred Cash's shirt sleeve. The coming evening would bring winds. Cold ones. He would look for Travis later. Everything else

could wait. Nothing would make him move away from this moment...
nothing.

The first thing they did upon leaving the dusty rodeo grounds was head for
a diner. As the truck came to a stop on the gravel parking lot, one more
cloud of dust resurrected around the vehicle. Neither of them had really
gotten a good meal all day; and by now, they were both starved. Like
his dad always said, "The only thing they know how to serve at a rodeo is
stuffed pig guts and a side order of shit."

Walking into the restaurant, a young girl with long brown hair pulled back
in a pony tail, quickly led them to a table. With clopping shoes and thick
glasses, she somehow reminded him of Jennifer.

"Your server'll be with you in a minute. Can I bring you anythin' to
drink?"

"I'll have water." Looking over to Mr. McCollum, he prompted.
"Dad?"

Rubbing his eyes with his cracked, weathered fingers, the older man looked
up at her and forced a weak smile. "Make that two."

With a spin on her heel, she set off to the service area.

Glancing around, Cash decided to keep his hat on. He could only imagine
how disheveled he looked. "I'm gonna wash up." A big yawn escaped as
he pushed himself out of the booth.

The jingle from his spurs drew stares from various parts of the dining room.
Tired and sore as he was, he cared less about being conspicuous. All he
wanted at this point was clean up and chow down.

In the men's room, he stood at the sink—gawking blankly at the mirror.
With a groan, he took his hat off. *Fuck*, he told himself. He looked rough.

Running raw, blistered fingers through sweaty hair and across his face, he brushed red-caked dust from sun-scorched cheeks—fiery stings biting into his flesh.   Turning the faucets, water began to fill the basin. Splashing the warm, soothing liquid against his skin, it delicately trailed across his eyebrows and sideburns—down his chin and neck.

"You should be more careful when you lean over a counter like that." The gentle touch of fingers slipped quietly around his waist.

What the…?! Quickly standing straight up, the collar of his shirt became wet.

"I've missed you so much today." Travis' words floated effortlessly, like a feather, into Cash's ears. He looked great—with a black Stetson, rodeo shirt, and snakeskin boots.

"Yeah?" the stunned cowboy replied—completely side-tracked from the task at hand—water still dripping from his chin and nose.

"Yeah." Travis' teeth gleamed against the hint of sunburn on his nose and cheeks. Flipping the latch, he locked the door—eyes riveted to Cash.

The silence of the room became alive.

And as if casting cuffs and chains upon a willing, spellbound body, Travis brought his fingers slowly to touch the soft curve of Cash's cheek. With the gentleness of a kitten's purr, he spoke words of a picture, thoughts of a dream…

"Oh, the love, embrace and flow—

over me, warming heart and soul…"

Cash closed his eyes.

"…To you I ride, my love, my *love*—

to you, I ride a moonbeam from above."

Lips on lips—warm and wet. They kissed. Swimming in their lover's pool—tongues diving without fear, they tasted the sweetness of dreams and hope. Wrestling with desire, drunk from the passion, they could not stop—swallowing whole until their flesh was entirely ablaze from each other.

Then, without a word, Travis turned, unlocked the door, and left the room. He was gone.

My God! Cash gasped for air. Quickly, he caught himself from falling—slamming his hands squarely on the counter.

Sunday seemed like a daydream. After Travis' kiss, everything following seemed surreal. Even the bull riding event, in which he had done well, tended to be shrouded in a misty haze…

"Well, folks, the man we've all been waitin' for this entire weekend is ridin' out of chute number one. He'll be on bull number eleven, Tombstone. Let's all give him a hand—Mr. Cash McCollum!"

Instantly, a wild applause ensued.

With the well-worn buckskin covering his hand, Cash situated his fingers into each customized groove and fold of the glove. Loving the feel it gave to his skin, he carefully wrapped it securely to his wrist and with a punch from the other hand; he excitedly took in a deep breath. Giving one last glance to the guys assisting, he shoved his hat low. He was ready to fly. Quickly, he sized up the situation. Something told him this was going to be the ride of rides—instantly, there was explosive energy between his legs. Nodding to the gateman who swung the chute door open, Cash drew up on the rope preventing his arm from straightening. A ton of cross-bred fury blew out of the chute. Ducking off with a series of angry belly-rolls and spins, Tombstone dropped its shoulders, pretending to go for a spin to the right. Suddenly, it threw itself into a fast left turn with several kicks from behind. It became apparent this bull had a mission as it bucked with a furious, arm-jerking force. Struggling to throw Cash forward by either hitting him squarely in the guts with its head, or hooking him good with the end of its horns, it became evident he had himself a hot-headed hooker. Getting somewhat in tune with the bull's vindictive nature, Cash managed to throw in several clean spurring licks. The crowd cheered louder. And what seemed to take forever, the buzzer finally blew with a wary bullfighter jumping into the scene with his usual distracting act. Cash broke free from the raging bovine with a less than graceful tumble then quickly scrambled out of the arena.

Whew! Cash caught his breath. There was *nothing* else that compared to a real-live bull ride. For several moments, Cash leaned against the arena railing in an effort to stave off the dizziness in his head.

"Well, ladies and gentlemen…it looks like our man has done it again." The announcer's voice seemed unusually loud to his ears. "Nine zero… that is an exceptional score for Cash, and if I might say so myself, I believe he is paving the way for a great career in the professionals. Let's give him another great hand!"

After a horrendous deluge of 'buckle bunnies' and fellow competitors wished him congratulations, a rare moment of silence fell around him. It was unnerving—and Cash couldn't put his finger on why he found it unsettling. Looking around, he shrugged his shoulders, not sure what he was exactly searching for. He began to walk back to the trailer.

"Cash?"

The voice was unfamiliar. Turning back, he found himself surprised to be faced with a black-haired, lean-faced cowboy looking as if he were decked out for a night on the town. Noticing the Chesney-type hat, black-and-white striped shirt, and an expensive looking pair of western boots, Cash became intrigued. It was all appropriately ensembled on the young man's somewhat lanky frame. Off the cuff, he concluded, this guy was stylish… and rather good-looking. What definitely stood out were those eyes. Mysteriously dark, they had the resemblance of two olives on a white china plate. In fact, he sensed there was something behind them, but could not see beyond their veil. "Yeah?" He was hesitant.

Quickly, the boy extended his hand and proceeded to speak in a somewhat subdued tone. "You did very well out there today." A smile crossed his lips, revealing two rows of pearly white teeth.

"Thanks." As they shook hands, Cash continued to feel strange—a peculiar awkwardness. *What was this all about? Who was he?*

Taking Cash's hand and vigorously shaking it, the cowboy went on to say, "I'm sorry, I should have introduced myself first. My name is Lee. Lee Biruni."

Putting his brain into high gear, Cash felt his heart leap. *Jesus,* he thought, taking in a sharp breath—quickly trying to gather himself back into the corral. He knew this person! Sharing the same piece of priceless turf for the past six months, he instantly realized this was his closest competitor for the state title.

"From Great Falls," Cash spoke his words half-dazed by the unexpected nature of this visit.

"Correct," Lee acknowledged, standing squarely in front of Cash, hands thrust deeply into his jean pockets. "I decided to drive over here and see who it was in the Eastern Division that has been giving me a run for my money." On the surface, the inflection in his voice made his words sound light and breezy, as if almost made in jest, but a definite structure was woven between them, making Cash realize this guy was focused on serious business.

In spite of the shock of actually meeting him face to face, Cash admittedly understood the reason for him to drive hundreds of miles to see who it was that had finally stripped the title from his grip. If the boot was on his foot, he'd probably do the same thing. "Nice to meet you, Lee."

"Likewise," the other cowboy replied, his eyes continuing their sharp focus.

An uncomfortable spell of silence fell between them. Cash wondered where this was going. Reaching up to his shirt pocket, he grabbed his pack of cigarettes and proceeded to light one up. He inhaled the smoke—holding it in his lungs for a moment before exhaling it from his nostrils. The rush from the nicotine seemed to put a soothing edge over his feeling of self-consciousness.

With an astute eye, Lee watched Cash shift his weight from one leg to the other. "You smoke the same brand I do." There was a half-smile on his lips with certain eagerness in his eyes.

"You want one?" Cash quickly offered, pulling the pack back out of his pocket. *Here was something else they shared in common...how ironic,* he thought.

"Sure," replied Lee, reaching out.

Firing up his lighter, Cash leaned forward and lit Lee's cigarette. There was something about this guy which he found to be strangely attractive. The way he stood, the movement of his arms and hands, and the slow glide of his hips as he would rest weight on one leg...it all had a disarming appeal.

"I've been keeping up on your success this year." Smoke slid from Lee's lips. "Your riding skills are very impressive."

"Thanks," Cash replied. Becoming keenly aware of the troop of gawkers gathering around them, he knew they had better find another spot to talk. From the crowd, he overhead several comments that made him edgy.

"That's Lee Biruni talkin' with Cash...yeah, he's from the Western Division..."

"You wanna grab a bite somewhere?" Cash was suddenly eager to get out of the area.

Shrugging his shoulders, Lee exhaled a long stream of smoke and said, "I'm not really hungry, but I think we should get outta here." The expression on his face revealed he was thinking the same thing as well.

Together, they made their way out of the chute area to an undeveloped section of the rodeo grounds. As they walked, small talk found its way between them.

"You do a lotta ridin'?" Cash flipped his smoke to the ground.

"Yeah, I practice ridin' after school and on weekends. Nothing else better to do, I guess." A faint hint of sarcasm seemed to emanate from him.

"You from around here?" Cash asked with great curiosity. Up until this year, he had never heard of Lee in the Association.

"No." Lee abruptly cocked his head, throwing Cash a narrow side-glance. "Why do you ask?"

Aware that he had crossed a certain line, Cash noticed a defensiveness emanating. "I didn't mean anything by it." Cash felt the need to clarify. "It's just that I've never heard of you before this year."

Remaining silent for a moment, as if trying to regroup, Lee finally spoke apologetically. "I'm sorry, it's just that a lot of people ask me that wherever I go." Sucking in the last bit of burning tobacco from the butt, he forcefully tossed it to the ground and stomped it out with the heel of his boot. "We moved to Great Falls last year from the West Coast."

"Which part?" Cash was hesitant to ask, but as usual, his inquisitiveness got the best of him.

"Yakima."

"Over in Washington?" Cash delicately tip-toed on his quest to learn more about this mysterious character.

Without giving Cash eye contact, Lee nodded. His gaze strategically shot into several directions. Suddenly, he blurted out, "I better be going. It's a long drive back home and I just wanted to meet you—find out who you were." Holding his hand out, he allowed a carbon-copy smile, like the one exhibited during their introductions, to cross his dark, mystifying face. It was obvious—something was preoccupying his mind.

"It's nice meeting you." Cash didn't know what else to say.

Looking intently at Cash, Lee firmly replied, "Likewise." After a momentary pause, he quizzically asked, "You mind if I call you sometime?"

"No." Instantly, Cash was taken aside. "...Not at all." *That's an interesting request*, he told himself. "My family's in the phone book under Eugene McCollum."

"Great." Lee said as he turned to go. Stopping at the end of the pavement, he called out with one last wave, "Thank you, Cash."

It was a great relief to see the old, familiar gates and pull into the driveway. Things had turned out a lot better than anticipated. And even though it had been an exhausting haul, the last two days had been, indeed, fantastic—almost surreal. As Cash pulled the large white pickup and livestock trailer up alongside the barn, he felt his arms quiver from exhaustion. He was worn out. A nice hot shower, something to eat, and a warm bed sounded very good.

His father looked equally tired—rubbing his eyes with those cracked, weary hands. Letting out a long sigh, he spoke with a raspy voice. "Thank God."

Grabbing for the door handle, Cash stopped. Something tugged at him inside. He looked over at his dad and said. "Thanks, Dad."

Eugene remained motionless for a brief moment, staring blankly out of the windshield. Eventually, he turned and allowed a small smile to scale over his dry lips. "Yeah, I have to admit I do this for myself as well...can't take the rodeo out of the man, you know."

"Yeah, I know." Cash nodded, his hand resting on the steering wheel.

For a moment, the two sat quietly in the warm cab—not speaking a word. It didn't seem right to break the spell.

The sun began its final decent into the western horizon—conclusion of an extraordinary weekend.

Finally opening his door, Cash's father pushed himself out into the still evening air. "Let's get these animals situated and grab some supper."

After a plate of warmed-up roast beef and mashed potatoes, Cash took a long, hot shower then headed off to bed. Even though the warm water eased a large portion of pain oozing throughout his body, he could barely move as he pushed himself through the tight fold of the sheets. All he wanted to do was remain still—allowing his abused muscles to loosen and relax.

As sleep began to overtake, his mind began to rehearse. How could so many things happen in such short time? The rabbit's foot and ring, the stolen kiss at the restaurant, the unbelievable rides, and Lee Biruni's unannounced visit—it was all too much. As he quietly lay in the soft, comfortable bed, Cash could not help but allow the questions to flood his mind concerning Lee. Leaving as quickly as he had come, Cash determined that boy was a complete mystery—casting more questions into his mind than answers. Why had he come all that way—to only visit for several minutes? How did his family end up in Montana? He looked like he came from money. How then, did he ever get involved with the rodeo? He certainly didn't seem like the typical rodeo type. And those looks... his dark complexion was unique. He didn't look Mexican, Native American, or Italian. What was he?

Down the road, he reasoned those questions would probably be answered. And even though he wanted to do some more thinking, it was time to hang it up and let his brain rest. He knew he definitely needed some heavy duty sleep.

CHAPTER 7

By Monday morning, the word was out. What had started out to be a simple observation from an astute, local radio announcer—about the phenomenon of Cash and Travis—soon became a hot topic of discussion in nearly every household of Montana. It seemed to spread like wildfire. Dubbed "The Titan Two of Miles City", they were instantly thrown into stardom... along with their hometown.

The question that was asked by everyone... Why of all places—Miles City? What made the town so blessed to have a championship football team, led by a charismatic tight end, and the top rodeo man of the High School Rodeo Association come out of the woodwork all at the same time? Was it the water? Some seemed to believe it was as the long-forgotten, prairie community appeared to wake up and stretch out from a long dreary slumber...

Tossing the newspaper on the cafeteria table, Travis pulled a chair out and plunked down beside Cash who was nearly done with his lunch. Allowing an incredulous smirk to cross his face, he let out a short sigh. "Can you believe this?"

Between mouthfuls of crusty, half-burnt pizza, Cash reached out and slid the paper closer to read the article printed across the first page of the sports section. "Nuthin' like bein' in the limelight." His voice was sour.

"You can say that again." Travis replied shaking his head unbelievingly. "Cash, someone from one of the Billings newspapers just called over my cell and they want to interview us this afternoon."

Cash looked up—shock written across his face. "What?" Not sure he had heard correctly, he continued. "Well, what are we gonna do?"

"What do you mean, what are we gonna do?" Irritation rose in Travis' tone. "We're gonna meet with them and answer a few of their questions."

Pushing himself from the table, he grabbed his tray. All of sudden he felt awfully antsy. "Hell, I won't know what to say."

Glaring at Cash, Travis went on to matter-of-factly reply, "Sure you will. You'll do just fine." Suddenly, his attention was steered to the other side of the room. Mr. Ryan, the school principal stood by the bulletin boards ardently looking about. "Oh, oh…" his voice trailed off. "Ryan's looking for someone. I'll bet it's for us."

"*How do you know?*" Cash was getting sick and tired of all the hype—having no patience in this celebrity thing.

Spotting them, Mr. Ryan proceeded to approach. The look on his face appeared urgent.

"Here he comes," Travis said observantly. Quickly, he sat up in the chair and cleared his throat.

"Christ!" Cash swore under his breath, tossing his food tray back on the table. With an unrestrained, insolent attitude, he threw himself back into the chair with a thud. Taking one more unwanted bite of the disgusting pizza, he felt like a cornered cougar at a city zoo.

"You two have a moment to talk?" The tall, serious-faced administrator gestured with his hand to follow him into the hallway.

"Sure," Travis replied, quickly rising to his feet. With a subtle kick against one of the legs of Cash's chair, he sent the unmistakable message to 'fall in line'.

Cash moaned, re-gathering his pop can and tray. Hurriedly, he bused them and caught up with Travis and the principal who were already halfway to the office. His boot steps echoed throughout the hallway. "Now what?" he asked himself. There was a sickening feeling in his stomach.

Gathering into the tiny office that seemed somewhat stuffy and overly warm, Cash huddled next to Travis. Quietly, he proceeded to pull up a chair closer to the large, cluttered desk. The first thing he noticed was the number of yellow post-its attached to various parts of the computer monitor. They all had illegible scribbling on them. *Encounters of the third kind*, he thought glibly. Strangely, he found the scene rather amusing. Each piece of paper seemed to take on the resemblance of little flags giving a certain degree of distraction to any endeavor of concentration. *How on earth*, he asked himself, *could anyone get focused with all that shit pasted around the screen?*

Resting a pair of wire-rimmed glasses on his pale-skinned face, the middle-aged man slowly folded his hands and let out a sigh. "The reason I called you boys here into my office is I got a call from one the TV stations in Billings and they have requested to meet with both of you either this afternoon or sometime tomorrow."

"We have a commitment this afternoon." Travis hastily interjected, throwing a nonchalant glance at his wristwatch. There was arrogance in his tone.

Mr. Ryan raised his eyebrows. "Excuse me?" He looked annoyed. It was apparent; *he* wanted to be in control of the itinerary.

"We're meeting someone from the *Gazette* after school," Travis endeavored to elucidate without throwing out too much information.

"The least we say, the least we'll have to explain..." had been the warning delivered to Cash by his boyfriend upon learning of their new-found popularity. Everything was so foreign; he determined to just sit silently—willing his spirit out the window. He would let Travis and Mr. Ryan duke it out.

Shaking his head, Mr. Ryan said with a swing of his hand, "I don't know anything about that, but the TV station talked about having you on a news spot. Travis, your mother has been notified, and I just got off the phone with your dad, Cash. Everyone is aware that the interview will be here at the school. We just need to determine a time and I'll get back with them." He was eager to wrap this up and get it off his desk.

"Tomorrow will work." Travis' voice remained low and very business-like.

"What time?" the principal asked without looking up, writing something on a yellow note pad.

"Three-thirty."

"Fine." Mr. Ryan spoke with finality. Briskly, he pulled the 'sticky note' from the pad and slapped it up on the computer screen with its other 'siblings'. "One other thing," he added before excusing them from his presence, "they mentioned an interest of having the two of you on "Montana Today" for next week's show. That means a trip to Billings during school time—so you will need to complete an excused absence request form from Carol before you leave so we can have that on file."

Cash could tell the entire scene was irritating to Mr. Ryan—one more thing added to a long list of urgent 'to do's'. In a way, he had to agree with him.

Details, statistics, and some bullshit thrown in between… the first in what would become a long freight train of interviews seemed to blow through Cash's world with a certain amount of ease. To his relief, it was much easier than expected. After interviewing Travis, the reporter's attention shifted to Cash.

"…so let me get this straight. Your current points for this year is One hundred and twenty-five points in bull riding, One hundred and seventy-seven in saddle bronc, and One hundred and sixty-nine in bareback. That puts you ahead how far from the next highest competitor in the Rodeo Association?" A young lady with spiked, highlighted hair quickly scratched information down on her notepad. Occasionally, she looked up and smiled at the boys; most of the time, however, she diligently focused on the questions written down on her pad.

"I believe seven." Having taken an uncomfortable position in one of the folding chairs at the large conference table, Cash had the feeling he was being interrogated in a police debriefing room. Their voices echoed.

Quietly, Travis sat with his hands folded, repeatedly checking the time from his wristwatch. Occasionally, he allowed a renegade yawn to escape from half-open lips.

"How long have you competed in rodeo events?"

"Since I was five."

With a look of surprise, she laid her pencil down and focused squarely on Cash. "Really?"

"Well, they have events geared just for kids that age."

"I see." The young gal grinned, keeping her sight fixed on Cash. From the twinkle in her eyes, she appeared fascinated by his story. "Like what?"

Hesitating, Cash bit his lip. "Mutton Bustin'..." A smirk snuck out. With all his might, he worked at keeping sober. *Why in the hell did he feel like burstin' out in a goddamn laugh?* He could feel that stupid, red-flush heat his complexion.

Instantly catching herself in a snicker, her voice quivered. "Excuse me?" Nervously, she repositioned in the chair—clearing her throat to regain composure.

Coming back to life, Travis threw a quizzical glance over to Cash then back to the girl—apparently trying to find out whatever it was tickling their insides.

"It's an event where kids between four and six ride sheep for six seconds." As Cash spoke his mouth broke out into a full-blown grin revealing those infamous dimples.

Unable to take her eyes off Cash, the reporter finally sat back in her chair and flatly stated, "My God, has anyone told you that you have the cutest dimples? And I just love your eyes!" Catching herself in the fall, she quickly sat up—struggling to regain a professional demeanor. "I'm sorry.... very sorry."

"That's all right," Cash casually replied, nodding his head. At first, taken off-guard by the unplanned humor, he eventually found it flattering. And as if being tickled by a dozen gremlins, he succumbed to what he would call—a 'Clayton moment'. Allowing a crazy smile to overtake, he blurted out something he had once read in an S. E Hinton novel, "God gave me my face, but He let me pick my nose..." *

"I didn't know what else to say!" exclaimed Cash on behalf of his own defense as they made their way across the parking lot.

Travis remained silent. Walking through the darkness, he spoke with a low, subdued voice, "Yeah? Well, you certainly had me fooled." His eyes spelled total disgust.

"Hell, she didn't mind my comment. If anything, she enjoyed it."

Travis' face became red. "What about me?" Stopping in the middle of the walkway, he brought his hands to his chest.

"What about you?" Cash was confused. He could feel himself get angry. The more Cash got to know this jock, the more it seemed the world revolved around him. *Bullshit!* He told himself.

Raising his arms, Travis' words shot forth words flat and choppy—as if being laid on a cutting board. "Look, Cash, I don't want to start something right now. I'm sorry I brought it up."

With fire blazing in his pants, Cash was determined to press on. Blocking Travis' way, he demanded, "No, I asked you a question and I wanna answer."

"It's not important. Just forget I said anything—it's nothing." Skirting by Cash's fury, Travis turned back to the parking lot and resumed his renowned strut.

"Like hell!" Cash snapped. Even though his boyfriend was twice his size, there was no way he was going to let the matter rest. "You wouldn't have brought it up if it wasn't something that bothered you."

Swinging around and facing Cash full front, Travis leaned forward and said with a twitch in his eyelids, "Well, how would *you* have felt to have someone googlin' over me and I egg them on with a dumb-ass remark?"

"You're jealous!" Cash let out an incredulous laugh. "That's what it is! You're fuckin' jealous over that broad!" It was the first time Cash became aware of Travis' possessive nature. It shouldn't have been a surprise, but it was.

"You just can't drop an issue, can you, Cash?" Travis' eyes were dark from the furl in his brows, his voice rising to a level never heard before.

Stubbornly, Cash refused to answer the question.

In silence, the two walked toward their separate vehicles. Apparently, he had hit Travis' threshold in dealing with confrontation. Something told him there would be no more to this discussion. Where it was second nature for a McCollum to carry on a good argument to the bitter end, Travis on the other hand, would rather shove it under the rug. In a way, it made sense—saving a lot of wear and tear on the nerves as well as the voice box. The only problem with that sort of thinking…it just wasn't a part of him. He had always been taught the get-it-off-your-chest-or-it'll-eat-at-you way of life… at least from his father.

Reaching his pick-up, Cash grabbed for the door handle—but stopped, allowing a tiny, unexpected thought to work its way into his mind. *Travis needs you. He needs to know you love and appreciate him. He's done so much for you by bending over backwards and going out of his way all the time. Get over to that damned vehicle and show him how much he means to you. Let him know he's your number one.*

Releasing the handle, Cash turned on his heels and ran to the Viper. "Travis!" He signaled with a waving arm.

Revving the engine, Travis, rolled down the window and looked at him with a heavy expression. "What?" The blue of his eyes matched a chilly detachment that radiated from his wounded spirit.

Cash crouched by the small sports car and leaned his head close to the window. Awkwardly, he bit his lip and took a deep breath. It was as if it took everything inside to speak the words he knew he should have said from the beginning. "I'm sorry."

For a moment, Travis sat quietly—looking straight ahead, his hands gripping the wheel, the engine smoothly idling. Finally, with softening of the muscles in his face, he turned to Cash and replied, "I'm sorry too."

Wait a minute…was there a tear in the corner of Travis' eye? Cash couldn't believe what he saw as he fixed his gaze on his boyfriend. Silence gripped at him.

Thoughts, feelings jumbled and collided in a wild hodge-podge as neither could find words to say what they felt so deeply. Even if they could come up with something to say, would it be appropriate?

"Can I get in?" Cash humbly asked. The still, small voice inside continued to whisper gently at his spirit.

Travis reached towards Cash's neck, pulling up on the silver chain that buried itself within his shirt. Slowly the ring appeared, resting easily against the little crucifix Cash had received for his confirmation years ago.

Suddenly, he knew.

Releasing him, Travis reached over and unlocked the door. They both knew.

As they headed out to the levee, Travis and Cash coupled their hands the entire way—blending their touch.

The evening breezes began to pick up—howling through gnarled, brown branches. Shadows danced precipitously across the car. Around them, cottonwoods stripped of their leafy cover, stood fully exposed against a black, ashen sky. It seemed lonely, so very sad and lonely—yet expectant.

Knowing what was desperately needed, they obeyed orders from within. It was clear what had to be done.

Slowly, Cash reached over and gently touched the back of Travis' neck. The big-muscled man seemed to let go, allowing his head to fall forward, his body releasing tension. Cash did not stop. He continued to drift his touch until it became a hold. From that hold, it gave birth to an embrace. That single embrace reproduced to create a churning sea of gasps only to be shared between two who dwell as one.

Cash healed Travis.

With tales revealed... a moon not withholding any more, gentle beams spread across the heavy blackness with a warmth that melted deep and pure. Forever, their love was forged, more powerful than imagined. Indeed, this was home.

CHAPTER 8

It had been a long time since Cash had ventured into the "big" city. His brother Clint seemed to get along pretty well there, but for himself, it was always a happy moment when he would see the looming skyline from the rearview mirror. Driving in and around Billings was unnerving for a simple country boy; so it was a jubilant moment when he found out that Travis would drive.

They were to be interviewed on the Friday show. From the high school, to the Co-op, the entire town was buzzing. It didn't matter where they went; people stopped to comment about hearing about them on the radio, seeing them on the TV news, and reading about them in the newspapers. And now, to appear on the state's premier daily talk show, well, it seemed to fling them into real stardom. Travis appeared fine with their new-found status. Cash, on the other hand, found it strange—almost stifling. As if being placed under a microscope, on a Petri dish, he felt as if every move was under scrutiny.

"Heard you're gonna be on television with that Hunter boy." Jennifer Evers, in her usual rare form, approached him in the hallway after school one day, yanking on her ratty brown hair and wrapping it around her finger as if succumbing to a nervous twitch. It was like she had nothing else better to do than sit around and dig up shit—then come to him with her fake, sincere-appearing concern.

Slamming his locker door, Cash instantly felt impatience overtake him. He was in no mood for her—or her likes that afternoon. "Don't you have a bus to catch?" his voice was crackly and high-pitched. She stood steady, determined to carry on the conversation. Quickly, he side-stepped her and made his way to freedom. It was scary; he was beginning to know her all too well

Taken off guard, Jennifer let go of her hair and hastily looked around as if searching for something she might have lost. "Uh, it won't be here for a few more minutes." She spoke as if in a daze. "Are you in a hurry?"

"As a matter of fact, I am," Cash briskly replied, zipping up his coat. "I have to be somewhere in a few minutes."

Eyeing him closely in the well-worn sheep skin jacket, her expression softened a bit—as if what she saw was quite appealing. A tiny laugh escaped her lips as she quickly brought her hand to mouth in what appeared to be embarrassment. "You look really good in that jacket, Cash."

Sideswiped, Cash turned to her and said in a rather astonished tone, "Why thanks." *That was unusual*, he thought to himself. *Was that an actual compliment minus any hidden agendas?*

"Yeah, you really do." Her voice seemed to trail off in a sea of lost thoughts.

Now it was his turn to smile back at her. It wasn't normal for anyone to side track her from what she had going on in her mind. For a fleeting moment, Cash caught himself—seeing an uncommonly rare side to this generally obnoxious girl. And in a strange sort of way, it was this setting he discovered a cuteness about her that made him soften a bit. Taking a deep breath, he let out a slow, deliberate sigh. "What's on your mind?" He knew he was treading on thin ice, remembering Travis' words after one of the interviews. "…you have a weird way of setting yourself up." That boy was certainly getting to know how he ticked.

"Well, you know…" There she was, messing with her hair once again— twisting the end of it mercilessly with a forceful finger. "I just wanted to say you sure have made it big and I think it's great." She had a difficult time focusing on his face. "The entire family is very proud of you, I'm sure you know."

"Thanks." Cash said warmly. Somehow, he could tell she was genuine.

Looking up into his serene countenance, she went on to say, "I think what you're doing is fantastic, and well, I wish you the best on that show in Billings this Friday."

Cash wished he could cut those damn locks of hair off—or handcuff her to keep her from messing with it anymore. It was so distracting. "I appreciate that." He replied, trying not to focus on her fingers.

Suddenly her attention shifted to the clock on the wall and jumped with a start. "Oh my!" she exclaimed. "The bus is probably here. I better be going."

Allowing his smile to remain, Cash called out to her as she twirled around and hurried down the hallway. "Don't be late! Who knows, if you miss the bus, you'll probably have to ride home with me in the Pound Puppy!"

"You know I'd like that!" she hollered back at him with a big grin.

"And *that's* what scares me…" Cash softly spoke under his breath as he watched her heave the doors—letting out a sharp whistle to the bus driver to hold on.

Travis suggested heading into the city the evening before since the program was early in the morning and they needed to be there prior for make-up. They would scout out the studio location, find a hotel, and perhaps have dinner at a nice restaurant without having to rush—or be in a panic the next day. But as best laid plans are usually scrapped, his intentions were swept away by the frenzy of another winter storm. And as if the wind, rain and sleet weren't enough, they had something else to contend with—rush hour traffic.

Leaving school early Thursday afternoon, they got on the freeway heading west in order to give them ample time before dusk. Earlier that day, the weather forecast had predicted another Pacific front barreling onto the Great Plains from the Rockies. As they traveled down the lonely ribbon of pavement, Travis began to complain of merciless cross winds batting against the side of the car. His knuckles were white from the tension of his grip on the wheel. "My God, this wind is something else!"

Feeling the rocky effects of the unyielding force, but sitting rather removed and somewhat aloof in the smooth leather seat, Cash replied, "They said there's a blizzard warning posted for Eastern Montana tonight."

'Yeah," stated the big burly jock, shifting down in hopes to gain more control. "Well, I hope this isn't gonna be a repeat of the crap we got several weeks ago."

When they reached the outskirts of the city, the storm was in full force. Snow was mixing with a hearty concoction of freezing rain making the roadways that much more difficult to see and navigate.

In spite of the treacherous weather, Cash sensed a surge of excitement—realizing this would be the first time they would be together all alone. He had looked forward to it since the meeting in Mr. Ryan's office. What was even better—no one from either side squawked about them traveling un-chaperoned. That, in itself, was a miracle.

"...you two are going to have to be responsible," Mrs. McCollum had stated as she folded clothes on top of the dryer—Cash standing quietly by the doorway. "In a few months, you'll be on your own, and neither Dad nor I will be able to look over your shoulder. Lord knows, when you get out in the circuit, you'll need to be able to use your common sense and remember all the stuff you've learned under this roof."

To be alone with Travis, all night... he could hardly wait. There would be no worry of someone barging in on them. No hiding in stairwells. No making out in the woods. It would be just the two of them—all alone.

Weaving the red sports coupe through the congested, downtown traffic, Travis became silent. They could scarcely see out from the windshield for all the slush and ice caking against the glass. "Those damn wipers are worthless," he angrily complained, signaling to get into the next lane.

Without warning, a bus ran along side of them splashing a wave of dirty sludge across the car—engulfing the windshield and the entire passenger side.

Allowing a stream of swear words to escape from his usually temper-controlled mouth, it was apparent that Travis' patience was wearing thin. "I hate those fuckin' city buses!"

For fear of having his head get bit off, or the car getting smashed up like a pancake, Cash remained quiet in his seat.

They finally came to the entrance of a large parking garage and Travis steered the Viper up the wet, slushy ramp. Grabbing a ticket at the metered gate, he gunned the engine- burning a bit of rubber from the tires as he shifted into gear. "Thought we'd never get here," he muttered under his breath. He swung into the first available slot and shut the engine off. Letting out a long, fatigued sigh, Travis stared straight ahead and said, "God, this place is about as bad as Frisco."

"I thought you liked big cities."

Tossing him a glare, Travis said with low, stern voice, "Don't push it. I'm not in the mood."

Retrieving their bags from the back, the two boys made their way to the service area and pushed a button for an elevator.

The doors opened up, and unexpectedly, a number of people exploded from the car—all wearing suits and rain coats. Some of them clutched umbrellas along with their briefcases. With glazed looks of determination, each of them passed by the two boys completely unaware of their presence. This was one hell of a different world, thought Cash as he followed Travis into the small confines of the elevator. Selecting a button from a long row of buttons, Travis seemed to know where he was going—as if he had done this scenario countless times before.

One thing was for sure, Cash knew if he was doing this trip alone, he'd be lost... right from the get-go.

The car stopped—opening into a large lobby that sparkled with polished marble, mirrors and glass. Leather chairs, sofas, potted palms and ornate rugs furnished the center of the room by a trickling fountain. Funny, it looked a lot like Travis' house, Cash told himself. Making their way across the large open area, they approached the front desk area where there were a number of clerks worked with several lines of guests.

As they waited, Cash noticed a tuxedoed guy playing a large grand piano in one corner of the lobby while a number of boys in uniforms carried bags or pushed luggage carts from a separate counter to the elevators nearby. When it eventually got to their turn, a young man from behind the counter asked for the reservation name.

Clearing his throat, Travis whipped out a credit card. The clerk busily searched in the computer. "Mr. Hunter, we have you staying one night in concierge. Is that correct?"

"Ah, yes." Travis briskly scanned the registration form and signed the bottom.

"Great, we have you on the twenty-fourth floor. Here is your key card, sir, and the room number is printed inside the folder. Will you be needing assistance with your bags to your suite?" The clerk politely asked, quickly clearing the counter and giving Travis a broad, admiring smile.

"No." Travis replied, returning the gesture.

"Thank you, Mr. Hunter. Enjoy your stay at the hotel."

Cash was speechless. He had never seen anything like this before. Everything seemed so elegant and formal. Looking at his reflection in the highly polished glass of an end table, he suddenly felt grossly out of place. The sound of his boots echoed on the marble floors as they walked to the guest elevators.

"Jesus." Cash whispered under his breath as the elevator whisked them up to their floor. "Maybe I should have dressed up." Rehearsing in his mind of the items in his closet, he couldn't think of thing that would be acceptable in a place like this.

The elevator slowed and finally stopped. They walked down the quiet hallway past small tables with lamps and stone figurines. Halfway, they passed a lounge area where a woman sat behind a desk. "Good evening," she smiled courteously to both of them. The smell of food drifted throughout the floor. Until now, Cash hadn't been aware how hungry he was. As he followed Travis, hunger began to gnaw at his guts—he was famished.

"Here we are." Travis said, looking over to Cash with a sparkle in his eyes. Throwing him a wink, he opened the door and gestured with a nod to go in.

Letting out a gasp, Cash took his cowboy hat off. He'd never seen anything like this before—it was a complete apartment. "Travis…" Cash caught his breath. This was definitely out of his league.

Coming up from behind, Travis slowly slipped his arms around Cash's waist—drawing him into a gentle embrace. "Just enjoy it," he whispered into the stunned cowboy's ear.

"This is too much!" A feeling of intimidation swept over Cash as he turned and stared unbelievingly at his boyfriend. "Way too much."

"Don't worry about it." Travis reassuringly grinned, taking hold of his hands. "This is for us."

"What do you mean don't worry about this?" It was impossible for Cash to comprehend. "My God, this is probably a fortune!"

"It's okay… it's all taken care of." Travis laughed. "Come here… I want you to see this." He led Cash into the livingroom. Extended from floor to ceiling, the windows commanded a view grander than the rimrocks. "Come with me… I want you to see this."

Shaking his head, Cash was at a loss for words. As he approached the glass and watched the city lights below, he became mesmerized. The view was unbelievable—countless car and bus headlights snaked along deep narrow passageways below, as office lights from neighboring buildings peeked through low hanging clouds.

Travis slipped his arms back around Cash. "This is our first night together—just you and me. I want it to be special, babe." Softly, he buried his face into the warm security of Cash's neck.

The warmth of his breath… that indescribable smell… and the creamy touch of his fingers—it melted any reservations Cash had about the penthouse.

"Hey!" Travis softly whispered, leading his cowboy man into the bedroom. "I think there might be something for you in here…"

There, lying on the bed was a long stem rose, card, and bottle of wine.

"Could this be something of yours?" A smile swept his face.

Looking into those azure eyes, Cash sat down on the sofa. *How in the hell did he get this stuff in here?* Slowly, he reached out and gently took hold of the flower. He brought it close and inhaled the supple scent—feeling the silky petal dance across the tip of his nose. No one had ever given him a flower before. Picking up the card, he opened it. Like everything else that evening, he was taken aside by the picture—having never seen anything like it before. Two guys asleep, naked on a bear rug, by a glowing fire… all he could say to himself—it was beautiful.

Inside, were Travis' handwritten words… words more powerful than the assailing storm outside… yet quiet, as the silence within shadowy room they sat.

What is a day that is spent near with you?
That I ask of myself-
Ah, the count
Is too few.
As a moonbeam slides,
Serene or' my soul,
Your heart that it heals-

Becomes ever my whole.

In fleeting, the moment

From deep in your arms,

Becomes all of my breath

As it fills every charm.

What is a day that is spent near with you?

It's but a tale...

...of my dream

Of a hope that is true.

So listen my love

And be still to the call,

It is only my glory

Of a prayer-

Lest I fall.

What is a day that is spent near with you?

It's my desire

Oh, my love,

All my life...

...That is you.

Tears clouded Cash's eyes. Clumsily, he brushed them with his hand. "Travis, what on Earth do you see in me?"

Taking Cash's hand, Travis slowly brought it to his own face. Softly, he brushed the tips of the cattleman's fingers against his wet lips—allowing a stray touch of tongue to tease and tickle. "I see my world, Cash... I see my entire world in you."

The wind and rain slammed against the massive sheathing as Cash gasped. Never had anyone come into his life like this—so powerful, yet so gentle.

"I've wanted to do this right... for so long." Travis explained.

Staring at the rose—a single, perfect, blood-red rose, he finally separated the seal of his lips and spoke the words that had been pursed against his tongue since that afternoon on the levee. "Travis, I love you."

An explosive gust pounded the glass. "I know." He softly spoke, caressing the back of Cash's head and running his burly fingers through those fiery Irish locks of hair. Smoothly, he breathed into Cash's ear what blazed deep inside, "I love you too… I love you *so very* much."

Twinkling lights from the tranquil city below delicately crept through the silky sheers casting an opaque hue throughout the large room. In spite of the huge, soft, comfortable bed—the piles of down pillows and exquisite comforters, Cash found it impossible to sleep. Afraid that one moment of this unspeakable beauty might be lost forever to an idle second of sleep, he lay still against Travis' smooth, warm skin, quickly finding this particular area to be his favorite place—head resting tenderly in the gentle slope of a chest carved of steel between the top of its massive crest and the comforting cradle of a shoulder designed to defend and protect. With lips barely clutching the delicate tip of a rigid nipple and his nostrils becoming drunk with the mesmerizing masculine aroma of an eloquently adorned arm pit, it seemed like a portrait painted of heaven itself.

Morning would soon arrive and he realized slumber needed to subdue him. Pushing the covers back and sliding from the sheets, Cash rose from the bed and walked softly to the window—peeking hesitantly down at the world below. The wind had stopped—gracefully replaced by little snowflakes that silently fluttered aimlessly against the glass. Eventually, each flake found their way home—falling on the white, blanketed rooftops and deserted street.

This was the happiest he'd ever felt—so loved and protected.

His thumb fumbled with the ridge of the ring that rested on his neck chain. Drawing his hand closer so he could see it in the diffused light—the stone glistened boldly. Tingles swept his spine. Belonging to someone... Having someone to call your own... It was truly neat. Where would this take them? Cash didn't have a clue. All he wanted now was to be with him for the rest of his life.

Suddenly, he sensed a touch against the back of his neck.

"Hey." Cash whispered—continuing to stare through the drapery's sheer into the deep city night.

"Hey." A tender voice replied from behind. Slowly, deliberately, Travis drew him in.

Leaning further into the hold, all Cash wanted was to submit. A flame burst into an inferno—an unbelievable conflagration—and with it, a primal challenge to his masculinity. Something raw—more carnal than ever imagined licked and sucked within his flesh. It brought him closer than what a dream could ever dare.

"Forever..." Cash breathlessly sighed.

Allowing his tongue to play smoothly across Cash's flesh, Travis created a stream—returning the sacred chant with his own prayer. "Forever..."

CHAPTER 9

Morning came too quickly as the two boys pushed themselves sleepily from the huge, sprawling bed. Room service trays, plates and glasses cluttered the dining room table. All intentions of scouting beforehand for the studio had been effortlessly put aside—as had been the plan to go to the restaurant for a formal dinner. Neither one had poked their nose out of the suite because of one reason—each other.

Putting his best clothes on, Cash felt an overwhelming sense of anxiety. Until now, the thought of being on live, statewide television seemed somewhat routine—like standing before a classroom, stating your name and telling everyone what you had done over the past summer. As he snapped the pearl buttons of his white western shirt, he grabbed his trustworthy black hat and shot one last glance into the large vanity mirror—feeling his heart pounding heavily within his chest. He was nervous.

Travis, as usual, looked great. Wearing a long sleeve, baby blue, button-down dress shirt, black tie, Dockers, and a pair of loafers, he radiated that typical college prep look. Carefully, running a brush through his perfectly sculpted flat-top hair cut, he cast one last inspection at the mirror as well. "We better be getting over there, the show starts at nine."

"What time do we have to be there?" Cash asked as he busily packed things into his bag. Looking out the window, he noticed a white layer of snow on the rooftops of the buildings below. The entire world appeared different from the hotel suite. It was strange to look directly into the office buildings across the street and watch people working at their desks while everything down below looked like a world in miniature, with Matchbox Cars and tiny plastic figurines.

"They said we need to be there at seven-thirty." Travis mumbled through a mouthful of scrambled eggs and sausage. Room service had come a little late with their breakfasts, forcing the boys to eat on the go. "You better finish your pancakes," he suggested to Cash, knowing how hungry he'd get by showtime.

There was no trouble in finding the studio. They got there in plenty of time. The director, a young man with a strong New York accent, quickly greeted them at the lobby, leading them to a back area where several dressing rooms were located. By the time they got situated into their chairs, Cash's stomach was doing some serious churning. Looking over at Travis, he felt a surge of envy fire up. Damn him! He looked so calm and cool. Obviously, this didn't phase him a bit. A staff of people began working on them—brushing a bit of make-up on their faces and checking various shades of lighting on them through an off-line camera.

"Are you planning to wear your hat on the set?" a girl innocently asked Cash as she straightened out his shirt collar and turned him around in the chair.

"Huh?" Cash was dazed. *What was she jabberin' about?* The attendant smiled. "Your hat, do you intent to wear it on the show?"

"Oh!" He felt dumb. Forgetting that he had it on, he yanked it off and replied apologetically, "I don't have to."

"I think you should!" she heartily exclaimed. "I think it looks great. It's hot!"

Nodding with embarrassment, Cash replied "Okay, if you think so."

Suddenly, Travis' attention was captured from across the room. Casting a wary eye, he silently watched the girl who seemed to make a come-on to his boyfriend.

Cash glared back at him. Quickly, the football player looked away as if trying not to let it get under his skin. Indeed, Travis was the jealous type.

Before they realized it, the show began. Third on the line-up, it seemed just the right amount of time for Cash to get totally knotted-up. He could hardly wait to get through it as he worried about what he would say and how he would act. Had he known what this would have entailed, he would have declined to do it.

Finally, their time was up—they were on.

Quietly, they stood nearby the set as show hosts Daniel Livingston and Sharon Wills enthusiastically introduced them...

"Today," Daniel announced to the cameras and small audience, "we have an interesting pair of guys joining us from Miles City. They've been labeled 'The Titan Two' and it's quite interesting how they've come to inherit this name. The first one is a tight-end on the high school football team. Extremely talented and versatile on the grid iron, he is up for the coveted Offensive Player of the Year title as well as Most Valuable Player for the state this season. He has assisted in thrusting his team into the current number one ranking of the Montana Eastern Division—Class A. The other fellow is a rough rider who has gained the top recognition of being best All Round Cowboy in the State High School Rodeo Association. He has three rankings in Saddle Bronc, Bareback, and Bull Riding. Not only do these two boys come from the same city, but they are best friends and

S. Bryan Gonzales

seem to feed off of each other's dynamic synergy. Let's welcome to our studios Travis Hunter and Cash McCollum!" A large round of applause rose from the audience as they walked out on the stage and shook Daniel and Sharon's hands.

Settling into the high, bar-stool chairs, Daniel looked at the boys and began by saying, "Well, you two have really created a stir around the state recently."

"Indeed, they have." Sharon acknowledged, looking attentively to her co-host, nodding her head. Then turning to the boys, she switched her focus and directed a general question to them. "How does it feel to be in such a center of attraction?" There was a sparkle in her eyes.

"Weird." Cash blurted without thinking. He could hear several chuckles from the audience. Instantly, he felt his face begin to burn with embarrassment.

"It certainly has taken us by surprise." Travis politely jumped in.

"I'm sure." Sharon acknowledged.

Daniel cleared his throat. "Travis, in looking over your stats, they're nothing short of incredible."

"Thank you." Now it was Travis' turn to blush.

"You've played the tight-end position for the past two years and for this season you've had fifty-four receptions for 1,062 yards and sixteen touchdowns."

"Yeah," Travis said thoughtfully, "It's been a really good year. My workouts have been very productive...I currently bench 285, with a 390 squat. I feel I have been focused on each game and I find myself being a strong encouragement to my teammates."

130

Noticing Travis' size and the packed-on muscles through his shirt, Sharon asked, "Do you work out every day?"

"I usually work out five times a week." Travis seemed very nonchalant. "My routines are varied."

Daniel asked the next question. "Travis, your coach told us that you are extremely athletic—as we can readily see." As he let out a small laugh, the audience began to applaud. "You're also exceptionally fast for your size…a great blocker and rather unbelievable with your hands as a receiver."

No shit. Cash caught his breath on that line. *Those fingers have the ability to catch anything!*

The show host went on to say, "He also told us he considers you one of the best athletes the school has ever had. You have developed a tremendous talent as a complete tight-end and you seem to possess all the physical skills to emerge as a top collegiate—and perhaps eventually professional player. Could you elaborate your take a little on that?" He pushed himself forward in his chair.

Travis took in a deep breath. "First off, I want to say it's not just me, but every player on our team that is making this year such a great success. When I go out with the others on the field, my mind is not on what I am going to do for myself as much as what will I do to be the best player for the team. We have an explosive offense and I love it." He spoke enthusiastically. "I love the way we throw the ball—and I love the way we block and open up holes. Most of all, I love working with each of the fantastic offensive linemen on our team. I believe we have learned how to work together for a common goal."

"And what is that goal?" Sharon asked.

"To win great."

Travis went on. "I'm tough and I love to go out there and hit. I'd like to improve my lateral movement and get stronger—you know, bust through blocks easier. I also have good speed for my size and great vision. I know what's going on around me..."

Boy, he's not kidding there. Cash mused to himself; recalling the scene back to his personal attendant and the dagger look Travis had thrown her.

"With your ability, have you ever considered switching to the quarterback position? You certainly seem like you'd be capable in managing it." Daniel asked.

"Numerous times, but the thing that keeps me where I'm at is I love digging in the trenches. I find more control in supporting others than directly controlling them."

"That's amazing."

Cash could tell the show host was clearly impressed with Travis, his outlook on football and life itself.

"What about college?" Sharon quickly interjected in an effort to keep the momentum going. "Have you been approached by any scouts?"

"So far, I have heard from USC, Colorado, Arizona State, and Oregon as well as from MSU and the U of M."

"Have you had any offers?" she continued on the same topic.

"One—from the U of M." Travis said, casting a quick eye toward Cash. "I guess I'm holding out to see what else might come."

Cash felt the blood drain from his head. *He hadn't said a word about that to him.*

"Do you have any wishes of where you'd like to go?"

"I'm not sure, the Pac 10 is a great conference, but I know that there are outstanding schools in the Midwest and back east—such as Oklahoma and Virginia that I'd like to consider. Sometimes in football you can tell by your talent what college will want you. Some players know that by their size and speed, they can go to this school or that. I guess the bottom line for me at this time is to be patient and wait it out a little bit longer."

Glancing at one of the cameramen who gave him a gesture with his hands, Daniel took over the remainder of the interview on Travis. "Do you have any personal goals in your life that you would like to share with us here in the studio and with the viewers throughout the state before we go on a break?"

Thinking for a second, Travis replied, "Well, I'd like to go into business administration. Both my parents have been in that field and I seem to have a good understanding of operating things. I guess it comes pretty natural for me because of my background."

"What type of businesses do your folks run?"

From the ceiling, a light began to pulsate—counting down each second from one minute. Cash found it difficult to pay attention to the dialogue due to all the subliminal activity that was developing around the set.

"My mother is a bank manager and my dad was the CEO of a law firm in California."

"You're living with your mom," Daniel carefully noted. "Do you keep in touch with your father?"

At once, Cash's attention was corralled in. His guts quickly tightened. *No one else knows...how's he going to work through this one?"* As a sick feeling came over him, he silently prayed, *"Dear God, give him words."*

Without hesitation, Travis nodded attentively and smiled. "I'm in close contact with him on a regular basis."

"Where's he at?"

"Close enough." A reassuring tone carried strongly in the steadied football player's words indicating no further information needed to be asked.

Timing could not have been better as Daniel looked out to the cameras and said, "Don't go away, folks, we'll be right back in several minutes to talk with Travis' friend, Cash McCollum, who is currently the Montana High School Rodeo Association's top All-Around Cowboy and possesses some of the highest scores ever seen in the state."

The cameraman signaled for the audience to applaud as he scanned the various portions of the room.

"Travis, you did very well." Daniel came over to him, heartily shaking his hand. "You have quite a story." He went on to say.

You don't know the half of it. Thought Cash as he remained quiet like a mouse in the chair.

"Thank you, sir." Travis politely replied.

Looking over in Cash's direction, Daniel smiled and jostled his shoulder. "I can tell you are not used to this."

"Hell no," said Cash, fidgeting a little with his collar. With the heat blasting down from those stage lights, he felt like he was burning up.

Sharon came over and joined the others. Choosing her words in a friendly, reassuring tone, she assisted Cash with his shirt collar by offering several small, adjusting tugs. "Just relax and have fun. We'll ask you the questions and you take your time to answer. If you have a brain fart, don't panic—it won't be the end of the world." Allowing a little laugh to escape from her lips, she continued to speak. "You know, something tells me you won't have a problem doing this at all."

Looking at her quizzically, Cash asked, "Yeah?"

"Yeah." Her face beamed. "You look like you have a lot of life scurrying around inside and I have a feeling you are going to absolutely *love* talking about yourself. In fact, I'm just dying to know more about you."

"Thirty seconds from air time." The cameraman called from his perch.

Cash's heart was pounding. He could feel his fingers tremble. *God have mercy,* he silently prayed. Lately, he knew he couldn't be labeled a good Christian church-goer. In fact, he couldn't be labeled *anything* in that department largely because of the rodeos every weekend. It didn't mean he didn't believe…in fact, he had strong faith in a God ruling over everything in existence. How he dealt with his faith and belief, however, was a little less than orthodox in the eyes of many church members where he had grown up—and that was where the conflict started. In spite of it all, his creed could be summed up into one sentence—*Love the Lord with all your heart and treat everyone else the way you want to be treated.* End of the doctrine class, and back to the talk show stage.

"…three, two, one—we're on the air." The cameraman called out.

"Welcome back, everyone." Sharon warmly greeted—smiling into the cameras. "Just in case you've joined us in the past couple of minutes—this morning we've had the unique opportunity of visiting with two young men from Miles City High School. They are best friends. Both are very successful in their fields of interest; yet their worlds are completely different. We've talked to Travis earlier, and now it's time for us to learn a little bit about Cash McCollum." Tossing him a tiny wink, a broad smile swept across her face.

"Cash, thanks for coming on our show today," Sharon began.

"Thank you for having me," Cash politely replied. He liked her. She made him feel very comfortable.

"You know, I just have to say this… I *really* love your name. Is there a story behind how you inherited it?"

"I'm really not sure," Cash replied, shrugging his shoulders. "I guess my dad liked it. Mom said it was because I turned out to be a good return on the deposit."

Instantly, everyone in the studio broke out in laughter.

Whatever behooved him to say that? God only knew—because it had certainly not been planned.

Wiping a tear of hilarity from her eye, Sharon regained her composure and went on to say to the cameras and audience, "Well, that serves me right…I asked and I guess he told me, huh?"

"That'll teach you." Daniel said, still chuckling.

"I guess." She replied. "Well, moving right along…" She quickly caught her breath and proceeded to carry on a lively chat with Cash.

Reviewing his rodeo stats and ranking, Cash could tell everybody's interest was roped in. Both Sharon and Daniel seemed amazed at the amount of preparation, not to mention risk a cowboy had to go through in order to participate for a single rodeo rough-stock event.

"…In other words," Daniel finally summed it up, "it's either an addiction, sheer determination, or complete insanity that a person takes up rodeoing. Am I right?"

Cash smiled, acknowledging the show host's statement with a nod. "Pretty much."

The cameraman gave their signal and the board on the ceiling began flashing its numbers.

"Wow." Daniel could not keep from adding one more thing, "You know, I have a whole different outlook on cowboys and rodeos. They really work their butts off. And who ever says the cowboy way is a piece of cake, I'll be able to say they need to walk in their boots for a day to discover the raw truth." Giving him a big smile, he said, "Thanks, Cash."

"Thank you." Cash let out a small sigh.

A surge of clapping instantly followed as Travis and Cash made their way off the set into the back area.

"Whew!" Cash breathlessly exhaled as he grabbed his cowboy hat and wiped the heavy perspiration off his brow. *Thank God*, he gratefully thought to himself. *The granddaddy of them all—down for the count.* He felt like he'd been through the ringer.

"Great work, guys!" One of the stage crew men praised, as they continued down the hallway to the dressing rooms.

Giving him a quick smile, Travis replied, "Hey, thanks!"

A brew simmering on the back burner of Cash's mind quickly got shuffled to the front. *What was up with this college shit?* Why the secret—until now? Not a word had been mentioned about the university offer... not even a hint! Was there a reason why Travis was holding this back from him? Perhaps looking for a *better* offer? Well, hell! Did that mean he's planning to leave? What about him? One thing was for sure, Cash had no intentions on leaving the state. Everything he wanted was here, why go someplace else? He couldn't wait to address this matter in the car.

Without warning, a very familiar voice floated into Cash's ears. "Hey there, little brother!"

"Clint!" Cash's eye lit up. He hadn't seen his brother in awhile.

The tall, sandy-blond man wearing a rather grungy, white baseball cap—bearing a "severe" curve in the bill, ran up to Cash and excitedly threw his arms around him. "Bucky, you looked mighty good there on TV! I am so proud of you!"

They hugged each other excitedly as people milled about them in the busy hallway.

"Did you see us?" Cash asked. It made him feel good to know his brother had taken the time to watch them.

"Did I see you?" There was a credulous tone to Clint's voice. "I wouldn't have missed it for the world!" Reaching out, he lightly punched Cash's shoulder.

Looking over in Travis' direction, Clint quickly stuck his hand out and warmly introduced himself. 'Hi, I'm Clint—the oldest of the McCollum brood. And you're the 'better half' I've been hearing about who has the dirty job of keeping this one in line!" Pointing to Cash, he made a silly face.

"Cut it out!" Cash laughed, coughing lightly with embarrassment.

"Travis, it's really nice to meet you." The citified, country boy spoke sincerely as he affectionately put his arm around his kid brother.

"It's a pleasure to meet you, Clint." It was obvious, the astonishment Travis had regarding Cash's oldest brother. "Wow, the two of you have a lot of the same mannerisms," he spoke, shifting his look between Cash and Clint, a big grin sweeping his face.

"I hope that's good!" Clint laughed. "I've always thought of Cash bein' a cool little brother, pretty good-natured."

"Unlike Clayton..." Cash spoke the name sourly.

"Hey, come on," Clint jumped into the line of defense. "Give him a chance. He's got some great qualities, you know."

Cash let out a quick snort. *Yeah, right....*he thought to himself.

Looking at his watch, Clint spoke up and suggested, "Hey, it's almost noon. Why don't we go someplace and grab a bite?"

"That sound's great." Travis wholeheartedly agreed. "I'm starved."

Together, the three of them walked out of the studio with high spirits, joining their paths—if only for a brief afternoon—on the grand journey of life.

Cash was really happy to see his brother. Having a totally different make up than Clayton, Clint was a sensitive individual who had a certain honest, warm nature woven throughout his being—giving him a sincere interest in other people. Cash had a lot of respect for his oldest brother. He seemed full of wisdom—careful of thoughts and words—guided with a tender heart of conviction. In many ways, he reminded him a lot of their mother. Cash believed it was this combination of cherished qualities that would eventually make him an outstanding teacher.

"There's a diner at the end of this block," Clint suggested zipping up his sweatshirt to protect himself from the cold breeze.

They entered the small eating place and discovered there was only one remaining available booth left. It was a good thing they arrived when they did because a flock of people followed in behind them who were unable to find a place to sit. *Gosh, this place must be pretty popular*, Cash quietly told himself.

Travis and Clint instantly plunked themselves into the opposite seats.

"Come over here," Travis spoke softly—his face beaming.

Cash slid in next to Travis. It was funny, he just couldn't get close enough to the big, muscular youth who situated himself—shoulder up against the wall with a relaxed arm resting easily on the back of the long seat.

Clint noticed the private rapport between the two boys and gave a big grin. "You know, I thought this would never happen in our family, but I have to say you two really do look good together—you compliment each other well."

An expression of surprise came over Travis' face. "Thank you," he smiled back at Clint—obviously very grateful for the affirming comment.

"I mean it," Clint spoke openly.

An older lady wearing an oversized, flannel plaid-shirt and a tight French-braid in her graying hair came to the booth—handing each of them a menu. "Can I get you boys anything to drink?"

"I'll have a coke." Clint replied.

"Make that two." Travis added.

"Three," Cash followed the suit with an impish smile.

"You guys are way too picky," she spoke with a deep, hearty laugh. "I'm not sure I can handle this."

Everyone at the table chuckled.

"How's Dad taking this?" Clint gave Cash a searching look.

Fidgeting with one of the corners of the laminated menu, Cash shrugged his shoulders and muttered, "I dunno... I guess alright. He doesn't talk about it." Pausing for a moment, debating whether or not he should bring it up, he finally decided to continue. "It's Clayton that's bein' an asshole."

Staring intently at his younger brother, he said in a light tone, "Be easy on him. He sees things differently than the rest of us. That doesn't make him a bad person—in fact, he has a lot of fine qualities."

"I busted his nose." Cash had to make his confession. It had been eating at him for weeks, and today seemed like the perfect time to get it out in the open. He wanted to tell Clint everything, especially about the talk at the Co-op, but with Travis present, he felt restricted. There was no way he wanted to be responsible for any battle that would ensue if Travis were to learn the 'rest of the story'.

"I heard about that." Clint laughed quietly to himself. "When mom told me, I could picture the whole scene in my head."

Cash pushed himself up in the booth—a flare of anger shooting from his eyes. "Well, damn it, Clint. You know how he can't keep his trap shut. Sometimes, I wish I could just super-glue his goddamn mouth."

"He probably deserved it."

The waitress came back with the pop and promptly took their orders.

Clint took a sip of the drink and continued to speak. "Just remember, he's your brother and you both need each other."

"Yeah, I know." Cash looked down at his lap.

"You two need to get along 'cuz Dad's not getting any better and stuff like this wears on him terribly." There was a serious tone in his big brother's voice.

Cash nodded—acknowledging Clint's stern words of wisdom.

"I'm sorry..." The tone in Clint's voice soften a bit. "I don't mean to come down hard on you, Bucky, but I know you'll find a way to work through it. Clayton's a good guy with a good heart—but maybe he's findin' himself a little jealous over you and your rodeo success."

Cash had never thought of it that way. Hell, he never thought of himself better than Clayton—or anyone else for that matter.

Letting out a big sigh, Clint reached over and tapped Cash's shoulder. "Hey, you're one of my favorite little brothers in the whole wide world and I'm proud as hell in what you've done."

Cash allowed a wide grin to grow across his lips and cheeks. He loved Clint so much. He couldn't have asked for a better brother.

Turning to Travis, Clint chuckled and asked, "So, Travis, what do you think about gettin' all tied-up with this eccentric family?"

"I think it's great. Cash comes from a very exceptional home." Travis replied thoughtfully. "Each of you seem to be really cool."

"Well, I'm glad you're becoming part of the clan." Clint flatly stated. "I know mom thinks you're the cat's meow..." he laughed at his own choice of words. "Just give Dad and Clayton a little time..."

Thus, in a world where him and Travis couldn't demand people's support and respect of their relationship, Cash considered it a blessing that Clint was so open. Moreover, the fact that Travis and Clint even *liked* each other—well, *that* in itself, truly meant a lot.

Later that afternoon, settling once again into the smooth leather seat of the sports coupe, Cash picked up the thought he had safely tucked away since the time of the talk show. Now, he found it to be a perfect time to sit on it like an old hen—waiting for it to hatch.

Noticing his partner extremely quiet, Travis looked over from the wheel and innocently asked, "Hey, why the silence? You tired?"

Cash did not reply. The embers were beginning to ignite into a slow burn.

"What's up?" Travis continued to mine. "You not feelin' good?"

Still Cash said nothing. Straightening up slowly in the seat, he rubbed his forehead; the sound of the engine roared steadily on the highway.

A look of concern flooded Travis' face. "What's wrong?"

Remaining speechless for several long moments, Cash let out a sigh and asked, his words icy and cold, "Would you mind tellin' me what that was all about at the show with you sayin' you're plannin' on holdin' off about the U until you see what else might come along?"

Instantly, Travis' face grew red, his fingers tightening on the steering wheel. Looking straight ahead, he replied. "What are you saying?"

"Exactly what I mean." Cash's voice elevated in anger. "You have plans to leave this state?" He knew he had him trapped in the corner.

"Cash," Travis' voice lowered, "I have to see what my options are out there." He tried to calmly explain, "I didn't mean anything by it in regards to you."

"Yeah," said Cash, picking up the fork and dagger. Slowly, he selected his next words meticulously—to jab and cut deeper than anything else on earth. "Seems all I'm good for you right now is providin' a safe, reliable hole until you can get away to some Ivy League school 'n find a more suitable fuck to drag around with your 'incredible fingers'."

"Don't go there, Cash," Travis warned. "I tell you—that's not fair."

'Not fair?!" Cash finally exploded. Turning to his boyfriend, he threw him a fiery start. "Like hell!"

"Listen," Travis tried to lasso him in. "No one's said anything definite about me leaving the state; so let's just drop the subject."

"Well, then," Cash pushed himself forward in the seat and leaned closer to Travis, "tell me what that was all about back at the show?" Pausing, he collected himself—gathering more ammunition for the battle. "What exactly am I going to do if you get accepted someplace like Virginia and I'm left out here ridin' ponies? Rust in my ass?"

"Knock it off!" Now Travis was mad.

Cash knew he had him caught. He had every right in the world to pursue this issue. Turning away, he sat back hard in the seat and stared out at the empty countryside. "You know damn well I have no plans on leavin' this area."

Silence passed between them like the barren wheat fields that zipped by the window.

"I'm not gonna leave you." Travis finally spoke, in an honest effort to reassure his other half. "You know that. I love you too much."

"Yeah?" Cash snorted. "Well, I'm beginning to wonder." His mind went back to the red rose resting wonderfully in his fingers the night before. *Am I nuts?* He hopelessly thought to himself. *Was this whole thing nothing more than an insane dream?*

Chapter 10

The subject of colleges and universities quickly became a don't ask, don't tell topic. As Cash and Travis had seemed to reach an impasse—much like a dangling participle to a fragmented sentence, a thick, tough callous seemed to develop over the small festering sore of distrust and resentment. Cash felt blocked out, and it quietly nibbled at him one bite at a time. Since their conversation in the car, coming back from Billings, Travis had seemed to shut down—refusing to talk. Cash on the other hand, became bitchy. The bottomline—neither one was willing to concede to the other's viewpoint. Over and over, Cash asked himself if he was demanding too much. Why couldn't Travis be content to attend a local state school instead of traipsing clear across the damn country? Pride? That's what it seemed. It was Travis' freakin' pride that seemed to make him vigorously cling to the possibility of getting an offer from a big, prestigious institution—even at the cost of their relationship.

Seeing it from *that* perspective was simply too much for Cash to comprehend.

Two critical games lay ahead for the Cowboys. The first one was on the home turf. Even though Billings Central was notoriously one of the best teams in the division, expectations in town were nonetheless high.

As expected, Cash made his appearance—sitting faithfully in the bleachers trying to muddle through all the foreign jargon and plays of each quarter. Because of the unspoken standoff between him and Travis, it felt more like an obligation than an honest desire to watch him and the rest of the team play. In spite of it all, he still cheered energetically. Deep inside, however, he knew his heart was not in it. How could he go ape-shit over the very thing that was forcing its way in between them? Certain resentment was beginning to fester as he knew it would be football that would take Travis away—perhaps far, far away. *Then what?*

What irritated him the most was how he had been seemingly tricked into this relationship. If his memory served him right, it was Travis who had said he was in this for the long haul—for life. He had also said that even though they were coming from different worlds, they would be able to work through everything—hell or high water. Had he forgotten that this would entail adjustments—with a lot of give and take? For Christ's sake, there appeared to be no compromise concerning this issue.

Then, there were all the *whys.*

Why in blessed 'H' had Travis showered him with all this romance? Why the rabbit's foot. Why the ring? Why the incredible kiss in Glendive? Why the unforgettable night at the hotel? Cash could not stop thinking of all this shit as he sat on that icy bench. One thing was for sure…he certainly felt like a fool.

When Travis had ordered Cash to drop the subject, did that mean for good—as in subject dropped, case closed? Or was it just being conveniently put aside until he felt like dealing with the issue. Surely, they were going to hash this matter out in more detail, but when? Until that time, was Travis expecting him to bite the bullet, or sweep it under the rug?

I don't think so! Cash flatly told himself.

As the game dragged on, he felt increasingly out of place sitting and watching something he knew little about—let alone have an interest in. He debated whether or not to push himself off the riser and get the hell out of there. To him, there was no reason to remain and be taken for a goober.

Pushing himself to his feet, his ears picked up a voice shouting his name from several bleachers below. His stomach knotted.

"Hey, Jen," he mustered, saying her name half-heartedly.

"Thought I'd find you here." Jennifer bounded breathlessly up the steps two at a time.

Jesus, thought Cash. *What a graceless cow.*

"What's up?" A tightness shot through his chest. Clearly, he needed to keep this short, lest he betray himself.

"I've been looking for you all day!" She pushed the thick glasses back up her frosty, beet-red nose. "I haven't seen you since you've been on TV." It was as if she had perused through a daily keeper and discovered he was one of the to-do items not yet checked off.

Looking out over the playing field, no place in particular, only to keep from focusing on her, he indignantly said, "Well, I've been here."

"Oh." Not picking up on Cash's disinterest to visit, she continued. "You looked great. Were you scared?"

"Naw," Cash casually replied.

"They let you wear your cowboy hat on the set?"

She was stalling, fishing, Cash could tell. She wanted more information. He knew how she operated. Her goal was to find out about the real stuff—the juicy details. "Yeah, they said I looked good with the hat so they let me wear it."

"I was talking with Clayton at the Co-op last night and he said he'd been real worried about you staying with Travis."

Cash nearly choked from the sound of her words as he silently sat, frantically trying to regain his wits. She sure wasn't pussy-footin' today, he thought cynically—just get right in there and dig. Perhaps it was the cold weather. Off and on, throughout the game, stray specks of snowflakes whisked around their noses. *Not a day for hangin' around outdoors if you didn't need to.*

"Surprised he would even care." Cash said blandly; which was the truth. Rarely did his older brother show any interest in what he did, let alone shoot his mouth off about Cash's business to other people. Or, was this an exception? A tiny, uncomfortable itch settled in his spirit, making him feel uneasy.

Adjusting the stocking cap stretching over her matte of hair, she went on, "Yeah, he was pretty soused. You know, I'm worried about all his drinking." She made it a point to express her concern.

Cash felt the anger surge inside. "He knows how to take care of himself." *Damn her,* he hotly thought. *Couldn't she figure out when to drop it?*

Looking over at Cash who was trembling from the cold, she said, "Yeah, well I'm not so sure about that. Somebody needs to look after him..." her voice trailed.

At that, Cash was convinced he had had enough—enough of her, the game, the weather, *everything*. "Well, I better be splittin'," he sourly announced. Quickly, he pushed himself up off the bleacher. "Good talkin' with you, Jen. Tell your parents hello."

'You're not stayin' for the rest of the game?" Shock was in her voice.

"Naw." Cash tried to act calm as he carefully stepped around her. "I need to take care of some things before it gets too late."

"What about Travis?" She blurted out.

There it was…what he had suspected all along. She had the two of them coupled up in her mind. Suddenly, he knew exactly where she was coming from.

Turning in the aisle, he threw the question back at her. "What about him?"

Pretending to act nonchalant, she replied, "I don't know, just seems you should be here to watch the rest of the game."

"Like I said," Cash cast one more quick glance out over the field, fighting his nervousness, "there's some things I need to take care of."

With an indifferent shrug of her shoulders, she impassively stated, "Whatever."

His mother knew the second he made his way quietly through the front door that something was amiss. Looking up from a book she was reading, her face became gaunt—washed with an uneasiness that forced her to pick up the concern of an intuitive parent. Perhaps it was the reflection Cash saw of himself over her eyes as he stole a glance in her direction. Slowly, repeatedly, he drew his boot heels across the surface of the living room floor to the staircase.

"I'm going up to my room."

"Is the game over already?" Surprise was in her voice as she cast her eyes quickly to the clock on the mantle.

Cash declined to answer. Every step up the stairs seemed like an excruciating effort within his weary muscles. He wanted to crawl into a hole. Was he making more out of this than needed to be? How was Travis going to react? His heart pounded a rhythm completely foreign to him.

In perfect stillness, in the dark bedroom, he sat on the edge of his bed—thoughts jumbled up together senselessly. Travis…the class ring…football and colleges…and then Jennifer and Clayton…why, even the goddamn talk at the Co-op—nothing made sense. *Nothing made sense!* He didn't know what to do. He certainly didn't know what to say. Everything had been said that needed to be said in this scenario—with no results. *So what now?* He asked himself. Wait? Talk more? Forcefully beat it into them until they all got it, understanding and accepting his viewpoint…*his way?* He didn't know…he just simply didn't know.

The phone call eventually came. Cash had been expecting it. From the moment he left the stadium, with a flood of raging emotions engulfing him, he knew one of the impending consequences would include an inquisition.

Answering the phone, Mrs. McCollum paused briefly and called up the stairs to Cash's bedroom. "Cash, you have a phone call."

Driving himself off the bed, Cash went downstairs—picking up the receiver, he drew it to his ear. "Hello?"

"Cash?" It was Travis' voice.

"Hey." Cash honestly didn't know what to say.

There was an awkward space between them. "I looked for you after the game." He began; pausing for a response from Cash.

Cash remained silent.

"Did you go to the game?" Travis started probing.

Cash knew this would be the first in a string of questions that were going to come down the trail. He had been waiting for them—anticipating their arrival.

"Yeah, but I left early." Cash's voice lacked the usual tone of excitement which he carried when talking with Travis.

"You left early?" By the sound of Travis' voice, he was having difficulty in trying to figure this conversation out.

"Uh huh."

Cash knew Travis wanted to ask why. Instead, he said, "I see…You knew we won?" Travis changed the subject—lightening the heavy atmosphere.

"I expected as much?" There was lack of emotion in Cash's words. He sure wasn't going to go wild over the newscast. "That's great."

Once again, there was a gap in the conversation. Finally, Travis came out and asked, "Cash, am I missing something here? You're acting pretty strangely."

"I dunno, you tell me."

"You're still upset about me and this university thing, aren't you?" There was a note of impatience rising in his voice. "Look, this is not the time to talk about it. I have to be at a celebration party that is being sponsored by the 4-H at the Dakota Inn—you should be there, too…" His voice drifted off. Travis was obviously not yet ready to talk about it and Cash didn't feel like pretending everything was hunky-dory.

"Do you want me to come and pick you up?" Travis' manner of speaking came off more demanding than suggestive.

"That's all right." Cash impassively stated. He hated where this conversation was heading.

"That's all right, what?" Irritation raised one pitch higher from the voice coming over the line. "All right, you want me to pick you up? Or, all right, you do your own thing and I can go to hell?"

Don't tempt me! The anger finally flared up in Cash. "You don't have to get smart."

"I didn't think I was getting smart." Travis quickly retorted. "We're both expected to go to this thing tonight, and all I'm doing is asking you whether or not you wanna lift."

"You can leave out the comment about goin' to hell," Cash said, lowering his voice so his mother would not hear them arguing. "You know, this is the first I've heard of this little gatherin'."

Silence engulfed the line. Cash knew Travis was mad. There was no way he was going to sell out on this issue, however. Travis' arrogance and all-assuming attitude would *not* win out.

"What do you want?!" Travis yelled over the phone.

"You already know." Cash was unmovable, his voice remaining monotone. "You just need to act on it."

Another period of silence overtook the line. Cash could feel he was pushing his limits with the indignant jock.

"*Hell!*" Travis' voice boomed through the receiver—instantly, a slamming click followed, signaling the end of *that* conversation.

Standing there for an eternal, excruciating minute, Cash held the receiver in his shaking hand. *What the fuck?* He asked himself. He could just go to his goddamn party by himself. Placing the phone back on the cradle, he let out a long, exhaustive sigh.

"I'm sorry." Behind him, Cash's mother's voice sounded from the doorway.

Cash couldn't look at her. Countless thoughts were banging and colliding wildly in his mind. He wanted to die. Or something. Only the faithful ticking of the clock by the fireplace was the single sound penetrating the hanging stillness within the room. There was nothing to say, nothing to do—too bad he couldn't hold back the emotions as well.

As if reading his thoughts, she quietly went back to the recliner and picked up her book.

Cash knew she felt the pain. He also was aware she knew the issue at stake. One of the first things that had come out of her mouth after Travis had deposited him from the Billings trip was, "Had you been aware that he's seriously lookin' at going to an out-of-state school? You know, that really surprised me."

Remaining at his stance by the phone, his mind thought of the possibility that Travis might decide to call him back to apologize for the rude cut-off. He even played with the idea of making the phone call himself and directly demanding it. With a snort, however, he tossed the second option out as there was no way he would be so manipulated. *Maybe other people would come back groveling to his highness, thinking they couldn't possibly exist without his handsome, gifted, and popular graces!* That simply wasn't the case here. Cash had come to live his life being quite content with himself, his family, and his animals, and by God, all of *that* was still here.

It wasn't long until the sound of Travis' Viper roared into the yard. Instantly, Cash's stomach tied into knots. He had just settled down at his desk to do a bit of Internet browsing on his computer—something he hadn't done for ages. Everyone else seemed so glued to their PCs, but Cash never found it to be an addiction. What seemed to trap him was spending time out in the barn or corral with the animals—and lately, being with Travis. Refraining from appearing too eager, Cash remained upstairs in his room as his mother went to the door and answered it.

"Good evening, Mrs. McCollum. Is Cash here?" He sounded so respectful and formal.

It was sickening!

She politely requested, "Hi, Travis...please call me Janice, ok? We're all pretty laid back here."

Cash could picture the two at the entryway.

"He's up in his room. Why don't you go on up," she suggested, stepping aside—allowing Travis to come in.

"Thanks." Travis replied.

Cash listened to the footsteps come up the stairs. There was a knock on his door. "Yeah?" He called from his desk.

Travis slowly pushed open the door and stood rigidly in the doorway. "Hey." The tone in his voice had simmered down considerably since the conversation over the phone.

"Hey." Cash repeated, even though his insides were crawling with nervous hesitation. He calmly pushed himself from the desk.

Travis looked extremely uncomfortable—the wrinkled brow, his inability to look Cash in the eye, and his fingers nervously fidgeting with his keys revealed he was not accustomed in seeking out others after a confrontation. Cash thought it was rather funny. There was a certain satisfaction seeing this great baby squirm and do a little groveling.

"May I come in?" Travis humbly asked, still not looking up.

"Sure, have a seat." He gestured over to the bed. "Welcome to my office." He let out a small chuckle.

Travis stepped over to the bed and sat down. Letting out a sigh, he finally looked up at Cash and awkwardly said, "I—I had to come over."

Cash remained silent; seated sideways in his chair, his arm rested easily on its wood-framed back. He wanted to hear Travis continue.

"This isn't easy for me," Travis appeared compelled to explain. "You know, coming over here and telling you I'm sorry—not that you don't deserve it, because you do." He cleared his throat and went on to say, "I've never known someone like you." Letting out a sigh, he stopped playing with the keys. "I don't know what it is, but no one else has ever had the control in my life that you have."

That took everything for him to say, reasoned Cash. He could tell Travis was not used to going to others to apologize, let alone admit they had control over him.

Thinking for a moment, Travis went on with his soft, gentle voice. "Cash, I really don't know what to say about the university thing, but all I ask is that you please be patient as all I want to see is what offers I'll be getting in the coming months."

Cash listened, allowing what Travis said to soak under his skin and into his being.

"Right now," he went on to speak, "I cannot promise you I will be going to the U, or to MSU for that matter. Neither one of us knows what the future will bring. What I *can* promise you, Cash, is my love and complete devotion to you. I'll *never* leave you, and you must believe me on that. You know, I've told you that I've wanted a relationship with you since the first day I laid eyes on you...that hasn't changed, and it never will. All I know is we'll work through everything as it comes. Sometimes, we just can't have the issues we face solved in one setting. I believe this is one of them. You and I just need to have the faith and trust that the best will come out for the both of us."

Cash remained quiet.

"It's one day at a time." Travis finally added, taking a deep breath as if relieved to get it off his chest and out in the open.

Allowing his tense muscles to relax, Cash smiled and said, "I love you."

"I love you, too." Travis returned the smile.

They sat peacefully in the small bedroom looking at each other. Eventually, Cash pushed himself from the chair and went over to Travis. Putting his arms around the gigantic shoulders, he embraced him and they shared a long, overdue kiss of reconciliation.

This relationship was a whole new thing for both of them. Prior to that, neither one had to go out of their way to think of another person before making a decision. Their worlds had seem to consist largely of 'doing your own thing'. Period.

Cash decided to go with Travis to the 4-H celebration. Hurriedly, he got cleaned-up and dressed. It was strange; there was becoming an expectation from the community that the two of them needed to appear *together* when out in public. *Like a couple.*

The two boys made their way down the worn steps to the living room where Cash's mother was still busy reading her book by the fireplace.

Looking up, a soft look of satisfaction crept over her face. Getting out of the recliner, she stretched, and said with a large grin, "I gather you two are goin' out?" The larger question answered.

"Uh huh." Cash answered.

"Yes, ma'am."

"Be careful," she spoke with concern, reaching out and giving Cash a hug, and sharing one with Travis as well—her warm gesture catching the burly football player somewhat off guard.

Within a flash, a thought passed through Cash's mind. He wondered how affectionate Travis and his mother were in that big, exquisite house. It was conceivable that two people could possibly go for days without seeing each other. That would be lonely, he reckoned. Awfully lonely.

CHAPTER 11

Miles City High won the state football championship—undefeated. It was record breaking not only for the school, but for the entire division as well. As the officials had stated, the feat was phenomenal. The season had definitely placed the town back on the map for top athletic prowess and community spirit—invigorating the region.

There were celebrations, convocations, and parties—one right after another. And there were awards— one bestowed on both Cash and Travis for outstanding community spirit, which Cash's dad immediately labeled it as a 'crock of shit'.

"You know damn well the city council scarfed that one up just to look good." His words were acidy. "Bein' that it's gonna be a re-election year."

What they couldn't dismiss, however, were the expectations placed on them. Cash honestly thought he was going to get an ulcer from the endless number of public appearances. From the Boy Scouts to the Toastmasters, it was invitation after invitation to various civic groups and organizations.

The most revered gathering of all was the official parade, dedication and hanging of the State High School Association's Football Championship banner in the school's gym—right by the brand new score board and large mural of a cowboy riding a bucking horse. Everyone would be there, and Cash awoke that morning to see the clock already showing ten. Puzzled, he wondered why his mother hadn't called him for church. Dressing as fast as he could, he rushed down the stairs only to see his father taken up at his usual space in front of the television, some boring political talk show yammering away.

"Mornin'," Cash called. He noticed his mother sitting on the couch, newspaper folded across her lap. "You guys didn't go to church?"

Mrs. McCollum glanced up from her newspaper. "We figured you would appreciate sleeping in today," she said, turning her face back down. "There's donuts in the kitchen."

Cash wasn't ready for sugar just yet; instead, he grabbed himself a glass of milk.

It was true. He felt as though he hadn't slept all night—constantly opening and closing his eyes, looking in the direction of the clock that never seemed to change time. At first, he had planned calling around midnight, anxious for the bus load of players careening over possibly slick, two-lane highways from Havre, but then, thought better of it. Travis would probably be tired after such a long trip. Or maybe they would have some kind of late night party, reliving their victory through illicit beers and laugher. So Cash determined, despite himself, to wait until morning—perhaps make the call at seven. But actually that wasn't any good either, because after either a late night of carousing, or just plain exhaustion, Travis wouldn't appreciate being woken up early.

Cash finished the milk then bounded up the steps to the upstairs phone.

It rang and rang, with no answer. Annoyed, Cash slammed the receiver down. The parade wasn't beginning until one. Why wasn't he home? Then he figured maybe the coach had taken them to breakfast—a little treat before everything started. If that was the case, then Travis might not be coming back home, and the thought sat with bur-like annoyance in Cash's brain. It would mean he wouldn't even see Travis until the ceremony at the gym, and *that* was after the damned parade. Cash slumped his way back to the living room.

"You going to the parade and stuff?" he asked both parents.

"We don't think so." Mrs. McCollum looked over at her husband. "Your father isn't feeling particularly well so we'll just probably sit it out."

Cash was disappointed at their inability to see Travis in his moment of glory.

"Where's Clayton?" He suddenly realized his brother's absence. After all, Clayton was never one to pass up donuts.

He heard his mother give a sigh. "Dunno. He went out early."

Well, Cash couldn't convince himself that he was in any way concerned. He walked into the kitchen and perused the box, helping himself to anything chocolate; eating so many he was barely able to choke down a few slight helpings of a fried chicken dinner at noon.

"Sure you're not going?" he again asked his parents. Clayton hadn't yet made his reappearance. Mrs. McCollum commented that she would just put a portion back in the refrigerator for him.

His father chewed on plump thigh and smiled, "And here you were, so worried about them not winning and everything being called off. So prepared for the worst—and now you're busting your pants ready to get out." Which was true. Cash had carried forebodings the entire week— visions entering his head of uniforms put silently away and crepe paper thrown into the dumpster.

"Like losin' would've made any difference to a good party!" He waved his fork in Cash's direction.

Immediately after dinner, Cash rushed to his room to change. He looked about in his closet for something he might consider extra nice, but realized he didn't have much to choose from. There was mainly the stuff he wore to school, the stuff he wore to church which was pretty much the same as for school, and then, work clothes. Shrugging, he put on his black jeans with a red and black checked flannel shirt, topping it off with his sheepskin jacket because after all, he wanted to be warm. Giving a quick polish to his best boots, he turned, admiring his lean frame in the mirror, and then, hurrying out the front door—calling "bye" as he slammed it behind him.

When he got to Main Street he could see a crowd had already formed up and down—lines of children and their parents, old farmers and ranchers, students from school and pre-teens just looking for something to do. Cash excused himself towards the front of what he thought might be the best vantage point, people smiling at him with recognition and easily giving way. In the distance, he could see members of the band gathering in formation, warming-up their instruments with occasional toots and trills, the cheerleaders hopping up and down to limber themselves.

Right on schedule, a whistle blew and then like ants to a drop of honey, the band, cheerleaders, and dance team assembled themselves—beginning their well-practiced approach. There were screams and cheers as one barely recognizable tune after another blared forth. The cheer squad leaped and danced their routine, acting oblivious to the afternoon chill in costumes that never varied by season. Shortly behind, followed one fire truck, then another, escorted in front and back by sheriff's cars. The trucks politely waited until the band placed their instruments to their sides before starting up their sirens.

And there was Travis, front and center on the very first one, smiling his biggest grin, wearing his favorite bomber jacket. Cash didn't wave, but willed Travis to find him in the crowd. Travis gave only the briefest of recognitions—if he actually saw Cash at all. With nothing more to look at, Cash turned aside, noting Harlan Jens sitting high atop the second truck. He felt his stomach tighten. Well, he's certainly in *his* glory, he noted dryly to himself.

Working his way over to school, the doors were already open. Inside, the gym was decorated with banners bearing a stern likeness of each player in serious business mode. Travis looked particularly uninviting in full-uniform, a solid mass of determination and grit. Streamers in blue and white fluttered about; balloons were tied to the backs of the chairs along the isle. Cash parked himself, and soon he heard the rest of the crowd rustling in, clamoring among the metal chairs—the heat of their bodies in their warm winter coats immediately raising the room's temperature.

The band assembled on the stage, with seats for the players behind and alongside. Mr. Ryan took his place behind the lectern, waiting patiently for the crowd to settle and quiet. When everyone finally got the implied message, he said a few words about the great victory that had occurred and formally presented the gold trophy and banner from the State High School Association to Coach Smith who gratefully took the awards and gave a short inspirational speech. Finally, it was time for special awards to be announced to those individual players who contributed toward this victory in a special way. Everyone's eyes turned to silently watch as the Montana's Most Valuable Player trophy was carried from the wings onto the stage by the Superintendent of Schools and the mayor. Holding it high aloft, the assembly cheered, and Cash swore it looked like some old timer's were crying. Then the coach grandly presented it to Principal Ryan, who placed it on his podium with loving care.

"We have a special trophy, of course, for our most valuable player. Travis Hunter, can you step over here?"

Travis, with characteristic modesty, had taken a seat near the curtains, unlike Harlan Jens who managed to be conspicuous. When he rose and walked towards Mr. Ryan, clapping and whistling started. A small figure from the front-row rose, encouraging those behind her to rise as well. Cash recognized Travis' mother, with her short, unnaturally blond hair and casual-but-still-expensive suit of school colors.

He stood as well, watching with pride as Travis slowly moved forward to take his gold cup—head bowed as though in prayer.

"I just want to thank you all," he began—stopping to wait for the applause to die down. "Thank you all. As you know, this is nothing without the team because we worked as a team, and without you fellas—" he looked behind at the other smiling players, "none of this would have been achieved." Travis gave a dramatic pause, his features becoming serious. "I want to also thank the people of Miles City, Custer County, and most significantly, the students of Miles City High for accepting me so warmly here. Thank you, with all my heart."

It took a moment for the crowd to quiet after that, Coach Smith standing patiently once again at the podium. Cash felt a mixture of thrill and warmth flowing through his body; his heart pounded so hard he was afraid it might be audible to the people around him. Coach Smith then continued his speech, introducing each of the other players and reading their statistics—allowing them and their families to bask in this perfect moment of glory. The band then started up the school anthem.

"If you would," Principal Ryan yelled into the microphone, "those in the first four or five rows fold your chairs and place them to the side so we can have some room up front here."

When the space was cleared, the group on the stage dispersed to the floor. Cash began a slow maneuvering towards Travis, now standing close by his mother who was being greeted by well-wishes to the right and left. Cash didn't want to be obvious, noting the occasional glance his way by those he knew and those he didn't. When at last he worked his way to Travis' side, Mrs. Hunter gave him a nonchalant smile, saying, "And here's Cash!"

Travis turned, face flushed with embarrassment at the outpouring of congratulations.

"Cash," Travis stopped and breathed his name. They clasped hands. Then Travis said, in a softer voice, *"Cash."*

They stood awkwardly for a moment—Cash uncomfortable in the presence of Travis' mother. He then went on to say, "Congratulations Travis. I'll have to get a closer look at that trophy later on."

A slightly-cool expression crossed Mrs. Hunter's face, before she turned her grin back on. "Yes, please stop by later." She then grabbed her son by the arm and turned him in the direction of the math teacher.

Cash walked back to his seat and plopped heavily down. She could have simply taken a goddamn knife and thrust it into his guts—it would have felt better, he thought miserably. If it wasn't the fact she had given birth to him, he would have told her to go to hell!

Almost everyone else was standing and milling about. For a second, he thought he caught a glimpse of Clayton going out a side door; then he was aware of a small touch on his shoulder.

"Cash," Jennifer leaned down to whisper in his ear, "Tiffany and me have some beer in her car. Want some?"

Without looking up, he shook his head 'no'. "Thanks, Jennifer, think I'll pass." He was suddenly sullen—annoyed at the entourage that had become a wedge between him and his boyfriend. He couldn't help looking in their direction—Travis and his mother—in her school colors suit. *She probably had it made special for the occasion*, Cash thought, brooding.

"You look a little lonely there, cowboy." Next up was Jens, talking to Cash, but looking at Jennifer. From the slight sway of his body, and unfocused stare, Cash knew he had already taken a trip to Tiffany's car. *Nuthin' like bellying up to the bar,* Cash cynically thought, slightly disgusted. He started to rise.

"Congratulations, Harlan," he clapped Jens' shoulder. "Good job."

Travis was coming towards him, making a break from the admirers, his mouth moving before Cash could catch what he was saying.

"We're going to go now." He repeated, louder this time. Cash stood still, trying not to look surprised. "Mom is ready to leave, says she has stuff to do at home. So, guess I'm gonna go too." There was a pleading to his manner, evidence that he wanted Cash to understand something.

Cash only shrugged, saying, "Maybe I'll see you later."

Travis grinned a "Yeah" and left.

Cash went out the door he had come in—passing a little group gathered around the trunk of Tiffany's car. Starting up his truck, he allowed the Pound Puppy to rattle him all the way home.

"Heard you coming halfway down the driveway," his mother remarked from the kitchen as he ambled through the front door. "How was it?" She popped her head briefly around the corner, then back.

"Ok," was all Cash could manage, before starting the slow ascent to his room. His entire being felt heavy and hollow.

In the midst of all this fanfare, Thanksgiving seemed to come upon everyone by complete surprise. The grocery store merchants even commented in the newspaper that sales had been the lowest—ever. It wasn't until practically the night before that God and a host of heaven came out of the woodwork to purchase the required items for the sacred holiday tradition—including Cash's mother. The market was a madhouse with grocery carts, darting children, and harried stockers running all over the place blocking aisles and creating endless lines at the checkouts.

"I can't believe this." Janice commented to Cash as they stood for what seemed like eternity at the check out. "I've *never* seen this place so crazy."

Cash had to agree with her—loosing count of the number of times he had been bumped and sideswiped by grocery carts being pushed by ignorant, impatient, and down-right irresponsible goons frantically trying to get from point A to point B. It reminded him of the stock yards.

Thanksgiving Day arrived with gusts walloping throughout the early morning hours and on into the better part of the afternoon. Clint bragged how little gas he used in driving home due to the tail winds.

"Just wait till you have to go home." Clayton smugly said. "Then we'll see how great a gas mileage you git."

What an ass, thought Cash. That boy could never say anything positive. What Jennifer had shared about Clayton's talk at the Co-op bugged him greatly, and now having to be in the same room with him, through the entire day, was a little more than what he could handle.

Everyone gathered in the living room watching the parades and then on to the football games. *What a treat*, Cash told himself—pushing himself off the sofa, and making his way out to the kitchen to see if there was something he could do to help his mother. ANYTHING was better than watching football, he concluded.

Eventually, it was time to eat, and Cash's mother beaconed the clan to huddle at the dining table. "Everyone just grab a seat. We're not formal around here as you'll soon learn." The voice in Mrs. McCollum was light and quite cheery as she looked over at Clint's girlfriend, Rebecca—giving her a small wink.

No sooner had they settled, however, when Janice suddenly bounced up from her chair, hitting the palms of her hands against the table.

"Damn—that's the dressing burning!" she exclaimed, and rushed off.

Cash smiled with this latest imagined holiday disaster. His mother's cooking was always perfect, and yet she had a need to dismiss some aspect of it as faulty, or less then presentable. The rest of the family silently waited for her return, Clint and Rebecca smiling at one another as they sat side by side. Cash felt a little jab in his heart, managing to avoid looking at either of his brothers. Travis had made plans to celebrate the holiday dinner with his mother and her family. He said he would stop by later, though.

"Well, not so bad," his mother announced on her return, placing the hot pan on its holder. "Have I forgotten anything else? No, I think that's everything."

Satisfied, she sat and they all automatically reached for one another's hands. Cash recoiled a little as his fingers touched Clayton's. Just then, the phone gave a loud jangle, startling the assembly.

"Who the hell can that be?" Cash's father mumbled.

Clint rose quickly, saying, "I'll get it."

Their hands detached as they listened to Clint telling the caller, "Yeah, he's here. Just a minute." Clint popped his head around the corner—holding the receiver in Cash's direction.

"It's for you."

Cash mouthed *who?* But Clint just shrugged. Getting up, Cash excused himself, taking the phone from Clint.

He was expecting the sound of Travis' voice on the other end, but instead it was one he didn't immediately know.

"Cash?" The clipped, lowered tone aroused a memory in Cash that he couldn't quite bring to the surface. "Am I interrupting anything?"

"Uh, well, we're just gettin' ready to eat…" He decided not to say anything more.

"Shit, I'm sorry. I guess I wasn't thinking since we've already eaten."

When Cash didn't reply, the caller continued. "Son of a bitch! I forgot… this is Lee."

Cash wondered why he hadn't recognized the voice right away. Lee's image instantly jumped into his mind. It wasn't an unpleasant one.

"Hey, what's up?" Cash's heart bounded. Hearing some whispers coming from the dining room, he turned his back to them.

"God, I really am sorry about calling now. I can call later if you'd like."

"No," Cash sort of lied, yet at the same time, sort of told the truth, "It's okay." Taking a breath, he continued, "They can wait for a minute."

"It's just, we're already done with our dinner," Lee continued. "I guess we eat earlier than most people. Plus, my dad didn't show like he had said he would. So we got on with it rather than…" There was a hesitation, then, "Well, that's not why I called. I just wanted to see how you're doin'."

"Hangin' in there," said Cash, talking directly into the phone so the others could not listen in. "How 'bout you? Still tearin' up the turf?" He let out a small chuckle.

"Not bad. Yeah, I've done a couple of local shows around here... nuthin' to hoot about. Hey, I saw you on television a couple of weeks ago. You looked great." There was a strong tone of admiration riding through the phone line.

"Thanks," replied Cash.

"So is that your buddy you were on the show with?" Lee asked without hesitation.

That was a rather peculiar thing to ask, reasoned Cash—nervously looking back at his family who were all patiently waiting for him to end the conversation and come back to the table. "Uh, yeah, ...we're pretty close."

"That's cool." Lee responded. "Before I split, did you hear about Trevor Green? ...last weekend in Modesto?"

Cash knew immediately who he was discussing—one of the top pro-rodeo contenders of the year. He felt a cold chill go over him.

"No, what?" was all Cash could say, since he honestly didn't know anything. How could he—with all the shit he had been contending with since the last qualifier?"

"Died. Sunday, he fell off a bull 'n got trapped in the stirrup. Bull pounced right on his head. Died the other day, so I found out."

"Jesus, Lee, that's a tough one." Cash felt slightly sickened at the thought of the great bull rider—Green dying like that. "How old was he anyway, all of about twenty-four?"

"Yeah, well," Lee gave a little cough. "I don't want to keep you. But I kind of needed to talk to someone about this, because it's been really bothering me."

"Why?" All of a sudden Cash felt curious.

"See, I hear about this, and I'm thinkin' of maybe droppin' out. I don't know if I want to keep on doin' this, if risking my life is worth the rodeo."

This news should have pleased Cash instead of startling him—giving him concern. If Lee was a rival, he was also a challenge—the source of effort.

Plus, there was the little pleasant tingling he felt from just talking to Lee.

"That's crazy," Cash's voice took on the gentle, chiding tone he had heard all of his life from his mother. "You can't let something like that spook you. It happens—you just have to accept it, and go on. I don't like hearing it either, but I'm not gonna give up."

Far from it, he thought, wondering why he shouldn't be encouraging Lee in his doubts instead.

"So you're gonna be riding this spring?" Lee asked softly.

Cash sort of liked the tone of his voice, as though Lee was pleased with his response. Quickly, he conjured up the darkly attractive boy in his head. "You betcha, I am. Why would I wanna give up? Hell, this is my life!" His voice rose with excitement.

He heard Lee chuckle and could easily imagine that wide, teethy smile.

"When you put it like that, yeah. Makes me feel kind of foolish wanting to jump off the saddle… you know, it's the only thing I seem to do well."

The phrase rang in Cash's head with recollection.

"I feel that way all the time, Lee. I didn't realize anyone else did." Cash blurted out his thought before thinking, but then, he didn't regret it. Somehow, he felt okay talking like this with Lee.

"Oh yeah?" the vulnerable way Lee said his words—with a certain smallness, warmed Cash.

"Yeah." It was a sigh coming out of Cash now. "I can't talk for the other cowboys, but for me, yeah. Why sometimes..." then he remembered Thanksgiving dinner on the table and his waiting family—which was now an annoyance. He wanted the conversation to continue. "Never mind about that," he continued, "we can talk about this later. But the thing is, Lee. Don't give up on rodeo, because if you're like me, it means too much to you. Just think of how happy it makes you, then the scary stuff about it just sort of goes away on its own. Know what I mean?"

"Hell yeah!" Lee seemed excited when he said this. "I just needed someone to remind me. Around here, around my house, there's no one. And my dad never understood it. I'm glad you're letting me talk to you like this, Cash. I really appreciate it."

The way Lee said his name made Cash suddenly shiver in the way a gentle touch on the back of his neck would.

"Sure you're gonna be okay?" Lee's earlier remark about his father returned to Cash. He realized he knew next to nothing about this boy, and suddenly wanted to learn more. "I mean, we have to eat now; but you can always call me." He laid out the invitation.

"Hey, thanks." Lee's voice trailed off—then said a slightly lingering goodbye. Cash returned the goodbye and hung up. The room was suddenly still and strangely empty.

"Lee Biruni," Cash remarked when he returned to his family crowded around the feast.

"Oh?" Janice raised one eyebrow slightly—then lowered it again.

Mr. McCollum snorted. "What the hell does HE want? You can't trust that little fucker further than you can toss a stick."

"Eugene," his wife whispered—trying to steer him in.

"How do you know?" A flash of defensiveness swept through Cash.

"Christ, everyone talks about him—all the contractors that have ever had to work with him. They all say he's a double-dealin', knivin' little shit—always trying to make arrangements on getting assigned to certain stock."

Cash's mother put her arms out across the table. "We need to say the blessing," signaling an end to this particular conversation.

CHAPTER 12

Who would have guessed the day would turn out as it did when Cash hopped into the huge, mudder pick-up—igniting the roaring engine? Barreling down the driveway, out to the rural road and on into town for school, something ate at his senses. He couldn't tell what it was, but without a doubt, an unknown force held a shadow over his head like a dark cloud.

It was a cold, blustery December morning, and he pulled the wool pile collar closely around his neck to keep from catching a chill. Instinctively, he checked the dash to see if the heater was on. The cab sure wasn't warming up. With a sigh, he told himself he couldn't wait for spring.

Spotting Travis' little sports car parked way-off in a distant corner of the parking lot, he heaved a huff. For the sake of avoiding scrapes and dents from other vehicles by thoughtless drivers, how far would it be taken? Babied… that was what he called it—Travis protected that car as if he had given it birth.

Inside, midst the warm confines of the crowded school hallway, Cash strolled by students visiting or retrieving books from their lockers. Reaching his own locker, he wearily worked the combination—pulling the door open.

"Hey!" It was Travis voice softly sounding behind him. "You're almost late."

Tossing his hat in the locker, Cash turned to face a full-view of plaid flannel draped tightly over an immense chest. It took him by surprise. "I had to feed the animals and milk the cows… Clayton woke up sick today, so he asked if I could do his share." Stepping back, Cash admired Travis' new shirt. It was a white, tan, and black flannel shirt with the sleeves rolled halfway up a pair of colossal arms. As usual, he looked really good.

"You should have called me," Travis instantly replied. "I would have come out and helped."

With a distracted smile, Cash said, "That's alright." Looking down the length of the hallway, he could not deny the feeling that something wasn't right. An odd feeling hung in the air.

"You all right?" Travis picked up on Cash's unsettled behavior.

"Yeah," was his response, but it was not convincing—not even to Cash himself.

Suddenly, the bell rang, bringing the boys abruptly out of the trance they had crawled into. "Looks like we're late…" Travis said, pointing to the clock.

"Oh well," spoke Cash, empty and dry.

Cash got to the classroom and quickly went to his seat. Fortunately, the teacher had not arrived yet so he couldn't be counted as a tardy. The room was busy, but not with class work. Everyone seemed squirrelly. Today was definitely a strange day. Finally, the English instructor came in with an armload of books and a stack of papers.

"I'm giving back everyone's test. I want each of you to see where your problems were on yesterday's exam. I'm also passing out a study guide breaking down certain highlights concerning essay composition." Walking slowly into the center of the room, he looked around with piercing eyes. "In going over everyone's papers last night, I have concluded it's imperative we all review the basic principles of paragraph structure, thought progression, grammar, and spelling." With a pause, he finally concluded—saying, "With the games behind us, I think it's time we focus back on the basic skills of written communication."

There was an uneasy stillness throughout the room—feet shuffling, a random cough here and there, and a repetitive thumping of a pencil erasure against the workbook coming from Cash's own desk.

Without a word, the teacher turned and shot Cash a sharp look. Cash instantly stopped—blushing from embarrassment.

Having the student's attention riveted to the handouts, neither the teacher nor the class seemed to take notice of the principal who opened the door and hurried in—lines of worry crossing his forehead. "I'm sorry for interrupting, but…" Mr. Ryan's eyes quickly shifted from the instructor to Cash. "I need to talk with you; you'll want to bring your books as well."

The stillness of the classroom was deafening as Cash numbly gathered his things and pushed away from the desk. He felt lightheaded—like after riding a wild bronc or bull. Following Mr. Ryan out into the hallway, the principal closed the door and said, "I just received a call from your mother. You need to meet your family at the hospital. Your father has been taken there by paramedics."

His brain began spinning—a cold chill sped through his guts—tightening every muscle in his body. *"Oh, God."* Cash gasped. "What happened?"

"I don't know, she just said you need to get to emergency right away." Mr. Ryan was usually a cold, detached individual, but on this occasion, he wore a look of deep concern. "Do you have a way to get there?" he asked.

"Yes, I have my pick-up." Cash called out, already heading to his locker.

He couldn't think right. He felt crazy. The only on his mind as he ran out the school doors was getting to that hospital.

What happened? Dear God, he prayed over and over, *let everything be okay.*

He reached the pickup—starting the engine with an explosion. Gunning the pistons, he tore out of the school parking lot and continued to pray—like he'd never done before. "Hear my prayer, oh Lord… hear my prayer! Let everything be okay!"

Thinking back on it later, he honestly did not know how he got to the hospital. He couldn't remember a thing en-route except running through a couple of stop signs and one red light.

When he walked into the waiting room, Clayton, his mother, and two uncles—his father's brothers, were huddled in the far corner. Mrs. McCollum looked up at the sound of Cash's boots scuffing on the smooth linoleum. Her face was void of the peaceful countenance it usually bore. Eyes red from crying, and lines deepened from worry streaked across her brow speaking emphatically of her turbulent emotions.

"Mama." Cash's voice was boy-like.

"Cash," she softly said, reaching out to her youngest son. "They're working on him right now."

"What happened? How is he?" His words tumbled out as he sat down by her side.

"We don't know." She simply replied, her attention distant. "Clayton found him in the kitchen… he must have fallen off the chair."

Cash looked over to his brother who was sitting—blankly staring off in space. His eyes gripped Cash with a start. Glassy and wide, they looked like a couple of shiny marbles tucked neatly in a ceramic statue. Cash could smell the faint hint of lingering alcohol waif from Clayton's body. Instantly, the memory of Jennifer's words came back to his mind concerning his brother's recent increase of drinking.

Quietly, Cash continued to pray—suddenly wishing he had his rosary beads.

Eventually, a young man wearing light-blue scrubs entered the room and politely asked, "Mrs. McCollum?"

All attention shifted to him as he approached Janice. "We've stabilized your husband for the time being, but his situation is critical."

Unexpectedly, a young man bounded from around the corner of the hallway and stood in the doorway—breathless from running.

"Travis!" Cash exclaimed. *How did he know to come here?* His presence was a shock.

"I'm sorry," he apologized. Catching enough air, he went on to say. "I didn't mean to barge in."

The doctor turned and looked at Travis with intrigue, then focused back on the family and continued, "It appears he is going to need to have immediate surgery regarding the arterial blockage to his heart. I've requested for Life-Vac to take him to St. Vincent's in Billings and the cardiac team has been arranged to receive him for a bypass operation the minute he gets there."

"Well, we better head out." Janice stated rising to her feet. Looking over at her middle boy, she voiced a note of concern, "Are you okay?"

Clayton was still in a daze. It was as if something in his brain had popped.

"Clayton!" Cash's mother elevated her voice to a tone she rarely used.

Wakened from his stupor, Clayton blinked—looking over to his mother who was becoming more annoyed with him each passing moment.

"Janice, you and the boys can ride along with me," one of the uncles offered.

"Thanks, Carl," Mrs. McCollum politely replied to the tall, slender cowboy standing by her side.

Uncle Carl didn't look at all like Mr. McCollum. This younger brother had a look all to his own—with a lankiness much like Cash or Clint's, but with thick, dark hair.

"It probably would be best if we went separately just in case we have to stay overnight."

Cash could tell even in the midst of all the tension and stress, his mother was still in control. Being the logical thinker of the family, it was no surprise. That woman always seemed to have a cool head on her shoulders.

"Whatever's going to be better for you," his uncle responded, resting a grey cowboy hat on his head and drawing it low against his eyebrows.

Before leaving, Travis pulled Cash privately aside. Taking Cash's shaking hand into his warm fingers he spoke, "Would you like me to come?" There was a soft look telling Cash he wanted to be a part of this matter—that he understood completely how the family felt.

Cash shuddered. He knew. Once upon a time, on a sunny September morning, Travis had been there, and done that.

Hesitating for a moment, Cash struggled with the inner debate. His thoughts were too jumbled up to make any decision. "I don't know." He fought back tears.

Without hesitation, Travis pulled his cell phone out and dialed a number. "I'm coming with you," he stated decidedly. "You need me. I'll drive separately… you should be with your family." Turning away, he walked to a secluded corner and spoke in a hushed voice. "Hello, Mom? There's something that has come up… I'm with Cash and his family at the hospital…" His voice trailed off into a near whisper.

"Are you ready?" Janice's voice was so close to his shoulder, it took Cash unexpectedly. He had not heard her footsteps approach from behind.

"In a minute," Cash replied, looking at her with wet eyes.

Giving a sigh, she said, "Travis can come as long as it's okay with his mother."

Within minutes, everyone was making their way to Billings—by helicopter for Mr. McCollum, by car for everyone else.

Cash drove.

"You're in no shape for anything," Janice had stated to Clayton as they walked out to the parking lot. "What in God's name did you do last night? Drink up half the town?" Exasperation rode heavily in her voice.

The ride to Billings seemed to take forever… enough time to stoke imaginations—get them running wild. Eugene was already prepped when they arrived at the Coronary Unit. Clint was there waiting silently. Embracing his mother, he began to weep. "I had a feeling…" his voice cracked as he held his mother tightly. "…the way he's been acting."

"It's gonna be okay." Her voice remained steady, reassuring even though the look in her eyes revealed cold fear. It was obvious, her strength was waning—Cash could tell.

Looking at his two younger brothers, Clint went over and hugged them.

Cash could not help noticing Clayton's hold with Clint—unexplainably brief and blocked. Clint instantly reared up—casting a glare of bewilderment and concern to Cash.

The minutes sitting eventually drew into hours as each McCollum settled into a rite of waiting… the vigil. Eventually, perhaps from the sense of creeping flesh, Cash could stand it no longer. Rising from the chair, he announced, "I'm going for a walk."

Throwing a wary glance into Travis' direction, Mrs. McCollum remained silent—knowing this was not the time to speak. Travis quickly pushed himself to his feet.

Cash's mind raced as he silently walked through the quiet hallway. He could not stop the wild thoughts. They swirled around him, clenching with iron claws into his scorching flesh, into its unforgiving undertow, covering him with a force so powerful, it was beyond words.

Was this punishment from God? The Almighty's way of getting back—a *lesson of what you sow is what you shall reap*? According to the Church, his lifestyle was an abomination—pure and simple, he knew that. Was this then his first step toward punishment—to strike down his innocent father? He felt an icy chill creep up his spine.

Or maybe he was taking too much for granted, and now, was the time to learn the lesson on being grateful. *'Be ye thankful...'*

Perhaps it was because he was nothing but just a spoiled, little boy—thinking the world revolved around him?

Hearing the solid thud of Travis' boots, Cash looked over his shoulder. "Hey."

"Hey," Travis softly breathed, catching up with his partner.

Everything had been fine this morning... who would have guessed the world would be overturned at the drop of a hat? Had there been warnings—hints of the impending storm? Of course, his dad had looked tired for weeks; as if everything he did was excruciating. How could they have missed it? Like buzzards floating vicariously through a dark sky—the evidence had been clear, but the message flagrantly ignored.

Finally, Cash broke the silence by thoughtfully saying, "You know somethin'?"

"What?"

"There *are* no guarantees, are there?"

"Nope." Travis knew... indeed, *he knew*. "Each day's a gift. The key is to take time and appreciate what we have when we have it."

They continued past the cafeteria and lobby. Eventually, they came to a small prayer chapel. Cash stopped. He looked at Travis—nodding his head in the direction of the double doors. His eyes were yearning. "I wanna go in."

"Okay." Travis followed him into the dim, candle-lit room. Silence overtook them.

Cash mechanically dipped his fingers into the small font by the entrance and quietly made his way down the aisle to a bench near the altar. Dropping to his knees, he made the sign of the cross over his forehead, shoulders and chest. Travis sat in the pew with his head bowed. No words were uttered—there didn't need to be. It was a time for prayer…a request to the Father of Spirits to ward off those circling birds, and spare one treasured life.

In the faint glow of the votives Cash looked up at the crucifix. His eyes shifted effortlessly to a nearby statue of the Virgin Mother Mary. Where would the strength come? How would he and the rest of the family cope? What was going to happen to his father? There seemingly appeared to be no power to chose, no option for control. Time… and something else rode in the saddle—everyone else could only sit and wait to see how the ride would end.

Rising from the bench, Travis slowly approached the altar. With his fingers, he clutched a tiny cup cradling a candle. Picking up the taper, he ignited the wick and carefully rested it back in the row. Instantly, it became part of the visual symphony of silent prayers offered by anonymous seekers of faith to a higher power—petitions to change situations spinning out of control.

Father God, Cash prayed within his heart, *if you can see fit, please spare my dad and strengthen his heart in this surgery. In the name of your Son, Amen.*

A thought passed through his mind in the stillness. What was Travis thinking? Did he see his own father in a murky memory? It must have been the stark pronouncement of finality—things unable to be changed coming back to haunt him in the dark visitation of this moment. What was it like? Cash couldn't imagine. He didn't want to.

Now was the time to wait… to be strong for his mother and the others. Drawing a deep breath, he got to his feet and said, "I think we should go back."

Travis followed out into the blinding hallway. It was such an antithesis to the chapel. There seemed to be so much light.

Cash wasn't sure what time it was; but probably well into the early afternoon when a weary looking doctor shuffled his way into the quiet waiting room, instantly catching all eyes. Cash felt Travis' hand rest on his. Mrs. McCollum sat up in her chair.

Inhaling a deep space of air, the physician announced, "Janice McCollum?"

Rising to her feet she approached him, a wary look riding heavily in her eyes, the color draining from her usually rosy cheeks. Cash could tell she was bracing for the worst.

The young looking doctor extended his hand and shook hers as he quickly introduced himself. "I'm Doctor Friedman. Eugene is recovering from the surgery right now."

"How is he?" Janice allowed the air which she had nervously held in her lungs to escape slowly—the tension in her muscles releasing as the man's statement seemed to sink into her mind.

"He's still critical, so we'll keep him in CCU for awhile under observation." Doctor Friedman paused, then went on to say, "Your husband is a strong man. He went through the procedure quite well."

"May I go see him?" She asked straightforward.

"In a little bit," the doctor nodded reassuringly. "He's been through a lot today."

"We all have…" Janice expelled a sigh—looking exhausted, but extremely relieved as she turned to her boys.

Cash and Clint both got up and gave her a hug. Clint was crying—always considered the 'softy' of the family. Oddly, Clayton remained motionless in his chair, his face frozen like an ice sculpture. *What the hell was wrong with him?* Cash angrily asked himself. He wanted to walk over and smack him a good one in the worse sort of way.

Mrs. McCollum must have picked up on Cash's facial expression—reading into his thoughts. Quickly, she grabbed his arm, and said in a subdued tone, "Let him be."

Wiping a residue of perspiration off his brow, the physician thoughtfully suggested, "I'd say in about an hour or two you can see him. For now, I suggest you let him rest."

"Thank you," Janice replied, tears filling her eyes.

Eugene's recovery would be slow. What the heart attack hadn't taken, the surgery had. Fortunately, it had not been that bad, and if Clayton hadn't stumbled into the kitchen when he did, the situation would have been worse. Janice determined to stay in a nearby hotel until her husband's release to low level rehab therapy. She allowed her boys to make up their own minds about what they wanted to do, but with snow expected to fall through the night, she expressed her concern about anyone making the trip back to Miles City that evening.

"There's hardly a soul who takes that highway at night and I really don't want any of you risking yourselves."

For Clint, it was a good excuse to stay off campus and get a respite from his roommate at the dorm. Rebecca encouraged him to be with his family during this time, stating she would keep in touch with him throughout the next day.

Clayton seemed upset about the decision as he sat up rigid in the restaurant booth. Impatience rode in his tone, "Well, I need to get back to work. Henry's gonna wonder why I'm not comin' in tomorrow."

"Call him up and tell him you plan to stay here for at least another day." Mrs. McCollum held firm to her patience. "He'll be able to handle things at the center—he's done it before."

"What about the animals?" He went on to ask, frustration rising in his voice.

"Your Uncle Carl said he would take care of them." Looking at Travis, Janice thoughtfully chose her words, "Travis, you might want to call your mother and let her know you'll be staying tonight. I'm sure she'll like to know what's going on." Pausing, she looked over at Cash then back to Travis. Her stare locked into those deep blues. A smile snuck across her lips. "You are welcome to stay with us as long as you like. You've been an encouragement for us all." She made it quite plain she liked him and respected him immensely.

And now on the decision of *who* would stay with *who*, well, that was a little tricky as the family was not yet comfortable having Cash and Travis together in the same room—in the same bed. After several awkward moments, Janice tossed her napkin on the cafeteria table and gave a resolute sigh. "We'll get a suite, or adjoining rooms. You all can decide who's gonna sleep where."

Allowing a snort to shoot from his nostrils, Clayton gave a low moan and crossed his arms. "This is sickening," he muttered—looking out over the dining room.

As if immune to Clayton's continual irregularity, his mother stated with finality, "You're going to have to just deal with it. We can't afford to have everyone in their private castles!"

And that was that. The CEO had spoken. With the plans rolled out, any further discussion was now closed. As the dignified red-head went back to her dessert, each boy tossed each other looks of amazement.

Since Clayton wouldn't consider sharing a room with Cash and Travis, he settled for his own double bed in their mother's room. The door that connected the two remained open, with Clint happily traversing between them.

"Don't do nothin' to keep me awake," he winked at his little brother.

"As if we'd even feel like it," Cash forced a weak grin.

But no sooner had the lights gone out when Cash heard a shuffling beside his bed. Lifting his weary head, he saw Clayton standing there silently, waiting to be acknowledged.

What now?

"Sorry to bother you guys, but I didn't get any toothpaste from the front desk and I can't seem to find Clint's. I don't suppose I could borrow either of yours." Clayton smiled sheepishly, his intent look briskly scanned over Travis.

"Sure," Cash replied, getting up.

"Hey," Clayton seemed unusually fast to acknowledge Travis, who was now awake.

"Haven't you been to sleep yet?" Cash asked a bit irritatedly—looking at the clock on the nightstand.

"Naw, I went down to the lounge to watch TV....can't sleep." He cast a glance around the room then back over to Travis.

Cash handed him the tube and waited for him to go.

There was hesitation. "Thanks," Clayton said, his eyes continuing to rove over Travis' body appraisingly.

"Yeah, sure." Cash suddenly caught on to Clayton's visual fixation. *What the...?*

Allowing a grin to cross his face, his brother blossomed with a captivating smile—full and brilliant. "See you all in the mornin'," he finally said, retreating back to his room.

"Now, what hell was that all about?" Cash whispered as he got resettled—his ears and cheeks feeling a peculiar burn.

"I dunno," Travis replied. "That brother of yours... he's one strange cat."

"You just have to get know him." Cash spoke, mildly defending him despite a tinge of jealousy that seared at the edges of his spirit.

...Lying quietly listening to the rhythmic series of snores coming from the young man lying beside him, Cash began to unwind. Even though the day had been an emotion upheaval, it ended up being pretty good—with exceedingly much to be thankful for. One thing was for sure... it could have been an absolute nightmare. Thank God. Cash told himself... thank God it hadn't become one.

Chapter 13

Cash felt a wild-mix of emotions during Christmas. What he had come to take for granted was now greatly appreciated each and every day—knowing his family was a rare and precious gift.

It would be long time, if ever again, that Eugene would be able to get out and do the things he used to do—especially working around the ranch with the stock, equipment, and maintenance. As a result of those limitations, more responsibilities were placed on Clayton and Cash—forcing them to work together. This was awkward, especially considering all the things that had settled between them.

"You two seem to be hittin' it off pretty good." Clayton had made a stray comment one afternoon while they were hauling hay out to the horses in the corral.

"Whadiya mean?" Cash asked, trying to act ignorant—his defenses going up immediately.

Jabbing the pitchfork into the gut of a bale, Clayton aggressively broke it apart with several more thrusts. "You know what I'm talkin' about." There was a tightness in his voice.

"So?" Cash tried to hold his brother's endeavor to get him riled at bay—knowing it was the last thing anyone needed at this time.

"So, I'm just sayin' you 'n Travis seem to be slidin' into a real comfy corner." Sarcasm tainted each word.

Jennifer's comments returned to Cash. It was true; she wasn't lying. This whole thing between him and Travis was a real bugaboo to Clayton.

"What's it to you?" Cash pulled several more bales down from the loft, his adrenaline beginning to pump a tingliness throughout his body. "It's not like we're hurtin' anybody. Besides, it's really none of your business."

"Yeah?" Clayton's voice was challenging. He wanted a fight. "You think so?"

"Oh, I know so." Cash struggled to remain outwardly calm even though his insides were exploding apart at the seams. He wanted to kick his brother's fat ass in the worse way. "The talk I've been hearin' from down at the Co-op is a little disturbing. And you seem to be headin' up the center of it."

Clayton stopped and shot Cash a fiery glare, "How do you know?"

Continuing on the job at hand, Cash avoided the stare-down and flatly stated, "I have my ways of findin' out."

"Jennifer." Clayton hotly retorted. Spitting at the ground, he went on to ask, "You've been listenin' to her shit, haven't you?"

"I'm not sayin'." Cash could feel himself dig heels into the ground. "What I'm tellin' you is, you better be careful 'cuz you might be bitin' off more than you can chew." He raised a pointing finger at his elder sibling, thinking of the consequences if Travis ever got wind of his tales.

"Well, as if I'm really scared." A cockiness rose in Clayton's tone.

"You should be... he could tear you apart." There, the warning was out. Clayton was now responsible for his actions from this point on, Cash considered. Something told him, however, this wasn't going to be end of the matter... knowing Clayton, there would have to be another force to rope him in. "All I'm sayin' is, you better be careful."

"I'll keep that in mind," Clayton angrily tossed the pitchfork against the wall of the barn, giving off a sharp, somewhat explosive noise, "...little brother."

Cash's hopes of spending time with Travis over the vacation break were smashed against the granite and sandstone boulders of the mighty Yellowstone the day he went to visit Travis after doing chores. He should have guessed the encounter would end up on a sour note as he quickly recognized Mrs. Hunter's BMW parked in the driveway of the massive house...

"Hey!" Travis greeted, gesturing him to come inside. Exchanging a kiss, he invited Cash into the kitchen where he was finishing up breakfast at the food bar. "You're done pretty early." He resumed eating his eggs.

"I woke up at four and decided I couldn't sleep anymore, so I decided to get up and get started on feedin' the stock," Cash explained as he watched Travis munch on his food. "Besides, it's more peaceful when I do it alone. You know how Clayton can be."

Travis grinned and gave a quick nod. "Oh, yeah." Grabbing for the salt shaker, he looked over at Cash and politely asked, "Have you eaten? I can make you some toast and eggs."

His offer was tempting. "Thanks, but I just chowed on a stack of pancakes and some of leftover ham."

"Hey, that was a great dinner your mom prepared," Travis complimented with a mouthful of food. "I had a lot of fun with your family."

Janice had invited Travis for the Christmas day dinner. As usual, she had put on huge spread.

Cash smiled. "See, I told you it would take only a little time for them to accept you." Pausing for a brief moment, he went on to say, "Mom really loves you. I can tell."

Travis' face lit up. "I know. She's a neat lady."

Without warning Travis' mother walked into the kitchen with her usual brisk gait. Looking at the clock over the counter, she exclaimed, "Oh my, I didn't realize it was this late!" Going to the refrigerator, she pulled out a carton of milk. "Do you have plans today?"

"Not specifically," Travis replied.

Grabbing a box of cereal from the pantry, Mrs. Hunter hurried to the bar and laid down a bowl, the milk and cereal by the newspaper which she had been apparently reading earlier—totally ignoring Cash's presence. "Well, I was wondering if you could give Casper a bath later this afternoon. He's starting to shed and smell." She wrinkled her nose and gave a little laugh. Glancing up from her breakfast, a look of surprise came over her face. "Why Cash! I didn't know you were here."

"Hi," Cash greeted half-heartedly, shuffling a little nervously on the other side of the bar. Travis' mother was not a bad woman, Cash had reasoned. It was just that her mannerisms were so fast and determined. She always seemed to be in a scurry, like a prairie grouse, making him feel like he was in the way.

"Don't pay any attention to her." Travis had once told him. "She's always been that way." He also went on to say, "Her hyperness used to drive dad nuts. He'd always tell her she'd have an aneurism for not learning to relax."

"Did you have a nice Christmas?" she asked over her bran flakes.

"Yes, thank you," Cash fidgeted.

"How's your dad?" She took a moment from her paper and gave him a direct look with her eyes.

"He's getting better," Cash spoke hopefully. "He's in rehab on Mondays and Thursdays."

"Well, that's good," her voice sounded sincere. "I guess those things just take time for recovery." Rising from the stool, Mrs. Hunter went over to the coffee pot on the counter and poured a mug-full of the hot, dark liquid. "Travis, I forgot to tell you last night, I got a call from the Halvarsons when you were at Cash's. They're coming up to do some skiing at Big Sky and wanted to know if we would join them for this week end." As if fixed to the counter, Travis' mother remained by the coffee pot while continuing to speak, "I said we can meet them on Friday."

Travis looked up from his food and stopped chewing. A look of frustration flooded his face.

Without turning, she continued to speak while stirring a pile of creamer into the mug.

"Marcia said Jason is coming too. He told her he's really excited about seeing you again," her voice was implicating.

At the mention of Jason's name, Travis' face grew ashen.

Instantly Cash froze. Something was happening here... something he obviously would not like.

Turning around, and coming back to her breakfast, she looked at Travis and gave him a light, perky smile. "I guess Jason has been asking about you for ages, and has wanted to come up and visit for some time now. I told her let him come up—that I'll take care of the flight plans. I have him scheduled to fly in Wednesday, and you two can spend time together till we head out to meet his parents in Bozeman at the airport on Friday."

She pushed herself back off the stool and retreated once again to the counter to clean up. Turning on the water at the sink, she began rinsing the plate and mug. "Consider this another one of your Christmas presents, honey!" Even though there was warm cheeriness to her words, an undeniable bite lurked just beneath the surface.

"Oh my!" she exclaimed, darting a quick glimpse back up at the clock. "I've gotta go!"

Travis still remained silent. It was as if his flesh had petrified.

Planting a small peck on the back of her son's neck, Mrs. Hunter grabbed the newspaper and said, "You two boys be careful today, and Travis, don't forget to give Casper his b-a-t-h." With that, she was gone.

Cash remained quiet. He couldn't move. This was part of the movie where a lot of explaining was going to be done. He braced himself for the story.

Looking over at Cash, Travis' voice was weak and labored. "You have smokes on you?"

Automatically reaching for his shirt pocket, Cash replied, "Uh, they're in my jacket."

The front door opened and closed with a click. A car engine started and quickly faded from earshot.

"Let's go outside," Travis suggested, pushing himself away from his unfinished food.

Cash wondered what was up as they went to the foyer. Grabbing their jackets, Travis looked at Cash and nodded for him to follow. They went out to the back sun-deck, and Travis gestured, "Let me have one."

Cash handed over his pack of cigarettes and watched Travis light up—taking a deep inhale of the thick tobacco smoke. It was strange to see Travis smoke. Consistently athletic, with an obsession of healthy habits, this behavior was unthinkable.

Cash lit one up for himself as well.

Together, they stood outside and smoked in silence. Cash had to admit it was rather hot seeing the big jock suck down a Marlboro. Travis never seemed to mind him smoking, but until now, he had never joined in on the bad habit.

Half-burned, Travis looked at the remaining portion of the cigarette between his fingers and sighed, "Wow, I feel dizzy."

"That's cuz you're not used to the smoke," Cash explained—allowing a small chuckle to escape.

"I guess." Travis took another hit and blew the white smoke out from between his lips. "Well, I suppose you're wondering what that was all about with Mom," he began to volunteer.

Cash looked away; tightness cramped in his stomach. Something inside told him he was not going to like hearing what Travis was about to say. "Yeah." It was a lie. He really didn't want to know.

Painfully, Travis began the saga, taking another drag from his smoke. "The Halvarsons have been really good friends of ours for as long as I can remember. They used to do a lot of stuff with us when we lived in California. Jack, the father, was co-owner with my dad for the law firm.

He took over when my dad died. They have one son—like my parents, and as you've probably guessed, his name is Jason. He's a couple years older than me. Last time I heard, he's attending Cal State."

Cash gave a shiver and tossed the cigarette butt out on a snow bank. He still remained speechless.

"Let's go in," Travis suggested, flipping his smoke out on the yard as well.

Entering back into the warm confines of the house, Travis laughed, clearing his throat. "Gosh, I needed that."

"I've never seen you smoke before," Cash said observantly.

"I haven't for a long time." Travis went on with his confession. "I used to smoke a lot after we lost dad. I didn't know what else to do with myself." Suddenly, he hesitated, as if thinking what his next sentence would be. "Jason got me started, and before I knew it, I was going through a pack a day. I decided to quit when Mom and I moved up here."

Cash stood unmovable. He suddenly discovered he couldn't look Travis in the face—hot, stinging tears swelled in his eyes. He knew smoking wasn't the issue, it was something else—or rather, *someone else*. A portion of the past was now wedging its way between them—he could feel it. Suddenly, he felt embarrassed—embarrassed thinking that there had been no others before him. What an assumption!

Travis must have felt obligated to continue since Cash found himself at a complete loss for words.

"Okay, here's the story," Travis began, gently leading Cash into the living room where they could sit and talk. "Jason and I started messing around when I was about fourteen. It wasn't until Dad got killed, however, our friendship grew into something more. I fell apart, and it was him who gave me a lot of support. He listened to me cry, and took me under his wing like a big brother. Well, I suppose it was more than that."

As Travis spoke, Cash could not help thinking how all this should have been shared at the beginning. He should have realized a guy like him would have had a past with someone. How silly he was in believing that he was the 'first' in Travis' existence.

"We kept it a secret until my mother found us in bed one day after school. At first, it caused a big ruckus, but eventually everyone grew to accept us. Like I said before, our lives got messed over by the media and crackpots— and dad's ghost everywhere. Mom wanted to leave right from the start, but stayed because of me. She felt I needed…you know." Travis sighed. "Eventually, she couldn't stand it any more so she decided to move to a place remote—away from everything. When we moved here, Jason and I kept in touch, but over time, we seemed to drift apart. Eventually, we both decided it was best to go our separate ways. It actually shocked her when I decided to call it quits with him. She thought the world of him."

Travis stopped and waited for a reaction from Cash. Cash couldn't talk. He couldn't move. The persistent silence of the room seemed to make Cash's ears ring. He felt a headache coming on.

"Cash, you don't need to worry… you know I'm in love with you." Travis reached out and grabbed his hand, linking Cash's fingers between his own. "I chose to leave Jason. He's in the past." Travis worked hard in showing his sincerity. "Look, you're the one who means the most to me now."

Once again, a deafening silence fell between them. It was obvious; Travis didn't know what to do. He was trapped in a very precarious situation and Cash could see it.

"Hon, you've gotta believe I will never leave you. Jason means nothing to me now. He hasn't for a long time." He tenderly touched the side of Cash's face.

"Yeah, but Jason must still have feelings for you. If he didn't, he certainly wouldn't be coming *here*." Cash paused to regain his composure. He felt like crying. "You both will see each other in two days. You'll be spending five freakin' days with him—talkin', reminiscin', and skiin' on some isolated slope—God only knows where... He'll talk you into gettin' back together again. Oh yeah—getting' you to come down 'n join him down at Cal State. You'll probably get a fuckin' football offer from there. And he'll *always* be by your side—every goddamn Saturday givin' you all the praise 'n support you'll ever need. Hell, there won't be any shit-ass rodeos competin' against your time." His voice ever rising, Cash began to reign himself in. "You won't have to deal with someone traipsing across the fuckin' countryside, week after week, scroungin' out a subsistent existence." What began as thunder drifted into a quiet breeze. Cash knew he was just projecting, but at this point couldn't stop.

"What do you want me to do?" Travis asked, flinging out his arms to symbolize his complete surrender. "Tell my mother *no*? No, he cannot come here? That I don't want to see him?"

Backing up, Cash cast a stony glare into Travis eyes, and quickly replied. "That's up to you. It's not for me to say." He could not believe this. He truly wondered if this was a dream. Perhaps if he pinched himself, he would wake up and the world with Travis and him would come back to normal—whatever that might be.

It was one thing to find out you're gay. It was another to find out your brand new boyfriend had a first love—and that love was coming back into his life with possible intentions... a*t the invitation of good-old-mother.*

What a plotting, two-faced bitch! Well, at least Cash knew without a doubt where she was coming from now. Obviously, he was not good enough for her precious little son. He didn't come from money, and certainly not from a world of high-class fluff. Today, she made it quite clear without saying one damn word. She hated country boys, dirty little rodeo rings, and loud noisy pick-up trucks.   In her eyes, she was out to protect her son from all this low-life shit and set him back on the original course.

"You know, Travis, you should have let me go the day of that snowstorm."

"What?" Travis' brow wrinkled, his eyes darkening.

"Out there in the driveway, when I said we were comin' from two different worlds… you should have set me on my merry little way and let be."

Putting his head down, Travis said, "I would have never been able to… I want you so badly, Cash. I can't begin to tell you how much you mean to me." He hesitated, fighting back the emotions that wanted to surface. "I need you."

"What about Jason?" Cash could not completely buy-in—his defenses were too raw. "You needed him. What made that change? The fact you moved away? It's apparent your mother believes that something is still there or she wouldn't be forcing you into this situation."

"Cash, we can work through all this. God, I can't let go of you… *you're my whole world!*"

Squinting with sharp, searching eyes, Cash leaned forward, and asked, "How?" He felt confused. "How can I be your whole world when our worlds are so fuckin' different? None of this makes any sense, Travis."

"Oh God, can't you see it?" Travis rose to his feet and went over to the large bay windows. "It's you… it's what's inside you, Cash. I love your being. You're so true and honest. You have nothing to hide, no preset games and manipulations. You are who you are and I want that so badly in my life. You ARE my inspiration." Tears began to trickle down his cheeks. "I can't live without you now… I'm in too deep."

Cash felt overwhelmed. He needed space. They both needed space. Whatever Travis' mother had intended to do this morning turned out to be quite effective.

Rising to his feet, Cash shoved his cowboy hat over his head. Angrily, he grabbed for his jacket.

"Cash, what's wrong?" Travis followed him. There was a never-heard-of-before tone of panic in his voice. The muscles in his face began to nervously twitch.

Cash shrugged without looking back. "You need space. It looks like you have some homework to do."

It was cold, but fortunately no wind as Cash and Brownie made their way down to the frozen river bottom. The last time he had been here, the world had held more brilliance—a wider variety of dazzling colors in the background. The deep blue sky was now exchanged for a softer gray, as the countryside had equally given up its radiant shades of autumn for an undeniable cast of burnt ash, dirty white, and patternless mix of shaded brown.

He had done the right thing; he reasoned to himself, recalling the horrible scene at Travis'. One fact was sure—if Travis truly wanted to be with him, he would have to stand up to his mother and set her straight. This type of shit would simply have to come to a halt.

Brownie's hooves clomped rhythmically over the frozen wasteland—allowing a snort or two to escape his nostrils. From time to time, he would rear his head back, cocked to the side to look at his buddy to make sure Cash was enjoying the ride as much as he was delivering it. Cash reached down and reassured his horse, stroking his mane with gloved fingers.

"You're my true 'n faithful, you know that?" Cash whispered lightly to Brownie. He liked speaking love words to him by the edge of his soft, auburn-laced ears—horse hairs tickling the tip of Cash's cold nose.

God, it was so peaceful out here, he told himself. This seemed to be the only place where things made sense. He knew he loved Travis—with his whole heart. There was no doubt; he had a total commitment for him. But at times, he needed a breather. As far as he was concerned, there was nothing wrong with a little time to be apart. In fact, he felt it was good for everyone to break away from time to time. Hell, even his dad and mom occasionally needed space.

The ski trip would be good for Travis, Cash tried to convince himself. But a tightness gripped at his stomach—admitting that he couldn't lie to himself like this. Yes, the trip would be good if that was all it was. Former boyfriends and past ghosts, however, could only spell trouble. Even though Travis was trapped by his mother in the situation, he couldn't be taken completely off the hook. When would this malarkey stop? What would be the next ploy of that manipulative blonde? The only thing Cash could tell himself as Brownie and he wandered through the empty, quiet riverbottoms was eventually Travis would have to crawl out from under the stamp of being 'momma's boy'. "Grow some balls," as his father would say.

Letting out a long, weary sigh, Cash tugged on the reins and steered back toward the ranch house. He was beginning to feel the frigid chill of the winter air settle deep in his bones.

Immediately, Cash noticed the infamous Viper parked by the house as they came around in the bend of the driveway. He wasn't surprised. In fact, it was rather strange—the hot little sports car was beginning to look like it belonged there parked beside the Pound Puppy and his dad's white truck. It seemed Travis came over a lot more often—not just to hang out with Cash, but to spend time with his mother, and sometimes help his dad out with some of the chores around the ranch. At first, he thought it was simply a novelty to see Travis here so often, but now, as Cash got to know him more, he discovered there was a lot to be desired at the Hunter residence. The house itself seemed very sterile and empty, void of any emotional warmth except for Travis' bedroom where there was the picture of his father and the trophies he had earned throughout the years resting on his desk. Now, after learning about Jason, and seeing how his mother operated, he could understand Travis and his ways a whole lot more.

After getting Brownie settled in his stall, Cash slowly made his way back to the house. His heart began to beat heavily as he entered the back porch—hanging his chaps up against the wall, and quietly opening the door. Eavesdropping on the kitchen conversation—his mother and Travis appeared to be totally unaware of his presence.

"I don't know—" Travis spoke in earnest, "I couldn't believe it when mom said they were coming up."

With the clinking sound of glass and china, Cash could picture his mother standing at the sink doing her usual mid-morning routine of washing dishes.

"Well, it certainly must have been quite a surprise to you," she said, thoughtfully.

"I didn't know what to say." Travis allowed his deep voice to raise a level. "She had already made the plans without even consulting me."

The sound of dishes being washed continued as silence fell between them.

"Cash is pretty upset," Travis volunteered. "I guess I don't blame him." The tone in his voice fell off.

"Upset about you going to Big Sky?" she asked, trying to gain more understanding of the matter.

"Well…" It was apparent Travis was having difficulty in sharing the rest of the details. "There's more to it than just that."

"What?" she asked. The clinking stopped.

"They're bringing their son with them," stated Travis with resignation in his voice. He paused, trying to figure a way how he could tell her the rest of the story. "Actually, he's coming early—this Wednesday to be exact, and he is expected to spend time with me until we head out on Friday."

Once again, Janice remained silent, allowing Travis to continue.

"Mom invited him; in fact, *she* is paying for the air fare."

Cash could tell Travis was hoping his mother would read between the lines without having to go into the sticky details. Whether she did or didn't, Mrs. McCollum quietly resumed the task at hand with the sound of running water and an occasional clunk of a plate being rested in the dish rack.

Allowing a sigh to escape his mouth, Travis finished his story in one sentence. "I used to go with him before we moved here."

Janice completed rinsing the dish that was in her hands and then placed it softly aside.

As Cash stood silently by the washing machine in the laundry room, his arm resting on a stack of folded towels left from the last load, he could visualize her trying to assimilate all the information. He knew she would remain calm.

"Janice," Travis obediently used her first name, "I don't want to see him."

"Then, don't you think you ought to share that with your mother?" Janice's tone was one of genuine concern.

"She's already purchased the tickets…she said this was a Christmas present."

It was her turn to let out a long sigh. Cash could hear her shoes scuff across the linoleum. "Well, it certainly sounds like you're in a tight spot."

"I don't know what to do." There was a lot of pain coming from Travis' voice. "I love Cash so much; I don't want to do anything to jeopardize it."

"I know that," Janice's words were gentle and reassuring. "You're the best thing that's come into his life. I can see it in his eyes—the way he walks, and talks—Travis, you're good for him." Allowing a moment to think, she concluded, "I know for a fact he thinks the world of you. He won't do anything hastily. He may have a hot temper…" she let out a small laugh, "but he knows how important you are to him."

"Thanks, I need to hear that," Travis flatly stated. "Can I tell you something?"

Cash could tell Travis really trusted his mother. Didn't he have this type of relationship with his own mother?

"I guess I have been pretty spoiled. People usually come to me. I rarely have to go to them. They search me out, and sometimes, they can be downright clingy…smothering." His voice was matter-of-fact, not arrogant. "You know, I've gotten so used to this and I've come to expect others to need me—often to the point I want to pull away. With Cash, however, it's totally different. He is so damned independent, Janice, sometimes it scares me. I constantly wonder if he could leave me and simply go back to his old ways—as if I never existed."

Silence filled the room as Travis paused to reflect. "I've never known anyone like this before and at times it really drives me nuts—I don't know how to react."

"Cash has learned to live contentedly with himself," Mrs. McCollum shared, her voice steady. "In fact, he's always been that way." Pausing, she let out a chuckle. "I just wish Clayton could be a little more like that."

Another wordless spell filled the room as Cash shifted his weight from one leg to the other. He debated whether or not to come out of hiding and face Travis, but realized he really didn't want to hash this over anymore. The ball was in Mr. Hunter's court and there really wasn't anything he could say or do at this time except wait and see where Travis would bounce it.

"Well, I better be going," Travis finally sighed with sullen acquiescence.

Cash could hear him push the chair away from the table—the sound of his heavy boots walking across the kitchen floor followed.

"I'm sorry," Mrs. McCollum apologized, her voice getting lighter as she followed him toward the front door. "I thought Cash would have come back by now."

"Would you mind telling him I stopped by?" he asked. There was a hopeful ache in his voice.

"I sure will."

Cash could tell she was smiling. He could envision her warm face looking into Travis' sad eyes.

The door opened and suddenly Travis stopped and said to Cash's mother, "Thank you."

"You're most welcome. You know you always have a home here."

With that, the door closed and Cash could hear his mother's footsteps come back to the kitchen. A few moments later, the sound of the hot-rod growled outside.

He knew his mother would be upset with him for going under-cover. Playing games was not a McCollum trait and she would certainly call him on it—not pulling any punches. Giving a sigh, Cash pushed himself forward from the laundry room into the kitchen. He braced for her reaction.

As expected, turning herself from the counter, a look of surprise crossed her face. "Cash! When did you get in?"

Looking down at the floor, he scuffed his feet—making his way to the table. "I've been here awhile," he answered honestly.

"And you didn't come out to talk with Travis?" There was a note of astonishment in her voice.

Cash remained silent. He knew what was going to be said next. Pulling-up the chair where Travis had been sitting, he settled himself down, still feeling the warmth remaining of his boyfriend's body in the smooth woodwork.

"Cash, I'm disappointed in you," she said, keeping her voice low, but allowing her irritation to surface. "He came over here in good faith to try to get things straightened out and you avoided him like the plague. That's not like you."

"Mom," Cash began, fighting back tears. She had a way of making him cry too easily. "I didn't know what to say to him." He continued to stare at the floor.

"Well, avoiding him isn't the answer." She walked over to the table and pulled up a chair opposite of him.

"I know," Cash thoughtfully replied.

"There's a lot hitting that boy right now, and not talking with him is really not fair."

"Not fair?" Cash sat up, his muscles tightening. "What about me? How do you think *I* feel about this situation?"

"Jealous," she spoke frankly, "...probably a little threatened."

"I can't believe his mother did that." There was a sharp bite to his words. He felt so angry towards that woman.

Resting a calm hand on her son's shoulders, Mrs. McCollum said, "But not talking with him will only make matters worse."

"He's going out there with Jason!" resentment radiated from Cash.

He couldn't hold back any longer. With his body shaking from all the intense emotions built up inside, he lowered his face and began to cry. Pain of the morning's events hurt so much. The room fell silent as Janice tried to console her boy.

"You two need to talk," she concluded, her hand gently shaking his neck. "It's the only way you'll be able to work through this."

And so, the holiday week seemed to miserably drag as Cash struggled to find a way to deal with the situation. Between a volley of phone messages, Monday evening through Tuesday, it seemed impossible for the two of them to connect. Wednesday eventually came, and with it, knowledge that the enemy was alive and present in *his* playground. It took everything in Cash's stead to refrain from heading over to the Hunter house and blasting his way into the reunion. The mere fact that those two would be spending time together *alone* for two days nearly drove him insane. There was no denying it—the hurt seemed to be more than he could bear—swearing there would be one hell of a pow-wow after all was said and done.

Chapter 14

On New Year's Eve there was more snow, more wind, and a phone call from Lee, which turned out to be the brightest part of the holiday.

"Hey, Cash, what's up?"

"Lee, how's it goin'?" Boy, it was great to hear his voice, thought Cash—pulling his attention away from the TV sitcom.

"Am I interrupting anything?" Lee cautiously asked, perhaps recalling his untimely call during Thanksgiving.

"No," Cash quickly reassured. The McCollum's had just finished eating dinner—with Eugene retreating to his usual spot in the recliner, Janice putzing in the kitchen and Clayton in his room primping for a night on the town. "We just got done eatin'…everyone's just hangin' 'round."

"You goin' out tonight?" the soft-spoken voice floated easily through the phone line into the curves of Cash's ear.

"Naw," Cash replied, thinking cynically, what would he have lined-up on a night like this—being that his boyfriend was out frolicking around with little Boy Blue? "How 'bout you?"

"Nope."

For some reason, Cash was pleased to hear that answer. Surprising him a little bit—he would have figured a guy as attractive as Lee would have an extensive social life. Evidently not.

"Guys have a nice Christmas?" Lee went on to ask.

"Yeah, we had a few guests…nice dinner." Instantly Cash pictured everyone seated at the dining table. Travis at his side—with his wonderful smile—those eyes reflecting the soft glow of the candles resting in the holiday centerpiece created by Mrs. McCollum. "'N you?"

"We don't celebrate it," Lee flatly stated. His voice was low and expressionless.

"Really?" That surprised Cash, bringing up a few questions in his mind.

"Well, not like you guys do," Lee tried to sound nonchalant. "It's nuthin' big."

There was a brief pause over the line between them.

"Tried callin' you two weeks ago; no one was around," Lee continued with the conversation.

Thinking, Cash tried to figure out what had been happening during that time. Suddenly, it came to him. "We were in Billings."

"For another interview?" A chuckle came over the receiver.

"No, my dad had a heart attack and they rushed him to St. Vincent's for surgery that week."

"Oh, wow!" exclaimed Lee. "Gosh, I'm sorry to hear about that. Is he all right?"

"Yeah," replied Cash, feeling a chill run through his spine. "Scared us pretty bad, though."

"I can imagine," Lee's voice was thoughtful.

Once again, there was a quiet spell between them. Cash wished he could see Lee's face—look into those dark, mysterious eyes.

"Hey, you headin' down to Rapid City next month?" Lee asked in an effort to steer the topic to something lighter.

"You mean the Black Hills Stock Show?" Cash asked. "I hadn't plan to." *Who would he go with?* Travis wouldn't want to go, and he certainly didn't want to traipse down there by himself.

"I'd like to go." There was a hint in Lee's voice.

Cash thought for a moment. *Why couldn't they go together?* That sounded like a damned good idea. If Travis could sashay around with his old boyfriend on some deserted mountain slope, why couldn't he spend a couple of days with a rodeo partner watching a professional show? "Lee, you wanna come down here and we can head out together?"

"Really?" There was excitement in his friend's voice.

"Sure. Why don't you come over after school on Friday. You can spend the night here 'n we can make the show on Saturday." Cash was beginning to like the idea even more as he spoke. "We'll come back Sunday afternoon."

"That sounds great," Lee said. "Sure your family won't mind?"

"Hell, no," Cash spoke casually, not thinking about the brash comment made by his father at Thanksgiving. "You can crash out here…nobody'l mind."

"What the hell you do that for?!" Mr. McCollum yelled at the top of his lungs, tossing his fork on the plate. *"For Christ's sake, Cash, are you out of your mind?"*

The piece of steak Cash was chewing got stuck in his throat as he tried to swallow. Oh God…he frantically thought. He could see it now—front page of the local newspaper—Cash McCollum dies at New Year's dinner from choking on beef steak.

"Gene," Janice spoke up; a furled brow clouded her visage. "You don't need to scream."

Waving his arms from the frustration exploding inside, Cash's father looked at his wife and explained with a continued, elevated voice, "Well, damn it to hell, Janice, what's he thinkin'? That kid is his top competition. Besides, I don't trust the little shit." It was apparent he was not going to let this one go.

"We're just going to attend the Saturday's rodeo. It's not like we're gonna be hittin' the bars, or floppin' around some dirty motel," Cash tried to logically explain.

"You better not or I'll whip your ass!" An angry fist plowed itself on the table, sending knives, forks and plates mid-air.

"Stop it!" His mother's voice rose to a demanding level.

"Don't tell me to stop it! I tell you, he's pushed this too far." Shooting a fiery glare across the table to his son who sat quietly, head down, Mr. McCollum continued along with his tirade. "Furthermore, he's not staying here in this house."

"Why don't you and Clayton go?" his mother thoughtfully suggested. "You haven't done anything with your brother for a long time. I'm sure he'd appreciate doing something with you—especially going down to Rapid City."

"But I've already invited him to come down." Cash felt a frantic fear that he was losing this one.

Allowing a sigh to escape his lips, Mr. McCollum looked up at the ceiling and spoke to Cash in a lowered tone. "What's gotten into you…thinkin' you can pull all this shit?"

Cash remained quiet—running his fork aimlessly across the plate sitting before him.

"There's no way I want you hangin' around with Lee Biruni. I don't want him stayin' in this house either!" There was no budging—no flexibility— his father had made his mind up. Looking back at Janice, he went on to say, "I tell you, that boy is trouble."

"Gene—Cash's already invited him. It wouldn't be polite to change that now." Mrs. McCollum sat up in her chair and turned to her son. "Have you talked to Travis about this?"

Instantly, her son glared back and said with sharp, biting words, "He's still at Big Sky."

By the tone in her son's voice, and the surly look on his face, she picked up on the implications, and slowly bit at her lip. Suddenly, she understood what was going on. "When are they coming back?"

"Tomorrow," Cash replied, staring at the table. "Sometime…I don't know." He shrugged his shoulders, his voice trailing.

Mr. McCollum tossed his wife a critical look. "What the hell does this have to do with our discussion?"

Cash looked up and gave his mother a desperate look. Arguing about Lee was one thing, but tossing Travis into the mixing bowl and spinning him around into this mess was simply too much to handle.

Allowing an indignant look to sweep her face, Mrs. McCollum replied—turning midway in her sentence to Cash—while initially directing it to her husband. "I just wanted to know when he was coming back."

"I won't have that kid sleeping here and that's my final word!" Mr. McCollum couldn't drive the point deep enough into Cash.

Suddenly, there was a knock at the front door. Looking out the window, Janice let out a painful sigh. "Oh boy... guess who it is?" Rising to her feet, she left the table and made her way out to the living room. "Hon, grab some more plates out of the cabinet. I'll get more steaks ready. The Evers are here."

Cash lay beneath the warmth of the thick comforter deciding which malady he could possess for the day. He could have a sore throat and say he needed to stay home and drink lots of orange juice, or he could take up the story that he had an upset stomach with chills and fever. Lastly, he could use the old alibi of the hurtin' ankle—inherited from an incorrect fall. Cash was always able to make it hurt to the point he couldn't *possibly* go to school.

This morning was definitely one of those selected days.

There was no way he could face Travis. Seeing a winter tan radiate boldly from that handsome visage was the last thing he needed. He certainly did not want to hear how fun it had been blazin' through virgin, powdery snow with good ol' Jason. His mother must have picked up on the hedging as she quietly poked her nose into his room to see if he was up and getting ready. Pulling the covers over his head, Cash pretended to play a game of 'opossum'. The ploy, however, didn't work as she came over to the bed and sat down on its edge.

"I don't suppose you have any desire to go to school today, hum?" Janice's voice was light and pleasant, in spite of how horrible the situation seemed to be.

He pushed himself up, avoiding her look by rubbing his eyes—pretending to be sleepy. He didn't respond to her statement.

Knowing that the two boys had failed to talk the entire week before, she sighed and said, "I know today's going to be tough, but you'll get through it."

'I'm glad you have faith in that," Cash replied with a yawn. He shoved the covers back and swung his legs out over the side of the bed.

"Just watch your temper," she soundly warned, her eyes conveying a certain seriousness to her words.

Pushing himself to his feet, Cash spoke—not making any stray promises. "I'll do my best." And *that* was the most he could offer.

"Hey."

The familiar sound floated across Cash's shoulder. He could feel his blood pressure kick into jump-start. Without acknowledging Travis' greeting, he continued to work the combination to his locker—fingers trembling.

Travis waited for a response. The air grew extremely thick.

"I'm sorry I didn't call," Travis began; his voice was shaky.

Grabbing his notebook and pencil, Cash closed the door and turned toward Travis—avoiding eye contact. "That's all right…doesn't matter." Mechanically, he scooted around the stunned youth and began making his way to his first class. As he walked down the hallway, he could feel a set of piercing eyes riveted to his back.

Determined he wasn't going to get into it with him at this time, he reasoned they had had an entire week to discuss the matter—for Christ's sake. They could gracefully wait until the end of the school day and duke it out in private. The thing that really irked Cash was that Travis could have taken one fuckin' moment to call from his cell, but had he done it? *No.* The bottom line—school hallways were certainly *not* the place to have a lover's quarrel.

Ironically, they hadn't made it to the second period when Travis grabbed Cash's arm after class, hissing in a deep voice, "I wanna talk with you… *now.*" He motioned for the two of them down the hallway and up the staircase.

Remaining quiet, Cash hotly yanked his arm free from the hold—shooting him a look of fire.

Jerking his head, Travis seized his hot-headed cowboy and led him down the hall—to their stairwell. Bounding two steps at a time, they reached the top landing, breathless.

"What the hell's your problem?" The confrontation started with Travis throwing the first bomb into Cash's territory.

"I just *love* how you return phone calls!" Cash snapped—his words coming out sharp and cutting.

"I told you I was sorry!" Travis' brow was dark with anger. "Besides, I tried calling you back several times before I left."

"And you couldn't call from Big Sky?" Cash was not going to let this one drop. "What happened? You flush your fuckin' cell down the toilet? *Bullshit!*" Catching his breath, Cash continued to slice away at the stunned jock. "I can't believe it...you couldn't even take one single minute from your goddamn precious little social life to give me a fuckin' call 'n tell me you're okay?" He turned his face and spit at the floor.

"Well, you said we needed space." Travis grabbed the only excuse he knew.

Furiously shaking his head, Cash raised his hand and thrust it up to Travis' face. "Oh, don't give me that shit...you knew what I meant."

"Well, why don't you just tell me to go to hell?!" Travis yelled, the veins in his neck standing out.

Cash completely ignored his boyfriend's demanding question by changing the subject entirely. "So, how was your time with Jason?"

With a gaunt and drawn face, Travis replied, "I'd tell you if you'd stop being such a smart-ass."

"Like I'd *really* want to know."

"Fine, I won't tell you." Travis threw his arms out from his side in frustration.

"I'll bet your mommy's thrilled you two are back together again." Cash pushed his way past Travis—starting for the steps.

"She doesn't have anything to do with this," said Travis in a defensive manner. "Besides, we're NOT together."

"Like fuckin' hell she doesn't!" Resting his hand on the stair railing, Cash's eyes blazed with anger. "She planned the whole goddamn thing, and you didn't have enough balls to stand up to her." Feeling the adrenalin shoot

wildly through his body, he felt he couldn't stop at that point. "You know what your problem is?"

"*What?!*" Travis' jaw was tight, rage seething from his countenance.

"You're a momma's boy, and you jump every goddamn time she snaps her fingers."

"That's not true!" Travis stepped toward Cash, leaning uncomfortably close to the fiery Irishman—his fists clenched.

Take your best shot, you son-of-a-bitch, Cash thought to himself. He was ready for an all-out fight. "*Damn right it is!* You do whatever she says without question."

"You shut the fuck up!" Travis' temper was now fully exposed.

"Make me, you son-of-a-bitch," Cash replied, completely undaunted—not moving a muscle.

Travis suddenly raised his arm back for a powerful slug—then suddenly stopped. His body began to shake, tears welling in his eyes. Letting out a growl, he turned and slammed his fist into the wall. "*Damn it, Cash, you make me so fuckin' mad!*"

"Well, get over it! How in the hell do you think I felt all last week?" Cash asked, offering no reprieve from his vented anger. "And you just fuckin' sail off with your ex to a ski resort and leave me high 'n dry to nurse my wounded thoughts? That's cheap, Travis—goddamn cheap."

Once again, Travis repeated the words that simply couldn't pay the price for his crimes. "I'm sorry, Cash, I really am sorry." He put his head down.

"And why can't you stand up to your mother whenever she slices and dices me?" Cash continued—a stray tear ran down the side of his face. "If you really think I am '*your world*' then why do you put up with that bullshit?

You know what I think? I think you get a fuckin' kick out of those put-downs."

Travis began an explanation, but Cash was unhearing. "I'm not puttin' up with this any more!"

"You shouldn't have to," Travis said, agreeing.

That shut Cash up. *Was he hearing correctly?* Had the message finally gotten through to Travis' brain, or was he being released from this relationship? Cash quickly prepared himself for the I'm-sorry-but-I-think-we-need-to-go-our-separate-ways line.

Travis continued, softening his voice to avoid attention from the lower portions of the stairwell. "Mom and I had a disagreement last night." He took a deep breath in an effort to calm down. "I told her I love you with all my heart, regardless of how she feels and that she needs to treat you with respect from now on."

Cash was speechless. *Well, that's a first,* he thought to himself. *It took long enough, however.* And just exactly what *did* happen between Jason and him? The question quickly jumped back into his mind.

Reading him, Travis went on. "As for Jason," he took a deep breath, "we had a good time, but nothing happened between the two of us."

Cash turned away, fighting back tears. He hated hearing the words, but all the while, he felt somewhat relieved.

Turning once again to Travis, he bluntly asked, "So did you sleep together?" Cash wasn't going to beat around the bush. He was determined to see if Travis would lie.

Without a blink or stammer, Travis replied emphatically, "No. Jason stayed in the guest bedroom at the condo—with his parents while I stayed with Mom upstairs." He hesitated. "There's something I need to tell you, however…" Travis' voice trailed to a near whisper.

Cash remained motionless. Suddenly a thick, dark and very heavy feeling came over him.

"Cash," Travis' voice was low. "Jason shared something with me…" there was cold fear in his eyes. After a long moment of pause, he finally pushed the words out of his mouth.

"He's HIV positive."

CHAPTER 15

At first, Cash couldn't imagine all the ramifications those words would mean to him. It was as if they had gone in one ear and out the other. There were so many other issues bombarding him at the moment; this added factor seemed to flick a safety switch in his brain that simply made him numb. *What the hell was Travis saying?* What were his implications?

So Jason was HIV positive. What did this have to do with them?

Cash stood there in the stairwell staring blankly at Travis—not uttering a word. Travis must have been waiting for a response. He finally sighed and went over to the window to gaze out over the bleak winter setting. The school parking lot was wet and slushy from the freshly fallen snow while the rooftops from the nearby houses were still pristinely coated white—casting a gentler hue to an otherwise gloomy, dreary day.

The bell rang for the next period. *What a way to start a new quarter*, thought Cash—an unexcused absence.

"What are you trying to say?" Cash was a little angry at himself for coming off so ignorant. He really wasn't sure what Travis was trying to get across except that his former boyfriend was infected with the virus.

"Jesus, Cash." Travis turned from the window with an incredulous look. "Don't you understand?"

"Yeah, you just told me he's infected with HIV." Cash felt his defenses surface. There was no need to talk down to him. Quickly, his mind raced back to those boring lessons of Basic Health—trying to recall the things he had learned about AIDS and HIV.

"Right," Travis spoke; a look of worry flooded his face. "He's not sure when he got it."

Cash braced for a barrage of ridicule as he struggled to follow Travis' train of thought. "What are you trying to tell me?"

"What I'm saying is, Jason is not sure when he got exposed. He told me he had been messing around with several guys before and *during* our relationship." Raising his arms out in frustration, he painfully continued, "I had no clue he was cheating on me, but I guess that doesn't matter now—except for the fact that he may have been infected while we were together."

Suddenly, Cash saw where Travis was taking this. The implications became frighteningly apparent and a sick feeling squeezed into his belly. He could sense his muscles freeze. "What are you going to do?" he asked.

Hesitating, Travis drew in a deep breath and said with a hushed tone, "I guess I'm going to have to be tested."

"Well, what if you have it?" Cash already knew the answer to that question, but he just wanted to hear it for confirmation.

"Then *you'll* need to be tested as well," Travis' reply was short and candid.

Cash couldn't describe the gratitude in his spirit when the last bell rang for the day. Gathering his belongings, he pushed himself from the desk and headed straight for his locker. He was not in any mood for people. All he wanted was to be alone—find a safe, secluded place and sort things out in the solitude of his mind.

Everything was damned jumbled up—his feelings about Travis, the near death of his father, the curiosity created by Lee, the trip to Rapid City, Mrs. Hunter, Clayton, Jennifer, and last but not least, Jason with his 'wonderful' gift of HIV—it was all too overwhelming.

What did all this mean? Did Travis have AIDS? Then his thoughts quickly progressed. *Do I have AIDS?*

This was all too much to comprehend. *For God's sake, I'm not ready to die!* His mind went crazy.

"You comin' over?" the words broke into his intricate, private world of thought.

"Huh?" Cash was startled by the intrusion as he made his way out to the truck.

Travis caught up with him; his jacket was unzipped revealing the haste involved in trying to catch up. "You comin' over for a little bit?"

"I can't," Cash spoke with numbness. "I need to take care of some stuff at home."

"Need some help?" Travis was eager to please. It was obvious that he wanted to get back on the right track. "Besides I told your dad I would stop in and see him this week."

Cash stopped in his tracks. "When did you talk with my dad?"

"Last week, one time when I called you before I left."

Letting out a long sigh, Cash mustered up a feeble smile—replying politely, "Travis, thanks. Let's see how tomorrow goes."

"Are you sure?" Travis was determined with the offer. A look in his eyes revealed how intense he wanted to be with Cash.

Damn it, Travis! Cash's brain exploded from the struggle going on inside. *Why do you have push things?* Nodding his head, he softly replied, "Yeah."

Reaching for the pick-up door handle, Cash turned and looked at him. There they were—those sad eyes and slumped shoulders. It stabbed at his heart—razor-blade sharp. Where anyone else would absolutely die to have this sort of attention from such an individual… Cash found it exhausting.

Feeling a stress-induced twitch play against his eyelid, Cash squinted in a fruitless effort to hide the nervous strain he felt flooding his soul. Travis was not letting go. *"What?"* he whispered from dry lips.

Travis began to reach out, but stopped midair with an extended arm. "Cash," he paused, searching for the right words. "I know what I've done to you this last week was horrible. You have every right to be mad at me. You should hate my guts. The fact of the matter is—I am *very* sorry for all of this."

Cash remained silent… unmovable. It was as if the air itself was freezing his flesh.

Travis slowly drew in a breath and continued—staring square into Cash's pale face. "Please listen to me…I want so badly for things to be right between us. I love you very much."

With the overpowering desire to get things sorted out—make sense of all it, Cash stared at Travis with a deep, penetrating gaze. Holding the words stored at the edge of his lips, a portion of his own life—something deeply hidden within his spirit broke free. It seemed to dance with its separate, silent rhythm into the frigid winter air—resting safely against his lover's chest. What he couldn't do from his own initiative—volition was carried by a translucent power. *He felt it. He knew it.*

Travis caught his breath. "God..."

Gripping the handle, Cash opened the truck's door. His eyes still locked to Travis'. "I'll see you tomorrow." The words were warm and gentle.

One thing was for sure, he told himself as he ignited the roaring engine—recalling their strange moment—none of that had been of his own doing.

Over the passing of days, Cash could tell Travis really regretted what had happened over the holiday break. He seemed to regret even more the lack of action he could have done to prevent it. Knowing that—made Cash feel good. But he knew it would take time for the hurt to heal.

So as Travis was committed to make Cash feel special—loved, it only made Cash feel odd—pressured. And even though his father had not yet conceded with him in going off with Lee, his mind became all the more set in doing just that. The real hurdle would be breaking the news to Travis—although, in the secret crevices of his heart, he couldn't wait to let the cat out of the bag. Now, it was *his* turn to see how it felt to be left alone.

"Whadiya mean you're going on a trip?!" Travis barked, stopping midway in a bench press—tossing the bar back onto the rack with a clanging thud. His face suddenly darkened with lines of irritation.

"I'm going to the Black Hills Stock Show in Rapid City," Cash calmly replied; watching the news sink into the huge jock's brain while diligently working on a set of concentration curls.

"The last week-end in January?" Travis made sure he had the date clarified before pitching his fit.

"Uh huh," Cash said, replacing the dumbbells.

"Well, hell, that's when I planned to take you to the Monster Truck Show at MetraPark."

"In Billings?" Cash couldn't hide the shock upon hearing that. He knew Travis wasn't the type who would who would relish going to something like that. "I thought stuff like that didn't interest you."

"I bought the tickets because I knew you'd like going to it." Travis sighed, looking away from Cash. A hurt countenance quickly came over him.

"You already bought the tickets?" This floored Cash—a sense of remorse quickly swept him. He couldn't change, however. He knew he had to continue with the plans created with Lee.

"Yeah," there was a heavy, indignant tone in Travis' voice as he wiped his brow with a towel.

"I'm sorry, but I've already made a commitment." Cash admiringly looked into the wall mirror and flexed. He loved looking at his muscles. Because of his leanness, he always looked incredibly ripped during a workout.

"A commitment..." Travis swung around, shooting him an incredulous look, "...with who?"

Instantly, Cash knew his arrow had reached its target. "A friend of mine from the Association," Cash cautiously replied. He didn't want to give out too much information.

Walking over towards Cash, Travis began to pump questions—his eyes narrowing with suspicion. "What's this all about?"

"I'm going to Rapid City with a guy from Great Falls."

"He's coming all the way down here?" Travis groped to comprehend this unexpected arrangement—veins popping up on his neck.

Cash grabbed the dumbbells and began another set of curls. "Yeah, he made plans to see the show that week-end and asked if I wanted to come along."

"Who is he?" Travis lowered his voice—his body completely tense now.

"Lee Biruni."

Pausing for a brief minute, Travis tried to associate the name with something else present in his mind. "Isn't he the guy that you've been tied with for All-Around Cowboy?"

"Yeah, it's not *that* big of a deal," Cash tried to sound as if it were a rather insignificant event.

"Like hell!" Travis' voice boomed. "Why haven't you told me about this before?"

"I was planning to."

"When..." Travis seized a large plate off the bar that rested on the bench press and tossed it angrily on the rubber matted floor, "...the day you leave?! Jesus, Cash, the least you can do is *ask* how I feel about it!!"

"Why should I?" Cash came back defiantly. "Did you ask me whether or not you should go to Big Sky with Jason?"

"You don't even know this dude!" Travis' voice filled the entire basement of the usually quiet Hunter residence. "How in the fuck can you make plans to go on a trip with him when you don't even know what type of person he is?"

"It's only for the week end. It's not like we're going to be together for *five whole days!*" There, he had gotten his dig. It had seemed forever waiting for the moment to come when he could take that stab.

Travis winced at the sharpness of Cash's words. Remaining silent, he slid the other plate off the bar and placed it dutifully on the rack. It was at this point Cash could tell he had cornered Travis with his own trick.

"Damn it, Cash!" Travis finally yelled; his eyes fought back tears. "You know I would go with you."

"I'm sorry," Cash once again replied; his sincerity—he felt was true. "I've already made a commitment."

Travis needed to be tested. Miles City wasn't exactly at the forefront of alternative health services, nor was confidentiality held at the top of that list. Neither of them knew where to go—let alone who to contact.

Fortunately, Tina Hunter had the drive and determination to seek out the nearest resources. After a lengthy search on the Internet and a few phone calls, she finally located a clinic that specialized with this issue. Once again, it meant another long and tedious drive to the city.

Cash, of course, had requested to come along for support. Making a special trip to the Hunter residence, he wanted to ensure his intentions were known—letting both of them know he wanted to be by Travis' side through it all. At first, Tina had balked at his offer, saying it was really a family issue.

About the time he was ready to give it to her, Travis stepped up to the defense. "Mother, Cash *is* family." The tone in voice was strong and extremely firm. It was obvious there would be no budging, no room for give.

Taken by surprise, the slight woman stood frozen in the middle of the dining room, unable to utter a word and completely shocked that her boy would dare stand up to her.

Proceeding on, to drive the point home, Travis rose from his chair and walked over to where Cash was sitting at the table. "I want him to come with me and that's that." His lips were tight, and his brow was dark from the heavy lines of seriousness radiating across his forehead.

"Listen…" she began, but then realized she had crossed a line. "Of course," she said slowly, as if something had been knocked out of her—her eyes darting searchingly between Cash and her son.

After a moment of silence between the three of them, Tina turned on her high heels and muttered a half-hearted, "Whatever," leaving the room and retreating to the quiet, pristine confines upstairs.

Cash remained still, riveted to his chair. Even Casper sensed the stony, thickened atmosphere—fleeing to the living room.

Continuing to stand, staring blankly into space, Travis finally spoke; his voice once again softened to the level he usually addressed, "Cash, "I'm sorry."

Cash didn't know what to say. He found himself quite overtaken by the scene and rather proud of Travis for standing on his own two feet. Another step in the right direction, he thought to himself.

"…An important meeting's come up," Mrs. Hunter explained. She couldn't possibly go with them—without an excuse. And this was one she wasn't willing to share with her employers. Sadly, she kissed her son's cheek as she walked the boys to Travis' car.

"It's going to be fine, just fine," she mumbled. "Fine-fine-fine."

Just as well she didn't go, Cash dryly thought.

"So, are you still planning on going to Rapid City?" Travis' fingers clenched the steering wheel with a death grip.

They reached the freeway with Travis shifting down.

"Yeah," Cash wondered quizzically, casting him a suspicious look. "Why would you ask?"

"I talked with your dad yesterday and he said the entire thing was called off." Travis continued to look straight ahead at the highway.

Suddenly, Cash could have sworn his head had been forced into a vise as he felt the pressure in his brain explode. This close communication with his parents was becoming a real threat. "Well, that's what *he* thinks," Cash hotly replied, squirming a little in the soft, leather seat—feeling that old Irish stubbornness creep into his bones.

"Well, that's what he told me while we were out in the barn," Travis flatly stated, never once looking aside.

How was he going to get through this one? Cash's mind kicked into overdrive. There was no way he was going to call this off. He had made plans—establishing a commitment with Lee—and hell or high water, he was determined to carry them out.

Continuing with his inquisition, Travis appeared quite pleased with the knowledge he possessed. "He also told me that you invited Lee to stay at the house."

Glancing at the panel, Cash wondered if Travis had cranked the heat up in the climate control. He felt like he was burning up. The heavy sheepskin jacket seemed to burst on fire as his body broke out into a nervous sweat. He wished he could have a smoke.

"Is that true?" Travis finally turned—blasting Cash with a cold, rigid look—his eyes horribly dark.

Drawing air, Cash solemnly replied with a more than subdued, "Yes." He had a good inkling what would follow—bracing for the rest of the storm.

"Would you mind telling me why?" Travis seemed to remain calm despite the fact he continued to clench the wheel—knuckles white.

Cash could hold his anger in no longer. He knew he was cornered and there was no way out. *"What is this?* Did you just bring me along so you could nail me to the cross?"

"No, but I want a damn good explanation for what you have planned." Travis' voice raised another level—clearly revealing his disgust over the matter.

"There's nothing between me and Lee," Cash blurted out. "If that's what you wanna know. I told him he could stay at the house Friday night because it would be a long drive from Great Falls to my house and it'd be late when he'd get in. What else am I supposed to do? Tell him to stay at a motel?!"

"Well, you might want to tell your dad that 'cuz he's thinking otherwise."

It was a solemn trip following Travis' check mate. Cash realized everything was quite out-of-control and something inside told him he should just hang it up and back out on Lee. But his anger at the entire situation caused his stubborn nature to settle into the trench. He was determined to dig his heels into the dirt on this one.

When they got there, Cash could not stop feeling the creeps. Entering into the plain-looking building, they located the floor and rode the elevator in silence. The undeniable question kept gnawing away at the back of his mind—*what if?*

Travis signed in, and together they sat down for the long wait. A young girl, perhaps about Jennifer's age sat quietly in a seat across from them. She looked weary—and quite pregnant. Tossing them glances, Cash figured she was sizing them up... determining what their arrangement was. *Was it obvious they were a couple?* He had never thought about it before, but at that moment, he felt somewhat exposed—knowing that everyone else in the room probably assumed they were gay.

Eventually Travis' name was called and he quickly rose to his feet. Cash didn't know if he should go with him, or stay in the lobby. The woman with a clip board looked over the rim of her glasses and asked, "Are you together?"

"Uh, yes," Cash's awkwardness could not be hidden.

"You can come with Travis if he doesn't mind." A hint of a smile peeked from her face.

"I'd like that," Travis quickly jumped in, motioning Cash to come along.

In the small examining room, they waited. Before long, a small grey haired man entered the room, looking over Travis' chart. "I see you want to be tested for the HIV antivirus?"

"Ah, yessir." Travis sat up in his chair.

"I guess my next question is—are you aware how HIV is transmitted?" The man looked directly into Travis' eyes, void of emotion on his face.

Travis nervously cleared his throat. "Yessir, I've read up on the disease as well as studied about it in health class."

"Have you carried out any sexual activity that may lead you to believe you might have come in contact with it?"

Suddenly, Travis' face turned ashen—eyelids twitching. Nervously, he swallowed. Nodding, he replied, "I think so."

The doctor went on, "Now, the virus can reside in the body for awhile before it can be detected. Has this activity been carried out six months ago or longer?"

Nodding once again, Travis weakly responded with a half-hearted, "Yes."

Cash could feel himself become antsy as he sat quietly watching this scene.

Casting a sincere, searching gaze toward Travis, then to Cash, he went on to say, "Well, first I must advise you that by getting this test, it will make you responsible with the knowledge of the results. Do you understand what I am saying?"

Not moving a muscle, he replied, "Yessir."

Something inside Cash wanted to take hold of Travis' hand, but he was too self-conscious. Damn Jason! He was the one starting all this shit.

"Travis, I don't want to scare you, I really don't," the doctor went on to say, "but I want to you understand what it is you're asking for. I want you to be prepared for what the results of this test might mean for you."

"I understand."

Pausing briefly to allow Travis time to change his mind, the physician let out a slow sigh. The lines in his face allowed a grin to move in. "I see you have some good moral support with you." His look directed toward Cash.

"Yessir, I do," Travis said proudly, a smile flooding his face.

Reaching for the door, Doctor Collins concluded by saying, "That's good. The nurse will be in to draw your blood, and the results should be back within ten days. You'll need to schedule a time to find out what your status is as we are unable to give that information out over the phone, okay?"

Travis nodded, "Thank you."

The doctor left, and within a few minutes a nurse came in to take his blood.

As they walked out of the building, Cash felt like the rest of the world had become completely detached from what they were being faced with. For one thing, this was something neither of them could talk about with their friends let alone family members. It was like being placed in a tiny bubble with no one able to come in, and more frighteningly, no one able to get out.

Crawling into the secure confines of the little sports car, Cash looked over to a very withdrawn boy. Quietly, he asked, "You okay?"

"Yeah," Travis sighed. He looked worn.

Without a word, Cash reached over and grasped Travis' hand—holding it securely with his fingers. Travis stared at the dash board, not blinking, not moving. There was a lot on their minds these days, reasoned Cash, a hell of a lot more than anyone would dare dream. Suddenly, he wondered if any other kids in their high school had concerns like this in their lives.

CHAPTER 16

To Cash's amazement, the discussion with his dad regarding Lee had been conducted with relative ease with only a couple of moments when elevated voices had been exchanged along with one single bang on the arm of the recliner with an impatient, angry fist.

From the beginning, Janice had made it quite clear she wanted to be left out of the conflict. The heavy lines of concern on her face indicated everything but a neutral stance, however. Not having to say a single word, Cash could tell she saw the entire situation from Travis' viewpoint. Before going into the living room to confront Mr. McCollum, she had quietly pulled her belligerent son aside and said, "I don't suppose you've considered someone else's feelings regarding this matter."

Feeling his impatience kick into high-gear, Cash hotly replied, "Mother, that's not the issue."

"Oh, it isn't?" A high look of surprise draped across her face. "Well, please forgive me for assuming that this entire get-together with Lee has been primarily designed to get back at Travis."

For once, he honestly felt angry at his mother. She needed to keep out of this and allow him to work the problem in his own way.

Approaching his father about Lee would be a phenomenal feat, Cash concluded as he entered the large, dimly lit room—the fireplace radiated a warm heat, casting a lively animated glow into every corner.

"Dad?" Cash nervously asked as he crossed over the large Indian-woven rug to the sofa.

"Yeah?" Mr. McCollum looked up from his newspaper.

"Can we talk?" He could feel his fingers tremble.

Taking his glasses off and placing them on the lamp stand, Cash's dad cleared his throat and said, "What's up?"

"I want Lee to come down so we can go to the Stock Show together."

Instantly, Eugene bristled, the expression in his face lighting up as bright as the fire blazing in the hearth. "I thought we already determined this issue was over." He placed his arms squarely on the arm rests and gripped the ends as if he were being catapulted into space.

"I'm sorry," Cash respectably replied. "I don't feel that it is."

"What in the hell's got you chompin' at the bits to do this?" Irritation soaked every word that came out from his mouth.

"Dad," Cash put all his attention at remaining calm and respectful, "I know how you feel about Lee, but I swear he's okay and I just want to be able to go to South Dakota and see the show with him, then come back."

"Why *him*?" his father asked with squinted eyes. "Can't you go with someone else?" He paused, staring at the fire dancing merrily over the logs. "Travis told me he'd like to go down there with you. The way I see it, you need to be goin' with him."

The manner in which his father took up for Travis intrigued Cash. It was as if his parents had adopted him and made him their own.

"But I've already made a commitment to Lee, and I don't think it's right for me to back out now." The logic that spewed from his own lips took Cash by surprise. It sure sounded good… McCollum mannerly good.

Eugene let out a long, slow sigh—still focused on the flames in the fireplace. "I don't trust that Biruni boy… he's sneaky." After a brief minute of thoughtful reflection, he continued, "How do you know he won't turn on you if he were to learn the truth about you? You know damn well he could get you thrown off the Association in a heartbeat as well as destroy your reputation."

"I don't think Lee is that type of a guy."

"Well, even if he isn't, what would you do if he tries to pull something on you?"

With a non-understanding frown, Cash asked, "What are you saying?"

"You know what I'm saying," his father's face closed.

Cash stopped. He didn't want to think in that direction. "It's just a friendly thing. You know, go to the show and that's it. I'll be careful around him."

Plowing his fist on the soft padding of his chair, Eugene growled, "You better! I won't have him messin' you up! *I mean it!*"

Silence overcame the room for a few moments as both of them sat reflecting on what had been said. "What I don't understand is why you don't want to go with Travis. If you two are what you claim to be… well, if I were him, I'd tell you to take a goddamn hike. It's not like he doesn't wanna go."

Cash remained quiet. He knew his dad was right. There was a part of him that wanted to openly admit it. Deep in the most private recesses of his heart, he also knew the right thing to do was pick up the phone and back out from his plans with Lee. There was no doubt; this had the potential to hurt Travis unbelievably.

Breaking the silence, Mr. McCollum turned to his son and finally said, "I don't know, do what you want… but I'm warnin' you, that little shit has the potential to mess you up. You're number one right now in the state competitions and he'll work at draggin' you down so he can get the title—even if that means destroying your reputation."

"I understand all that," Cash whispered. But all he could think was, *I'm too young to be married… after all—I have the right to make friends.*

The day finally arrived. Not a word was uttered about the trip back to Billings. And even though neither one had chosen to talk about it, it still hung heavily in their minds. Over and over, Cash told himself that this whole thing didn't seem fair. With neither of them having the reputation of playing around, he thought it was ironic that Travis' health had been flagrantly put on the line. Jason seemed to be one selfish bastard. Did he even really care about Travis? And why wait until now to break the news of his infection? If Tina hadn't made the arrangements for the boys to get back together, would Jason have ever said anything to her son?

Cash found himself praying like he had never done before hoping that the test would come back clean—not only for Travis' sake, but for his own as well.

From the beginning, it was decided that nothing would be said to Cash's family. With the alibi that they were working on a group science project, he knew there was no need to get them all worked up—especially if the test was negative. If it turned out positive, well, then it would be a different story. He would cross that bridge when it arrived.

"I sure wouldn't have gotten involved with him had I known about the cattin'..." Travis lamented as they made their way down the hallway to the drab, oppressive clinic.

Finding themselves in the same examining room, they revisited the awful wait. It was an omen, Cash told himself. A horrid sense of finality nibbled away—destroying their endurance.

Before they knew it, Dr. Collins walked in with the clip board. Their eyes locked on him—not a muscle was moved.

Both of their lives rested upon what was written on the surface of that paper. They both held their breaths.

"How are you boys today?" The doctor asked as he pulled up a chair and sat down.

"All right," Travis replied. His words came out as a squeak.

Cash tried to read the physician's face, but an expressionless countenance veiled his eyes.

Clearing his throat, Dr. Collins looked down at the report, and with a sigh, he finally glanced up toward Travis. "Your test results came back negative."

For a moment, both boys sat frozen—not responding to the news. It seemed to take time for the verdict to sink in.

Cash wasn't sure which emotion needed to come out of him first. Feeling as if he were going to fall out of his chair and collapse flat on the floor from shear exhaustion, he also wanted to jump up and scream Hallelujah at the top of his lungs with an inexpressible joy flooding his soul. Somewhere in between, there was a burning desire to lean over and hold Travis with all his might—perhaps letting loose with a few tears.

Travis was already crying. Looking out the window, he blinked away the pool forming in his eyes—sending them down a trail across his cheeks and neck.

"I'm sure this is quite a relief for both of you," the doctor noted—scribbling something on the report then rising to his feet.

"You have no idea," Cash instantly replied.

"I think I do." The man smiled and slowly reached for the door. "I see either this or the other scene every time I volunteer here."

When they stepped out into the blinding afternoon sunlight, Cash suddenly felt like he had been reborn—as if he and Travis had just received a new stamp on life. Walking to the car, Travis suddenly stopped. Throwing his head back, he looked up into the weightless, blue sky, and took a deep breath.

Without a word, they simply stood in the middle of the parking lot allowing the warm winter sun's rays to blanket their bodies as the frosty air gently, quietly floated around them. Cash wondered what the by-passers thought, but he really didn't care. It felt good to simply enjoy the moment for what it was… it felt good just to enjoy life.

The weather looked ominous as clouds moved in early that morning, darkening throughout the afternoon. There was no wind, but it was evident there was a lot of moisture saturating atmosphere. The morning news had given out the statement of a severe winter storm warning for the entire eastern Montana region. A cold, artic front which had lots of time to develop in Canada was moving down upon a warm, wet pocket of Pacific air that had pushed its way across the mountain ranges and settled across the northern plains. Ice warnings had already gone out for areas west of the Continental Divide the night before. The cities of Missoula, Butte, and Helena were already socked in with a heavy thick layer of ice and freezing rain. The mountain passes were closed.

The entire day, Cash found himself on pins and needles. He could barely endure the long progression of boring periods at school. Knowing Lee would soon be heading across the treeless prairie, he wondered if this whole plan needed to be scrapped. This was dangerous weather which was nothing to play around with—especially when nightfall would arrive. The part that really irked him was the fact he had his heart set on spending the weekend with his new rodeo buddy. Now, with the storm slamming down off the Rockies, he knew the chances of those plans becoming a reality, was slim to none.

Looking out the windows during his last class for the day, he watched the overcast sky become heavier—more foreboding. In spite of the shit-assed weather, his mind instinctively wandered back to hazy memories of a golden afternoon. He could still visualize the handsome cowboy all decked out—enjoying a deep, slow smoke from his cigarette and walking with the easiest sway. And then there was that smile. *Goddamn.* Between those beautiful full lips, were a set of teeth that just seemed to jump out from nowhere. He could feel his tongue slide across them drinking in Lee's taste like it was aged bourbon.

When the bell rang, he sprung to his feet—unaware that he was the first one to exit the room. He couldn't get out of school fast enough. By the time he pushed the doors and breathed the outdoor air, Cash could swear he was exploding. The storm couldn't have come at a worse time, he sadly reasoned to himself.

Big fluffy snowflakes were now beginning to flutter across the parking lot—a few of them landing softly on his long eyelashes. When he reached his pick-up, it was coming down heavily. Looking back, he could barely see the school or any of the neighboring houses nearby. Jumping up into his truck, he started the engine and slid it into gear. Without warning, a loud bang from the passenger's door jarred him to reality. *Jesus!* He jumped in his seat. Through the snow-covered window, he recognized Travis' face. *What the..?* He wasn't in any mood for hounding. Reaching over, he unlocked the door and flipped the handle. Travis quickly swung it open and hopped in.

"What's up?" His voice was impatient.

Pointing to the exit of the parking lot, Travis cocked his head and undauntedly ordered, "Let's go."

Cash stared at Travis with wondering eyes trying to figure out what was up.

"Just trust me, let's go," Travis repeated.

In spite of rising anger and a strong yearning to arch his back, Cash complied. "Where we goin'? Morocco?"

Travis allowed a smile to glide across his lips, but spoke in a commanding tone, "Just shut up and drive... turn right at the corner."

Suddenly, Cash knew where they were heading. Taking it from there, he headed the 'Puppy' on its pre-destined course.

Leaning closer to Cash, Travis slid a possessive arm across the back of the seat. Devilishly, he allowed a wandering finger to play gently across the cowboy's ducktail and neck.

Cash could feel the ice melt—his tension wane. That damned touch could work a candle down at the North Pole. *Not now!* Frustration screamed inside. It was what he wanted... what he always longed for... *but not now!*

The snow piled—relentlessly, purposefully—making their world completely white.

Not stopping, Travis drew in further—his warm, moist lips caressing Cash's cheek—allowing a hot, thirsty breath to lap against the soft flesh of his boyfriend's ear and sideburn.

Cash pulled away—frightened of being spotted, but soon, he gave in—succumbing to this battle of passion. Turning the bend, he viciously pushed the truck through the fresh, unmolested coat covering the land. He knew full-well where they would end up.

Coming to a stop, Cash shut down the engine. Quiet engulfed them. The only sound was their hearts beating—pounding. Soon, the chill from outside began to work its way into the cab. A shiver ran through Cash.

Travis took Cash's hand and carefully wove it between his fingers. At first it startled him, as most things did when it came to Travis.

"Cash," the big youth broke the stillness. His voice was tender. "I don't know how to start this, but I want you to know, that this thing with Lee is very difficult for me to take." He paused, looking intently into Cash's emerald eyes. "I can't tell you not to do this, and I don't expect you to back out on him at this point… but you have no idea what this is doing to me."

"We're only goin' down to see a rodeo…" Cash started to explain, then became quiet—staring at Travis. He didn't know what else to say. Travis' love, …hard to understand, but impossible to quit.

"Just remember how much I love you."

Nodding, Cash bit his lip. "I will."

When he became buried in the protective hold of Travis' arms, he couldn't quite remember; but before he realized it, he had lost control. Totally.

S. Bryan Gonzales

With gasps and moans, they became one with explosive obsession.

"Oh, God!" Cash cried.

Outside, the pick-up's windows became blanketed with snow while the steam of passion collected delicately inside from two boys who could not stop.

"I can't get enough of you!" Breathless, sweating, Travis took one more plunge.

There was no denying it, Cash loved being overtaken—subdued by the great wolf. With eyes of fire, and strength of steel, only the wolf-man knew how to do it, and do it well. No one would be able to replace him—he was sure of that. Absolutely no one.

With the dimming of the sky, Cash pushed away from Travis and lit a cigarette. "You know, I'm sure Lee is straight."

By the time he got home, the snow was in full force. It was dark now and nearly impossible to see the road. Hell, there was no way Lee would make it through all this shit, Cash finally admitted to himself. *Damn it!* Of all the weekends of winter, why did it have to storm on this one? *How it holy sucked!*

Brushing the snow from his pants and slipping his boots off in the back room, Cash slid across the kitchen floor with sweaty socks. "Any phone calls?" he asked his mother who appeared to be cleaning out the refrigerator. He chose not to be specific in order to avoid any stray comment or look of disgust at the mention of Lee's name.

"Nope," his mother replied, leaning over with her head halfway in the ice box, meticulously checking each item to determine its worthiness to remain as part of the McCollum food supply.

That surprised Cash. Surely, he thought Lee would have called him to cancel out. Now, he really wondered what was up. Should he call? He debated what the next move needed to be.

Throughout the evening, Cash felt the agitation increase. He tried not to make a scene in front of his family. Quietly, he crept to the large living room picture window, a number of times, to see any sign of headlights coming down the long driveway.

Unable to keep anything hidden from an observant mother, he was approached by the thoughtful woman who bore a look of slight irritation. "Did he say he was going to call before leaving?"

"No," replied Cash, in a disheartened—yet expectant tone. Staring out into dark, wintry night, his heart sank deeper into a pit. There was already a foot of the white stuff resting on the ground with a steady dump still continuing. *For God's sake*, he dismally thought to himself, *was there going to be any reprieve from this soon?*

"Well, maybe you should call his home and find out what's going on," she suggested.

By ten o'clock, there still had not been any word from Lee. Cash knew he should have called earlier. Now, he was worried. If Lee had intentions of canceling, he would have done it by now. Picking up the phone, he dialed information and got the only number under the Biruni surname.

Working the number with nervous, shaking fingers, Cash allowed the call to ring a number of times before it was answered by a soft-spoken female voice.

"Hello." A heavy, foreign accent came over the line—her voice almost a whisper.

"Is Lee there?" Cash asked.

"Huh?" The lady responded.

Not sure if she could hear him, he spoke louder. "Is Lee there? May I speak with Lee?"

Muttering something unknown to Cash, she finally spoke in broken English. "No… no Lee is heer."

Thinking he had gotten a wrong number, he was about to hang up when she continued. "Lee drife to friend long whay…."

Cash could barely understand the words for the sake of her accent, but what he could make out sent his heart back into the expecting mode. Wondering how much she comprehended, he debated to ask any more questions. "This is Cash," he said, almost shouting through the line. How stupid, he reprimanded himself, speaking louder to her would not help her to understand any better.

"Who?" The voice asked from the other end.

"This is Cash… Cash McCollum… from Miles City. Lee is coming here?"

"Who?" She asked again, followed by another string of words he couldn't make out.

"I am Cash McCollum…" *Whew!* Cash hopelessly thought; he felt desperate. "Is Lee coming here?"

"Lee, yes… he drife much time early to you."

In the background, Cash could hear a young child start to cry. Talking quickly in a language Cash didn't know, the woman momentarily left the phone. His mind became saturated with curiosity. Questions by the dozen flooded him. *What was this all about? Who was she? Who was the child crying in the background?* Hell, there was so much about this mysterious cowboy he found to be a brain-bustin' puzzle.

Thanking her as well as he could possibly think of, he ended the call and rested the receiver back on the cradle. Well, *that* was interesting, he told himself—standing frozen by the phone.

Cash's mother came out of the laundry room with an arm load of folded linen. "Well, what did you find out?"

"He's on his way," Cash said, still staring out in space.

"Who did you talk with?" Janice stopped, resting the stack from her arms on the counter.

Shaking his head, he replied, "I don't have a clue." He paused, looking at her with a blank face. "It was a lady, but she could barely speak English."

Mr. McCollum hollered from the living room, "I'm headin' for bed." It was clear he would not be part of the welcoming ceremony. That was okay, thought Cash. He could do without his father's surliness.

Listening to the scuff of his dad's slippers on the stairs, Cash went on to say, "I guess he left early this afternoon."

Letting out a long sigh, Cash's mother retrieved the fresh laundry and headed for the stairs behind her husband. "I just hope he makes it here safely," she muttered under her breath. "Of all times..."

Cash remained by the phone, not knowing what to do with himself.

It was nearly midnight when Cash heard a vehicle head down the snowy driveway. Feeling his heart jump into high gear, he couldn't believe that Lee was finally here. He was awfully excited.

As he bounded for the front door, he could still smell Travis' scent waif off his face and body. *God, what was he doing?* This was insane, he told himself—feeling a tinge of remorse briefly gnaw at his conscience.

Opening the door, he waited for the travel-weary cowboy to make his way across the snowy drive and up the steps to the front porch. Instantly, the feelings of guilt were shoved aside like a bulldozer barreling through a pile of dirt. "Hey!" he heartily greeted with an extended hand.

"How's it goin'?!" Lee burst forth into a broad, toothy grin. Taking hold of Cash's hand, he shook it with revived energy.

As expected, Lee looked good... real good. Wearing the same black western hat that he had worn the last time they had been together, Cash felt himself kick into overdrive. He fixed a gaze into that lean, handsome face, taking note of the start of the full beard and mustache. Lee looked exhausted.

"I'm glad you're here," Cash said, gesturing for his buddy to come inside.

"I am too," Lee quickly replied, taking his jacket and cowboy hat off— revealing thick, shiny black hair which draped lazily over his forehead. He wore a sharp-looking creamy-white shirt, slightly unbuttoned.

Instantly, their eyes met and locked. Neither one blinked.

Cash's nose picked up the scent of stale cigarettes, strong musk and cologne. At that point, he knew this would be tougher then herdin' a nervous flock of sheep to a roarin' waterfall.

Breaking from the spell, he nodded, "Come on."

Together, they went to the kitchen. "You hungry?" Cash knew there were no eating places for hundreds of miles. He was probably starving.

"I could probably eat a whole calf," Lee laughed as he rested his bag on the floor.

"Well, I dunno if we have one here in the fridge, but I'm sure I can round you up a sandwich or two." He pulled a package of sliced meat and some mayonnaise from the refrigerator, placing it on the counter. Going to pantry, he got a loaf of bread off the shelf. "Anything to drink?"

"Beer."

Together they laughed. Cash liked his humor. "I could go for that myself," he agreed, thinking what would happen if he snuck two cans of his father's stash.

"Water's just fine."

Weighing out the consequences, Cash stalled at the fridge then went with his guts. He couldn't resist. Opening the door, his arm slid in and grabbed two brews. Retracting his catch, he turned and handed one to Lee. A wink flashed from his Irish greens.

Lee's eyebrows raised and his face lit up with pleasure. "Thanks."

Flipping the tab, Lee lustily guzzled down a good portion of his beer by the time Cash finished making the sandwiches. At the table, Cash spied Lee's every movement. His entire essence seemed so smooth and easy. From the occasional slight rise of his left eyebrow, to the gentle, relaxed—yet very masculine movements of his hands and fingers, his entire body sent out an invitation. Cash could feel the web tighten.

As Lee finished off the second sandwich and the rest of his beer, Cash broke their quiet. "Surprised you did the trip."

Lee gave a sigh. "I had my doubts." He turned and looked out the window, watching the snow steadily fall against the reflection of the yard light. "It got pretty bad around Jordan."

"I called your house and talked with somebody... said you were on your way here."

Nodding his head, Lee spoke indifferently. "You must've talked with my mother."

"She seemed nice," Cash added, trying to be positive in spite of the fact he could barely understand her.

"When she wants to be," Lee's voice soured. The look in his eyes darkened.

A moment of silence slipped in between them as the ticking of the clock in the living room filled the empty space with its steady, rhythmic beat.

Cash was hoping he would volunteer some information as to the foreign accent and lack of ability to communicate in English. Inside, he was just itching to know where they hailed from.

Sensing Cash's curiosity, Lee pushed himself from the table and took a deep breath—resting his hands behind the back of his head. He cleared his throat and began to speak in a lowered voice. "My family's from Turkey. I'm first generation, born here in America."

That certainly answered one question, Cash quietly told himself. He didn't know what to say.

"There's a lot I can tell you, but I won't bother you with all that shit right now," Lee bluntly stated. He didn't want to talk about himself—or his family.

The clock chimed and Lee looked at his wristwatch. Allowing a yawn to escape, he looked at Cash; a slight grin slipped along the gentle curves of his mouth. His words were easy. "You wanna share a smoke?"

There was an undefined stimulation from the proposal that set Cash reeling over the edge. It compelled him with suggestive implications—setting his mind on fire and his mouth watering. "Sure," he replied, feeling himself overcome with excitement and anticipation.

Rising from the table, they got their jackets and quietly slipped out onto the back porch.

Reaching in his shirt pocket, Lee pulled out a pack of cigarettes and proceeded to fire one up with a hard, deep inhale. Looking at Cash, he offered him a hit. Smoke slowly crept from his nostrils—curling momentarily around his well-trimmed moustache, then across his cheeks and on out into the chilly room.

Cash took a drag, copying Lee's technique.

Slow, smooth and downright tough... that's what it was. Every stitch and corner of Lee was something that attracted Cash like a moth to light. He couldn't get enough.

Lee sucked in another long breath of hot, thick smoke then whispered with a deep-throated voice. "You like to watch me, don't you?"

From the dimness of the room, Cash couldn't tell if there was smile or a gleam on his face. Only a faint glow of the yard light's reflection shined from Lee's eyes.

Cash nodded, remaining silent from embarrassment.

Handing him the half-burned cigarette, Lee blew the rest of his smoke out into the night air—his eyes now locked to Cash. Softly, he went on to say, "That's alright. I like it."

Cash was lost. As reason and logic seemed to abandon him, he realized he didn't know where he was going, or what he was doing. Fucked up, and out of control—Travis would call it. Instantly, he knew he was in way too deep. His guts began to ache.

Opening the back door and flipping the butt out into the freshly fallen snow, Lee roped him in and said, "Let's get some sleep." There was a sad weariness that weighed heavily to his words.

Slipping their boots off at the base of the staircase, Lee and Cash tip-toed up the steps to Cash's bedroom. The arrangement had been set—Lee would have the bed and Cash, the sleeping bag on the floor. Cash didn't mind, knowing that Travis had been the last one to sleep in the bag… naked.

Faster than a lightening bolt from a cloud, Lee had slipped off his clothes and was sound asleep. And as he got ready for bed, Cash could not believe how beautiful his friend looked lying in bed, under the covers, with only his head exposed to the cool of the room.

Sleepily, Cash slid his body in between the soft, fuzzy confines of the bag and pulled the pillow up behind his head. Looking up at the ceiling and listening to Lee's breathing become slower, he told himself he couldn't believe this was actually happening. Was this a dream, or a nightmare? At this stage, he couldn't tell… but something was for sure, he certainly didn't want it to stop.

He couldn't have fallen asleep since the feel of the body behind him was more than real. Recognizing Travis' strong arms tighten into an embrace, and the light touching of his tongue along the large vein in his neck, he sighed and eased back—reaching behind to run his hand along a firm, solid hip. Suddenly Travis grabbed him by both wrists, holding him bondage—positioning him a manner to make it easy. Cash could feel his body shake as Travis worked him deep, the way he liked. At that moment he was aware of a movement on the bed that was neither his nor Travis', and when he looked up, there was Lee—fully naked—sitting, watching them both. For some reason, his presence didn't surprise him, which was probably the strangest thing about the encounter. Instead, he admired the lean boy with muscles grouped like rocks and tethered vines under his skin. Lee moved forward while Cash allowed his head to fall back against Travis' shoulder, feeling hot breath. The other boy's mouth worked its way down the front of Cash's body, finally stopping at his most sensitive part, feeling the electricity shoot through him. He let himself be rocked by both boys, one forward, the other back, until his body jerked so hard it flung him aside and brought him fully awake...

The sound of Lee's breathing in the tiny bed was reassuring, and Cash knew he was alone. Arranging himself in the sleeping bag, he cursed himself repeatedly, both embarrassed and angry. As he lay there perfectly still, he became keenly aware that something, indeed, was growing inside of him needing to be either completely rooted out, or dangerously nourished. Once again, he stared up at the mysterious shadows scaling the ceiling, only vaguely aware of the approach of morning light.

CHAPTER 17

Overcast rays of daylight eventually crept into the small, simple bedroom. It had seemed like such a short night as Cash stretched and yawned, wiping the sleep from his eyes. Family members began to stir throughout the house with his father being the first to make his way downstairs to start a pot of coffee. He hadn't heard Clayton come home and wondered if his wayward brother had even made it in. Pushing himself up from the sleeping bag, he glanced over to the bed and discovered it empty—the comforter and sheets pushed back. His head turned, scanning the room, looking for Lee.

At Cash's tiny desk his friend sat motionless, staring out the window— apparently lost in a sea of thought. It had stopped snowing sometime in the night, but the entire landscape outside seemed completely bleached of color. Shifting his focus from the window, Lee allowed his eyes to scan over the desktop. A jar of pens and pencils along with a stapler, some tape and a calculator were strategically positioned at one side of the desktop—while the rabbit's foot, a framed graduation photograph of Travis, and the card which he had given Cash the night they had stayed at the hotel in Billings rested on the other side beside a small laptop computer.

Suddenly, Cash panicked. He had forgotten to remove Travis' stuff earlier the day before. *Oh God*, he frantically thought.

Hearing Cash stir, Lee turned to him and smiled. "Good morning." The tone in his voice was light and expectant.

"Hey." Cash got to his feet, grabbing his jeans and shirt, and running his hands through his thick strawberry-blonde hair. *How long had Lee been sitting at the desk?* He had an overpowering instinct to leap across the room and retrieve everything of Travis' that was resting by the computer, but he knew if Lee had seen anything—especially the card—it was too late now. The secret about him and Travis would be out in the open, and Lee would have knowledge about their relationship. The only direction he could go from this point was forward.

If Lee had noticed the card, and if he had any pre-meditated intentions of trying to bring Cash's reputation down, the ammunition was now delivered. One thing he quickly told himself, if he over-reacted to Lee's discovery, it would only give the other boy more incentive for sabotage. It would show a weak spot—egging him on, giving him a reason to see Cash squirm. On the other hand, by appearing not to be affected by the possibility of Lee's new-found knowledge, it might send out a message that nothing could phase him... not even the fact about spreading the word that Cash might be queer.

Picking up Travis' picture, Lee looked at it closely and asked, "Wasn't he the one you were with on TV?"

Cash calmly nodded, zipping up his trousers, and fastening the button snaps to his shirt. "Uh huh."

"You two are very close," Lee said observantly, resting the photo back on the desk.

"Yeah," Cash tried to make his voice sound smooth and casual. "We're like brothers," he helplessly lied—knowing that if Lee had noticed Travis' card and message, it would be evident of a false cover-up. *Oh well*, he told himself, *it was worth a try.*

"What's his name?" The dark-haired boy asked still staring at the picture.

"Travis." Cash was feeling awfully uncomfortable. He needed to get Lee out of this room as soon as possible.

Lee remained quiet. Looking at the cork board hanging against the wall in front of the desk, his eyes slowly traveled from one object to another—first inspecting a 4-H award Cash had received from a project he had done several years before, then photos of him riding rough stock at various rodeos along with a certificate for bull-riding techniques. On the dresser were a couple of trophies he had won in the Association the previous year along with a family photograph that had been taken outside in the front yard during the last Fourth-of-July picnic.

"You have a lot of history." Lee turned to Cash—there was a note of envy in his voice. "Your family is close."

Rolling his eyes, Cash quickly replied, "Oh, not all the time... there's usually someone in the clan that has their undees in a bunch... We're just human," he added.

Thinking of a good reason to get Lee out of the room, Cash instantly thought of Mrs. Biruni. "You think you might want to give your mom a call 'n tell her you got here safely?"

Lee's face went dark. A sour scowl swept over his brow. "What for?" His words were stinging. "She won't be concerned."

"Really?" Cash openly asked—once again, his curiosity aroused.

Lee shrugged his shoulders with irritation. "She'll just bitch at me."

"Why?" Cash wasn't sure how far he should carry this.

Lee pushed himself off the chair and walked over to the dresser. Resting an arm on the top, by one of Cash's trophies, he cleared his throat and said, "Because she thinks I'm not being responsible."

Shaking his head—not understanding, Cash couldn't help himself. "About what? You seem pretty responsible to me. Hell, anyone who has gone as far you have in the Association has to possess a good share of responsibility."

Lee's agitation increased. "You don't *know* the situation. There's a lot more than what I can explain to you." With that, Lee made it evident he wanted the subject dropped.

As expected, Lee's interaction with Cash's family was somewhat strained—especially with Mr. McCollum.

"You know my dad from the Association?" Cash asked Lee, trying to make formal introductions the moment they stepped into the kitchen.

"Yes." Lee took a step back the second he spotted Eugene—as if he were the devil himself. A shocked look came over his face. Extending a respectful hand, he said reservedly, "You're one of the stock contractors."

"How ya doin'?" Eugene asked—ignoring the comment and exerting all the energy he could muster to shake the boy's hand.

"Lee, this is my mom," Cash gestured with an extended arm in her direction. She was busy talking on the telephone. Raising her hand, she gave a slight wave and smiled. Covering the mouthpiece of the receiver with her palm, she whispered to Cash, "I'm talking with Clint. Did you have anything you want to say to him for a minute?"

"Tell him hi," Cash said as he went over to the stove to check out what was in the skillet. Lifting the lid, he discovered it was scrambled eggs and sausage. All of sudden he was really hungry. Looking over at Lee who had quietly pulled a chair out and sat at the table, he asked, "Want some scrambled eggs 'n sausage? It's real good."

Thinking for a moment, Lee finally said, "Sure, thanks." He looked rather uncomfortable in the presence of the senior McCollum.

Cash got a plate and scooped up a good portion. "Here you go. How 'bout some frosted flakes?"

"That's fine." He glanced up at Cash and gave him a big smile.

Cash could tell Lee was not used to having someone wait on him like this.

Without looking up, Mr. McCollum continued to read the newspaper while nibbling on a piece of toast. It was apparent; there was no way he was going to extend himself to the house guest.

"Did Clayton come home last night?" Cash asked his dad, making an effort to lighten the heaviness hovering around the table.

"How would I know?" Eugene responded with a slight edge of sarcasm to his voice. "Can't keep up with that kid."

Mrs. McCollum concluded her call and placed the receiver back on the cradle. Walking to the table, she looked over at her husband and said, "Clint said Billings is under a snow emergency today and tomorrow."

"I'm surprised the whole damn state isn't under one." As if what he had just said brought something to mind, Cash's father looked up from his paper and directed his full attention to his youngest son. "Speaking of which, you know that most of the roads are closed this morning."

Cash stopped chewing his eggs. His stomach sank. If it wasn't one thing, it was something else, he thought to himself. Glancing over to Lee, he could tell his buddy was not surprised.

"The roads were pretty bad last night," Lee tossed in.

"Mom, this is Lee." Cash made a quick effort to change the subject at hand.

"Hi, Lee," Janice smiled, making an effort to be cordial as she pulled up a chair and poured herself some orange juice from the pitcher on the table.

"Hi." Lee looked up from his eggs and returned her greeting with a grin bearing two cheeks full of food.

Redirecting her attention back to the original topic, Janice looked at her son and asked, "What time were you two planning on leaving?"

"As soon as I get finished feedin' the animals," Cash replied. He knew where this conversation was heading. There was no way he was going to sit around the house with Lee, Clayton and his parents.

"Well, you better find out how the highway is between here and South Dakota before you go galivantin' outta here," Eugene flatly stated.

Janice threw her husband a look of concern. "Gene, do you think the boys should be going down there at all?"

Sitting up in his chair, Eugene snapped irritatedly, "*How would I know?* Cash needs to call the Highway Department and see what the conditions are out there."

Suddenly, the telephone rang just as Clayton shuffled his way into the kitchen. Mrs. McCollum got up to answer it while her middle boy looked over at Lee—scratching his bed-messed hair and slowly sauntering to the cupboard.

"Lee, this is Clayton," Cash offered.

The two boys exchanged simple "hi's".

"…just a moment," Janice said over the phone, looking impishly over to Cash. "Cash, it's Travis."

Oh, Lord, thought Cash, pushing himself away from the table and walking over to the telephone. As his mother handed him the phone, a tiny hint of a smirk crossed her lips.

As Clayton poured milk over his cereal, he looked up and allowed his mouth to spout off the first smart-assed comment of the day. "Nuthin' like gittin' caught between a rock 'n a hard place—huh, Cash?" His eyes traveled from Lee to the telephone, driving his ball into home.

"Hello?" Cash's voice was weak from all the stress he felt inside his guts.

"Hey." Travis' soft, gentle tone sailed through the line directly into Cash's ear.

"Hey." Cash returned the greeting—holding his breath. This definitely was *not* the time to have a chit-chat with him.

"How are you?" Travis asked.

Cash could picture him now—sprawled out on his bed, dressed in one of his collegiate sweatshirts and a pair of worn out, loosened football tights.

"I guess all right," Cash awkwardly replied—knowing what the next question was going to be.

"Did Lee make it down last night?"

"Yeah," Cash answered. "He was pretty worn out though."

There was silence from the other end as if Travis was trying to read between the lines.

"Are you still going down to Rapid City?" he finally continued.

"Plannin' to…" Cash sighed. He was tired of hashing over the same subject, "…as soon as I get finished doin' my chores."

"That's the reason I called…" Travis began.

Right, Cash indignantly thought to himself. There was more to this call than valiant concern over chores. With his other ear, he could hear his mother start up a bit of conversation with Lee at the table.

"So, you're from Great Falls?"

"Yeah, my mom and I live in town."

"That's a pretty area."

"It's all right." Lee conceded. "But I like getting' outta the city and ridin' my horse."

Janice remained silent coaxing the boy to share further.

"I have a horse boarded out at a guy's place, and he lets me ride in his corral any time I want."

That was the most information coughed up by the dark-haired cowboy since they'd met, Cash observed, trying to focus back on Travis.

"…tell your dad I'll be over tomorrow morning to take care of Brownie and the rest of the stock." Travis' voice seemed to trail off—as if distracted by something else.

"Do you wanna talk with him?" Cash offered, wanting to get rid of the phone as if it were a hot potato.

"No, that's okay." Travis paused.

Cash could sense tenseness creep in between them. Travis was fishing.

"You can let him know."

"All right," Cash said, wanting to end this call in the worst way.

Hesitating a bit more, Travis finally went on to say, "I love you."

Turning his back toward the kitchen table, Cash leaned into the mouthpiece as if he was going to eat it and quickly replied, "I love you too." He could sense Lee and the other's attention honed in on the phone conversation.

"Be careful," his boyfriend thoughtfully added.

"I will," Cash replied. God, he needed to end this call.

Cash hung up, taking a deep breath—followed by a heavy, long sigh. Coming back to the table, he announced to his father that Travis would be out the next morning to do his portion of the chores.

Janice allowed a big grin to flood her face. "That's really nice of him." Her admiration of Travis was obvious.

"Just wait," Clayton spoke up, directing his words to Lee. Leaning forward, he crossed his hands—both elbows on the table. "That's what you'll git rewarded with when you move into Cash's inner circle."

"Clayton!" Janice instantly jumped in.

The rest of the morning was dedicated to chores. Lee pitched in, quietly helping Cash make the rounds from the barn and stables out to the corral and pasture.

"You have quite a spread."

"Yeah, it's days like this that sorta suck." Cash threw a bail of hay from the truckbed onto the icy ground. "But over all, I love it here."

Cash gathered that Lee was not a talker. Nearly the entire time they worked was shared in silence—which was okay, he thought—not being in the mood for empty chatter.

By noon, the boys were able to head out for South Dakota. Cash was relieved.

After calling the Highway Department and the Sheriff's office, and having it determined by *everyone* that the roads were passable, they finally received a blessing to hit the road. Mr. McCollum had quietly pulled his son aside and told him they could take the white pick-up—only on one condition—that Cash drive all times. He made it explicitly clear that under *no* circumstances was Lee to operate the vehicle.

"It's because of the insurance coverage."

Cash knew it was more than that.

Thoughtfully, Cash's mother had prepared a cooler-full of food for them. Giving him last minute instructions, she finally directed him back to the kitchen—particularly to the garbage under the sink.

Pointing to the two empty cans of beer, she looked at him seriously, then closed the door. "Don't ever pull that stunt again," she sternly warned. "I almost brought it to your father's attention this morning."

With a sparkle in his eyes, Cash leaned over and hugged her. "Thanks mom."

Janice let out a sigh of exasperation. "Sometimes, I just don't know what to do with you boys."

The quiet that had started with the two boys in the barn yard, traveled with them along the snow-packed highway; perhaps because a lot was on their minds.

For Cash, the concern that Lee probably read Travis' card made him paranoid. It continually gnawed at his thoughts—making him wonder if this entire get-together was nothing more than one huge mistake. One thing was for sure, if Lee had taken note of the card, he had not let on of his discovery—making Cash even more nervous.

Finally, on the other side of Broadus, Lee opened up. "Your family is very dynamic." His voice was thoughtful—and for Cash, extremely intelligent.

"What?" Blankness shot from Cash.

"There's a lot of social interaction within your family."

"Too much of it, if you ask me." Cash snorted.

"No," Lee continued, staring out into the vast horizon of snowy, empty bluffs and fields, "I think that it's good."

They traveled down the road for quite a spell before either of them said anything else. Cash could not get the worry out of his head. What if Lee knew he was gay? What would happen next? Was there ANYTHING he could do to in the 'damage control' department? He wasn't sure. The only thing he could think of was to wait.

As expected, the drive took them longer—getting them into Rapid City later than originally planned. What normally took three hours on clear roads turned out to be five, slow hours. Both boys were hungry, a little tired, and in dire need to take a piss. With the show beginning in less than an hour, it didn't give them much time to do all three.

Glancing at his wristwatch, Lee gave a sigh. "Think we should grab a room before hittin' the show?"

Instantly, Cash's stomach knotted up. *Did anyone think of making reservations at a motel for this week end? Jesus.* Knowing how vacancies magically disappeared during these events, he knew that it would be virtually impossible to get a room last minute. "That's if we can find one."

"Huh?" Lee threw him a bewildering glance.

Suddenly, it became apparent to Cash that Lee had never attended a professional rodeo before. *My God*, he thought to himself in wonderment. It was downright strange that he could make it as far in the ranks of the Association, yet never take the time to see a real-live professional competition.

As they pushed their way through the crowded traffic, Cash got mad at himself. He should have made reservation. He knew better. *Travis would have had this base covered*, he dismally thought to himself. Now, it would be only a miracle if they could find a place to stay.

Like Cash had predicted, all the motels had their no vacancy signs turned on. A sweat broke out underneath his jacket. *Damn it!*

Without warning, Lee sat up in the seat, pointing at an approaching motel. "Turn in here." His voice was commanding.

Swinging into the turning lane, Cash hastily steered his father's rig into the drive. Obediently, he slid into an open spot and threw the truck in neutral. Whatever Lee saw he didn't see. The large sign hanging by the road read *No Vacancy*. *What the hell?*

Lee opened the door and hopped out. Looking back at Cash, his words were emphatic. "Wait here."

Running into the lobby, Lee talked with a man behind the counter who looked like he too was from Middle Eastern decent. Cash watched intently. Occasionally, hands flew out in rapid movement—appearing to be talking up a storm. Within several minutes, Lee came back with a key and receipt.

"Come on!" he said excitedly. "Let's go dump our shit in the room and head over to the Convention Center." He pointed toward the back-end of the building. A residue of a thick accent lingered over his tongue making Cash glance with a look of intrigue.

As Cash navigated the pick-up toward the back entrance, he couldn't help asking, "How'd you do it? How did you get us a room?"

Giving him a sly grin, Lee said lightly, "Never mind. I have my ways."

Hauling their bags up the flight of stairs to the second level, they made their way down the hallway to their room number. Unlocking the door, Lee walked in and flipped the light. Cash followed, lugging his bag and the cooler filled with food. By this time, he was famished, plus he had to piss in the worst way. Walking into the room Cash suddenly caught his breath. There was only one bed. *What was up?* Thoughts came crashing into his mind.

Lee noted the surprise, tossing his bag on a nearby chair and heading for the bathroom. "I know it's only one bed, but it's the *only* unit they had available." The tinkle of a hard piss sounded from the toilet as he went on to say, "We'll just have to make do." His voice was apologetic.

Cash was motionless, remaining quiet, trying to assimilate the arrangement in his head. *Well, this would prove to be interesting*, he thought to himself—looking around the rest of the room with inspecting eyes. It was simple, but neat—very clean with a view overlooking the back lot and a large grove of leafless trees beyond the property fence.

Lee came out of the bathroom still zipping his jeans. "This is okay, no?"

Taking his jacket off, he scurried to the bathroom—feeling as if he was going to explode. "Like you said," he called out to the other boy who had begun to work his way into the cooler. "We'll make do." Somewhere, deep inside, his mind ran wild with possibilities as he could feel the energy between his legs become increasingly excited—making the leak job awfully difficult.

Quickly, they gobbled down some sandwiches and potato chips with a couple of cans of pop. It was what they needed. Cash's stomach was aching for food.

"You're mother was kind to make this," Lee said. Respect weighed in each of his words as he spoke of her.

"She's a sweetie." Cash smiled.

Glancing at the clock on the lamp stand, Lee wiped his mouth with the back of his hand—letting loose of a healthy belch from his guts. "We better be splittin'… parkin's going to be a bitch."

When they got to the Convention Center, Cash took the first available spot and they ran up to the ticket office.

"Wow," Cash exclaimed breathlessly as they finally spotted the ticket area and slowed down to a brisk walk, "this place is pretty big."

"Yeah, no shit," agreed Lee, pulling his wallet out.

They got their tickets and proceeded to find their way to their seats. After milling through a throng of people in the concourse, they finally located home base and planted themselves respectively.

"You know, I wasn't sure we were going to make it here this morning." Cash offered.

"You can say that again," Lee heartily agreed, slipping his jacket off and readjusting his hat. "I had my doubts yesterday evening."

The lights dimmed and spot lights were thrown down on the arena. The music started, blasting from large speakers suspended from the top of the dome while a group of decorated horse riders, each carrying an American flag, came out and rode in dual circles, going in opposite directions. It looked really neat.

Cash was happy they had come. He had looked forward to this for weeks, and now, he told himself it was worth all the crap he had experienced along the line. His eyes scanned the crowds amazed at all the people that were there. The place was packed.

As his gaze wandered aimlessly, he suddenly noticed a couple of cowboys looking in their direction—one even pointing. *What the hell?* he asked himself quizzically. *What were they staring at?* A defensive spirit crept into his flesh. Quickly, he looked away—his eyes darting into another section of the large hall. Ironically, he caught several more individuals gawking at them. With that, he began to feel self-conscious. *What on earth was going on?*

Glancing over to Lee, Cash could tell he was completely engrossed with the program—paying no attention to anything else other than the group of performers in the arena.

With a sigh, he redirected his attention back to the opening activities. Suddenly, there was tap on his shoulder. Sitting back up, he noticed close by his side a young boy standing—hovering over him with a piece of paper and pen.

"Excuse me, sir… are you Cash McCollum?" The kid appeared nervous.

Catching the disturbance from the corner of his eye, Lee turned—honing in on the interesting scene unfolding beside his friend.

Looking at the child, Cash hesitantly smiled, and then went on to say, "Yeah, last time I checked."

The little cowboy beamed with a big, bright smile—minus one front tooth. "You're the number one cowboy in Montana!"

Cash was blown away—dizziness overtaking his senses. He didn't know how to respond.

Shoving the paper and pen into Cash's face, he went on to ask, "Can I get your autograph, sir?"

Cash stared at him—trying to gather some reasoning back to his mind. *Was he for real?*

Lee remained quiet, watching closely with wide eyes.

Taking the piece of paper and the pen into his numb fingers, Cash continued to gaze at the child in disbelief. "I-I guess so." He really was not prepared for this. Quickly, he wrote his name on the sheet and started to hand everything back.

Timidly, the lad went on to ask, "Could you write somethin' on there? My name's Travis and I rode in my first rodeo this last summer." A smile broke out across his face. "My brother's say you're gonna make it big in the Pros soon."

Thinking at first he had been just hit with a full sack of feed, Cash froze at the mention of the little guy's name. *Was it an omen?* He could feel his heart shudder. "Yeah, …sure." Trying to think of something to write, his hand scribbled a hasty— 'Keep on riding!' and addressed it to Travis.

God, he told himself, this was unbelievable.

"Thank you, Cash!" Travis beamed. "You're gonna make it big someday!" With that, the young lad bounded up the steps to where the rest of his family was sitting.

As Cash proceeded to focus his attention once again to the arena, two more people came up to shake his hand and give him best wishes for the coming spring season.

By this time, Lee was fully-turned in his seat, staring in unbelief at Cash and his admirers. He didn't say a word—his face, however, hid no shock.

People from all over continued to gather around Cash and Lee to acknowledge their respect—sometimes asking for an autograph or a couple of informal snap shots. Then, at one point, a big, heavyset kid approached and said, "I've been watching you two this entire year. Best of luck." Vigorously, he shook both their hands. Then, with a hearty grin, he went on to say, "You know, both of you will make one hell of a great team if you stay together."

Cash quickly glanced over toward his partner. Lee let out a gasp. *Wait a minute,* he blinked away the camera flashes to focus better, w*as he seeing things?* Cash instantly froze. *Were there tears welling up in those black eyes?*

Lee instantly looked away.

Not until the first event did the commotion die down. Grateful that they were alone again—neither of them spoke—probably from the bolt that had just struck. *Who would have guessed?*

Several passing moments and Lee finally got up from his seat—softly muttering, "Gonna get a drink. Want anything?"

Cash noticed Lee's hat veiling his eyes. "No, thanks anyway." Intently, he watched his buddy shuffle down the aisle to the concourse. A strangeness settled in and sadness flooded his soul—something was eating at Lee.

Before reaching the motel, Lee ordered Cash to stop at a convenience store. Bounding out of the truck like a wild deer, he ran inside—bee-lining to the coolers. Cash had hardly blinked when his buddy came back clutching a bag against his chest; a rowdy, unmanageable gleam sparkled from his face. Something inside told Cash he was in for one hell of a night. Sort of scaring him, yet finding it rather tantalizing, he could feel his body kick into overdrive. Tonight, he told himself, looking into the crystal ball, a force as powerful as a hundred mustangs would play against him, trying to unravel every construct knitting his trustworthy character. *Father, forgive me…* he earnestly prayed.

"Come on," Lee commanded with a quick nod. "Let's get back to the room."

Cash steered the truck back onto the street and drove to the motel.

Walking into their unit, Cash suddenly felt overwhelmingly tired, a-deep-in-the-bones exhaustion. What a day! He told himself. He sure wasn't ready for what Lee obviously had planned. Plunking himself wearily on the bed, he lowered down as slowly as possible—every muscle in his body aching from all the tension that had built up.

"Jesus," he gasped with effort. "I feel like I've just done the whole circuit."

Lee closed the door behind him, making sure it was locked. "What's the matter? You winkin' out on me?"

"I feel beat." Cash's voice trailed off as he raised an arm over his forehead—covering his eyes.

"Hey, come on there, little cowpoke," Lee chuckled softly as he placed the beer on the small table and walked over to what apparently had become Cash's side of the bed. "We've got some brews to slam down before we hit the hay." Reaching into his shirt pocket, he pulled out his pack of crumpled cigarettes—firing one up. With his head thrown back, he blew the smoke out into the room with a steady stream. "Fuck, this tastes good," he sighed, sitting down on the edge of the bed, close to Cash. "Wanna hit?" He took another drag and held the smoke out.

Nodding, Cash weakly replied, "Yeah." Taking the cigarette from Lee's fingers, he drew it slowly to his own lips.

"Here," Lee said, jumping up from the bedside and going over to the table. "This'll perk you up." Pulling a couple of beers out of the case, he opened the cans and handed one to Cash.

Grabbing the pillows, Cash pushed himself up on the bed—his back resting against the head board. He took the beer and gratefully guzzled several swallows of the chilly brew. Lee was right; it sure hit the spot as he had worked up a mighty-big thirst at the rodeo. He had gotten so caught up with the events; the last thing he had thought was boppin' down to the concession stands to buy a soda. By the time he sucked the can half-down, he noticed Lee finishing his first one—starting on another. It shouldn't have been a surprise that his buddy was such a hard drinker—considering how intense his nature seemed, but it caught him off-guard. In many ways, Lee seemed older, even though he was still in high school.

"How old are you?" Cash asked, half-expecting a defensive retort to come his way.

"I'll be nineteen next month." There was no distrustful attitude in Lee's tone.

The beer must be working its way into that rough-edged personality, Cash reasoned to himself. Going ahead and finishing off the cigarette, he watched Lee light up another one—drawing the smoke in and blowing it out as a series of perfect smoke rings. It looked neat.

"I was held back a year because I was having a difficult time with school. Nothing much to it, really. We only spoke Turkish at home, maybe that was part of the problem."

"So you speak two languages?" Cash gazed at Lee with amazement; he found himself impressed.

"Actually, I can speak four." Lee gulped down some more beer and took another drag from his smoke. "I understand English, Turkish, Arabic, and a little French."

Cash laughed. He could feel himself getting loosened from the beer. That was incredible, he told himself. He had never known anyone who could talk so many languages.

"At the mosque they usually speak Arabic, and I've been to France several times to visit relatives with my parents."

"How did you end up here in America?" Cash, once again, was tickled by his curiosity. Lee was interesting—with a lot to him not revealed on the surface.

"My dad is a medical doctor," Lee freely answered, sucking down more smoke. "The Turkish government had sent him here to get his degree—expecting him to go back and serve the homeland. Some things happened and he decided to stay in the States to start up a practice on the West Coast." Tossing Cash another beer, Lee swallowed the last of his second one and flipped open the tab to his third. "So," the words from Lee's mouth began to slur a little bit, "what about you?" He gave a small wink from a smiling eye.

Shrugging his shoulders, Cash slid over to the side of the bed, throwing his boots to the floor. He started to drink down his next can of beer. "Not much to tell you. My family's nuthin' but a bunch of roughnecks that hale from the river bottoms of the Yellowstone River."

Locking his gaze on Cash, Lee allowed a grin to shape his lips. "You're too humble."

Cash gave a snort and smiled back at his friend. For the umpteenth time, they caught themselves staring at each other—not shifting their eyes away for one second. Cash could feel whatever it had been possessing him the night before resurrect itself from dormancy. Seeming to rise from slumber, it stretched out with full-force—pounding away at his will. He knew he was growing weak.

Emptying out his third beer, Lee mechanically reached for his fourth. "Tell me, Cash, why is it you'd spend your time with someone who's second best?"

"Huh?" Cash gulped down several huge swallows of the golden liquid—tingling in his mouth and throat as it slid down. Frowning, he tried to figure out where Lee was coming from.

Keeping on track, not wavering to either side, Lee zeroed in on the boy sitting at the edge of the bed. As he worked nearly half of his newly opened can with several hearty swallows, he froze in his attention and asked with a raspy, deep-throated whisper, "What the *hell* do you see in me?"

Cash allowed a small chuckle to escape. His brain started to feel a little fuzzy. "Funny, that's what I ask of people all the time." The thought of one particular person came to mind as he continued to eye Lee, wondering where this conversation was heading.

Lee's eyes narrowed—prowling, pacing the situation with precise calculation, Lee allowed his stare to penetrate Cash like fangs of a hungry mountain lion. Pushing his cowboy hat back, he asked with a soft, low voice, "You could have easily blown me off—many people do, but you haven't. Why?"

Cash shrugged; the force of the beer continued to work away at him. "I dunno, you seem like a nice guy."

Lee snickered, evidence of his succumbing to the alcohol flooding his veins. "Yeah, right," he said cynically. Instantly, he reached over and grabbed another can, throwing it to Cash. "Here, have another one."

Cash gulped the remainder of what was in his hand before opening the next one. It wasn't long until his body began to feel things. Something was happening. Like being plunked into a big bowl of Jell-O, his world began to wobble and weave. It was a weird sensation… but a sweet one, he determined.

Lee stared, his gaze riveting. From that point on, there was no retreat. Firing up another smoke, Lee shot the smoke out of his nostrils like an angry bull. His words, however, continued to be smooth and easy. "Cash, can I ask you a question?"

"Yeah." Cash was defenseless.

"What is it that you want?" Lee continued to stare straight into Cash.

Slowly, Cash pushed a smile across his lips—taking another drink from the can. "I dunno what you mean." Inside, he knew damn well what Lee was driving at. In all honesty, he was hot for it—fuckin' crazy for it. Since the last rodeo, he knew he desired this Biruni kid in the worst way.

Neither boy moved. The room became still as Cash imagined Lee's fingers over hungry flesh. Owning, possessive, he yearned to submit to his power.

Gaping silence passed between them. Finishing the beer he had in his hand, Lee methodically rested it on the table and took another one from the case. "Fuck," he hissed—his impatience rising. "Let's go at this from another angle."

Rising to his feet, Lee unsnapped his shirt, slipping it off to reveal a well-developed chest carpeted with a layer of soft, flowing hair. He was delicately covered from one nipple to the other, from the base of his breasts, to that warm, soft area Cash always called 'the valley of the neck'. Flexing his muscles, allowing an ocean of ripples and ridges to flow out from his flesh, Lee stretched out his arms—resting his hands behind his cowboy hat.

He's posing, Cash desperately told himself. His mouth fell open. *He wants me to see his body.*

Eyeing Cash closely, Lee took a step toward the bed, allowing his arms to fall back at his side. "You like what you see, Cash?"

Cash's heart pounded. He wanted another beer—another smoke... something.

Lee went on. "Does this look good?" He swiveled his neck for a glance at the dresser mirror. "I think I look pretty good." The words slid from his lips smooth and extremely seductive; underneath, however, came a bite.

"Maybe not the best, but I've had my share." His smile was full of teeth, but the look in his eyes was something different. "What about you, Cash?"

It was one of those questions that couldn't quite be answered because it wasn't quite understood, so Cash remained quiet on the bed, suddenly finding his focus narrowing, his eyes dimming. Nearly dropping the beer can onto the bed, he hastily drank it up, placing it securely on the nightstand.

"There's one thing that's eating at me." Slowly, Lee sat down on the bed beside Cash—his leg pressing strongly, deliberately up against the thigh of his half-drunk buddy. He did not pull away.

"What's that?" An edgy, nervous feeling quickly came over Cash. It came with such a start that for a few seconds he was sober. But just as rapidly as it had appeared, it subsided.

Slowly, Lee leaned in towards Cash, and without a blink, he said, "It's you."

Without warning, Lee grabbed Cash's shoulders and shoved him down on the bed with an unbeatable, full force—sinking his mouth hard, firmly across Cash's. The kiss was rough, wild, and unpredictable. Gasping for air, Cash pulled back instinctively, wary of what was going to happen next. Instantly, Lee grabbed Cash's golden, silky hair and anchored his head—sinking his tongue deeply between trembling lips. Lee's strength was unrelenting—giving no break, no reprieve.

In spite of the onslaught and Cash's will to bring it on, his eyes suddenly envisioned a burly jock coming upon him with magnitude force. *Travis!* Instantly, his conscience awoke. He instinctively countered Lee's grasp, turning aside just enough to cause Lee to fumble his hold.

"What the fuck…." Lee pulled up. "What the fuck you doin'?"

"What the fuck YOU doin'?" Cash cried, once free—feeling like a damned hypocrite.

Lee spat into the room and fell onto the bed beside him. With an arm over his head, he closed his eyes and asked, "Would you mind tellin' me what's your problem?"

Cash didn't know what to say. Stalling for time, he jumped off the bed and headed to the bathroom. Calming himself, he dispensed some beer.

"I can't do this," he called, his words echoing off the tiles. "I mean, I'm not…."

"I know what you are and what you're not."

When Cash returned, Lee was lying still, half-dressed. "Don't bullshit me." Suddenly his arms fell to his side, and he turned his head slightly on the pillow, eyes watery. "I know…" Then his voice fell away.

Still unsure, Cash stood for a second looking in Lee's direction. He didn't know if he should attempt to get back into the bed, or continue to stand there swaying and simply pass out. Reluctantly, he settled atop the covers, resisting the sudden urge to touch Lee's arm, or any part of his body for that matter, Cash turned out the light and spoke into the darkness.

"What you know and what you think you know, well I'm not gonna deny...
but just remember there are reasons. Deep ones. Don't forget that."

For a long time Lee was quiet. In fact, it seemed so long that Cash thought
perhaps he had fallen asleep, until the cold words blew from his mouth.
"Christ, I feel wasted." Eventually, after that, he started to snore.

Cash awoke to the sound of the shower, and almost just too soon, the
water snapped off. Lee strode into the room, toweling himself casually,
comfortable in his nakedness. Cash instinctively checked to see if he was
still dressed, now remembering that he had gone to bed with his clothes
on. Trying and failing to sit up, he fell back on the pillow and exclaimed
"Jesus" because his head suddenly shot through with a billion tiny buckshot.
"Jesus" as he tried again, hearing Lee's soft chuckle.

After a take-out breakfast at a fast food place, they rode home in strange
silence. Lee pushed himself down in the seat, pulling his hat over his eyes,
and quickly falling asleep. Cash could hear his rhythmic breath almost the
entire way home and was curious how Lee managed it. Glancing over now
and then at his strange new friend, he asked himself over and over what
had happened last night. But as many times as he asked that question,
he couldn't come up with an answer—at least one that was honest. They
drove straight to Miles City, not stopping again except for gas, in a quiet
suitable for a church.

"No," he said, he didn't want to come in. He needed to get home.

Cash stood astonished as he watched Lee load his gear into his pick-up.
"You don't even want anything to eat? No dinner? *Nothin?*"

Lee kept his head down and focused on the task at hand. "Nope. Gotta
hit the road."

That would mean he would spend most of the night driving, not getting home until morning. The action cut through Cash cleaner than the sharpest steel.

"Well, let me know if you get home okay."

With that comment Lee turned back, ready to step into the cab. "Thing is," he said, "if I don't get home okay, that's when you won't know."

Puzzled and hurt, Cash watched Lee drive off, and when he went into the house he avoided both parents, not hungry and not tired and not even wanting a bath. He just made his way slowly up to his room, each step with an anchor attached. He thought he would just fall, clothes and all into his own bed and lay there to rot.

The call came early in the morning as Cash was getting ready for school. *School!* He thought with amusement when he woke in the morning. *I still have to go to school!* Travis would be there, waiting for him, angry that he hadn't called the night before. Well, he reasoned, Mr. Hunter could have just as easily called me, and he didn't. He was drying off from a hot shower when his mother's voice announced from the other side of the bathroom door that the phone was for him.

"You asked me to call, so I am." His tone shooting from the other end of the line was bullet-sharp. It was Lee.

"Great. Thanks, Lee. I was worried." Cash pulled the phone into his bedroom and closed the door.

"*Were you?*" Defiance reigned from the ear piece.

The sarcasm was jarring, but Cash was beginning to realize it was something he would have to get used to with him. After all, he had gotten *more* than used to it with Clayton.

"Yeah. Why do you have to say it like *that*?" He paused and nervously swallowed. "I was." He allowed the small hurt to escape from his voice. He could hear the child crying in the background again. "I'm glad you made it okay," relenting, not allowing Lee's attitude to get to him. As if the relationship seemed born of it, silence came between them. Cash was ready to say his good-bye, when Lee's voice crept through the line.

"I need to talk to you." There was an odd, distant longing in his voice.

"What about, Lee?" Cash pressed the receiver tight against his ear.

There was the sound of a deep sigh being released, which was comforting, in its way, because it reminded Cash that Lee must be having *some* emotions stirring beneath that frigid surface of his.

"What's your relationship with Travis?"

Cash was taken back. *What a strange question to be asked while getting ready for school.* He almost said something, but reined himself back. "What do you mean?"

"Tell me, what's Travis to you?" Calmly, Lee chose his words with accuracy. Cash could detect a hot jealousy snapping through the telephone cord.

Trying to shut down his emotions, Cash hastily replied, "Ain't nonna your business, Lee, about me and Travis."

"*What?*" The question from Lee was sincere, throwing Cash.

"You heard me…."

"That's not what I meant." Lee interrupted, in a lowered tone.

"Well, what did you mean?" Cash turned to look at the clock, realizing if he didn't hurry he would be late. *Why hadn't this been brought up at the motel?* Then, he thought, the hell with it. This relationship was becoming a sea of confusion, anger, impatience and, trumping everything else, the specter of desire—threatening to start an unbridled fire that could ignite his entire world.

It was all returning to their night at the motel. Cash knew it would never be allowed to rest.

"Do you see yourself as being too good for anything else but the best?" Lee drove in his stake.

"I don't make comparisons in my friends." Cash was amazed it was coming to this. Quietly, he began gathering up his books on the desk, needing an outlet for his adrenalin. "You're just as successful as I am. I've just lucked out on a couple of rides… that's all."

Lee sneered. "Like hell. You're better and you know it. You don't act it out, but deep down, you damn well know it."

Silence, once again, engulfed them. Where was Lee taking this? Cash helplessly asked himself.

"When am I going to see you again?" Lee finally asked, throwing a complete curve. There was desperation in his voice.

"Well…" Cash's voice trailed to a whisper. His mind was blank—there had been too many kicks.

Lee hesitated, as if expecting more—demanding it. Then within the harmonic chasm of static, he shouted an explosive bull's eye, "God damn it!" and with a popping click, the call was ended. Cash felt shot down— dead on the spot—still dripping, the towel half-draped over his naked flesh.

Chapter 18

As usual, the wind across the prairie was harsh and cold. It even seemed to penetrate deeply into the protective ravines of the river bottoms. Although the sun was out—with only occasional, wispy cirrus here or there, the air carried a frosty sting, reminding everyone what time of the year it was.

Gathering himself together after Lee's unexpected, unnerving phone call, Cash got cleaned up. He slipped on his favorite pair of western jeans—the chocolate brown ones—with his well-worn, pointy-toed cowboy boots and the soft leather belt bearing the big, brassy rodeo buckle awarded him from the Association the year before. After a moment of deciding what shirt he would go with, he selected the solid-pale red cotton one with shiny-black pearl snaps. With a hasty last-minute inspection in the dresser mirror, he concluded that he looked pretty sharp—in spite of how he felt.

When he got to school, an unsettled feeling hung over his spirit. This should have been a day to call off sick, he told himself. He dreaded the moment he would have to face Travis. And as Murphy's Law went, that moment arrived a lot sooner than anticipated—with a tight-faced, flat-topped, muscle-bound jock standing at attention—as if stationed for guard-duty at the main entrance of the school building.

Spotting Travis approach with his brisk military step, Cash's stomach tied up in knots. *Oh, God,* he thought. "Hey." Cash tried to sound casual—his heart pounding heavily.

With a stony look of assumption, Travis spoke without a blink. "What's up? What's goin' on, Cash?" The look in his eyes blazed as if he could see right through the cornered cowboy.

"Not much," Cash hesitantly replied. Instantly, he knew he needed to bring together a quick plan. Defensively, he told himself, his winning strategy would be the withholding of information. Having two older brothers taught him well on that one. Secondly, he needed a sound, offensive plan… therefore, it would be imperative to show Travis that nothing—*absolutely nothing*—was going to get his goat. He took a deep breath.

"What time did you get in last night?" Travis' gaze was piercing.

"I was tired." Cash pretended to be nonchalant.

Front and center, Travis crossed his arms and spread his feet, his voice expectant. "I waited for your call…"

"Really?" Cash tried to act surprised—hoping his other half would know now what he had felt several weeks ago. "Well, the phone line works both ways." *If the shoe fits, wear it,* Cash went on to tell himself. In a sick sort-of-way, he found this rather fun.

Travis snorted like a brahma in the bull pen. "Imagine that."

"Yup, it's quite a concept, I think," Cash quipped, pushing his cowboy hat back and tossing Travis a big, dimply grin.

"You're pretty cocky today." Travis' face became flush with anger. It was obvious he was prepared for a fight.

"Yeah?" Cash asked innocently.

"Uh huh." Travis nodded, his lips tighter than a lid on a Mason jar. "Oh, yeah... Speaking of calls, your family waited all evening to hear from you." Pausing briefly to allow his words to sink in, he continued, "Maybe they were expecting too much."

Cash pushed forward, making his way to his locker. As good as his intentions were, Travis was starting to get at him. Following right on his heel, his boyfriend kept working the same sore spot.

"It's just like what Clayton said to me out in the barn yesterday morning..."

"And what was that?" *This oughta be good*, Cash cynically thought.

"'Outta sight... Outta mind...'"

"Well, what in the hell do you think *I went through* Christmastime?"

Travis studied him closely. "So, how was your time with Tex? Did you both find a chance to get to know each other a little bit better?"

"His name is Lee, and don't go there. I'm warnin' ya." Tossing his jacket as if it were a horseshoe, Cash grabbed for his books and slammed the door.

"Ooh!" exclaimed Travis. "Struck a soft nerve." His voice dripped of sarcasm. "A little touchy we are this morning, huh?"

Looking at Travis with a bolt of fire, Cash shot his words as if they were rounds from a semi-automatic. "Back off, Travis!"

"So did you have a fun time down in Rapid?" Travis kept going—whittling away at Cash's barricade.

Cash ignored him, scooting around the defensive block, setting off toward his first class.

"Where are you taking this, Cash?" Travis called—still positioned by the lockers.

Something inside made Cash stop in his tracks. Staring blankly down the long corridor, he stood speechless, not turning back.

Travis continued. "What are you trying to accomplish? Too hurt me? Get back at me? Kick me in the dirt?" Nodding with a venomous resolution, he throated deeply under his breath, "You're doin' one *hell* of a good job."

"Why do you have to always push it?" Cash demanded, swinging around and facing him full-front. "You can't let an issue drop until you've driven it in the ground."

"Funny, I was just thinkin' the same damn thing about you."

Without warning, the period bell rang.

"I need to go," Cash awkwardly said, resuming his charted course. About a dozen hasty steps later, he spoke back to Travis, "We'll talk later."

"You bet we will." Travis' heavy voice boomed clearly throughout the hallway.

Cash thought he might drive home for a quick snack and then maybe take a wander around with Brownie. Besides, there was no way he wanted to revisit the entrée he had savored with Travis earlier that morning. He rushed through a few stoplights and eventually found himself on the main strip heading out of town. Realizing there was something silent, earnest, pecking away at his will, he pulled into a nearby gas station. It was apparent that a long distance call to Great Falls was in standing good order. He hopped out and went to a pay phone. Looking around the parking lot for a minute, he tried to gather thoughts that just wouldn't come. He let out a long sigh. With a quick prayer, he pulled out his card and dialed the number. On the first ring, he knew this call was already overdue.

To Cash's relief it was Lee who answered.

"Hey." He knew he didn't need to say more, Lee would know who it was.

"Cash," he responded, hesitating.

Suddenly all of the anger he had been feeling earlier in the day starting with Lee's abrupt hang-up, and roiling more fully with his encounter with Travis, faded with the sound of Lee's voice, which was soft now, almost quiet.

"Lee," Cash began, aware of his urgent craving for a cigarette, "I been thinking about what we talked about this morning. I thought I..." but then, the hurt broke through, never having left. "I don't know what I did to piss you off like that, and I think you need to tell me why."

There was a long silence. Cash was worried maybe Lee hadn't heard him.

"Are you there?"

He heard a cough. "I heard you, Cash. I heard you."

Cash could hear the sound of crackling paper, then a rough laugh. "I sure could use a smoke right now. Mom won't allow smoking in the house."

"I know how you feel." Cash was willing to wait.

"I'm not sure what you want me to say," Lee continued after a moment. "I think you..."

"I don't owe you anything, Lee." Cash interrupted.

"No, not that. I know you don't. But, I think I would...like to know more about where you're coming from."

Where I'm coming from? Cash was willing to let it slide, however. He suddenly had the feeling that this conversation wasn't really about him anyway. "Not sure what you mean."

"I'm not sure I do, either. It's just that..." Lee stopped. "This thing is really fucked up."

"I told you anything between me and Travis, or *anyone,* ain't your concern." His face was suddenly hot. "You just need to stay out of all that shit instead of gettin' mad at me 'n then hangin' up on me." A truck roared down the street nearby. Cash waited to continue. "I wanna know what the fuck I did for something like that."

"I just want to know where I...where we..." but then he stalled.

"You wanted to know if you were better, or somethin'. And you were trying to make these comparisons, and all, and then you got pissed at ME 'cuz I'm not havin' none of it."

Cash's breathing was coming hard now, the blood surging through his ears. "I'm willin' to be your friend, Lee, but Christ sake, I'm not gonna put up with shit like that."

"Just friends, Cash?" Surprisingly, Lee didn't sound upset. His voice was calm, almost still. "I see something more in your eyes when you look at me."

The simple statement managed to pull all the fight from Cash. Now it was his turn to hang up, but he wasn't going to do that. He wasn't going to leave this itch unscratched. "Listen to me, Lee." He paused to try to think clearly. "What happened..." Hesitating, he quickly reasoned with himself. What *had* actually happened? Truth be known, he was too honest with himself to blame it all on being drunk. He didn't think Lee would use that excuse either—although he might try. What had happened, however, they had *both* wanted at that time.

"What happened isn't important." There. He would just let the statement lie and see if Lee picked it up.

"Yep, no big thing," Lee agreed. "Was that why you called?"

At first, his blood started going again, but then Cash recognized the playful tone and relented.

"Course not. Just, why'd you hang up on me? That was a shitty thing to do."

"I'm sorry about that. I shouldn't have done it. I guess I was tired—had been taking something to keep me awake on the drive home and I was probably wired out. Probably kind of crazy too. I shouldn't have done that, Cash. I shouldn't have done..."

Cash cut Lee off. "Yeah, another thing... I don't want to talk about Travis. He's not a part of this." He wanted to ensure the point was driven home.

"If you say so." Lee had no other option but give in to the decree. "Somehow, I think...well, don't matter what I think on that, does it?"

An uneasy, peculiarly restrained silence now fell between them—providing little, if any, balm on their sore psyches.

Lee spoke first. "When we gonna get together again?"

Cash shouldn't have been surprised to see the Viper sitting in the driveway as he made his way around the bend, but he was. Once again, his guts tightened up. He had just begun feeling somewhat better after the phone call with Lee. All that, however, seemed to flee to snowy pasture as he pulled the 'Puppy' in beside the red jewel.

Setting the brake, Cash wondered how Travis managed to keep that fricken car so clean—even in the dead of winter. *Everything* about him was pristine perfect. At first, he had thought it was impressive, but the more he got to know him, the more it seemed just plain intimidating—if not irritating.

How in the hell did Travis get to the house so early? He must have skipped last period as well, reasoned Cash. *Did he see me duck out the back door after Government class?* The question popped into his mind as he stomped the snow and mud off his boots. Well shit! Was there *anything* that could pass by Travis without notice?

To his discovery, the house was quiet as he searched for signs of life either downstairs or upstairs. Everyone was probably out in the barn or the stables, he reasoned—going back outside into the bitter cold.

Opening the door, there they were—the two most unlikely paired characters. Travis and Clayton busily loaded hay in the back of the flatbed. To his astonishment, Travis was beginning to look like a real-live, working cowboy with his dirty-frayed jeans, Clayton's worn-out hat, and manure-caked boots. The scene warmed a cold part of his heart.

"… here, you take 'em like this." Clayton grabbed onto a bale and flung it squarely against the stack situated on the flatbed.

Travis silently watched.

He looked so damned cute. Cash allow a grin to sweep his face—erasing the wrinkles of annoyance that had been accumulated throughout the day. It was a true sight for sore eyes. What attracted that kid to this family? He asked himself, standing quietly in the barn entrance—hands thrust deep into his pockets. While this multi-talented, richer-than-snot, with-looks-to-die-for stud could literally go for the gusto—here he was, grunting away on a hay pile at a two-bit ranch. It just didn't make sense.

Cash stood there several minutes soaking in the scenery—admiring his boyfriend working hard with his brother. He would have never guessed in a million years those two would be hitting it off. Where Travis was so particular and refined, Clayton was the exact opposite. There wasn't another individual he knew quite like his older sibling. One look into his room would tell anyone that discipline and organization were not part Clayton's philosophy on life.

And while the McCollum's good looks had been divvied out pretty evenly between Clint and Cash—each bearing their share of rugged, easy-to-look-at masculine features; the genetic union creating Clayton must have kicked into hyper-drive as he had popped out of the womb with beauty that could make people stop in their tracks.

Those huge, puppy-dog eyes, rosy cheeks, a large, dimpled smile carried by full lips were just the start. The rest of his face appeared like it had been sculpted by angels. A sexy, cleft chin, heavy-brooding brows, sharply-angled forehead and feathered, chestnut-brown hair gave Clayton a movie-star appearance. Looking at him could take a person's breath away. In all honesty, it was his body, namely his gut that lacked appeal. Years of inactivity and increased drinking brought about a sizeable roll around Clayton's belly, stripping his edge of outstanding looks and great physical prowess. How he could let it all go, get out of shape, and drink so much, Cash would never know.

And while on the subject of Clayton, there were other things that seemed to come natural to him such as math, taking things apart and putting them back together. For Cash, all that stuff was like swimming up the river—being somewhat a struggle.

So, with all that said, it wasn't any secret that Clayton's greatest shortcoming seemed to fall in the area of social skills. His sarcastic, acidy nature could sting the most thick-skinned individual. Generally, he lacked any sensitivity towards others—especially their feelings. Perhaps that was why he had no girlfriend; or anyone in particular to hang out with. Considered pretty much of a loner through and through, he never seemed to talk about doing things with other people. Which made Cash wonder just exactly where did he go in the evenings? What did he do, and who was he with until the wee-hours of the morning?

Remaining by the barn doors, he continued to watch the scene unfold as if on stage. The raw truth, Cash knew he had taken his plan of the Christmas vacation revenge a step too far. He had never intended it to go to this degree…

Or had he?

Was he interested in Lee? Was he the culprit for what happened over the weekend? It sure appeared that way. A stinging pang bit at his conscience. What would be next? Would they honestly be able to settle into a casual friendship? There were doubts. Indeed, there seemed to be a compelling force pulling him deeper… deeper than just rodeo buddies. Perhaps his father was right; Lee was doing nothing more than setting him up to bring him down.

Clearing his throat, Cash watched Clayton and Travis' attention instantly shift from the hay bales.

Allowing a big, broad smile to flood his handsome face, Travis let out a small, "Hey," and took off his gloves—walking slowly towards Cash.

Eyeing closely, Cash noticed that Travis was getting a typical cowboy-swagger to his feet.

"Hey."

Clayton let out a loud sigh. "No smoochin', you two." He resumed his attention back to the hay. "Who knows, I might like it…" His voice trailed off.

Cash threw a quizzical glance at his brother. *Had he heard right?* Surely, he was only joking.

"You wanted to talk with me?" Cash felt schizophrenic. Caught between a major hard-on and cold terror, he held his breath. How was Travis going to approach this matter? From the sound of his words earlier that morning, he braced himself for the worst.

Gently leading Cash by the shoulder out into the yard, Travis took in a long breath. "You really disappointed me this weekend." He spoke bluntly, but the tone in his voice was sensitive.

Cash could feel muscles across his face tense up—those freakin' eyelids! Shivering and shaking, he could barely focus. He knew if he spoke, he would start crying. *Damn it!* Why did he have to get so soft each time they had a serious discussion? This just wasn't the McCollum style.

"Everyone thought you would call when you got there," Travis went on to say. The look in his eyes revealed more hurt than anger. "Your dad was worried that a wreck had happened to you two out in the middle of nowhere. He wanted to call the State Police several times to see if anything had been reported."

Putting his head down, Cash pushed out his apology. "I'm sorry." He felt badly about all the frustration he had caused. Being so focused on Lee, the thought of calling his family hadn't even crossed his mind. If the tables were turned, he would have been upset as well. No wonder his dad had been silent throughout breakfast. He didn't utter a single word the entire time they had sat together at the table. Now, he knew why.

"Cash, no one knew what to do. None of us knew what was up until you drove the pick-up into the driveway yesterday afternoon." Travis paused— looking squarely into Cash's jade eyes. "You had us all worried."

Fixing an intent gaze on Travis, Cash let out a heavy sigh. "I'm sorry, I really am."

Allowing the silence of the moment to sink in, Travis finally stepped up to Cash. And taking him into those burly arms, he softly spoke with a smile, "I'm just grateful you're okay."

Turning off Lee's memory and taking in Travis' warmth, Cash felt dizzy-crazy… schizophrenic. The questions and doubts seem to flee, vanish. Suddenly, everything seemed organized again—sorted out and back in place. Once again, he knew who he belong to. And thus, with the weekend being put behind him, Lee now looked awfully far away.

CHAPTER 19

With colleges temporarily put on the back burner, and Lee neatly tucked away in Great Falls, everything seemed to be falling in line and in its proper place. So the slow, winter-weary weeks passed, and Cash found himself busy with studies, chores, and Travis. Thankfully, the dust was settling between them even though nothing was being addressed. It was as if everything was in a holding pattern—or perhaps better said, swept under the rug.

A week after Valentines, a bombshell dropped. Looking back, Cash knew he should have suspected it—taking everything into consideration concerning Lee...

"Why can't I ever see you? There's gotta be a time we can get together." Typical of his recent calls, Lee's voice was a balanced drone of wheedling and pleading. "You never take time out to come see me."

Sensing the vise tightening, Cash instinctively served up the only excuse that could come to mind, "There's a lot of responsibilities I need to take care of around here. With Dad unable to pitch in... well, you know what I mean."

"No, you really don't want to see me..."

Now even though Lee live hundreds of miles away, there was one thing which Cash hadn't calculated... that his rodeo friend was a mobile creature—able and more than willing to transport himself any time, anywhere, or when so desired. And within that cowboy's timeclock, a trip to Miles City was now in good standing. Cash knew if he would have seen this one coming down the trail, he would have definitely headed it off at the pass. Unfortunately, with little foresight and no access to a crystal ball, the visit came as a complete and unexpected shock...

Bounding to his locker, Cash was looking forward to an afternoon at the Hunter house. Grabbing his jacket, he pushed his way through the throng of students in the hallway to the front entrance. As he turned the corner, he could see Travis' head scanning the crowd, occasionally talking with various individuals passing by him. As Cash got closer, something caught his attention that sent his heart into a tail spin. It couldn't be, he told himself, instantly shifting his attention to what captured his eye. Tip-toeing in his boots, he struggled to get a view over the milling heads. *That black cowboy hat sure looked familiar.* In fact, it looked like...

He couldn't believe it. Standing quietly by the door, directly across from Travis, was Lee. This couldn't be... it absolutely couldn't be!

"Tell me this is a goddamn dream," Cash muttered under his breath as he approached the two boys. Feeling his muscles turn to gelatin, he wondered if it was too late to duck out the back door. Surely, there was a logical explanation for all of this.

As if thoughts in his head were escaping telepathically, both young men turned and focused on Cash. He instinctively desired to recoil and slither into a dark hole like a cornered rattlesnake. *Oh, my God...* he helplessly thought to himself—*I'm dead!*

Who was he going to approach first? His mind shifted into hyper-drive. Shit, did it matter? Either way, he knew this was going to end up bad—*major bad*. Slipping by a group of kids jabbering in the center of the hallway, Cash strolled toward Lee, pasting on a frantic, last-minute smile. "Lee, w-what are you doing here?" His words came out in chunks and pieces—his eyes revealing cold terror.

Lee's grin froze. "I had planned to call." The look in his eyes instantly revealed his knowledge that a line had been crossed. "I mean, I was on my way to see a friend in Forsyth. Thought I'd stop by and see if I could find you."

Cash stood facing Lee, trying to force more words from his mouth. From the corner of his vision, he could see Travis quickly step in by his side. Each man took their stand. In a fast effort of survival, Cash gestured with a trembling arm, "Travis, this is Lee—Lee Biruni from Great Falls." Glancing over toward Travis, he could see his boyfriend's face become set in stone.

Lee extended a hand, but was met with only an icy vapor of air. Travis did not speak... he did not move. It was as if he had become a frozen statue of glistening granite.

"Saw you on television." Lee's stare riveted to Travis'.

Neither boy blinked, nor budged a muscle as Cash stood horrified—fumbling for something, anything to say.

'Yeah?" Travis spoke lightly—in almost a whisper. His face was beet-red.

"Yeah." Lee looked undaunted—a smirk creeping over his lips. It was obvious he had prepared for this encounter. "Looked good. You knew all the right things to say."

"I always do." Travis rigidly maintained his stance.

"I'm sure." Lee spoke in a condescending tone—nodding slowly in mock agreement. Keeping his gaze locked on Travis, he allowed a tiny chuckle to escape as he slurred out a cocky, "All right." He seemed to go out of his way to show he wasn't scared of Travis—or his size.

Turning to Cash, Lee drew a deep breath—the hardness in his eyes softening a bit. "How ya doin'?"

Feeling as if someone's fingers had been forged around his neck, Cash found it difficult to take in air. "All right." His words squeaked out. "I'm just surprised to see you."

Adjusting the hat on his head, Lee allowed a full, white-teethed smile to flood his face. "We haven't talked for awhile. Say, you still got that horse for sale? I'd like to see it." There was a sly gleam in the eyes; his mannerisms were slow and deliberate.

Travis quickly jumped in, looking over to Cash. "Thought Clayton decided not to sell that Paint."

"It's a different one," Cash hesitantly replied, not really sure he was heading down the right trail. They didn't have any horses for sale as far as he was aware of. It was worth a shot, he desperately told himself. He'd go for broken straws at this point.

"Well, I believe you should have made an appointment." Travis stepped in closer to Cash, blocking Lee. He wanted to make sure Lee knew he was taking over. "Cash and I have plans this afternoon; so I guess you'll just have to come back some other time."

Lee's eyes scanned Travis from head to toe, his face unreadable. "Nice to see you have it all under control."

"Always do," Travis spoke with strong assurance.

"Really?" Lee exclaimed in a low whisper. His eyebrows rose as if surprised. Pulling out all stops, it became apparent he wanted a direct confrontation. "You could fool me." His words came out sharp and sarcastic—slicing the big athlete into slender pieces.

With anger igniting, Cash had had all he could take. "All right, you two, knock it off." His emotions began to fire up at Travis, knowing that the case had already been reviewed and the verdict delivered regarding him and Lee. On the other hand, he was consumed with contempt toward Lee for assuming he could take his boyfriend on with a direct face-off. What made him think he could come in here and throw his weight around?

Several kids glanced over as they shuffled their way out of the building. Finally, the last of the stragglers sifted outside leaving the three boys alone in a very quiet hallway—standing silently as if huddled around a casket at someone's wake. For all Cash knew, it was his own.

Just then, as the tension reached its crescendo, a whining voice bellowed throughout the hallway followed by the clopping of waddling feet. "Hey Cash!"

It was Jennifer.

What timing, thought Cash. "Hey, Jen." One more coal added to the flame wouldn't make a difference at this point. This entire situation was out of control.

Travis turned and glared at her with a look of disgust. Lee's mouth dropped open—amazed at her brash, blatant behavior.

"Hey, I need to talk with you." She demanded, ignorantly barreling her way into the middle of the three boy's secret-coven of testosterone.

Cash let out a sigh, "What about?"

Looking at the other two with disdain, she spoke in an indignant tone, "Do you mind? I need to talk with Cash for a minute."

Cash pulled away from the group and followed his cousin to a distant corner. He wasn't sure how much more tension he could stand as his stomach felt like shoving dry-heaves. "What's up?"

Covering her mouth as if to whisper, she leaned up to his ear and said, "Have you thought anything about the prom?"

What?! He couldn't believe his ears. Was she out of her mind? Why was she talking to him about that? If she had any outrageous ideas of him taking her—she was barking up the wrong tree. Besides, it was weeks before the damned event; why was she bringing it up now? "Jennifer, isn't it a little premature to talk about somethin' like this? For Christ's sake, it's not until May."

"I realize that." She impatiently began to fiddle with a stray lock of hair with her fingers. "I just want you to think about it."

A touch of irritation slipped out of Cash, "Let's talk about it some other time."

Already leaving that subject, Jennifer focused her attention to the other two boys who were standing like wax figures in a museum. "Who's he?" She pointed to Lee.

"He's a rodeo buddy of mine from Great Falls."

Her face wrinkled. "What's he doing here?"

Damn, she's nosey, he thought. "He's interested in one of our horses."

Not satisfied, she continued with her inquisitiveness. "Does he know Travis?"

For God's sake! "They just met." Cash was ready to shove her out the front door.

Allowing her face to grow a frown, she observantly stated, "You know, it looks like they're ready to slug it out."

Cash swung around, casting his attention back in their direction. He could tell Lee was saying something to Travis, but he couldn't hear what it was. From the way Travis was standing with his fists clenched, he knew it wasn't good.

"Jennifer," Cash broke away from her in a dead run, "I've gotta go… talk with ya later."

She stood transfixed, completely fascinated by the event unfolding at the end of the hallway.

"…I don't know what the fuck you're talkin' about," Travis growled, taking a firm step toward Lee. In a stance—as if on the grid iron, he prepared his body for an all-out tackle.

"Travis!" Cash frantically called out.

"Cash, take care of this munchkin so he can get back on his happy little trail." Giving Lee a sneering glare, he continued by saying, "Hope you find the pony ride you want."

"*Oh, I will.*" Lee's words dripped of defiance. "Have no doubt about it."

With one last stare-down, Travis arched and tightened—bolting out the front doors of the deserted school house.

Cash could hear the Viper viciously roar out of the parking lot with burning rubber. Well, so much for the rest of the afternoon, he told himself with resignation. From the corner of his eye, he could see Jennifer's shadow remaining at the corner of the hallway. Damn her! He grit his teeth. She was unbelievable.

Taking one long, hard, deep breath, he shifted his attention to Lee— shooting him an explosive glare. "What the fuck are you doin'?" His lips were trembling.

"I had no intention of getting into it with him," Lee tried to sound innocent. "I just stopped by to say hello."

"Like hell," Cash could feel his face burn with a fury of emotions. "You knew who he was. You remembered the picture on my desk. That's why you planted yourself right next to him. You knew there would be a confrontation, 'n you damn well wanted it."

"I've waited for your call." Lee ignored his bitching. "What's it been, three weeks?"

"What are you lookin' for?" Cash rephrased the question. He wanted an answer.

"You know..." Lee's voice trailed off to a murmur.

"You keep saying that." He was tired of re-visiting the same conversation.

"Well, you do." Lee paused, looking back where Jennifer had been standing. She had disappeared. It was now only Cash and him. "I've left you several messages—how long until you return them?"

"You know I've been busy." Cash threw his arms out from his side.

Lee remained quiet for several moments then slowly turned for the doors. "Well, I better go. Sorry to have bothered you."

"Lee, wait," Cash softly called out. It was obvious that neither one was going to fess up to their end of the game. This was a battle of wills, and both were strong enough not to give in. And as there was a side of him that desired to let go of Lee and chalk it up to experience, there was something else that compelled him to hang on and give him another chance.

Stopping at the door, Lee rested his hand on the handle and continued to look forward through the glass.

"What's going on?" Travis sat across the empty table staring coldly into Cash's gaunt face.

As the words came at him like hurtling paint balls, Cash realized they couldn't come at a worse time—right at lunch. The fact that the issue was being addressed smack-dab in the middle of a crowded, noisy cafeteria meant this was the end of the line.

Travis' scowl seemed to bring the ridge of his forehead, brows and eyes into one heavy, dark, squinty line. To Cash, he resembled a GI Joe doll poised for sniper attack. Looking down at the food on his tray, he felt his hunger disintegrate like a bead of water on a red-hot skillet. The tuna noodle casserole could definitely wait.

Drawing in a stream of air, Travis continued to fire away. "Clayton told me you guys had no horses for sale and that you never came home the entire afternoon. In fact, you missed supper and you didn't get you're ass in until almost bedtime." With narrowing eyes, his sapphire-blue irises became black as night—suspicion clouded his face. "What are you doing, Cash? Are you messing around with him?"

"No." Cash couldn't look him in the eye. He had already caught holy hell from his father when he had sauntered into the house way past dinnertime. The remainder of that evening had been equally difficult. His brother had refused to talk with him and his mother had managed to keep her distance—not even offering to warm up leftovers—which in and of itself, was extremely out of character. Now sitting in front of his boyfriend, haplessly groping for words, he felt as if he was being ruthlessly interrogated by a shrewd prosecution attorney. *Imagine that*, he cynically thought to himself, *a chip off the old block*.

"Well, what did you two do?"

"We talked." Cash threw out a lame excuse.   At this point, he knew it was hopeless trying to sooth over ruffled feathers. There simply was no use in trying to preserve a dying trust.

"For five hours?!" Travis yelled, his voice carrying throughout the large room. Several students glanced over to them with quizzical looks. It was ironic, he didn't seem to care if anyone else overheard. "What the hell did you talk about?"

"Rodeo stuff." Now, Cash wasn't exactly in a cooperating mood and be damned if he was going to tell Travis the entire story. As far as he was concerned, his 'better half' didn't need to know about the drive to the levee afterwards... by himself... to think and sort through shit. "The first rodeo is in two weeks. It's up in Kalispell at the Carpenter Arena—we're plannin' on signin' up for the rough-stock both days."

"That's way out in the western division!" Travis' tone got louder. "Why in God's name are you goin' way out there?"

"Everyone's plannin' on goin'." Cash tried to explain.

"So?" Travis hotly exclaimed. "It doesn't make sense for you to attend that one when there will be plenty of shows on this side for you to register in."

"I promised Lee I would meet him there."

Moving in closer to the table, Travis watched Cash begin to tremble. Releasing all restraints, he demanded, "What the hell is goin' on between you two?" He was determined to squeeze the information he wanted out of Cash.

"Stop bein' so damned paranoid." Cash nervously backed up in his seat. He could feel Travis' hot, angry breath blow against his forehead and cheeks. "There's nothing goin' on between Lee 'n me."

Not taking his eyes off his boyfriend, Travis replied, "You know, I'd like to believe you, Cash, but my guts are telling me different." Taking a deep breath, he went on to speak with a shaky voice, "I think you're holdin' out on me." He paused, narrowing his eyes down to a squint. "Tell me why all of a sudden you're making plans on going to rodeos with him? And tell me, why would he come all way down from Great Falls unannounced to see you? To talk shop? Buy a horse? You can do all that on the phone or computer." Shaking his head, his eyes still fixed on Cash, he flatly stated in a conclusive tone, "No, things aren't addin' up, and your stories aren't connectin'. I think you're coverin' up." Travis looked at his once-trusted cowboy with a glare of crumbling disbelief.

"What am I coverin' up?" Cash held his breath. The defense he had resting at the tip of his tongue seemed to find itself stuck as Travis' continued to bombard with a relentless, accusing tirade. God have mercy... he could not push the words out.

The truth was—they *had* just talked. After Travis' dramatic stomp-off, they had gone to sit in Cash's truck to calm down from all the tension that had unraveled in the school hallway... to quietly gather themselves back together in a civil manner. Trying not to rehash Rapid City, even though it still hovered between them like a wrecking ball, they could only find themselves able to stare at each other with searching eyes. Lee had the look that begged like a puppy—making it exceedingly difficult for Cash to turn away...

Casually draping his arm across the steering wheel, Lee spoke into the air. "I didn't mean to create a scene back there."

Cash flashed him a 'yeah, right' with his eyes.

"Like I said, I was goin' through town on my way to Forsyth for business with a guy I know there."

Cash's attention was caught. "What kind of business?"

"Oh, ...just some stuff."

It sounded damned strange as Cash sat in the seat trying to assimilate it all.

"Anyway, I wanted to see you before I passed on."

"Well, you saw me," Cash's voice sharpened as he looked past Lee to the bleak landscape beyond. Peacefully, little houses sat in the growing dark, unattended just like small boxes in a closet. He suddenly recalled something similar that Lee had taken with him to South Dakota ... a little black box... Dr. Feelgood's Medicine Chest as he had called it. Was this somehow involved in the so-called 'business'? He shook himself.

"Damned near got me killed." There was an emotional flatness to Cash's voice.

"Yeah," Lee acknowledged. "This Travis..."

"Never mind about Travis," Cash snapped, all the recent feelings returning. "We discussed this already." One thing about Lee—he was never good at taking a hint.

Dropping his head, Lee's voice became quiet, "About what happened..."

"Nothin' happened, Lee. We were both drunk, but nothin' happened."

With his spirit once again shoved back inside, Lee bitterly laughed. "You say so, Cash. If you say so..."

There was no question; he didn't want anything more from Lee. He might be great to have as a friend, but the other stuff, that was too much to be handled.

He loved Travis in spite of all the differences. It was difficult relating to the things that seemed to come natural for the all-star football player, such as nice cars, clothes, and a bottomless pocketbook. Where Cash could take or leave all that in a heart beat, Travis seemed dependant on it. It was as if his entire nature expected nothing less than the *best* of material wealth and comfort. Moreover, Cash's world went no farther than windswept prairie of Eastern Montana. This was the only ground he knew. And where Billings seemed to be the ultimate in urban life, Cash could not fathom coming from a progressive, cosmopolitan city like San Francisco. In his mind, it seemed like another planet...

"What's this?" Cash had asked one afternoon at Travis'. His boyfriend had pulled out a box-full of pictures.

"This was our house in San Francisco."

Cash could remember being taken back. "My God, it's incredible. *It's a mansion.*"

Travis had nodded, not speaking.

Looking at him, Cash couldn't believe the world that Travis had come from. He couldn't fathom it.

"Your dad was a lawyer?"

"Yeah."

"He must have been pretty successful."

"He was good—one of the best in the country. He represented many big clients."

"Like who?" Cash had found himself mesmerized.

"Movie stars, politicians, CEO's, and several corporations…"

All Cash could ask himself back then was—*why Miles City?* Why would they want to come here? For Christ's sake, there had to be better choices.

…Putting that aside, he still found himself intrigued with Travis and this new way of life. There was a reassurance that made Cash realize he would be taken care of by a strange, yet wonderful world of affluence.

And while Travis had the ability to make him feel like a prince—giving him lavish things and saying all the right words, he could also be extremely controlling and harshly possessive. At times, it made Cash wonder if he was not more than another addition to the Hunter property—only uninsured.

It shouldn't have come as a surprise, therefore, to have Travis say, "I want you to tell him you won't be able to meet him in Kalispell at the rodeo," but it did. And it hurt. His words had been cut and decisive—no room for question or debate…

Holding the receiver in the palm of his hand as if it were a grenade, Cash dialed the number and let it ring on the other end. Except the fact that he was on the brink of loosing Travis, there was no other way he would make this call. And since he desired to avoid the impending consequences at all costs, the only thing he could do was follow orders. Willingly, he allowed the bit and bridle to be slipped over his head and straight into his mouth.

Lee answered. "Hello."

Cash cleared his throat. "Hey."

"Cash." There was the faintest hint of surprise coming from the voice on the other end of the line.

"Lee, I can't go with you to Kalispell." Cash felt so detached from the words coming out of his mouth.

There was no reply. Fuzzy static ruled.

"Are you there?" Cash wondered if Lee had vaporized. He held his breath.

"Yeah," his friend's voice came over the line faintly—as if distancing himself from the phone.

"I'm not gonna be able to make it with you up to Kalispell." Cash wasn't sure he had caught what had been said.

"Yes, I heard you the first time," Lee finally acknowledged. The disappointment was quite evident from the tone of his voice.

"I'm sorry," Cash was at a complete loss for words.

Time seemed to stand still as silence filtered over the line.

Suddenly, Lee's words traveled into Cash's ear strongly, clear as a bell, "I want you to come here... you need to come here."

Cash quickly replied, "I will." His head spun.

"When?" Lee was pressing.

"As soon as I can," once again, Cash could feel the pressure. Funny how Lee could do that. From his religious background, the word was 'obligated'.

"Travis made you call, didn't he?" Lee's words were bitter.

"That's beside the point," Cash tried to evade the matter.

"No, it's not," Lee began to drive the subject into an issue. "I know better."

"Lee…" Cash tried to pacify him with some bullshit.

"I know you were put up to this," Lee knowingly stated.

Cash's soul was vexed. "What do you want me to do?"

"There's nothing you can do," Lee's tone turned sour. "He has control over you."

Silence once again fell between them. They were both at a loss for words.

Finally, Lee continued. "Cash, you really need to come here." Seriousness rode heavily through every word.

"I will," Cash promised. He really would head up there at the first opportunity, he told himself. "I will."

CHAPTER 20

In high school, the coming of spring isn't announced by birds singing outside of bedroom windows at dawn, or the bright greening of the sagebrush, but rather the appearance of navels and midriffs. Travis had no sooner left the table with his tray leaving Cash to recover from another strained lunch and conversation in the cafeteria, when he felt an ominous presence next to him. Turning his head, Jennifer Evers' belly button was leering just inches from his nose.

"Hey Cash," she chirped. "Was that Travis?" She swiveled in a vague direction, then right back—nervously yanking on her wretched hair.

Like whom else could it be mistaken for? Cash dryly asked himself, his mood cascading further into a sour pool of acidy thought.

"Hi Jen," he replied, non-committal. It only took Jennifer a second to plop down into the chair across the table, swinging her backpack down with a loud crunch. He would have made an excuse to leave right then, except that his lunch was only half-eaten and he was hungry.

"Haven't talked to you in awhile," she began, oblivious to Cash's sudden intense involvement with his food. "In fact, it seems I don't see either you or Clay any more than once in a blue moon."

Gulping down a big swallow of coke, he cynically asked himself, *whatever a blue moon was...* "That's probably because we're both pickin' up the chores that Dad can't do."

Jennifer tossed him a dumbfounded look. "What?"

Letting out a huffy snort, Cash stared at her with disbelief. *Was she for real?* It was as if he was talking to a chimpanzee. "The heart attack? Remember, my dad can't do a lot of stuff now?"

As if a tiny light had been switched on in her brain, she closed her mouth and nodded. "Hummmmm."

Cash's comment, however, didn't seem to slow her down as she quickly bounced back to what was initially on her brain. "I need to tell you something." Leaning forward over the table, her eyes shifted throughout the lunchroom so see if anyone was watching them.

"If this is top-secret, perhaps we should take this out of the cafeteria." His eyes followed hers—feeling impatience overtake his attitude.

"Huh?" Jennifer turned back to him.

"What's on your mind?" He pretty well guessed it would probably be connected some way to the prom.

"You know," she leaned closer; her plump breasts hovered threateningly around the top of her tight tee. "Ever since Clayton talked about you and Travis at the Co-op, there've been a few individuals keepin' the flame-a burnin'." Jennifer's smile was tight and false.

Her all-to-familiar abrupt manner was disgusting, Cash silently told himself—struggling to remain calm, waiting for her to continue.

"Not that their talk amounts to much since most of the time it doesn't," she snickered.

Knowing she couldn't be put out with a fire extinguisher, Cash resigned himself to the flames—like riding Brownie on one of his tears, or holdin' down a bull from crashing into an arena. At first, he tried not to act interested. Leaning back in his chair, he finished chewing on his food. Inside, he was quaking. He was learning from hard experience that Jennifer's attention to him always had a motive behind it—being driven by a grander, more menacing force. This time, he was afraid to guess what it was, but something in his guts told him to brace. "Hummm..." he brought the sandwich back up to his lips and bit into it, moving some fries from one side of the plate to the other.

Reaching over uninvited, she took a slurp of his coke, knowing it would make him look at her. Cash pulled the coke out of her reach the instant she put it back down.

"I don't pay attention to much of what the guys say around there at the Co-op, in fact, a lot of it is just plain stupid. It's just that Harlan Jens..." At this, she suddenly stopped, waiting for Cash's reaction.

He couldn't help himself. Suddenly loosing his appetite, the burger rubberized in his mouth. "Jens?" His voice nearly yelped, giving her the opening she wanted. He was very much interested in what his round-faced cousin had to say about Travis' long-time teammate and closest rival for school stardom.

"Yeah, he's something else... I think he's a nasty sort, don't you?" She wrinkled her face.

Cash's gaze gripped on her.

"He likes to talk a lot about Travis, it seems," she continued. "That's kinda strange, doncha think?" She paused to ensure he was with her in this conversation. "Not that he talks much to me, even though he tells me how much he wants to take me out and show me a good time." She threw Cash a sneering grin. "He just talks to the guys—mostly a one note conversation, lately… about Travis and his relationship with you."

Cash's jaw tightened. *She's lying*, he thought. She must be. But what if she wasn't? What if she actually *was* trying to get something across? This was a game unfamiliar to him. If he acted interested, she might continue, but get suspicious. If he ignored her, she might get pissed off and do who knew what. So he tried to stand a neutral ground, putting his lunch down and simply looking at her. As hoped, she warmed to his focus.

"Are you going to the prom, Cash?" Jennifer aimed and fired her shot.

Pushing himself abruptly from the table, Cash grabbed his tray and began to make his way to the waste baskets. "I'm gonna be late for class," he said half-muttering his words, back to her front.

Jennifer jumped up, grabbing her bag and moving quicker than she seemed capable. She positioned herself in front of him, blocking his exit.

"Are you?"

Cash held his tray close to his chest, resisting the urge to whack it over her head.

"Haven't thought about it," he tried maneuvering around her, thinking that if he just kept going forward it would be like driving on ice—he would get where he was going—eventually.

"Haven't thought about it?!" she mocked shrilly. "You gotta be kidding." The cafeteria was emptying out now as it got closer to the next period.

"I'm gonna be late," Cash repeated, wondering why she didn't go away. Was she slightly retarded or something?

Instead, Jennifer fell into step beside him, sweeping past the surrounding chairs with her hips. "You HAVE to go, Cash—you and your buddy, Travis. Is Travis going?"

"How should I know?" Cash snapped, his irritation getting the better of him. She was definitely crossing the line now. *Damn her!*

"Well," Jennifer snorted, "I would THINK you would know—you TWO bein' together ALL of the time. " The way her voiced pitched up a couple of tones for certain words was making his left temple throb. "I mean, after all..." She trailed off.

"It's not something we exactly talk about, Jennifer," Cash turned to her after emptying his tray of half-eaten food. The burning sensation in his flesh made him feel as if he was being reduced to a pile of powdery ashes.

"Yeah, well," Jennifer looked slyly about, "that's kinda what Harlan says, too."

"What?" Was he correct in where he thought she was taking this?

She didn't respond; she just kept looking around like she was expecting someone to step up and visit with her.

"What did you say?" Cash repeated.

A smile crawled around her lips. "I didn't say anything, Cash." Jennifer finally began walking away from him, slow and sure—twirling a long strand of hair from her strangling ponytail with a pair of manipulative fingers.

Like hell, he angrily thought, fighting his emotions. She was playing with him. He knew she was aware of the power she possessed in this matter. With clenched teeth, he swung around and bellowed out, "What do you want, Jennifer?"

"I think you already know." Coyness swelled in her eyes, scanning him very closely.

"You want me to take you to the prom," he flatly stated. This entire proposition made him sick—making him feel dirty and cheap. She had such a way of not only lowering herself, but bringing others to the same level of deceit.

"For one thing, it'll shut Harlan up."

"How's that?" he asked knowing that each moment lingered was one step deeper into the web.

"You know, I know him pretty well. "

As if he didn't? God, he wanted to strangle her. She sure had a way of working a nerve raw. Without blinking, he gave her one of his silent spells—waiting for her to continue.

Instinctively, she threw back her head and let out an arrogant sigh. "Letting him know you're taking me to the prom will defuse whatever flame he has lit regarding the rumors about you and Travis. Besides, *I* have a way of convincing him of certain things."

A wave of cold fear swept Cash as he could envision the entire situation getting completely out of hand. With Harlan and his big mouth, there was no telling where it would stop. Not only were their individual reputations on the line, but their family's as well.

"Just keep me in mind, about the prom," she called from a few feet, loud enough for those nearby to hear.

"You're taking Jennifer Evers to the prom?"

Janice looked up only the briefest moment from her task of repairing once again an ancient quilt. Her hands stopped—stilled by her own question.

Cash sat quietly in the chair next to the fireplace. He could hear the flames working over the wood, going to ash. He hesitated, then "Yeah. So?"

"Well," his mother began, noticing she had left her needle in the air—mid-stitch. "Well, I guess I'm a little surprised. That's all."

"You don't need to tell me about bein' surprised." Cash didn't look away from the fire as he spoke, talking more to the logs than the woman close by.

"Still, Jennifer Evers?" Mrs. McCollum slowly shook her head.

"It's more like she asked me. That's all. It wasn't exactly my idea."

The quilt began to slip to the floor. His mother quickly pulled it back up as she spoke, gathering it close as if suddenly chilled. "You know, I've never had much to do with that family and there's a reason for it." The needle waved—flashing light in the air. It pulled Cash's attention. "When I saw Ellen Evers today and she told me about you asking Jennifer, well, I could have dropped my drawers. I mean, Cash, what on earth were you thinking?"

"Mom," he shifted slightly in the old wooden straight-back. "This all came kinda quick. I didn't feel I had much of a choice in the matter."

Now their eyes met.

"Believe me, I don't really want to go... with Jennifer or *anybody*." He paused, gathering air into his lungs. "It was kinda like she blackmailed me." A spark flew from the fire. "That's exactly what it was like, because..." again a breath quick-in, and then out, "she was there at the Co-op that night, and she believes she has the solution to the whole mess at her fingertips."

Mrs. McCollum paused long enough to show her son he had her complete attention.

"What do you mean? What night?"

"The night Clayton started talkin' about Travis 'n me."

Suddenly, Cash remembered his mother was ignorant of the situation. Now, he was committed to the telling of the tale. Besides, he owed it to her that she should finally know—giving silent thanks that she had never even asked about what had transpired the day of the fight—or before.

"Clayton was talking about you and Travis?" She swallowed, visibly, her head rising. "I don't think I understand. What does this have to do with Jennifer?"

"Everything and nothing." Cash resisted the urge to jump up from his seat and stomp upstairs to his room. Just thinking about the entire incident made his face ache. He felt himself reddening. This was a conversation best left un-had.

"Cash," she was pleading now, watching him try to shut down.

He knew his mother well. The topic would not be dropped now—he could only go forward, get it over with. "She was there at the Co-op. Trailing Clayton, no doubt. You know how she latches on to *anyone* who's male and walks on two feet." He rolled his eyes.

His mother nodded. She knew. Everyone did.

"And Clayton was talking—drunk talk. Said things about Travis. Said things about me."

"So," Janice sighed, "what exactly did he say to get you two into the fight you had this last fall?" She put it together so quickly, so assuredly—knowing her sons so well.

"That I'm not completely sure of. But Jennifer over-heard and made damn-well sure to let me know about it at school practically five seconds after it happened."

"So where does this fit into the prom?" Janice was still fuzzy on the connection.

"Well, when Clayton was sharing that night, Harlan Jens was there soaking it all in." Cash hoped and prayed his mother would put the rest of the story together.

Allowing the quilt to slide further down her lap, his mother cleared her throat. "And let me guess, Harlan has now taken the ball and is running with it at the Co-op and all over town."

He nodded.

"And I'll bet she thinks she can stop him yakking and has told you she will do it—if you take her to the prom."

God bless her... Cash earnestly thought.

"I gather this is where this it is all going. Am I right?"

He should have known his mother would make this easy. *I should have told her right away,* he reprimanded himself, *before being cornered.*

"I'm sorry I didn't mention it right away, Mom." He could feel the warmth of the fire hitting his face, covering his now furious blush. "I thought we could settle it, Clayton and me. You didn't need to know."

"I'm glad you can talk about it, son. It *is* important."

"Anyway," Cash settled back to tell the tale for what it was. "Jennifer said, in school yesterday afternoon, that Jens has been talking about us to others since then."

His mother shook her head, side to side. A small smile began to creep out on her lips, obviously unwanted, considering the seriousness of the conversation.

"And she's made it a point of telling me she wants to go to the prom. And if I take her, she will shut Harlan up. You see what I'm sayin'?"

Indeed she did. Janice McCollum needed no instruction regarding the Evers family. They were always on the outs with someone—even relatives.

"Still, Cash, taking her to the prom?"

"Mom, like I said—I felt I had no choice. What else was I s'pose to do?"

"Well, I realize you see it that way, son. What about Travis? What's he think of all this?"

It was just like his mother to think of Travis. How was it that every conversation with his family seemed to always head back to that big boy and how he felt about things? Cash suddenly felt like he was suffocating.

"He'll take Tiffany Jo Morton."

At that, the quilt was thrown onto the floor, Cash's mother's head thrown back with a hoot. He couldn't remember the last time he saw her laugh like that—hard and true.

"Tiffany Jo—oh, my God!" Her laughter echoed throughout the house. "That poor, unfortunate boy!"

If there was anyone worse in their tiny little community than Jennifer, it was Tiffany Jo. They were equals in totally disparate ways, complementing each other like sweet and sour sauce on a Chinese dinner. Without them, the town would be that much duller.

"Normally, I would say Travis can take care of himself, but regarding that girl, I won't go that far."

"Mom, you've gotta help me."

"Cash," his mother gave a long, drawn sigh, "I think you're on your own with that one." A spark of humor lingered in her eyes as she looked earnestly into her son's troubled face. "Not enough angels will keep him in line when you break that news out to him."

"Why the fuck'd'ya do that for?" Travis' voice rose to a pitch loud enough to set Casper off whimpering and yelping. The room itself seemed to vibrate with anger. "Jesus fuckin' Christ, Cash. What the hell's gotten into you?"

It was a dilemma he hadn't thought through yet. Not only was there the issue of the prom, there was the issue of the motive behind it. Fortunately, in Travis' room late the following afternoon, Cash desperately hoped they could find space and time to work it all out. Searching for an explanation that would bring Travis' into line, he was unable to find one. It was a delicate fence he was sitting. The last thing he wanted was the whole damned town knowing the truth about them... *or* having Travis on Harlan and Clayton's tail.

"Doncha see," Cash began, trying to keep his voice steady, facilitating a logic that wasn't truly there, "I had to do something. She was buggin' me."

"Then, why not just ignore her? You've been managing *that*, until now."

Cash instinctively knew he could have brought up some bullshit reasoning involving family loyalty. Hell, he could say his mother had put him up to it, with a poor-girl-she'll-never-go-to-a-prom-unless-you-ask-her appeal.

It would be perfectly believable, too. Popularity would never be in the cards for Jennifer Evers.

Or he could have taken another attack and explained that he really *did* want to go to the prom. Only occurring once in life, it was an unrepeatable experience. And Jennifer, being a relation, would be a safe date.

The light was going quickly—shadows coming as they always did—shifting around Travis' reclining form on the bed. It was a shame they had to have such a discussion on an afternoon like this. Damned shame.

Cash half-expected—hoped that Travis could guess for himself. Like Lee, however, reading between the lines was not one of his treasured talents.

Biting a lip in a manner he knew was attractive, Cash rolled to the side of the bed, swinging his legs over the edge with an intention to sit. The feel of Travis' hand on his arm kept him in a half-way motion. He turned to look at the boy who restrained him—defiance instantly swept over him. "I don't owe you an explanation," was what finally came out of his mouth. "I did it for reasons I don't expect you to understand."

A hurt look fled across Travis' face—suddenly disappearing. The anger returned. "Like fucking hell you don't! This is serious shit, Cash. If you don't tell me what's going on, it won't take much effort on my part to knock it out of you."

Cash jerked his arm free. Travis was big, but Cash was a solid work of fiery muscle—he could be mean and quick. He knew Travis would never really best him. "That attitude ain't gonna get you an answer." Even though he pushed himself to the edge of the bed, he made no effort to go anywhere.

"You know, Cash, you've gotta lotta room to yap at me like that."

"Whatdiya mean?" He tried to act ignorant, knowing full well what was going to follow.

319

"Here you've been messin' around with some shit-assed, Arab cow-poke from up around the north forty, and then you've taken it upon yourself to line me up for the prom with the skankiest chick in the whole fuckin' county. Now you tell me to change my attitude? You're something else, Cash, you know that? You're a *real* piece of work."

"First off, I haven't messed around with anyone!" This conversation was beginning to spiral into a nose dive.

"Right," Travis huffed skeptically.

"Travis, listen." It was getting dark and soon he would have to head home. He knew he was down to the wire and he *had* to get his wits in line—quickly. "How do you think it would look if we didn't go?" He paused, wanting Travis to take it in. Hopefully, it would be enough.

"I don't care how anything looks from here. This town is shit and you know it." A tone of bitterness crept out from the distraught jock's words. "You don't care what anyone thinks any more than I do."

"Hell, yeah, I do! I just don't talk about it. *You*...you're nuthin' but an outsider. But me—things are different. This is *my* home, and these are *my* roots."

Travis jumped up so abruptly Casper ran from the room, the little dog's tail neatly tucked as he scurried around the door. "*Stop with this bullshit! If you'da cared anything about what people here thought, we'd never have gotten this far. Now would we? Isn't that the truth?*"

Cash remained silent.

"What's *really* going on here, Cash?"

"We've gotta make a face, Travis," he firmly concluded. "We've gotta keep the talk away."

"I've not heard any talk." Travis moved around his room, closing curtains and turning on lights. "That's all in your head."

"Well, the main head it's in, right now, is Jennifer Evers'." He refrained from mentioning Harlan's name for the sake of not complicating things. "She's actin' mighty suspicious. She's family. Not necessarily anyone's favorite, but she's still blood. And you know, people in families talk."

"*Then shut 'er up, Cash!* Going to the frickin' prom isn't going to solve anything."

"No? Think not? Maybe it's not a big deal in California, but it is around here. And trust me, buddy—we don't make an appearance, and it'll look damned funny."

A light suddenly switched on.

Sure, Travis knew. Like Batman and Robin, a dynamic duo, there was so much attention in regards to their relationship. There really was no way out—*that commitment* was already made for them.

"You got a point." Travis sat back on the bed, arms outstretched to stroke Cash's lean frame. "I don't like to admit it, but you do. But—I still don't see why you—we—have to do this. Can't we just go—the two of us and no dates?"

"I thought of that, but that would be worse. I was hoping to have a rodeo that Saturday, but no such luck. It's almost like they were scheduling around the damned thing."

Now the logic was marrying the excuses, and Cash knew he was winning this one. "Who knows, you may be elected prom king. You couldn't possibly turn that down. Then the talk would *really* fly."

"Yeah, I get you." Travis flopped back heavily against the pillows, a sigh escaping. "But why do I have to take that stupid whore, Tiffany Jo? Shit, I don't even like girls. At least you'd think I be goin' with some cute, popular fox like Melissa Jacobson. At least I could look her in the face when I'm dancin' and not worry about catching something." He closed his eyes, long lashes brushing his cheeks. "What do we have to do in the meantime, go on dates for Chrissake? Or even after—we gotta break up with them?"

"Hell, no," Cash lay back alongside Travis. Glancing at the clock, he realized Travis' mother would be home soon. "Jennifer doesn't really like me. As it is, I think she's in love with Harlan—or somebody."

At that, Travis' eyes flew open, rolling on his side to give Cash an incredulous stare. Silently, his lips moved—uttering unhearable words.

CHAPTER 21

As Travis had dictated, Cash did not attend the rodeo in Kalispell. Even after several pleading calls from Lee, he still opted out.

"You won't change your mind?"

"Sorry, Lee," Cash's words had been warm, but firm. He knew Travis was stern about this matter and there was no way he would be able to rescind without serious consequences. "I promise I'll come up 'n see you the first chance I get."

In spite of it all, Cash diligently set his sights on the first Eastern Division rodeo scheduled in Glendive. He was focused on that title. By now, he wanted it more than anything else. And no matter how much it appeared that Lee was pushing for that unacknowledged something, he was still competition.

Countless hours were spent either in the corral, or at the college indoor arena being knocked around like a crazy pin-ball. Taking on any available bad-assed beast in order to improve his riding skills, or to learn a new technique was leaving Cash nearly crippled—leaving every muscle in his flesh torn with numbing pain. Every morning, upon waking up, he'd find himself taking extended spells in steamy, hot showers, followed by a religious ritual of rubbing ointment over swollen, achy joints. It was his hips, lower back and shoulders that seemed to protest the most. Sometimes the pain was so great he found he needed to take a pill to simply get out of bed and walk across the room.

"Are you sure it's worth all this?" His mother complained one day, watching her boy hobble down the staircase like an old man.

"I've come this far... no sense in fizzlin' out now." Cash's words were determined even though they came out like a yelp.

So, in spite of the pain, he continued to bite the bullet—not even letting Travis know how badly he felt...

"Are you set?" Travis reached down—grabbing Cash's heavy gear bag with a solid grip. He seemed excited about getting on the road—with a sparkly gleam in his eyes; there was an energetic lightness to his movements.

Lifting his saddle and swinging it over his shoulder, Cash looked around the tack room one last time. He could not help but think to himself that this adopted Californian was beginning to sound more like his dad each day. "I think so."

They loaded the last of Cash's gear in the back of the pick-up. Tossing a quick glance at the empty hitch, Cash realized it was strange not having the stock trailer attached with several raging bulls snorting and kicking in their stalls. As long as he could remember, his father had been a contractor with the Association. Year after year, he had spent countless weekends hauling obstinate animals from one rodeo to another in the old, weather-beaten, rusted-down carrier. Hopping into the cab, he felt things were just not right. It was his dad, not Travis, who needed to be sitting in the driver's seat—one arm positioned against the door handle while the other would lazily dangle over the steering wheel. Cash had been floored when Mr. McCollum whipped out the keys the night before, handing them over to Travis.

"I know you'll be responsible with the rig."

For Eugene to say something like that was unbelievable. He never let Clayton drive it, and until the trip to Rapid City with Lee, Cash had never been privy to the controls either.

Quiet ruled throughout the cab as the truck made its way down the long endless ribbon of freeway. Across the prairie, a hint of green was springing forth in various patches amid withered wood of fading winter. Secretly, Cash sat glancing over at the rugged figure at the helm. Like his father, there was a determination set in Travis' body that radiated a stalwart faith forecasting that the trip would be successful. However, he couldn't help thinking that he would probably have a better time with Lee despite the fact that they were competitors—fighting to get the same prize—reaching for the same goal. Cash wondered if Lee would try to submarine him—cut him down to make him fail. Cash could almost see it.

As expected, Cash did exceptionally well in both entries. Scoring the highest in both saddle bronc and bareback and walking away from the arena with a saddle-bag of satisfaction, he crushed the scores that Lee had earned the week before in Kalispell. Thus, he remained securely on the throne as the top-man in the Association. Travis, as well, was pleased—with a look in his eyes revealing pride for his little man. It was a light, giddy moment shared between the two as they triumphantly loaded up the last of the gear into the truck and pulled out of the arena grounds in search of a motel for the night.

"Guess we showed them today." Travis rose up from his quiet thoughts—throwing a hearty grin at Cash.

"Uh huh," Cash wearily agreed. "We sure did." Every muscle in his body cried as he sat crumpled in the truck's big, firm seat.

With Travis' unwritten call in life to provide the best for both of them, it was decided that they would stay at the nicest place in town. Stating he wanted to do some laps in the large, indoor pool, Travis also added it was only appropriate since Cash had done so well at the rodeo.

Finding Travis' path of reason rather humorous, Cash determined it was one of those tiny things which seemed endearing...

"What're you doing now?" Travis called from the bed—naked and eager for a little return from all the doting throughout the day.

Pulling the curtains and taking off his underwear, Cash propelled himself heavily onto the bed, shaking off the spring nighttime chill. He would be glad for summer, after all. "Just fixin' things."

Travis immediately reached over and pulled Cash close. His body was already warmed under the covers and he began an annoyed kicking to free up his movements a little. "Why are you always messing?"

By now, Cash had reached behind Travis' head, jerking him forward, quieting him with a hard kiss. "I'm not messin'." Deep down, he was beginning to hate that word.

In the sudden pause, Cash could hear the singing of tires on the nearby highway. He noticed a lessening of the traffic as the evening progressed, the cars coming at longer intervals, replaced periodically by the heavier roar of trucks. Cash wrapped both arms around Travis' neck, willing his body closer than was physically possible.

Travis' smile seemed to glow in the dark shadows amidst the stillness of things. "You know how much I love you?"

"I know exactly," Cash replied, slightly smug. Suddenly, an old spark ignited and his passion began to soar. He did indeed know the degree of Travis' love for him. He knew it very well… Brushing his long cowboy fingers softly across Travis' tightly-shaven, flat-topped head, gently embracing him closely by his thick, massive neck, he should have guessed the evening would turn out like this.

If there were angels, they were at play tonight.

Before hauling their bags into the motel, Cash had looked up at the clear, ebony sky, noticing more stars than ever before. Lighting their way, it seemed to be a night shared only between them. His heart had lifted— singing the ancient song that once filled his soul when he had first touched this mighty warrior. Unexpectedly, he felt himself fall back into love.

Retreating into Travis' sweet, manly scent, Cash whispered with a flame that could've burned Rome, "I love you with all my heart."

It yanked him from a deep sleep. *What was it?* Could it have been real? It seemed real. Sitting up in the bed staring wildly about the darkened room, Cash could still feel his heart pound excitedly within his chest. The skin on his body was chilled with a scalding sweat.

Looking down at the peaceful figure sprawled beside him, Cash concluded it must have been a dream. If there had been any disturbance in the room, Travis would have been the first to rouse since he was a light sleeper. His ears seemed to pick up everything. Whatever it had been that had disturbed Cash seemed so damned detailed; he could have sworn the voice had come from within the room.

Eventually, his heart went back to a steady rhythm, calmness once again took over his senses. Pushing himself back underneath the covers, his leg brushing flush against Travis' side, he rehearsed what he had just experienced in his brain in a hopeful effort to determine more fully what it was that he had heard.

As if drugged, Travis continued to soundly sleep—not stirring a muscle. As expected, it had been a big day of adjustments for him. Not accustomed to the world of rodeo and its clandestine culture, it was somewhat of a shock, mixing with farm boys, ranchers and rednecks. Smiling to himself, Cash had found it humorous watching his boyfriend trying to take it all in. At first, he just stood around awkwardly watching everything unfold behind the arena—like a new kid hanging at the edge of a playground. Moreover, not being recognized from any previous competitions, everyone seemed to take second hesitating looks—trying to size him up and figure him out. For starters, he just didn't seem like the cowboy type. Everything about him was too neat—too perfect.

As he lay beside Travis, trying to coax the sleep back, Cash continued to revisit the disturbance in his mind. Someone had cried for help. There had been no doubt about that. He had recognized the voice as well… it had been very familiar. Strangely, it had sounded like Lee's.

Morning came with a vengeance. Cash felt like he had been through the mill as he lay silently staring up at the ceiling. As if having a hangover from an all-night binge, his head throbbed, and his eyes were puffy. It had taken hours for him to fall back asleep after he had been awakened. Recalling now, a peculiar uneasiness had swept into his spirit—telling him *something* was really wrong. Pushing himself laboriously from the mattress and covers, Cash turned and looked at Travis who was still curled-up, breathing deeply in the last recesses of sleep.

Thoughts of what had spooked him earlier vanished into vapor as the warm water of the shower sprayed gently across his sore, tired flesh. He desperately hoped for a rub-down. As he briskly rinsed the shampoo out of his hair, he became distinctly aware of being closely watched. Peeking through the cascading water around his eyes, he spotted a warm, familiar face beaming from around the shower curtain.

"Hey." Inviting mischief twinkled from Travis' eyes as he watched Cash adjust the shower nozzle to spray off the last residue of soap from his body.

"Hey." Cash stopped the water, casting a big grin toward the boy who was admiring him in the buff. "You like seein' me wet?"

"I like seeing you in any way." Travis' words were soft. "You have an incredible body, Cash."

Pushing the curtain back, Cash reached for a nearby towel and began to dry off. It was their usual banter… "Oh, you say that to all the hot guys."

"No, I don't," Travis flatly stated, his eyes still fixed on Cash. "I've only said that to you." The tone in his voice revealed seriousness. "I love your body… and the one who dwells inside it."

Leaning forward, Cash stole him a kiss…hotter than any shower.

Why did he have to care? It certainly wasn't expected from him—and to do so, threw a question on his own integrity. The fact was—he *did* care. He cared a lot. Scanning the posted statewide scores for the previous day, Cash searched to see how Lee had done in Helena. There had been an instant mixture of joy, relief, curiosity and bewilderment as his eyes rested on the low numbers recorded for his buddy. He knew scores that poor were gravely out of character for someone as talented as Lee. Fresh memories of the dream flashed back into his brain. Something was wrong. He knew it… he felt it.

"Your entry's coming up," Travis' voice floated in from behind, startling Cash back to the here and now. "Are you all set?"

"Uh, I guess so," Cash replied in a daze. His mind was someplace else—nearly five-hundred miles west. *Damn it!* He thought to himself. He wished he could talk to Lee and find out what was up.

"Are you okay?" Travis suddenly looked concerned—his eyes closely scanning Cash's pallid face.

Nodding, Cash mumbled, avoiding Travis' gaze, "Yeah, just a little tired." Turning, he shuffled his way back to the truck—his boot heels dragging heavily through the dirt and occasional straw on the ground.

As if by sheer instinct, Cash mechanically went through his ritual of last minute adjustments. It was odd, the thought crossing his mind, of loosing Lee as tight competition. It was more threatening than loosing the title himself. To have someone so tight and close—nipping at his heels seemed to be the motivation he needed to be the best. It was fun. Without Lee keeping up—being focused, there was no challenge.

He wanted to know what was wrong. He would find out what the hell was going on if it was the last thing he did.

As he finished wrapping his glove, he was suddenly aware of someone's presence—a big set of fingers slipping around his waist, drawing his flesh firmly against a solid body. Warmth with warmth… he felt his senses flood—chill bumps breaking out. *Oh God…* his mind went wild. *Not here!* Not in front of all his buddies and rodeo fans. It was too late, however. Being led by a betraying nose, his nostrils drank in the sweet, familiar scent—this time blended with the pungent odors of stock, hay, and smoke. His will succumbed into a craving hunger.

Warm, sensitive lips wisped effortlessly against the crevices of his ear—Travis ever-so lightly breathed, "I believe in you, Cash. You've come this far… nothing is gonna stop you now. *Nothing.*"

Shockwaves jolted through his veins with purpose that burned. Cash was lassoed and roped in.

Boldly, Cash made his way from the practice arena to the lead-up alley. Climbing the railing, extending a wary leg into the chute, he rested upon the obstinate beast that ferociously reared-up against his crotch. Its force nearly knocked the wind out of him.

"Hold 'em! Hold 'em!" One of the assistants hollered as two others tried to quell the beast. Railings along the length of the holding area shuddered.

Jesus, he quickly thought to himself. This one seemed like it was ready to kill. Perhaps that was why it was dubbed, Cold Blood.

"Focus on your center of balance, son." Cash heard someone yell from behind the chute. "He's gonna work at settin' you up."

Nearly a ton of offensive power fought beneath him as his legs were thrown mercilessly against the sides of the chute. Sharp pain snapped inside his bones. A frantic prayer slipped from his lips. "Oh, God…" The snorts and growl of the animal seemed to make Cash's ears ring and his head twirled with adrenalin. His entire world instantly became one tempestuous caldron of seething frenzy. Cinching his gloved hand to the rope with a clenching grip, he shot a nod to the attendant. In a flash, he hollered out, "Let 'er roll!"

Before the gate could even swing open, the bull had kicked-out from behind, crashing its hooves squarely into the chute's rear rails, knocking a bystander clean to the ground. Angry foam sprayed from its mouth, spraying Cash's face as he frenziedly worked at maintaining a welded hold and balance. Each landing from its crazy bucks and spins felt like his arm was going to rip apart from the rest of his body.

"This is the ride we've all been waiting for..." The announcer's voice revealed a heightened level of excitement. "Ladies and Gentlemen, Cash McCollum from Miles City is coming out of chute four on Harrington Stock prized-fighter, Cold Blood. Let's welcome our number one bull-rider back to the arena for another outstanding season!"

The stands were wild. The bull was wild. *Everything* in Cash's existence seemed violently wild, and out of control as he was hurled into space by a raging eruption. As if being hit on the side by a streaking locomotive, the animal ran forward—suddenly jerking to the left—then to the right, throwing his balance off momentarily. Desperately, Cash struggled to regain center. Feeling his feet flay out uncontrollably from the brahma's sides, he suddenly lost his leverage. Seizing the rope, he thrusted his hips forward and leaned heavily into each throw with an effort to stave off the churning momentum. About that time, Cold Blood heaved and shot a mouthful of blood—bringing its head back with fiery resistance. With its rear still midair, it twisted its neck, digging a determined right hoof into the ground, allowing the hips to swing off to the left for a fast spin. Instantly, Cash wondered if he was in a tornado's vortex as crotch, belly and balls flew off the beast—all twirling around like a whistling top. *Jesus!*, he cried. If there was ever a time he needed help! Forcing his legs to come flush against the animal's turbulent flesh, he kicked out several swipes of his spurs across its rippling flanks. There had to be way to bring this son-of-a-bitch into some form of control, but he couldn't be lucky as it was apparent the bull was hell-bent on making him eat dirt.

Thinking the buzzer couldn't go off soon enough, Cash clung to what little support he had—praying his arm would stay attached to the rest of his body. Just when he thought he was going to be ripped-clean apart, the most welcomed sound finally echoed within his ringing ears. But the animal seemed to take up momentum. *What the hell?!* The hooky bastard was just getting started. At that point, Cash knew he couldn't let go or he'd fly. Bouncing up and down and every direction sideways, his eyes frantically scanned for the barrel man. *Where was he?* He could tell he was loosing it. From the corner of his vision, he spotted the rodeo clown wildly thrashing his arms and shouting at the top of his lungs. Angrily, the bull lunged, throwing Cash mid-air—tumbling him mercilessly to the ground. Feeling his shoulder crumple like an accordion, he heard uncontrolled hooves crashed beside his head—sounding like a round from a semi-automatic rifle. Miraculously Cash rolled away, managing to crawl back to his feet. Grabbing for his hat from the ground, he ducked-out for the chutes. *My God!* He had never been on such a vicious bull with so much piss and vinegar.

Amidst the thunderous applause, the announcer's familiar voice blasted from the speakers. "That was one heck of a ride provided for us by Mister Cash McCollum. Let's all give him a great hand!"

Dizzy and feeling like his legs were going to give out, Cash stopped to gather his bearings. Was he going to pass out? Struggling to regain his focus, he leaned up against a stall railing—taking in a deep, dusty breath. With pats on the back and congratulating jostles to his shoulder—countless fans surrounded him. In the worst sort of way, he wanted to break away.

Finally, along with the crowd, his head cleared. Focusing with squinted eyes, he noticed the quiet figure standing proudly at the end of the alley. He seemed to stand out from the rest—broad-shouldered and unmovable. Cash instantly knew who it was. He also knew he was in love.

He was about to hang up when a voice finally sounded from the other end.

"Hello?"

It was a relief to hear his voice. "Lee?"

There was a silent pause, then a muffled sound as if someone was trying to catch their breath.

"Cash," Lee's voice eventually floated over the line—weakly.

"What's up?" Cash got to the point right away. "What's going on? Are you all right?" He couldn't get home quick enough to make the phone call. Even though he had left Glendive feeling very satisfied regarding the scores earned over the weekend, the unsettled sense concerning Lee piqued at his peace of mind.

"I see you did real well at the rodeo this weekend." Lee worked at denying anything was amiss—an envious coating iced his words.

"I saw your scores." Laying the cards out front, Cash waited for an explanation for the slump.

"So?" Lee clammed.

"So, I'd like to know what happened to you in Helena."

"Don't worry about it. It doesn't concern you."

"Perhaps it does." Cash was undaunted.

"Look," Lee began. "I need to go. I'll call you later."

Cash was not ready to release him. "Lee, wait." Hesitating, knowing he was venturing on thin ice. "What's wrong?"

"I told you, don't worry about it!" Lee's voice snapped across the line.

"Lee, I'm not getting' off this line until you tell me what's…" but he got cut-off by a storm of fiery words.

"Damn it, leave me alone!" With that, there was a click from the other end followed by a sea of dead static.

As if the wind had been knocked out of him, Cash quietly leaned forward and gasped—holding the receiver in his hand. *Fuck him.* There appeared to be a disconcerting pattern to Mr. Biruni's telephone etiquette, and as far as he was concerned, it was bullshit. He wasn't going to put up with it anymore.

Walking away from the phone, he had no sooner gotten two feet down the hallway when the phone began to ring out. Instinctively, he knew who it was.

Picking up the receiver, Cash stalled, "…Hello."

"I'm sorry," Lee's voice barely came over the line.

Cash remained quiet. Admitting the degree of his anger, he refrained from saying what was on his mind.

"I don't know what's the matter with me," Lee began to confess.

Cash's heart began to soften, but he remained silent.

"I wanted to call you last week, but I couldn't," Lee continued.

"Why?" Cash asked—knowing it was not characteristic of him.

"There is bad news with my mother."

"What is it?"

"I don't know. She won't tell me." Lee paused. "I know it's serious." Suddenly, in the background, a small child began to kick up a heavy fuss.

Wishing he had a periscope—that he could see through to the other end of the line, Cash remained quiet. He wanted to know Lee's private world in the worst way. From his end, it seemed so detached and compartmentalized.

He couldn't conceive what his friend's home looked like—let alone who he lived with.

Lee's attention was eventually diverted from the persistent bawling. Several muffled sounds floated into Cash's ear followed by a string of foreign words spoken in a sharp, commanding tone—only making the baby more upset.

Cash could tell Lee was unraveling. "Do you want to call me back later?"

"Would you mind?"

"No, not at all." Cash could tell there was much more to this saga than what was on the surface.

A moment of empty space settled between them even though the fussing seemed to escalate in Lee's background. Neither knew what to say. Cash felt awkward—unable to help.

"Cash?" Lee's voice finally broke through—his voice shaky. It sounded like he was trying to hold and comfort the child while wedging the phone between his shoulder and ear.

"What?"

"I miss you." Lee's words were abrupt, but longing.

They caught Cash off-guard. Fumbling for words, he cleared his throat and said the only thing that could come to his mind. "I'll call you."

CHAPTER 22

The unmistakable sound of the Viper on the gravel outside startled Cash. Looking at the clock and seeing it was only eight, he wondered why Travis was here so early. They had made plans for the day, but hadn't discussed a time. The chores still needed to be done. Well, he figured, Mr. Hunter could just cool his heels in the kitchen—he wasn't about to rush. Surprising himself, because just not that long ago, Cash would have jumped through his morning ritual in order to have that much more time with Travis. As he scuffed into the bathroom, he could hear the quiet talking of Travis and his mother.

Listening to their voices rising and falling, Cash studied himself in the bathroom mirror. His eyes were puffy from lack of sleep, maybe even from worry, it was hard to know. There seemed to be a line forming at the edges of his mouth that he hadn't noticed before. Frowning, he vigorously scrubbed his face in an effort to make it disappear.

A lot had occurred during the course of the week. Besides being pestered by a couple of newspaper reporters for a rodeo interview, haggling over plans about the prom with Jennifer, there were the unexpected conversations with Travis and Lee.

The first discussion was with Travis. It had happened at the Hunter home on Wednesday. Cash recalled scanning the college and university catalogs littered about on Travis' desk—like the propaganda they were. He had felt his blood boil. Perhaps he misunderstood—had they not agreed they would both be attending the U of M? Travis had gotten the scholarship and *supposedly* he had sent in his acceptance… the rest was simple formality—placement testing, class registration, and dorm assignment. Why then, were all these catalogues staring him in the face?

"So, tell me—where are we at with this college shit?" Cash's eyes looked up at his boyfriend who conveniently began fussing with the DVD remote.

"Huh?" Travis pretended to be distracted.

"You heard me." Cash continued with his probing—his ire gradually increasing.

"There's nothing wrong with me keepin' the fleece out to see who else might be interested." Travis tossed the remote disgustedly on the bed and went over to Cash's side.

"But why lead them on? If you've already made up your mind on going to Missoula, why are you keepin' yourself open for other possibilities? Besides, I thought you promised me we would both go to the U together." Pausing, he finally went on to ask, "You *have* completed your admission work, haven't you?"

Travis began stacking the catalogs into a random pile, not looking at Cash while he spoke. "Yes. Nothing's changed concerning that. It's just I want to see if any other offers come in before the end of the school year."

"To nurse your ego…" Cash muttered under his breath, turning from the desk and plunking himself on top of the rumpled bed.

Instantly, Travis swung around from the desk—glaring at Cash. *"What?"* There was an offensive note within his voice.

"You heard me." Cash chimed in with the same phrase he had said only minutes before.

"Don't go there." Travis soundly warned.

"Wouldn't think of it," Cash coldly responded as if he had been offered a bowl-full of Cajun-flavored cockroaches. This would be addressed again… at a more convenient time, however.

And then there had been the unnerving phone call coming from Lee during the middle of the day on Friday…

Remembering the scene of being pulled out of class when his father had been hit with the heart attack, it nearly sent him into a cold panic when the school secretary buzzed him in the middle of study hall with the phone call from Great Falls. For her to have done that meant it was an emergency.

"Yeah?" Cash numbly spoke into the receiver. Everything inside him had been hesitant in taking the call. Suddenly, he could hear heavy breathing and Lee's broken voice.

"Cash, I-I need you."

"What's the matter?" Cash held his breath.

"I don't know what to do… everything's out of control right now." It was evident Lee had been crying.

"Slow down," Cash tried to calm him. "What's wrong?"

"It's my mother. She didn't tell me much what was wrong with her, but today she went in for surgery and they found cancer. They're not sure how much it's spread." He began sobbing.

Allowing a sigh to escape his lips, Cash felt his heart go out to the lost boy on the other end. "I'm sorry."

Lee struggled to regain composure, but his sobs were not stopping.

"What can I do?" Cash sincerely asked. He wanted so badly to reach through the line and hold him.

"Cash, I need you here." Lee caught his breath, his voice was urgent. "I can't take care of everything."

With thoughts racing wildly in his mind, Cash stood at the classroom phone, staring at the wall. He whispered lightly, "Let me see what I can do." He knew he had to go up and help his buddy out in this situation. There was no question regarding that. The problem would be... breaking news to Travis. He knew his boyfriend would become unglued...and now, here he was, early no less.

The talk downstairs caught his ear. It was Travis' voice—louder than normal. Carefully turning off the water and slowly opening the door, Cash tried to listen from the landing, but couldn't make out anything being said. Then he took a couple steps—still it was no good. Finally, he settled near the middle of the staircase, sitting himself down. If he went any further, the pair in the kitchen could easily turn their heads and possibly see him eavesdropping. And normally, he wouldn't have bothered, but there was something different in the quality of their conversation, Cash could tell immediately. It advised him to be cautious.

Frustratingly, things were quiet for a moment while Travis apparently gulped his coffee and rested the mug back on the table. He heard his mother asking if Travis wanted anything to eat. *"No,"* said Travis. "I'm not really hungry yet. It's still kinda early for me."

Cash was ready to get back up and continue dressing when he heard his mother say, "I thought the thing with UM was pretty well settled. I'm a little surprised to learn that this isn't true. What made you change your mind, Travis?"

Now Cash was all alertness, his morning grogginess completely vanished. It was shocking to have his mother break the confidence which existed between them—stepping into the personal arena between him and Travis. *What was she doing?*

Travis said something in a low voice, then "I guess I'm curious to see what my options are."

Janice was silent, and there was a long pause.

The wise woman carefully selected her next batch of words, "College is a big decision. Outside of marriage, it can be the *biggest*. And no one can make that choice except for you, Travis. You have to do what you think is best in the end."

"Tell me about it. What I find really funny is how some people freely toss out what they think I should do when actually they need to think of what they're going to do themselves. My mother is good at that." Cash heard Travis' voice catch.

The steps beneath Cash's rear seemed cold and hard—forcing him to shift a little. He worked at trying not to make any noise.

"You know, Travis, and I don't know what makes me think of this," Cash was attuned to his mother's subtle shift. She was good at playing the bumbly country housewife when she knew it would get someone off their guard. "But I remember one time when I was still a child. I maybe was ten or eleven. Anyway, I had these two good friends, Janie and Lauri. We always rode the bus together; we always sat together in school." The sun was slowly coming up and shining brightly through the living room window now. Cash watched a hopeful beam starting its day-long march across the floor.

"Anyway, one day in school, I saw them pass a note. Like kids do—or did do, back when I was in school. They didn't see me see them, because when they looked back over at me, after they had done it, I quickly put my head down, pretending not to see. And when class was done and we were getting ready to go home, I saw one of them throw the note into the garbage. I followed behind them and pulled it out. I decided not to sit near them on the bus that day so I could read the note on the way home." Cash knew from the expression in her voice that she was smiling now with the memory.

"And let me tell you, that note was something else. All about me and what a terrible person I was."

And then Cash realized that his mother was making a confession, except to Travis instead of him. His heart gave a little start. He felt light-headed.

"After I got home, I had to make a decision. I had to decide whether to tell my friends that I had read their note, or whether to just throw it away and forget about it. Of course," and here she really did laugh, "you don't ever forget something like that. You know how when you're a kid, things are a lot more important than they really are—especially when it comes to your friends. When you're that age, your friends are the most important thing in the world—more important than your own family. Well, so it seems to a kid."

"So what did you do?" Travis asked, as if he felt he had to say something to prompt her.

"What I decided was, to throw the note away. I never said anything to Janie or Lauri. I thought, well, maybe they had cause to write those awful things. Maybe I had done something, like talk to a boy they liked. Something. Because, they had never done anything like that before. And," Cash could hear her rising from her chair, "they never did anything like that again. To this day, Janie Miller is one of my best friends. Lauri left for Oregon shortly after high school. But we were friends until the day she moved."

Cash's mother began rinsing dishes in the sink, making listening difficult.

"Dunno why I started that old story," she continued.

This time it was Travis' voice that came softly through. "You think Cash and I are havin' some kind of problems?" he asked.

"That's for you two boys to decide," Mrs. McCollum replied, then said nothing more, giving Travis the opportunity to continue. Which, of course, he did.

"It's just that, any more, I don't know about things. I mean, not just with Cash. About things in general. It's like I can't talk much to him—as if there's this wall that's suddenly come up between us, and trust me, it's not me that wants it there."

The water suddenly snapped off. "Cash isn't the kind to put up barriers." Janice's voice was point blank. "If he's gotten like that, something must really be eating at him."

"It's like a guessing game anymore," Travis continued, ignoring her comment. "Always trying to figure out what's going on." He stopped, letting the sound of his words linger in the air. Cash began to fidget, using the powers of his mind to command Travis to continue, anticipating what he might say, and dreading it as well. The banister that he was gripping in his left hand was causing the fingers to cramp, so he pulled the hand aside and began rubbing it—waiting. Travis said something Cash couldn't quite make out, then he continued, his voice a rising tide.

"...Where he's been, or where he's going—or always *something*. And so often, I just feel left out."

Cash didn't quite know what to do. Should he just get up and go into the kitchen—confront Travis? Or sneak quietly back up into his room. After all, he really did need to get ready. His mother's voice drifted out, she was obviously thinking carefully of what to say.

"Well, Travis. I know Cash thinks a great deal of you. You're an important person to him. You just have to give him a little room now and again. He's not used to having another person so steadily in his life." Her footsteps became closer and Cash knew she was going to come to the stairs and call for him. "Before you, I swear, his best friend was that horse."

Cash scooted back to the bathroom as lithely as he could, heart pounding.

Janice approached the stairs and called out, "Cash, Travis is here."

"I'll be down in a minute," Cash hollered back—busily getting himself ready.

As Cash finished grooming himself, he knew he had to make a decision and go with it—regardless of the consequences. Considering the dream, Lee's lack-luster rodeo scores and the recent phone calls, he knew Lee was in a desperate situation. His friend needed help. Travis would just have to understand and trust him.

Recalling the heart-to-heart discussion with his mother the night before, there was an assurance he was doing the right thing...

After pouring his soul out—telling his mother about Lee's situation—how much he was concerned about him and his mother, the look on Janice's face seemed to disclose a motherly understanding of Cash's frustration. He would never forget his mother's thoughtful words as they spoke into the wee hours of the morning. "You need to do what your heart is saying, Cash. No one can make that decision for you. Travis loves you, but it appears Lee needs you as well. You've got to figure out what you should do—then go with it."

Pulling a t-shirt from the drawer and slipping on a pair of jeans, Cash ran a comb through his hair and sent up a quick prayer. This would be a difficult hurdle to cross, but it needed to be done.

His heart felt like it was going to explode from his chest as he took each step down to the living room where Travis was quietly waiting.

"Hey," Cash softly greeted, the sound of cowboy boots scuffing across the hardwood floor.

Travis sat on the leather sofa—his face heavy and drawn. Somehow, he knew what was coming. "Hey."

Cash went to the sofa and sat down beside him. A thick cloud seemed to suddenly develop over them. Travis stared off into space, his hands folded neatly over his lap. The house was uncanningly quiet—as if waiting, with bated breath, for the final word as well.

"Did you wanna go to Red Rock Dam this morning?" Travis pushed the words out of his mouth, hoping against hope, things would work out as they had been planned.

Cash hesitated. How was he going to start this conversation? "I can't," he breathed out.

Travis turned and looked at him. Silently, he waited for the explanation. His silvery-blue eyes grew wide—cold fear resting within them.

"Travis," Cash slowly began, "Somethin's come up."

"What?" Travis' lips wrinkled, the lines in his face tightened. Suddenly, he looked very small. That massive, big frame of his seemed to melt right in front of Cash.

"I got a call yesterday..." Cash paused, staring at the blank TV, avoiding his boyfriend's face. "It was from Great Falls."

"Lee?" The way Travis spoke the name it could have been any random word. There was no emotion to it—as if his mouth had become detached from the rest of his body.

Cash could see where this discussion was going to roll. They needed to head someplace private to hash this out, he quickly decided. Rising to his feet, he said in a gentle, but firm voice, "Let's go outside." There was no way he wanted the rest of his family hear what would be exchanged between them. Besides, the peaceful outdoors this particular morning seemed particularly attractive.

Stepping out onto the large veranda, Cash inhaled the sweet, fresh prairie air. Only a gentle breeze wafted past them while the warm spring sun began to peek through the budding leaves of the old oak tree that sat in the middle of the front lawn. A couple of western meadowlarks perched on one of its branches singing their pretty morning song.

Cash focused on Travis who stood rigidly at attention near the steps, his hand gripping the wooden post that supported the awning. Carefully, he continued, "I need to go up there." *Damn it*, he told himself. It was too beautiful of a day to dump something like this out in the open. "Lee's mother had surgery yesterday and they found cancer. They're not sure what the outcome's gonna be."

Frowning, trying to grapple with the situation, Travis broke his silence. Shifting his weight from one foot to the other, his arms extended out toward Cash in an emphatic gesture. "What does that have to do with you?"

"He needs my help," Cash flatly stated—reasoning to himself he couldn't go into any more detail. His gaze focused blankly over the heavily-worn wood planks on the porch floor.

"Well, where the hell is the rest of the family?" As expected, Travis' voice elevated with disgust. "Can't they pitch in?"

"There *is* no one else." Cash's words remained monotone.

"What does he need you to do for him?" There was an incredulous quality in the way he spoke. "Hold his hand and baby-sit him?"

"No." Recalling the sound of the small child crying in many of the phone calls, Cash's mind wandered off into a sea of speculation. "There's a small child in the house that seems to need a lot of attention."

"Yeah—Lee," Travis rolled his eyes, making no apology for the sarcasm.

"No, I'm serious," Cash ignored the comment. "There's like an infant in the background that's always crying whenever I talk with him on the phone."

Travis' squinted until his eyes were slits, "How many times have you talked with him over the phone?"

Once again, Cash felt trapped. Avoiding Travis' stare, Cash hesitantly replied, "Several."

"Several." Travis took a step towards Cash. It was obvious he was trying to control his anger. With a lowered voice, he hotly asked, "How many is that? Three, ten, twenty-two?"

"Stop it!" Cash snapped. He had no time for Travis' sarcastic shit.

"Why does he think you'll be able to help him through everything? You're not a day-care provider!"

Turning, Travis angrily stomped across the veranda staring out over the vast stretch of virgin grassland. It seemed so brilliantly golden from the angle of the morning sunlight. "I don't like this, Cash! This is not good."

His voice seemed to drift away into the unending openness of land and space. There was no place for it to roost—to rest and settle down.

"I'm sorry, Travis, there is no room for discussion concerning this. I'm going up there." An unbending force of resolve took over Cash's will. He was not going to budge.

Travis swung around, speechless. Panic gripped his face, replacing the boiling anger that had been building up. "What are you saying?" his lips quivering.

"Just what I said, I'm goin' up whether you like it or not."

Shaking his head in disbelief, Travis looked as if the wind had been completely knocked out of him. "You can't. …You can't be saying this."

"I have to do this." Cash could not be more explicit.

Instantly, Travis dug his heels into the dirt. "Cash, you go up and you can just consider us over and done.

"That's not right! I need to go up there and help him and his family." Cash paused, trying to gather his wits about him. He couldn't believe Travis would make it come to this point. "You can't place that ultimatum on me." His voice became pleading, his mind swimming. "I *don't* want us to break up—instead, you *need* to understand this is somethin' that *has* to be done."

"Why you?" Travis' impatiently flung an arm out. "Why does it have to be you to jump in and assist? Where the hell is his father? Didn't you say he was a doctor?"

"He's out of the picture… has been for years, I guess. Beside, I know Lee will never ask him for his help." Cash ardently, fitfully worked at remaining calm even though everything inside him wanted to rear up—scratch frantically at the netting trying to bind him.

"But that's not your problem! You can't make yourself responsible for the situation that family is in right now. They're gonna have to work through their own shit." Travis simply would not understand Cash's point of view.

"Why does everything have to be so black and white with you?" Cash poured his heart out. "Can't you just trust me knowin' this is what I've gotta do? I can't just sit by and watch an entire family fall apart. It's just not right! Lee's a friend. I have a right to have friends. I have a right to other people in my life besides you. What if Jason—" here he stopped, his mind twisting. No, he would say it—because it was true. "What if Jason had told *you* that he couldn't get involved after your father..." He knew he didn't have to complete the thought. Travis could finish it himself.

Travis let out a gasp. *"How can you say that?"* Tears welled up in his eyes. "I know you've messed around with him—how can you say I need to be understanding while you go up there and play house with him while I sit here alone wondering what's gonna happen next? You can't dump all the responsibility of our relationship on me, Cash. That's not right either."

"I haven't messed around with him!" It was such a hopeless situation—to be placed in the defendant's chair, have the charges delivered, and the sentence decreed. There was nothing more he could think of to prove his innocence. It wouldn't matter even if he could.

Silence engulfed them—as deep as the cavernous crystal-blue sky floating above them. Cash could not believe this was happening. He would have never imagined it in a million years. Was it only several memories ago he had vowed he would never leave this love? What had happened to the snow that gently drifted past the hotel window... the twinkle of city lights far below, and the touch of a hand so tender—it had made him cry? *God, had it only been a dream?*

It started as only one... a single tear stealing its way from his eye and slowly trickling down his cheek—blazing a trail for what would immediately follow. Suddenly, without warning, his guard broke. Completely. The mighty fell. There was no way he could stop it. It flowed from a dam opened wide. It came in streams and gasps. Travis finally broke down. "Cash, can't you see what this is doing to me?"

Refusing to accept the distance, the space falling between them, Cash reached for someone he once would have died for. *Was this a mistake?* Was he insane for what he had created? Perhaps he could reverse the clock and redo what he had just written. *No.* He was doing the right thing, and Travis was just plain wrong. His face grew hot with indignity. *How dare he!* But then, truth be faced, Cash could understand Travis' feelings, off-base as they may be. Tightly, frantically, he gripped a crumbling rock with his weak, shaky fingers. He couldn't let go. Even though he felt it softly sift through his fingers like the sand on a cold, deserted beach, he struggled frantically to hold the tiny pieces of Travis' heart from falling to the floor.

The road seemed endless. Time immeasurable. Mile after mile of rolling prairie and bottomless blue sky rolled past the window as Cash drove his pick-up down the empty stretch of pavement.

Alone. He was all alone. Was this what he wanted? When he had awakened that morning, did he have any inkling what would happen? Without a doubt, he felt isolated, separated—just plain dead.

It had been difficult to approach his dad and ask for an advance on his allowance since he could only scarf up a couple of bucks from his dresser. Looking less than enthusiastic, Mr. McCollum reluctantly forked out several twenties.

"You need to get rid of that piece of shit." Had been the only blessing Mr. McCollum could muster for an incomprehensible journey. As far as he was concerned, Cash was on his own for this one.

Hastily, he had tossed his stuff into the back of the Pound Puppy—pulling out of the yard with a pocketful of half-baked expectations, and a heavy-assed truckload of 'grade-A' confusion. Over and over, he asked himself was he out of his mind? He couldn't turn his buddy down. For starters, they were both fellow cowboys—that certainly had to count for something.

Eventually, the long, horizontal countryside of the Great Plains gave way to the outskirts of civilization. Off in the distance, Cash noticed the eastern front of the snow-capped Rockies. They were quite impressive. Recalling he had been to Great Falls once before, as a Sophomore, a few memories resurrected as he glanced around. It had been an Association bull-riding clinic and he had come up with his father and brother. He could remember it had been a fun time. One night, after trying to riding bulls all afternoon, they had gone to an all-you-can-eat buffet. Cash had never eaten so much in all of his life.

As he pulled into town, his heart kicked into overdrive. Churning with a hodge-podge of emotions, his fingers trembled as he clutched the wheel and steered his way through the busy streets. He had no idea what to expect.

Pulling a crumpled piece of paper from his jeans pocket, Cash tried to make out the worn-out writing. He had almost forgotten to bring along the directions to Lee's place. Recalling that Lee had stated they lived right in town, he decided to pull to the side and gather his bearings. Dusk was beginning to approach, and he considered it not a good time to shoot from the hip—trying to locate an address in the dark.

Just a few more blocks and around the corner at a Super Fill, Cash finally pulled up in front of a tiny duplex apartment bearing the same address that was scrawled on the wrinkled note. Scanning the area, he noticed it was older, but a rather well-kept neighborhood, with large, mature trees—branches extending over the parkway.

The building was nice, but small.

Cash pulled his mudder by the curb, gratefully shutting it off. He was amazed the cops didn't pull him over on the main drag. Sliding out of the cab, he sent up a prayer—stiffly making his way up the walk to the front door. From outside, he could smell burnt eggs and cigarette smoke. Inside, a soft cry of a child overtook the low chatter coming from a television set. He recognized the sounds from the phone. This was the right place. Hesitantly, he gave several knocks on the door, waiting for someone to answer. *Now what?* He asked himself. What was going to happen from this point on? *God only knew.*

The front door finally opened; and with it, a world of chaos spilled out through the screen door—pouring shamelessly over Cash's travel weary body—spreading onto the lawn and into the quiet street. It nearly took Cash's breath away. Whatever he had been expecting—certainly wasn't what came bombarding.

"Come in," Lee barked in a commanding tone. Gesturing for him to come in, Lee half-heartedly stepped aside, allowing Cash to enter.

At first, Cash didn't recognize him. He looked like a mess. With his hair disheveled, face unshaven, and bags under his eyes, it appeared that the young man had just gotten up. Shirtless, the only things on his slender frame was a pair of frayed cut-offs and a half-smoked Marlboro dangling precariously from his mouth.

With continued second thoughts, Cash took his first step inside—absorbing what lay before him. It was all he could do—stare at the shit before him. Never in his life had he seen anything like it—the closest, perhaps, Jennifer's house. *Oh, my God*, he told himself—taking a step back.

Stark—the apartment was cold and gloomy, with no pictures, plants or decorations anywhere. Toys and other 'stuff' were randomly strewn across the floor.

Regaining his senses, he spotted the toddler, a little girl sitting in a corner of the living room with a ragged doll—her eyes were round with wonderment. She looked like she hadn't been bathed in days as her long dark-brown hair was tangled and grossly un-kept—her face soiled from tears. Despite the untidy condition, however, Cash saw something deeper. It was quite evident. Her beauty was unmistakable. She possessed an elegance that immediately touched at his soul.

Lee took a hit of smoke and defiantly blew it into the stuffy, heavy air. He walked over to a dish that was lying on the TV and crushed the butt out amidst leftovers of a half-eaten fried egg and dried-out toast.

"I thought you told me you couldn't smoke in the house," Cash spoke observantly.

"I'm not supposed to," Lee said with an indifferent attitude. "But she's not here. She's still at the hospital."

With bloodshot-dry eyes, Cash froze—looking straight at Lee. "How's your mother?"

Coldly shrugging, Lee avoided his gaze, "Who knows."

Wondering if he had missed something, Cash leaned forward—tightening his stance. "What?" *Hadn't it been Lee sobbing over the phone—pleading for him to come up because he needed help? Well, what was up with this?*

"I don't know." Lee became impertinent—obviously not in the mood for probing.

Cash remained quiet. Was he out of line for asking? Considering all the shit he had gone through earlier in the day, along with the endless trek to

Great Falls, the least Lee could do was be courteous. "You know, I didn't *have* to come up here today."

Cash barely got the words out when Lee snapped, "*Fine*, then just get the hell outta here and go back home." Angrily, he swung his arm out—gesturing toward the door.

Gathering a look of fear and frustration, the little girl began to cry. Her fingers grew white from squeezing the doll's stuffed body. Cash could not help but notice the amount of strength those little hands possessed. Everything inside him wanted to walk across the room and pick her up in his arms. Was Lee oblivious to her whimpers? *For God's sake, she needed some attention!* Lee continued to ignore her.

Staring in unbelief, Cash said, "You're somethin' else, you know that?" Turning, he went for the door. *What a fucked-up day*, he told himself. It would be one shit-assed haul through the night back to Miles City, but one thing was for sure, he couldn't wait to get out of this dump.

"*Cash, wait,*" Lee's voice softened; his black eyes revealed panic.

Turning back to Lee, Cash shot a scorching glare. "You can't imagine what I've gone through to be here with you. The last thing I deserve is bein' treated like this."

Lee remained speechless.

Tired of waiting for introductions, Cash pointed to the child who was quiet once again. "Who is she?"

"That's my daughter." He could have been talking about business news in the Wall Street Journal, or discussing the latest price of hogs at the livestock exchange from his lack of emotion.

Cash was shocked. He couldn't move. Lee didn't seem like the 'fatherly' type—not at all.

As if reading his mind, Lee slurred out with a smirk, "You had no idea did you?"

Stepping across the room, over strewn toys and clothing, Cash squatted down and looked into her eyes. "Well, what's your name?" His voice was tender.

"Her name is Elena." Lee spoke out from behind Cash. He still kept his distance. "She's almost two."

He could see many resemblances of Lee in her features—the color of her eyes, the curve of her cheeks and chin—even her lips. It took his breath away. Together, they silently stared at each other. Then, unexpectedly, something very subtle strangely tugged at his heart. He could tell she wanted to be close—to be held. Having never sensed anything like this before, he went on to accept it.

"That's the quietest she's been in days," Lee dryly stated.

Instinctively, Cash leaned forward and gently gathered her into his arms—drawing her closely to his chest. Rising to his feet, he began to slowly rock her, stroking her tiny back. Within moments, her rigid muscles began to relax—releasing all the tension. Quietly, she rested her head against his boney shoulder. Soon, she fell asleep.

It wasn't long after, his nose picked up the scent of dirty training pants. She desperately needed to be changed.

"She needs a bath, some good food…" Cash spoke with a stinging bite of contention, carrying her to the bathroom in search of a cloth to wipe her face, "…and a lotta rest." He could feel disgust burn toward Lee. What in the hell had he done for the past two days? Didn't he have enough common sense to nurture and care for his own kid? Slipping her diaper down to take a peek of the smelly situation, he finally decided, obviously not.

Cash fiddled and faddled bathing, dressing, and feeding her—his lack of experience with small children stuck out like a sore thumb. And even though he had no idea what was the proper way of doing things, Elena didn't seem to mind. From her smiles and occasional giggles, he could tell she was having fun—being the center of attention.

Finally, laying her down in bed with crisp, clean sheets and blanket, he realized this was just the beginning. With a weary sigh, and a repulsed sweep of his eyes, he noticed there wasn't a corner that didn't need attention. The entire place was an unfathomable mess.

Heading back to the living room, Cash felt his temper kick-in—discovering Lee blank-faced on the sofa, watching TV, and smoking a cigarette. *What was the matter with him?*

"You know what a broom looks like?" A sour inflection oozed from Cash's mouth. He was ready for a fight.

"Huh?" Lee looked at Cash with an empty stare.

Cash bit his upper lip. Deer in headlights was all he could think of as a contemptuous attitude overtook. "What have you done since you called me yesterday?"

Without batting an eye, Lee brazenly responded, "My mother will take care of everything when she gets back."

Not sure he had heard correctly, Cash stepped in closer. *"What?"* He had to be joking.

"My mother will take care of all this when she comes back from the hospital."

"Are you for real?" Cash couldn't believe it—a cold feeling tickled at his brain. "She's gonna need rest."

"This is women's work," Lee's words were forthright as his arm made a broad sweep of the room. "She will do it."

"Whadiya mean, women's work?" Cash exclaimed. "Can't you do anything? You got a broken arm? Looks to me that ANYONE could take care of this shit around here."

Focusing back to the television, Lee pretended to ignore Cash's outburst. "If you're hungry, there's some fried chicken in the fridge."

Marching across the room, Cash stood by the couch, looming over the nonchalant boy with a searing stare. "You may think straighten' this place is a woman's work, but I can tell you right now, it ain't gonna hurt your precious little manhood to get off your lazy ass 'n do what you shoulda been doin' days ago!"

Instantly, Lee bolted off the couch and faced-off with Cash. With arms faster than bullets, he shoved Cash backwards across the room. "Shut up!" Fire blazed from his eyes.

That was it! Fearlessly, Cash came back on Lee with a lightening-fast right hook to the eye.

Sailing back onto the couch, Lee shouted, "You son-of-a-bitch!"

"Grow up, Lee!" Cash ordered with a strong, commanding voice. "You're actin' like a goddamn baby!"

Assuming a good pout, Lee remained on the sofa defiantly glaring at Cash with one eye—cupping the other with his palm and fingers.

Enough of this! Cash headed for the kitchen to start a sink-full of warm, soapy water for the massive task lying before him. How could a place fall in such a state? Tossing food-caked dishes into the suds, he felt his anger swell. Unwillingly, he began to wash.

After a sufficient spell of brooding in the living room, Lee eventually sauntered into the kitchen and stood quietly by Cash, his countenance drawn and surly. Pride had been wounded, but Cash didn't care. All he wanted was to get the house back into some semblance of order. "There's a towel over there if you wanna help me out with dryin'."

Slowly, Lee shuffled over to the end of the counter where an extra towel lay. Grabbing it, he went back to the rack and began to dry dishes. From the look on his face, Cash could tell it was killing him as he placed each finished plate back into the cabinet.

Looking up from the sink, Cash could see swelling and bruising set into Lee's left eye. The hook had been successful—making its target and leaving its mark. He hoped there would never have to be replay.

After washing, drying, and folding several loads of dirty laundry—plus performing a hefty scrub-down to the kitchen floor on hands and knees, he went forward to attack a seemingly endless effort of dusting. Finishing that, he remade the beds with fresh, clean linen. When all was said and done, Cash was ready to 'cash-in'. He was completely torn. Sending Lee out for some late-night fast-food, he helped himself to the telephone. His intentions were to call his family earlier, but walking into this shit hole totally side-tracked him.

"We were wondering if you were going to call." His mother's voice seemed to sail lightly through the line into his weary ear.

"Mom, you wouldn't believe this place." Cash tried to explain the scene.

"So Lee needed your assistance?" An affirming tone came from her words.

"Hell, yeah!" Cash exclaimed. "This entire apartment was falling apart. The baby's diapers hadn't been changed since yesterday." Cash still couldn't believe how dirty she had been.

"The baby?" Mrs. McCollum was lost. Cash had never spoken about a child.

"Yeah, Lee has a little girl." He had no intentions of going into detail about her over the phone. "She's almost two."

A gulf of silence spanned the line—the newsbreak catching her off guard.

"How is his mother?" Janice finally moved to another topic.

"She's still in the hospital." Knowing his mom was searching for more information, he went on to say, "I guess she's hangin' in there. Lee hasn't said much about how she's doin'."

"When's she coming home?" Janice continued with her questions.

"I'm not sure. I think sometime tomorrow or Monday."

"Were you planning on staying there until she gets back?"

Recalling Elena's condition when he had arrived, he knew he couldn't allow her to go through that experience again. He was resolved to stay until she'd be back in good hands again. It was clear that nurturing was not a gift of Lee's. "Yeah, I think I better. Can't leave the little girl unattended, you know—seems that Lee can't even change a diaper."

Another uneasy quiet settled between them. Cash could tell his mother was troubled. She was always one to read between the lines. Her questions and hesitation was the give-away she was aware that things were amiss.

"Well, keep in touch," she said with a sigh. There was no way she was going to make a scene. It was a time to trust her son and his decisions regarding this issue. Cash could tell she would hang in there and support him no matter what.

"I will." Cash promised and hung up.

Looking around the quiet room, a sense of heaviness took over. He felt so lonely. Was he doing the right thing? Could he have handled the scene with Travis differently? Something gently landed on his shirt pocket, just above his chest. Glancing down, he was surprised to discover what it was. Lightly brushing it with a sore, tired finger, he watched it quickly absorb into the woven fabric. Strange… he never felt it come out, nor was he aware it had slipped down his cheek. As if dropping from the empty sky… perhaps from heaven itself, he could tell it was a tiny, single tear from a totally numb eye.

CHAPTER 23

Cash slowly walked down the emptying hallway to his locker.

Thank God the day was done. He was exhausted from the moment he woke up. *What an unbelievable weekend.* He had no idea that cleaning a house could make him ache so much. His body felt like he had ridden a dozen wild bulls.

To be honest, he had been ready to head back home Saturday night. It was a miracle he had stayed. Thinking back, he remembered how hungry, tired and irritated he was waiting for Lee to come back with some food. Just as forever seemed to pass, the wayward cowboy finally meandered into the house with a bag-full of soggy hamburgers, cold fries, and liquor breath strong enough to knock over a horse.

"Here's your fuckin' food," Lee had slurred out his words—throwing the bag on the table with a plop.

At first, Cash had thought of raising a ruckus about him coming back so late. He was ready for a knock-down, drag-out since his defenses and temper were already worn raw from the build up of the day's events. He decided, however, it wasn't worth the hassle.

Recalling how surly Clayton could be after a few drinks, he knew it would probably be the same with Lee. In a peculiar way, they both seem to share a number of traits—including a tendency for heavy drinking and a touchy temperament. Kid-leather personalities was what he called it.

…Working the combination, the lock released. It took all his remaining strength to rest the books on the shelf and grab for his jacket. God, he couldn't wait to get home. Ever since he got back from Great Falls, the only thing he desired was to be alone. The peaceful solitude of his bedroom, his private fortress of protection, seemed more inviting with each passing minute.

But it was his mind that couldn't stop. He kept rehearsing the damned weekend as if trying find to some cryptic, spiritual message through it all. One thing was for sure, if there had been intentions to sort his feelings out at the Biruni's house, it certainly had not occurred. If anything, he left more confused, lost, and uneasy regarding his relationship with Lee. Somehow, he had known this would happen—his involvement would deepen, forcing him to take a high-dive with the hope of making a change… at least for a little girl's sake…

"You seem comfortable here," Lee jealously stated. He watched Cash play with his daughter on the floor with a set of blocks. "She loves you very much."

Sunday morning was a late start for both boys. Not a word was spoken of what happened the night before.

The little girl was already up fussing for breakfast and a diaper change. Cash was focused on her from the get-go.

"Yeah?" Cash smiled, glancing up with a sparkly gleam—taking note, this was the most fun he'd had in days.

"Yes, I'm really quite surprised."

"Why's that?" Cash's curiosity struck a match.

"I don't know. For one thing, she's never warmed up to anyone else but my mother."

"Really?" That was odd, Cash thought. He found her to be an extremely warm, affectionate child.

"Yeah." Standing in the doorway, Lee nodded—his thumbs lazily hooked into his jean belt loops. "She always screams if anyone else ever tries to pick her up. Even me."

"She's a good girl."

"Unlike her mother." As if overtaken by a sea of recollective thoughts, Lee's voice softly trailed off.

"Yeah?"

Pausing, deciding the worth of sharing the rest of the story, Lee reached into his pocket for a pack of smokes. "Let's just put it this way. Her mother is extremely selfish. She has wanted nothing to do with her, or me since the day she was born."

Cash silently fed the moment with anticipation.

"If it hadn't been for my mother, she would have been put up for adoption."

The look on Cash's face must have revealed bewilderment as he rose to his feet.

Acknowledging the questioning look, Lee took a hit—slowly unraveling a few more knots.

"We just finished our sophomore year, and it was summer. Her name was Christine." Stalling momentarily, as if gathering strength to continue, Lee took a hard swallow. "She was popular and intelligent, head cheerleader— you know the type. She was a member of Speech and Debate of which I got involved with too. We became friends. Our fathers were both docs and they worked together at the hospital. Her dad was in OB; mine was a surgeon... head of the damned department. Our parents hated us together, which was why we hung out. We liked pissin' em off. Buncha snobs, we called 'em. Tight-assed, bullshit-laden aristocrats. It was great. We were such rebels." Lee checked out his cigarette glowing against his knuckles. "Then she got pregnant and all hell appeared on earth." Obviously, he fought the urge to toss the lit butt on the carpeted floor.

"We're Muslim, you see. And they were Protestant... Christian. You can guess what manner of shit that caused."

Actually, Cash couldn't. He knew nothing about Islam and Lee seemed basically normal, so he couldn't imagine the big deal.

"She went away for awhile," he went on, "shipped back East to a relative— eventually returning with Elena."

Cash remained speechless, waiting for the rest of the saga.

"After that, her dad and mine acted like they'd never met, and Christine and her folks decided to put Elena up for adoption. By that time, my parents were in the process of splitting up since my mom discovered dad had been seeing another woman behind her back for a number of years...about half his age, not much older than me." Lee crushed out his cigarette. "My mother was livid. She went to a lawyer and filed for divorce. In our culture, it's not acceptable for a woman to divorce her husband. It is considered direct rebellion, and in some circles—harlotry. In many Muslim states, there are no legal provisions for such acts requested by women. The laws see females as property of their husband's households; it remains that way until their deaths. My mother had broken the rules."

"Well, do you blame her?" Cash found himself ready to come to her defense.

"That's not the issue. She broke the laws"

"What about your dad? He had broken the laws of marriage." Recalling the rules of the Roman Catholic Church, Cash felt himself develop a tinge of anger toward Lee and his father.

"He's still the man." Lee defended without emotion.

Coming from two different levels—separate mind-sets—Cash knew at that moment, they would never agree on this subject. He remained silent.

"Well, anyway," Lee went on to finish the story, "my mother eventually divorced my dad, and she adopted Elena. She was adamant."

For a moment, Cash stood completely focused on Lee, trying to assimilate all that had been said. This was quite a story, he reasoned. It shed a lot of light on a number of mysteries. Finally, separating his stunned lips, he allowed the only word he could think of to escape. "Wow."

"Yup... quite a story, huh?" Lee grinned almost in a sarcastic, cynical way.

"What happened to your dad?" Cash was unable to withhold the question.

"He's still here in town." Lee's emotions remained stable. "He's married to that gal and I think she's pregnant now."

Unreal, Cash quietly thought to himself slowly coming out of his spell. The entire ordeal was absolutely unthinkable.

Looking over toward Mrs. Biruni's bedroom, a thought suddenly jumped into his mind. They needed to go to the hospital. He wanted to meet this strong-willed, determined, rebellious woman. The rest of the puzzle needed to be pieced together. "We should go see your mother..."

Recalling her lying in that hospital bed, all Cash could think of was how tired and very sad she looked. For a woman who was probably not much different in age from his own mother, she had appeared so vastly older.

Except when asking her son how Elena was doing, she had been rather quiet.

Explaining to his mother the baby was with the nurses at the desk, Lee had gone on to say he was unable to bring her because of the hospital rules—no children in patient rooms.

Something had told Cash that her son would not relay the rest of the story—that upon entering the hospital, he had literally thrusted the screaming child into one of the nurses arms stating they were going to see Altiar Biruni. They would be back in several minutes.

Speaking with a strong Turkish accent, she had bombarded Lee—one question after another—of which he indifferently blew off by simply nodding.

"What you do weeth harr?" Anger blazing in her dark eyes. "You geef harr to complete stranger?!"

The more he did that, the more she got upset. Cash could tell from the squinted, dark shadows of her eyes, if she felt better, she would have reached out and slapped him with her hand. With what little energy she had left, she finally allowed a heavy, exhausted sigh to escape—shifting her attention to Cash, silently standing by Lee's side. Quickly, her face had lit up like a Christmas tree when Lee finally introduced him as his friend. An unexpected softness came over her.

Like Elena, Mrs. Biruni had instantly fallen in love with Cash.

"You are goot boy, I make you kibbeh when I get out a here." She had smiled warmly—continuing to speak with a heavy tongue, "Now, you be goot influence on Lee..."

Closing his locker door, Cash turned and headed for the entrance. Rounding the corner of the hallway, he spotted him—nearly taking his heart away. It was the first time seeing Travis since Saturday. Even though, outwardly, he looked the same—with his usual handsome build and extreme high n' tight—something was missing. There was no audacious spring to his step, no strut to his feet. Surprisingly, it caught Cash—the pain—plunging itself into his soul like an unforgiving knife.

Closely, silently spying Travis approach the doors, Cash stood at the bend of the hallway. How he longed for that smooth, wispy touch, the sweet, musky scent, and a soft, gentle whisper in his ear. There was something overwhelmingly powerful that wanted him to shout out his name and break into a run. Not from him... but to him. Right into his big incredible arms. Would he be able to move on from this? He really had his doubts.

Listening to the Viper start up, Cash's thoughts wandered back to the rest of that weekend at the Biruni house...

"Are you coming to bed?" Lee's voice was cool, assuming.

It was Sunday night.

367

Something in his eyes grabbed at Cash and would not let go. Was this an invitation or simply an expectation?

The night before, they had slept separately—Cash sleeping on the living room couch and Lee resigning himself to his own bed. It had been a decision demanding no discussion, since they were still on the outs.

Hesitating in the old recliner—staring at Lee, Cash fought with his thoughts. *Was this right, or wrong?* Inside, he still had questions, but Travis had said they were through. Kaput. So, now was he free?

Without a word, he obediently pushed himself from the chair and followed Lee to the tiny bedroom. In all its supremacy, silence overtook them.

Together, slipping off their boots, belt buckles and inner battles, they slid their bodies between the covers of the tiny bed allowing their flesh to rest comfortably against each other. They became one in effort and spirit—with the air of something rather eclectic culminating between them and their peculiar bond.

Afterwards, in the afterglow, Cash settled in next to Lee—moving close, but not too close. Raising his eyes in the darkness, finding sleep difficult in the stuffy little room, he struggled at putting his mind to rest. The sound of voices from the apartment next door drifted through the paper-thin wall catching his ear, bringing him rudely back from the sleep well-earned by a hard day. Looking over to the peaceful, reposed figure beside him, a feeling of envy overtook. His partner seemed to pass easily into that realm of steady, slow breathing.

Even though he was asleep, and of course, nothing had been said between them, Lee seemed to assume his rightful, new place as Cash's boyfriend— extending an arm across the blond youth's gracefully curved chest. As a symbol of possession, Lee unconsciously restrained Cash from getting up in the middle of the night.

When Cash tried to take a midnight piss, he had awakened and grabbed the stunned Irishman's forearm. "Where are you going?" The tone was quiet, yet domineering.

Cash recalled his response. *"Like where the hell do you think I'm goin?"* As much as he disliked Lee's controlling nature, he still felt it to be an odd comfort.

Occasionally, a car rumbled past outside, encouraging Cash to silently curse the intrusion.

He was mystified. Why was he here? Did he really want something from Lee? If so, what? Like Travis, they were vastly different—different cultures, different histories and different opinions. The thing they *did* share together was the world of rodeo, and *that* seemed to count for *something*.

Lee's personality was a bittersweet herb that permeated the food on his plate. With a determined dominance, and pair of keen eyes, he was like a mountain lion—calculating every smooth move, but with no gentleness. It was as if an entire canyon of emotion was skipped over by Lee's heart. A person could go directly from one side to the other, with no pause in-between—no chance to fall into the chasm...

The evening slowly settled into early black morning, and Cash's brain wavered confusedly between things perceived awake and asleep. Once, he imagined Brownie down by the Yellowstone in the bright sunshine of summer—except the river water was black and churning. As they picked their way across a cliff that was continuously crumbling down a forever distance, he began to look over, only to feel a movement arousing him. Once again, he became dimly aware of the tiny bedroom surrounding him.

Then he heard words being spoken into his ear.

I love you.

He quickly came awake, raising his head to look about. Turning to Lee, he knew the words had come from his direction. But Lee was still motionless, apparently asleep—eyes tightly closed. Cash looked at him for a moment, eyes traveling the length of the slender body lying languid under the sheets. He could have sworn he had heard it. At least, he thought he had. It hadn't been part of the dream—or was it?

Wearily, he flopped his head back onto the pillow—knowing at that moment he would never get to sleep. No, Cash reassured himself, he'd been asleep. He was in that confused place one gets between two worlds. If he had actually heard anything, it was coming from his own brain, maybe from his own desires. But, that thought was no more comforting than the conviction that it had belonged to Lee's lips.

What had it meant—this near silent middle-of-the-night 'I love you'? Why say such words? Cash tried to keep his eyes closed, but couldn't. He didn't want his mind to go in that direction—knowing it would be a mistake to do so. For one thing, it was too soon. What about Travis?

One thing he couldn't deny, he had feelings for Lee, certainly. But love? That had been reserved for Travis, or at least it had been before coming to Great Falls—*that* particular kind of love, anyway. Yet when his thoughts shifted back to Lee, aside from all of the external, away from the public display, the question hit him broadside… what, exactly, DID he think of Lee? More than a friend, now more than a brother, there certainly was an emotion, he had to be honest. Maybe he was just being softened by his tiredness, aching body, and rampant desire for sleep.

Chill-bumps ran through his body.

The idea that Lee loved him was beyond confusing. Until that night, Lee seemed to love no one and nothing… not even rodeo. What he did, he did either because he wanted to, or was good at it. There was no emotion involved aside from frustration and occasional anger. If he was falling into love, it would mean the falling into other things as well. Cash wasn't even sure he wanted Lee's love, truth be told. It would confuse everything, making his ongoing issues with Travis more complicated and irresolvable than they currently were. Cash didn't want to love Lee and he didn't want Lee loving him, it was as simple as that. And yet—there was always the *and yet*. Try as he wanted, Cash couldn't get the idea, with its attached emotion, away from him.

He was certain now—Lee had just told him that he loved him. Any reasonable person would have just shoved the sleeper and asked, what did you say? But that was impossible here. Lee had assumed Cash was asleep, *and yet* he had felt the need to...

The tear formed in the corner of his left eye, the eye closest to the pillow—closest to Lee, Cash pushed his face hard against the rough cotton, not knowing what it represented. If love was intruding its way into this relationship, and if that was true, what then?

Damn, damn, damn! Cash wildly thought—wanting to shout...

Making his way out into the quiet, school parking lot, Cash recalled how he was so utterly worn-out with all this complicated thinking. Where was this taking him? Was he making mountains out of mole hills—or was he on a true quest? Life was quite profound, when he dared confront it. Or maybe it was actually quite simple, and he just seemed to make it the other way.

Chapter 24

"Why can't we have our prom somewhere decent, like in the hotel ballroom or something?" Jennifer whined as they pulled into the high school parking lot. She eyed the gym building warily, a glum expression on her doughy, overly made-up face.

"This really kinda sucks." Her mouth was red and seemed swollen. Cash avoided looking at the repulsive orifice as she moved it.

"It's better than not going to the prom at all," Tiffany jabbed the back of Jennifer's seat with her elbow. "Come on, get your fat ass outta the car."

From the back seat, Cash heard a low moan as all the doors opened at once. Travis did an end-run so impressive he only barely managed to miss Tiffany as she stepped out—brushing the front of her gown with her hands. She glanced up—smiling in a puzzled way as though she was surprised to see Travis standing in front of her. Travis gave an almost inaudible sigh.

"At least Travis is a gentleman." Jennifer stood a few feet from the car, halfway in a turn towards the gym, halfway back towards Cash who was hurrying to catch up. He said nothing, already weary from what promised to be the longest night of his life. When he reluctantly reached out for Jennifer's arm, she moved forward with a small motion, uncertain what he wanted.

"Huh?" She glanced at Cash's extended hand, then said, "Oh," and giggled a little. Her breasts seemed to shake in their pink chiffon binding. Cash tried not to stare.

They handed their tickets off to the bored science teacher manning the doors. "Have fun," Mr. Woods mumbled with a distinct lack of sincerity as they passed.

Inside, the gym was decorated in the school colors—white and royal blue—purity and power. It all merged in an inharmonious celebration against the dismal grey and beige ceilings and floors. The basketball hoops had been garlanded with white and red flowers, even the seat railings were covered in crepe, all in a vain attempt to disguise the utilitarianism of the building itself. The ultimate decoration, if one could call it, was an over life-sized banner of Travis' likeness pictured with a football in hand, poised with a front tackle position right next to the original painting of a bronc-riding cowboy situated directly over the hoop located at the opposite end of the gym from the main entrance.

In jest, Jennifer drew the sign of the cross over her face, chest and shoulders as her eyes focused and shifted up at the brazen memorial. "My, gosh, you feel like you need to genuflect every time you come into this place."

Trying to ignore her thoughtless comment, Cash nervously bit at his lips as he guided them to a table at the far end of the floor.

Jennifer reluctantly trundled alongside him much like Brownie would when being led from of his stall inside the stables out to the corral. "Why do we gotta sit so far from the band?" Her sullen voice shot through Cash.

Trying to make himself emotionally detatched, he shook his head. "So we can hear each other talk, that's why." He didn't bother to look over at her as he spoke.

The tables were covered in white cloth along with the metal folding chairs. Cash plunked down, allowing the legs of the chair to scratch into the gym floor. Travis instinctively sat next to Cash, leaving the girls to face each other.

Jennifer immediately began fussing with her dress as she sat, muttering "I hope I don't get too wrinkled," the whole while.

Cash hadn't planned on them being nearly the first to arrive, but that would make sense since most of the other prom goers were still busy with dinner and last minute make-outs. Only their small party had come directly from home. Neither he nor Travis had been able to come up with an excuse to delay things.

"Why don't you get me some punch," Jennifer nudged Cash's arm. He looked around. "It's over there," she pointed, with something of a snarl, her wrist corsage shaking.

He and Travis stood together at one time, forcing a smile at one another across their date's heads. They walked off.

"You look so unbelievably nice," Travis whispered, appraising Cash's black tuxedo up and down. Cash, for his part, was the most uncomfortable he had ever felt in his life and wanted to scratch and tug at his costume.

"I feel ridiculous in this outfit," he hissed.

"You don't look ridiculous …anything but." In spite of his admiring smile, there was a hallow emptiness to Travis' voice and an undeniable sadness in his eyes. He was going to say something else, but stopped in the middle of his breath.

Cash stopped mid-stride and turned to Travis. Suddenly, he felt the pull at his heart. He could tell the other boy wanted to speak, but was fighting his emotions.

A deafening silence felt between them.

When they got back to the table the girls were whispering and pointing behind their hands.

"Who are we assassinating now?" Travis asked, a little too loudly. It was obvious he was trying to mask the inner pain.

They only giggled.

Cash drank his watery punch in one gulp—suddenly thirsty for another. He had sincerely wondered if this entire thing was actually going to pull off since the relationship between him and Travis had pretty much been laid to rest in a coffin. Being men of their word, however, neither one had backed out. Reasoning it over in his mind, it seemed to speak a lot of their integrity.

The band was still setting up and already he was restless. At least dancing would be a distraction.

"Isn't that Jimmy Atherton over there?" Jennifer nodded to another table.

Jimmy Atherton was the smartest kid in school, and the nerdiest, with glasses thicker than Jennifer's.

Cash immediately realized what a good match they might make.

"I'm surprised to see him here," she continued unprompted. "You know what they say about him."

Tiffany giggled.

Cash moved his chair closer to Jennifer. "No, WHAT do they say?" He looked hard at her, but now she was giggling as well. *When is that damned band going to start playing?*

As though reading his mind, Tiffany chirped, "The band looks like some of the same people who play for the football games."

Travis immediately turned his head.

"Ugh," Tiffany continued. "Naturally, we can't even get a real band. They probably don't know anything good. Just you wait."

Tiffany folded her hands on the top of the table. Her wrists were bare since Travis had forgotten to buy her a corsage, giving her a half-dozen roses instead, like she was a patient in a hospital. She had tossed the flowers next to her in the car with a disgusted *humph!*

"How should I know," Travis had lied. "They don't have proms any more in California."

They all drummed their fingers on the tabletop in unison, each finding the motion uniquely fascinating. "I think I need another punch," Cash declared over the humming of the amplifiers and *check, check.*

"They should have set up before we got here," Tiffany opined. "Making us listen to this is so rude."

Cash stole glances periodically towards Travis, dressed in a sharp, designer black tux and brand new oxfords. Looking down at his own worn out, but newly polished black cowboy boots, he sighed, thinking that on a night like this, it would be nice to have money. Even the cuff-links on his ex's French sleeved shirt appeared rich—pure ebony embedded in highest quality gold—probably refined and set somewhere exotic such as South Africa.

His mind traveled back to the ranch house where his mother had patiently assisted him in getting ready for the big event.

"Cash," she had pleaded, "you have to wear the cummerbund."

"Yeah, says who?" He had remembered how she had smiled and shook her head—folding the black satin in her hands. He thought that if she had said "Travis, that's who," he might have worn it.

The first notes from the band jarred him back to his surroundings. Jennifer jumped up so fast she almost toppled her chair. "About damned time," she yelped as she approached Cash—hand out.

Might as well get this over with, Cash thought, being led to the execution, Travis and Tiffany following slowly behind.

Naturally, the first song was a slow one, which annoyed Cash beyond reason. Jennifer latched herself onto him, arm up to his shoulder, the other working to find his reluctant hand. She then pushed herself against him, too close, and would have even leaned her head on his chest had he not managed to maneuver away. Neither spoke as they danced, which made the whole ordeal more tolerable. Cash didn't want distractions. His only desire was to watch Travis glide Tiffany around the room. He had to admit, they looked nice together—Tiffany with her white-blond head neatly contrasted Travis' dark hair and tux, her gown a sparkly midnight blue. Cash noticed others who watched them too—eyes riveted with envy, Cash's most of all.

"Cash," Jennifer interrupted his reverie, "do you ever think about what you're gonna do after high school?" She raised her chin up towards him.

What a time to ask that question, thought Cash—especially after the last month and a half. "All the time," he answered, continuing to stare at Travis. Between exhaustive drives to qualified rodeo events and spending the remainder of his free-time commuting to Great Falls, he honestly wondered which way his life was going to turn once he received that coveted diploma.

Jennifer waited a second, expectant, then bumped her forehead against his chest as she lowered it back without resolve.

Cash had never seen Travis dance. Not this kind of dancing, anyway. It was captivating because in a way, Travis' whole being was a dance, with the movements he made on the football field, behind the wheel of his car, and in the silence surrounding his bed. Little waves of energy, sometimes floating, sometimes emanating directly from somewhere deep inside— Cash continued with his close observance—appreciating, worshipping his every sway.

Finally, when Cash was just beginning to think the slow dancing was never going to end, it did. He released Jennifer abruptly and walked back to the table, Jennifer trailing a step behind. There, he met up with Travis.

"You're a damned good dancer," Cash smiled directly into those blue eyes, "—like everything you do." A longing, aching tone rode through his words. At the edge of his lips, it sat. Travis glanced over to Cash with a warm smile. It was obvious he wanted to speak, but he remained silent. His eyes said it all, however.

Tiffany was clinging possessively to Travis, her arm hooked in his. Cash admired his own restraint, because he wanted nothing more than to smack that arm aside. He wondered what kind of a world it would be if he could just push the bitch butt-down onto the hard floor, grab him—his first love, and dance—just dance, with no thoughts or concerns behind the action. Worried that his thoughts would cause him to start flushing, he quickly put them aside.

The band started up again, a fast song this time.

"Cash, don't you wanna dance?" Jennifer wheedled, forgotten by his side.

"No," he shook her away, "I don't like to fast dance. Don't much like to dance at all," he added, continuing to toss his gaze toward Travis, feeling his stomach clench. "You go ahead."

Jennifer tapped Tiffany's shoulder. "Let's go" she snipped with a look back at Cash that said *losers!* Cash saw her heading in the direction towards Jimmy Atherton. He wasn't displeased.

Travis sat with Cash at the table wordless for awhile, the blare of the music being a blessing since there was so much awkwardness hanging between them. Cash wished he was anyone else but himself this evening. Looking at the boy whose heart he had hacked apart, he really didn't know what he could say.

"So, how have you been doin'?" Travis swallowed hard, pushing the words out with a quiver. Unconsciously, he brought a stray hand up to one of his eyebrows—allowing his forefinger and thumb to fidget across the short, flowing hairs.

Jesus. Cash helplessly thought. This was a lot harder than what he had initially planned. With Jennifer hitched to Tiffany Jo, it was a true try on his patience, but facing-off with Travis, it was simply unbearable. It was difficult enough to wander through the halls at school, head out to the corral each evening, and even walk through the house without thinking of Travis, but to gaze deeply into his elegantly handsome face, with dimmed light, tuxes, and boutonnières, it was too much... way too much. "All right," was all he could muster. He felt something wedge itself in his throat.

Travis froze. His eyes locked on Cash. The silence thickened between them as he drew in a deep breath. Separating his sad, shaking lips, the words floated out into the air as a soft whisper—no, more like a prayer. "You know how much I miss you."

Looking away, fighting the wetness in his eyes, Cash was ready to bolt from the table—out of the room. He couldn't take any more. It was as if his soul was being cracked and broken—slowly ground to a mulch. A quick nod was the only thing generated. He could not talk.

In direct inversion to the slow song, the next one ended up way too fast, and in a flash, the girls were back—punches in hand. "Since you goofs can't get yourselves together enough to get us drinks…"

Cash noticed that any more Jennifer kept her voice modulated in a consistent whine. No wonder her family was crazy, he would be too if he had to listen to her like this day in and day out.

"Speaking of which…" Tiffany still stood, cup in hand. "I need to go out to the car."

When no one at the table said anything, she repeated, louder, "I NEED to go OUT to the CAR."

"Oh, yeah," Jennifer fumbled with herself. "We need to go out."

Travis and Cash remained where they were until two sets of hands yanked at their respective jackets.

"Not by ourselves."

Cash rose to his feet, "I need a smoke anyway," thinking this couldn't have come at a better time—besides, another slow song was starting.

Staying close to the front door while he lit up, he watched the others walk on. A minute, then two, passed. Cash threw his stub down and went back into the building. Some more time passed before the little band returned, Travis leading the way. Even from way across the room, Cash could read trouble on Travis' face.

Travis reached the table first, flinging his chair back. "Stupid bitch," was all he said.

The girls followed up, setting their drinks on the table, not bothering to sit back down, since they were in the mood for dancing. Cash looked up at Jennifer, then over at Travis. Good as he was with horses, he wasn't the best when it came to reading the body language of humans. Still, there was no doubt what he needed to do. He remained seated.

When they were out of ear shot, Travis moved closer. "Do you know what that dumb broad tried?" Cash wanted to ask which one he was referring to.

"When we got out to the car, seems Tiffany Ho had a bottle of whiskey back there. So she wanted to put some in her punch, which was okay with me. I don't care if the bitch gets drunk. I don't care if she passes out even, save me some headache. But..." Travis looked quickly about, then resumed, "she wanted me to sit in the car with her while she drank. So I sat for a bit and then she reached over and started putting her hands all over me, tried to kiss me." Cash watched a shudder overtake Travis. "Put her hands on my damned crotch, for God's sake." Travis took a deep breath, "Shit-fire, like I knew what to do, so I pushed her away, asking what the fuck was she doing? She said, didn't I like it? Didn't I want it? Christ, by then, I needed a drink myself."

Cash tried not to laugh, but couldn't resist. A guffaw quaked out of him.

"Dammit, Cash, it isn't funny."

Cash scanned the dancing crowd until he found Tiffany and Jennifer. As expected, they were talking together more than dancing, their faces turned slightly in the direction of the table. Cash felt a sudden chill and thought longingly about the whiskey in the backseat.

"Yeah, maybe not, Travis, but everyone in the school knows what a skank Tiffany is. Don't worry about it. She'll probably hit up Jimmy Atherton next." He knew his words were not going to comfort the upset youth, but he at least made an effort. Suddenly, without any warning, a pink chiffon bow almost jammed into his eyes.

"I want to dance," Jennifer said.

381

Distracted, Cash rose reflexively, leading her out to the dance floor while the band sacrificed some obtrusive tune to the indifferent crowd.

"You know what your friend Travis just did to my friend Tiffany a minute ago?" Cash wondered why she needed to mention names since there were only four of them and two of them were now dancing together. When he gave no response, Jennifer continued. "They were in the car having a drink and then Travis acted like he wanted something from Tiffany…you know! Then she was getting ready, and he pushed her away! He shoved her! Cash, your friend Travis shoved Tiffany!"

As if he had been personally responsible… well, it was a hell of a lot less than what he would have done, he hotly thought to himself. Wondering where Jennifer had been during the little encounter, he went on to ask, "So, what's your point?"

Jennifer let out a long breath, shaking her head the entire time. "Why do you *think* they went out to the car together? Just to get drunk?" making the statement as though it was the most logical thing in the entire world. "Jesus, Cash, I'm beginning to think…" but she was stopped by Cash's intense glare.

"Think what?" Cash was ready to take her on. He had had enough of this evening, and as far as he was concerned, he was no mood to put up with her shit.

"Nothing," she began, shaking her head. A nervous look quickly came over her face. She knew she had crossed a line. "I'm sorry. I didn't mean to get you upset."

Well, that was a first, Cash dismally told himself, guiding her across the dance floor, all the while closely studying her face. Calming himself somewhat in order to catch his breath, he went on to say, "Look, Jennifer, you better be careful where you go in people's lives. There's a lotta stuff we're probably not aware of with those we chum around."

In a silent moment, which seemed to last forever, she studied him closely. For once, he seemed to get through to her—that there might be more to the scene than what was visible.

Somewhere in her rough-mannered temperament, she somehow managed to gather some understanding of the situation and show some sensitivity to Cash's raw spirit. Taking hold of his hand firmly, reassuringly, she quietly rested her head against his chest—saying nothing.

Cash could feel those damn tears well-up in his eyes as he allowed the tension in his muscles to relax. Smoothly, they glided in rhythm to the beat of the music. *God, could anything good come out of this evening?*

"Got a monopoly on this young lady?" A voice unexpectedly came from behind Cash, who turned his head sharply.

"Not at all, Jens," Cash force a smile and slowly moved away from them. "You may have her..." His voice trailed off along with a corral-full of thoughts.

Back at the table, Travis and Tiffany continued their impasse—one waiting for the other to make the first move.

"Harlan Jens took my date," Cash announced casually. "Wanna dance?" He was shocked and quite amused when both Travis and Tiffany looked up.

"Jennifer can have that fat pig," Tiffany said, jumping to her feet. "Come on, Cash."

For the moment he chose to ignore Travis.

"What's with your friend, anyway?" Tiffany began, assuming Cash already knew the story from Jennifer.

He decided to act ignorant. "Whatcha talkin' 'bout?" Somewhere in his early upbringing, he realized from experience that most people equated a broad accent with a small brain. Probably from his Texas relatives…

Tiffany smelled vaguely of roses and some other sweet, nauseous scent. "I think you know what I'm talking about—Travis and me."

The song was quickly coming to a close, but rather than go back, Cash insisted they stand there and wait for the next number, subliminally nursing her to spill the beans on her little tale of woe. Inside, he really could have cared less, but outwardly, he pretended to be eager to hear what Tiffany had to say.

She lowered her voice once it became quiet. "He is SO damned hot, and yet when I got him alone in the car, he wouldn't do anything. In fact, the son-of-a-bitch pushed me away."

Cash cleared his throat. "From what Jennifer says, you weren't exactly alone in that car."

He watched her expression carefully—her pale complexion rapidly turning pink.

"What Jennifer says….Jennifer…well," Tiffany paused, mid-thought, reviewing the situation in her mind. "Jennifer was there? I guess maybe she was."

"So, you thought Travis was interested in a three-way or somethin'?"

Now, Tiffany was blushing a raging red. Hell, Cash thought, she was probably no stranger to three-ways.

"No, not at all, nothing like that." A quick beat rescued her in her embarrassment. "Just that…" she turned side to side, pretending to be caught up in the music, panting a little as she moved. "Damned that Jennifer." Tiffany's eyes darted anxiously around. Spotting Jimmy Atherton vaguely standing by the refreshment table, she undulated in his direction. "Hey, would you like to dance?" It was obvious she wanted to pair-up with a more agreeable partner.

Cash graciously allowed her.

"I think I got her good." Cash smiled, returning to Travis. "I think she'll keep her mouth shut now."

Travis's eyes were following Harlan and Jennifer. At first, he said nothing. Then he looked carefully at Cash. "I don't know, I guess I'm more concerned about those two," nodding his head in their direction.

Cash suddenly felt indescribably sad and tired. There was no more shit he wanted to deal with—no more Jennifer, no more Tiffany ...no more ornery boyfriends. All he wanted was to put his arms around Travis and hold him. He needed a healing, he longed for his heart to find a home. There were no words that could describe how much he missed Travis.

CHAPTER 25

Looking out the window of Lee's immaculate pick-up, across the numbingly, endless miles of tall, grassy plains, Cash couldn't decide if he enjoyed the traveling or was simply inured to it. He leaned his head against the headrest, hypnotized by the uniform beauty of the land, and its boring repetitiveness. At least it was spring. The thought of any chance in having to plow through snow was less than appealing.

"You going to keep doing this after you get outta school?" Lee had the annoying habit of driving long distances in total silence, only to interrupt it with a question or comment that required an answer.

Cash shrugged. "Haven't decided." He saw Lee turn his head ever so slightly in Cash's direction, then turn back to the road.

"Season's getting on. You're thinking about it, though. Right?"

That was another thing about Lee that annoyed Cash—the near perfect clarity of the way he talked. Cash wondered if it was the self-conscious by-product of being raised in a home full of embarrassing accents.

"Yeah, I think about it all the time, matter of fact. Why?" Cash gave Lee a suspicious eye. "Hoping I won't go pro and get off the circuit? Leaving the field that much wider for you?"

That got a chuckle out of Lee. "Sure. Makes sense. But, your brother went to college."

"Clint, yep. He went away." Cash pushed aside uncomfortable feelings. "He ain't me, though. He wasn't that good at it. Me, I figure maybe college can wait."

They drove a bit longer before Cash asked, "You?"

Lee spat a bitter laugh, shaking his head. "What do you think? What else do I have to do?"

Cash thought back to that last afternoon in Travis' room. Like rehashing through a freakin' bad dream one more time, he could envision those damn university catalogs on his desk...

"I don't get this thing with the football scholarship," Cash had complained, lying back on the rumpled bed. "Your mom's got money, you can go to any school you want. Why do you waste your time chasin' scholarships you might not even get?"

"Because, Cash," he spoke in a way like how could one boy be so dumb, "it'll look good on my resume."

Cash snorted. "I don't think the pros, who come scoutin', are gonna be lookin' at your resume."

Travis sat on the desk chair with a sigh. "Why are you such a fuckwit at times?" He waved his hand at the books, an acknowledgement of their power. "I'm talking about my life resume. The thing that's gonna go with me long as I live, Bucky." He pulled out the University of Oklahoma catalog, and fingered the already-worn pages. "Besides, getting that scholarship means they want me. No questions, no problems. The team is as good as got. Saves me a hell of a lot of work."

"Not like you'd have to work that hard," Cash interrupted. "Everyone's already convinced what you can do."

"Maybe. Maybe here—in this pit-stop of a town. Hundreds—thousands—of towns just like this one, all over the country. And thousands of guys just like me," at that, he slammed Oklahoma against the desk top, "all looking for their chance…"

A pothole in the road shook Cash back to the present.

"That's what I don't get about you, Lee," Cash wearily shoved Travis out of his mind for the millionth time. "Your dad was a doctor. Whatcha doin' this for? What'd your parents think when you told 'em you were gonna keep ridin' bull?"

Lee stayed quiet a minute, then said, almost like he was talking to himself, "You think it's easy being a foreign doctor around here?"

"Then why not just go somewhere else? Like the coast. Why stay here?" Cash gave Lee his full attention. He watched Lee blink a time or two, waiting a beat before returning Cash's stare.

"My dad needed to get away from some kind of political troubles back in the old country—I'm not really sure." He held his breath. "When we got here—we all wanted to fit in. With me, since I liked horses and I'm not half-bad in the arena, you know it would be crazy for me not to rodeo." Lee glanced a wide grin Cash's way. "Nothing like being a rodeo champ to get you to be one of the boys around here."

Once his curiosity was piqued, Cash could work at a bit of information like a scab. His mother had labeled it a bad habit.

"But your dad…" He blurted.

Lee laughed easily now. "Shut the fuck up." He put his arm up on the rest and placed his cheek against the palm of his hand.

"Yeah," Cash continued, undaunted, "seems a lot of people come out here, because they're tryin' to get away from somethin'."

The prairie was alive with the movement of the constant winds. Cash would have enjoyed the scenery, if he hadn't been so caught up now by the boy sitting next to him.

Lee had recently developed the affectation of referring to himself as a native American to dim bulbs who didn't know any better. A sportswriter in Butte had cornered them during an event and asked Lee, point-blank, if he was an Indian. Lee had put on an insincere smile and said, "Yeah." Then, after the reporter was gone, he had turned to Cash and asked, "Quick, what kinda Indian am I?"

The only tribe Cash could think of was Cheyenne.

"No good," Lee explained. "They can check me out too easy. What's some Canadian border tribe, no one knows anything about?"

Cash admired and disliked Lee's duplicitous nature. One thing he could easily see was how handy it came in when a guy needed to hide behind the truth.

"Rodeo life doesn't last long. That's the problem." For the most part, Lee didn't allow himself to sound weary. Now, however, he did. "But for me—it's all I got."

"Unless you get killed—"Cash interjected.

"Or worse, break your neck and live." Lee finished the worn wisdom.

They both chuckled.

The truck rattled down the road, a silence settling in the cab. Cash glanced Lee's way every now and again—feeling the strange attraction grip at his guts. Generally Lee handled the steering wheel tightly when he drove, but now his hands were relaxed and easy. He seemed so lost, but then, wasn't everyone? Cash could not help but ask himself the bitterly-raw question. He knew the answer, but he didn't want to say it.

"I hate you, Cash McCollum." Lee's voice was soft. "Why don't you just hurt yourself and go away for awhile—let me finish this up. You don't need this game like I do." Lee reached over and lightly laid his hand on Cash's.

The irony of it all raced into Cash's mind and he couldn't help but smile. The two most popular riders in the Association, the rivals that made every event that much more exciting... and, if the truth about them ever dared come out, they would be despised by those same cheering crowds.

Except in this case, Cash thought, he would be hated by a lot of these fans, but Lee... Lee would be hated by most of them.

Lee noticed Cash's grin, but he would never learn why it was there.

The plan had been a quick, simple trip to the automotive section of the local Shop Mart. The thermostat on the Puppy had been acting up ever since he had returned from his trip to Great Falls. Just short of drawing blood, Cash had finally resorted to the family mechanical expert for some insight. As expected, Clayton had initially reacted in his typical, old self. Caustic in nature, he had relentlessly bombarded him with a series of condescending questions.

"What did you do? Blow the fricken engine apart drivin' up there?" A smart-assed smirk sat across his lips.

Rolling his eyes in disgust, Cash had allowed a laborious sigh to exhale from his chest—throwing off his brother's thoughtless comment as if it was leftover food needing to be scraped from a dinner plate. "No." With Clayton, he once again had to acknowledge that nothing was easy.

After a little shaking, a couple of knocks and several startups, the elder boy had finally retracted his head from under the hood—shooting Cash an arrogant conclusive look. "Your radiator is overheating."

At least it was something Cash could deal with. The possibility of having the truck break down at this time seemed completely out of the question. His regular commute to Lee's, and countless rodeos, left him dangling on a thread. The question was not if, but when his worn-out truck would kick-up its heals and die.

Hopping out of the cab, he slammed the door behind and crushed out his smoke. As he made his way across the stiflingly parking lot, he felt the premature spring heat broil up from the pavement. Shit, it was already too hot for this time of the year. What in the hell was summer gonna be like? Quickly, he pushed the question from his thoughts as he walked through the automatic doors into the refrigerator-cold climate. Packed with people, the store looked like Christmas. It was as if everyone was retreating from the oppressive heat outside.

Reaching automotive, he cut into an aisle. Instantly, his heart skipped a beat. Less than a few feet away, stood Travis, holding an item, looking intently at the package label.

It was a fateful window of opportunity. Cash suddenly realized he could duck back out of the aisle from where he came, or he could face this connection head on. *What to do...* he instantly thought.

Going for it, he slowly stepped in closer and cleared his throat.

Travis glanced up, his cheeks immediately becoming red.

"Hey," Cash softly greeted.

"Hey," Travis instinctively responded. He fumbled to find something to say as a sterile emptiness hung heavily in his eyes. Replaced with a shaded gray, his crystal-blues resembled the prairie sky succumbing to a deep, entrenching Pacific front.

For Cash, it was awfully strange to jump back into their regular greeting. "Whatcha lookin' for?" He tried to break the ice—feeling his body grow clammy. *Damn it*, he said to himself.

Pausing, as if trying to regain control, Travis looked down at the box in his hand and shrugged. He seemed frustrated. "I dunno. I'm tryin' to find out what this thing does." He avoided looking up.

An uneasy spell settled between them.

A god-awful pain shot through Cash. It was unbelievable—starting within his heart, it sped and ricocheted wildly into every corner of his soul. Telling himself this had been a mistake, he stepped back, struggling to catch his breath. "It's good to see you, Travis," he mustered enough strength to speak. Turning to leave, he went on to say, "Catch you around later." With several awkward scuffs of his boots, he exited back out from where he had come—feeling as if his flesh was melting.

Outside, he grabbed for the truck's door handle and was surprised there was barely enough strength to pull it open. How was he going to make it to graduation? Dear God, all he wanted to do was curl up and die. The hurt inside seemed so excruciating.

Sliding onto the cab seat, he drew a deep breath. As he pulled the door shut, it quickly got stalled by an unexpected force. Blocked by a determined hand, Cash flinched—completely caught off-guard.

"Cash."

Travis stood, dark and solemn—his hand remaining firmly placed on the handle.

Gathering his wits, Cash replied, "What?" Instantly, his mind began to spin. He wasn't up for a fight today with him, or anyone else.

"We need to talk." The soft words floated carefully into the pick-up.

"About what?" Cash asked half-heartedly. He wasn't convinced. Hadn't they discussed everything enough? Two people can only hash through shit so many times before it's rammed into the ground like a graveside cross.

"Don't you see what this is doing to me?"

"What, Travis?" Impatience quickly took over the storm-weary cowboy. "What is *this* doing to you?"

"Cash, I miss you." Travis' strong voice caught.

Cash winced. "I'm not the one who separated us." He knew at this point there was nothing to lose by laying the cards out on the table.

The big jock threw him an incredulous stare, but the words failed to come to his lips.

"Travis, you're the one who's pushed me away. You haven't taken one goddamn minute to even listen to my side of the story. How many times have I tried to tell you... explain to you what it is I'm dealin' with, 'n you won't have none of it."

Travis remained quiet—the skin on his face bleached.

"All this time you've been blamin' me." Cash found it extremely difficult to speak. He fought back burning tears. "You've made assumptions about things between Lee 'n I, but the truth you won't hear. There's been nuthin' between us... at least not until the day you gave me your ultimatum."

Taking another deep breath, he slid back into the seat. There, with the truth having been said, he reasoned to hell with its consequences.

With that, Travis became erect—his muscles tightening. "What do you mean?"

"I've told you time and time again, nothing ever happened between us down in Rapid City. I wouldn't allow it. Not for my love for you. But you've been so dead-set on believin' we messed around back then, all you've tried to do since is put a damn rein on me like a fricken work horse."

"So we're all washed up."

"I didn't say that!" Cash snapped. "That's how *you* wanna see it.

"Sure, you have." Travis' words rang with hallow resignation. "You've given up on us."

Cash slid out of the truck—his blood sizzling. *"What the fuck you talkin' 'bout?"* Glancing out across the crowded parking lot, he went on to ask, "Tell me, Travis, how can you be so smart, yet have such a difficult time listenin'?" Pausing, Cash pondered about taking it one step further. Something sat in his mind and now it seemed a good time to throw it on the floor.

"I guess in *your* words it would be called a 'fuckwit'." Stepping back, Cash waited for the response.

"What?!" Travis must have recognized the word as his eyes grew wide—color returning to his cheeks. Indignantly, he continued, *"What is it you want to tell me? What is it you want to say?"*

Tossing his arms up in the air with utter frustration, Cash threw his head back. As he rolled his eyes, a sarcastic chuckle shot out. He had heard enough. Somehow, his friend was dealing with a major mental block and there was no way of breaking through. "Nuthin' more than what I've already said a million times before." Then, without warning, it came. All his thoughts of frustration and resentment surfaced and bubbled out onto the pavement and all over the parking lot.

"And since we're in the middle of this 'I miss you conversation', let's review the subject of colleges. I think it's confusin' you wanna commitment from me, yet you keep holdin' out on the school of your choice. What the hell you think I am? An easy pushover you can lead around by the nose? I've told you before, I have no plans on leavin' this state. This is my home, my roots, 'n I love it here. If you have ideas on convertin' me to somethin' else, you're barkin' up the wrong tree—cuz it *ain't* gonna happen."

"Well, how do you think I feel about you runnin' off to Lee's every spare moment you have?" Travis tried to change the subject.

"That's what I'm talkin' about. You can't seem to get it through your skull that perhaps I'm doin' this for other reasons."

"What other reasons are there, Cash? What in this big picture am I not seeing?"

"For starters, there's a little girl who needs me in the worse way, not to mention a poor lady whose heart's been cut a hundred times over and now is unable to bring all the loose ends together."

"What do you want from me? My blessing?" The tone in Travis' voice was bitter.

"Maybe a little understandin' and some support."

"Why you? Why does it have to be YOU?"

Cash was lost. "What are you talkin' about?"

"What makes you think you have to be their savior? Where in the hell is that good-for-nothing bastard you call a 'great friend'?"

Keeping himself in check, Cash deliberately explained, "Lee has his own issues. There's nuthin' anyone can do about that. The only thing I can do is be an encouragement."

Travis shook his head. "I think it's deeper than that."

"Perhaps in your mind."

"I know what's goin' on... I wasn't born yesterday."

"You know, Travis, for your information, I wouldn't be with him now if you wouldn't have pushed me away."

Instantly jumping on Cash's confession, Travis' eyes became round. "See, I told you... I *knew* there was something between you and him!"

"Only AFTER *you* told me we were through if I went up to Great Falls!" Realizing the level of his voice, Cash stopped and took a breath—closing his eyes. "If you recall, it was you who dished out the ultimatum. You wouldn't hear of the fact that I wanted to go up and help a family. Instead, all you could think of was me jumpin' in the sack with the competition. Well, that was *not* the case. God as my witness, the only thing I wanted to be was a true friend—nuthin' more." Wiping something that crept from his eye, he went on to add, "*Travis, I was faithful to you, even though you thought differently.*" Finally, after what seemed like eons, Cash successfully delivered his defense. His soul could now rest.

Travis turned away—gasping.

Cash could tell he was deeply struggling. "Look, it's not my choice that we're separated. I've *never* wanted to leave you... *not for one second.* But sometimes there are things a person's gotta do in order to help others... especially if they can't help themselves."

"Yeah, but Lee can help himself."

"Yeah?" Cash snorted. "Well, I'm not so sure about that."

A cascade of thoughts engulfed them as people milled about with whiny children and shopping carts.

"Now, if you'll kindly excuse me, I need to be gettin' this truck back on-line—so I can go wash diapers, cook some meals, and change colostomy bags. I'm sure *you* have enough to do gettin' your admission paperwork done for some big-star university back east."

With that, Cash hopped back into the cab and started the engine. Resting his arm on the truck door window, he leaned out and said. "Take care of yourself, Travis. It's a tough world out there." Shifting down, he pulled the Puppy from the stall and made his way out of the parking lot.

Lee had promised to be home when Cash arrived. *What a toad*, he dismally thought. It was no surprise, however, when Cash rounded the corner of the street to discover the big, black pick-up missing from its parking space in front of the duplex. Something inside, had told him that plans would not go according to Hoyle.

The little foreign lady was very glad to see him as she let him into the stale, musty quarters. With a labored gesture of her arm, she spoke with her thick Turkish tongue. "Come een! You moos feel tire from long drife."

Respectfully taking his hat off, Cash smiled and followed her into the livingroom. Taking note at how weak she was, he was amazed at her determination to navigate around the apartment. "I should have called." He apologized for any imposition.

With a wrinkled face, she grinned. "No, ees alright. No problem at all."

Cash could not help noticing the weary lines of failing health—how beautiful she must have been before all the misfortune. Her eyes bore a gentleness, complimenting the curves of her cheeks and forehead.

Suddenly, taking a deep breath, as if in much pain, she said, "Lee no heer." With another sweep of her arm, she continued with an irritated voice, "He go out. No tell me whare… he never say."

"That's okay," Cash reassured. "I've come to see you and Elena."

Mrs. Biruni glowed with a flush of embarrassment. "*Oh!* You sweet boy!"

At the mention of her name, Elena excitedly ran out of her room. "Cashie!" Instantly, she jumped in his arms. He was amazed she could say his name. The warmth of her tiny, soft body pressed into his belly and chest.

It was at that moment Cash realized why he had made the trip across the tedious prairie land. He gave her a long hug.

"How's my little bug in the rug?" The cowboy's voice was soft and gentle.

Not releasing Cash, Elena continued to grip—letting him clearly know of her starving hunger for affection and complete acceptance of his touch. In this department, she reminded him of her daddy. Rising to his feet, he instinctively drew her up—a small set of arms slipping around his neck with her head resting pleasantly against his boney shoulder.

"You moos feel hungry, no?" Lee's mother started to make her way to the kitchen.

"Actually, I grabbed a bite before I got here."

"Grab bite?" The woman was intrigued by Cash's choice of words. Obviously, she had never heard the saying before, so she found herself ignorant of its colloquial meaning.

Now, it was Cash who felt embarrassed as he fumbled for words she would understand. "I ate a hamburger before coming here." Rubbing his belly, Cash chuckled and went on to say, "I am okay."

Understanding, Mrs. Biruni smiled and nodded. "Fine, very fine."

The three of them sat in the kitchen—Elena drifting off to sleep on Cash's lap, and Mrs. Biruni asking a number of questions about Cash's family, school, and rodeo life. She seemed so interested to learn as much as she could about her son's new-found friend. Eventually, lines in her face deepened. Pain and exhaustion took over.

"Please forgif me... I moos lay down for rest."

Cash slowly assisted her to her room—for some strange reason, he did not feel awkward in helping her to recline and adjusting her pillows. He could not help noticing how thin she was—feeling her bones press up against his hands and arms. She couldn't weigh more than a hundred pounds, he figured.

Taking a hard breath, she looked up at Cash. Struggling to talk. "Son," she winced, "...een bathroom, pills—I need."

Cash darted to the bathroom and frantically searched the medicine cabinet for her request. Amid the number of bottles and little boxes, his fingers fidgeted. Which ones was she talking about? For God's sake, there were over a half a dozen prescriptions stuffed on one shelf alone. Suddenly, he was reminded of the small black box—the little bag of tricks. To Cash, it reminded him of Pandora's Box. Too much of a good thing was usually bad—he strongly believed. Deciding she could pick and choose the ones she needed, he grabbed for all of them, and along with a glass of water, he took them to her.

The look in her eyes revealed sincere gratefulness.

Selecting two bottles, Altiar proceeded to take her medications. Cash stood by, on alert. He really didn't know what else to do.

Afterwards, he went back out and spent the rest of the afternoon with Elena who eagerly ate it up. They listened to music, played a few hand and finger games; then watched a movie about a little pig staking out on a wild adventure to the big city. He even learned about 'Hello Kitty'.

All the while, his thoughts seemed to wander and pick into somewhere unknown—perhaps a dusty rodeo arena with a cantankerous bull, or a quiet place to sort shit out.

When was Lee coming back? Where did he go?

Preparing a dinner of macaroni and cheese, about the only thing he knew how to make, he ate in silence; then he went on to clean the kitchen, bath Elena, and finally, get her settled for the night. In the strange quiet of the evening, he plunked himself deep into the recliner, turning the television on.

Closing his eyes and shaking his head, he let out a puffy snort. If anyone would have told him a month earlier he would be doing stuff like this, he would have replied, "You're fuckin' crazy!"

Waiting for Lee eventually became a lost cause. *He's not coming back tonight,* he told himself.

Soon, he began nodding off—too tired to concentrate on anything specific. Knowing he couldn't wait up any longer for his buddy, he decided to head for bed as well. Instead of the couch, he chose to sleep in Lee's room, in his bed. At this point, he knew he owed nothing to Travis— fresh pain still stinging from their conversation earlier that morning. In addition, stressful knotting from endless corral practice pulled against every muscle throughout his body, making any idea of sleep on the couch quite unappealing.

Wrestling about the implications of Lee finding him sprawled out on the bed, sent his thoughts reeling into space. He knew it would send a message to the young Turk that would be voraciously consumed. It would spell out a new dominance.

But, who would care?

Even though this relationship was not his first choice, he found himself slipping into it quite easily—like a comfortable work shirt. And in spite of Lee's unpredictable behavior Cash knew he'd be able to handle it—much like breaking in a testy bronc. Undeniably, there was something that continued to draw him in deeper—with no stopping, no reprieve.

As Cash willed sleep to overtake, his mind played on something—piquing his interest. Had Altiar called him 'son'? He lay still, staring into the shadowy stuffiness of the room—his eyes wide with wonder. *Now that was something to say.* He certainly had not expected that. *What did she mean by it?* Suddenly, a strange feeling came over him.

By chance, did it have anything to do with Elena?

Inhaling the faint odors of Lee's body impregnated throughout the pillows, sheets and comforter, he turned on his side—curling up into a ball. Allowing his muscles to loosen, he told himself he could be in this bed forever. Closing his eyes, he let out a sigh as long as eternity—whispering under his breath, "Let be, let be..."

Chapter 26

Cash had already packed his bag and was preparing to say good-bye to Lee's mother and Elena when the pick-up rolled into the driveway. Without an apparent care in the world, Lee pushed himself out of the truck and grabbed his gear bag from the back. It was a dead give-away. He had gone rodeoing without letting anyone know. What a shit-ass, thought Cash as he envyingly watched him strut into the livingroom.

"Cash!" Lee acted surprised at his presence.

"Where were you?" Irritation shot from Cash's lips.

"I attended the Valier rodeo," he spoke with a big grin. "Chocked up some mighty big points too." It was obvious he was very proud of the accomplishment.

Cash couldn't say a word. A mixture of raging emotions twirled around in his brain—happy that the competition was back on track, and angry over the worry of wondering where the hell he was all weekend. The best thing he could think of at that moment was to remain silent.

"Hey, you wanna go for a ride? I'll tell you all about it."

Now, what Cash failed to do, Lee's mother completed. Instantly, in full-force, she began to shout with Turkish words at the insolent boy.

"Let's go." Lee headed back to the door. Cash stood the middle ground between Mrs. Biruni and her son, pivoting his head towards one and then to the other—bouncing Elena in his arms. Altiar continued to speak sharply in her native tongue, covering herself with a scowl while obviously fighting back a fantastic surge of pain. Standing with his back to her, Lee remained motionless. Cash could make out the little upward curve of his lips. The scene was tightly woven with defiance. Finally done with her tirade, Lee remarked, "My mother is making a comment about my hosting and parenting skills. They're not good, as you might have guessed."

"Why no tell Cash the whole trooth?" Lee's mother continued, her accent extremely heavy, but her words firm. "Tell you bad."

"Oh God, I don't feel like this right now, mother." He said something to her in their native tongue, then again to Cash, "Let's go."

The front door slammed heavily at their backs, Lee moving quickly to his truck. Cash didn't bother making conversation. When Lee took a moment into his hands, like he was doing on this occasion, Cash knew better not to consider resistance. Pulling their way up into the cab, Lee drove off toward the interstate. After only a few miles, he turned off onto a two-lane highway, and then just as quickly, made a sharp right onto a dirt road.

"I think this is private property," Cash commented as the truck rumbled over a cattle guard.

"Yeah, well, maybe. I know the people who own it. Don't worry."

Cash knew from experience there was only a fifty-percent possibility of truth to that statement. He remained silent while Lee turned off the road and parked the truck behind several large sage bushes—hiding it from view of the road. Lee opened his door and hopped out, already standing with the tailgate down by the time Cash shuffled his way around back. He reached across the truck bed and pulled what looked like a bed roll—corners of a brick-red Pendleton blanket hanging out between the folds. Securing the truck, Lee strode off onto what was clearly a marked path through a field of tall grass. It led around and behind a few large boulders worn from weather. When Cash finally caught up with Lee, after climbing up a small rising, he found himself standing in the midst of a tiny campsite, the dirt brushed and evened, protected by an overhang of the rocks. He could see traces of black soot underneath them.

Lee untied and spread the blankets, although it hardly seemed necessary, the area was already so clean.

"I come here now and again," he remarked while working, "…mainly to get away from the situation at home."

Cash said nothing. He just dutifully sat down.

"I won't tell you everything my mother said," he looked over at Cash, giving a wide, generous smile. "You can pretty much guess what she thinks of me."

"That don't matter, Lee. That's your business."

Lee sat alongside Cash, then hopped up. "Wanna beer?"

Cash was beginning to realize two things. Lee had no patience for his mother's nagging, but he loved beer. While Cash wasn't really used to drinking, the idea of a beer did sound good, so he nodded his head. Lee was off, returning in a flash, carrying a small cooler. When he opened it, there was a six-pack inside. Lee pulled it up and out. "They're kinda warm. Maybe better if we take them out to cool over here." He rested the cans on some rocks.

Cash agreed that while it was yet warm and pleasant in the sun, with early evening approaching, the winds would soon be coming up bringing with them a chill. Lee handed over a beer, then popped one for himself. He drank greedily, Cash had just taken a few sips when Lee was already pulling off his second. Cash allowed the warm feeling from the alcohol to drift through his body. It was relaxing. He leaned back onto the blanket to face the sky. Suddenly, he felt very good.

"My mother's a good woman, just sometimes she hates me. And I don't blame her." Lee started talking again in between gulps from the can. "I didn't want to take the kid. It was her idea, as I told you. Her Islamic sense of decency, I suppose." He looked off into the distance, then turned behind him, pointing to the bluffs at their back. "If you go up over the top of these rocks, on the other side you can see Great Falls. It looks nice lit up at night. Funny how we seem so far from everything, but the damned city's right over there." His laughter was wry. "We could walk it, if we had to."

He continued to drink, Cash mimicking his movements at a much slower pace.

"Mom doesn't understand how I don't want Elena. I figure if we would have given her up for adoption, she could have been taken by some rich couple, maybe some wealthy doctor like my dad. She would have been better off, my opinion."

A cool breeze brushed Cash's face. He suddenly remembered the need to call his parents. His stomach tightened. They would come apart at the seams if he failed to call and not show up as originally planned.

"I forgot to call my family 'n tell 'em I won't be back until tomorrow. They'll be wonderin' where I'm at."

"You can use my cell," Lee offered, tossing it into Cash's hands.

"Thanks." Cash replied.

"...we were wondering what was going on." Cash's mother's voice sounded broken from the static.

"Somethin's come up and I really need to stay one more day." Cash tried to make the tone in his voice sound urgent.

"Well, is everything okay?" she went on to ask.

"Yeah, but Lee's been gone all weekend and he just got back. There's a few things that need to be done around the house and it really calls for two people to do 'em." Looking over to Lee, he tossed him an impish wink. "We should be done sometime by noon."

There was a spell of silence—as if his mother was assimilating all the information in her head. "All right. You two be careful," she said warily. "And give us call before you leave."

"I will," Cash promised.

Silence bathed the two boys sitting on the blanket like the shadows that began to extend ominously from the eastern horizon.

Finally, Lee cleared his throat and said out of the clear blue, "I never told you that my dad molested me."

"Huh?" Cash couldn't believe his friend was sharing something like this.

"Just what you heard..." Lee verified, lighting up a cigarette and sucking in the smoke as deep as his lungs could take.

"Wow."

"Wow, you betcha. It was a mess, such a mess. You see, my father was…" he let the sentence trail off, fortifying himself with a jerking slurp of his beer before beginning again, "My father started coming into my room at night. Would come and sit on my bed. At first, it was just that. And then he started putting his hands under the covers. Doing things, you know. Anyway, long story short, mom came into my room looking for him one night, and saw him. She called him names in Turkish that even I couldn't understand."

Lee threw his head back and barked out a laugh.

"Dad was so pissed, he came up to her and slapped her silly. Told her to shut-up and go back to her kitchen. And you know what she did? You know what that little Turkish woman did? She stood right there and hauled her hand back and brought it straight into the side of his head." Lee was smiling from the memory—reliving this one moment in pride.

"Dad was so stunned that he just stood there while she pulled me out of bed and packed a couple of suitcases. When we headed out to the car, he still hadn't moved from my room. Funny. But…," he shook his head from side to side, "we lived in a shelter for a few days, while she got the court-order in place."

In the distance Cash could hear the sharp cry of coyotes beginning their evening haunt. He lay back, arms under his head, waiting for Lee's tale to continue.

"Anyway, he had the good lawyers, and mom didn't want to push it. She figured his sense of responsibility would take care of everything. Boy, was she sorely mistaken…" There was a pause, then a quiet "son-of-a-bitch."

Night came slowly this time of year, Cash realized. The sky began to deepen its blue—the cirrus glowing a brilliant orange. He reached for a beer.

Lee became silent for so long that Cash thought maybe he had fallen asleep from all the alcohol. But when he looked over, he noticed the young man staring up at the sky, eyes wide-open.

Cash knew not to say anything; instead he simply enjoyed the feel of the breeze drifting over his face, smelling the light scent that came with it. Things were beginning to bloom now.

Lee's story should have shocked Cash. It should have made him shiver, but he had already known from someplace deep inside, a piece of the tale… that something terrible had gone wrong in his friend's life—especially when thought was given to the evidence.

"That's rough, Lee," he finally offered. "But look at where you are now. Things are gonna get better, I'd guess."

The figure beside him remained unmoving. He had fallen asleep.

Soon Cash could hear the sound of heavy, rhythmic breathing. Turning to Lee, he was somehow gratified to see those features that he was coming to appreciate—relaxed and freed. Without plans or blue prints, he instinctively moved his face over the slumbering boy, barely allowing his lips to touch Lee's. Cash could feel himself warming from something other than the alcohol.

As the red wool of the blanket seemed to frame the darkness of Lee's coal black hair, there was created an intensity of both colors. Cash kissed him again, a little firmer this time. Lee fluttered his eyes, just briefly, giving only the smallest recognition, then closing them again. Bringing his mouth hard on top of Lee's, Cash kept it there, forcing the other boy to open. With quickening breaths, Cash reached for the buttons on Lee's denim shirt, unsnapping the one at his neck, then the one under that, and following, until the shirt was opened—completely spread against the evening-hued red.

There were no words spoken. Did there need to be? Cash could not stop as he pursued the very thing that had been forbidden to him by Travis.

Lee continued to lay, arms at side, legs relaxed. He seemed so willing to slip into such a quiet, undisturbed space.

Cash found himself excited, *determined* to violate.

A coyote yipped its craving song from the distance, only to be followed by a shattering, heart-throb silence. The moment felt like destiny as Cash seized desire and rode into the sky somewhere between a lonely, forgotten wheat field and a sacred levee nestled by the banks of a lazy, muddy river. Dreamed of, but yet, unplanned, Cash still went with it. In his mind, he knew this was a night for taming. Grasping his partner, he could see that twilight was coming on in earnest, the clouds having dissipated allowing for a full-moon night.

After all was spent, the band long since gone, they remained silent— together. With Cash's shirt blown into the dirt, and jeans tossed recklessly over the base of the rocks, it felt so good to hold the rodeo champ, second only to him, tightly in his arms. Cash wanted to sleep, but he knew it would be best that they leave.

Nudging Lee, who gave only the slightest moan, he was about to speak.

"Let's stay here for awhile like this. No need to hurry."

On second thought, Cash had to agree.

Cash was amazed he hadn't heard the Viper pull into the driveway, nor any of the conversation downstairs between Travis and his mother.

By the time he got back from Great Falls, his tail was dragging. It took everything inside to push himself out of the truck, and scoot up the stairs to bed. Hitting the mattress, he went out like a light. The next thing he knew, someone was quietly opening his door.

Listening to footsteps cross the creaking floor to his bedside, he struggled to open his eyes. With an unexpected bounce, something hit the mattress—making him jump with a start. Gaining his focus, he pushed himself up, letting out a long, hard stretch with his arms. Squinting, he looked over to the clock. *What time was it?*

Close by the bed, Travis stood at attention; his face was hard and determined. It was his eyes, however, that gave the secret away. Bloodshot and draped, with dark, hanging bags—they bore a look declaring undeniable surrender. *Was this the bringing down of the high and mighty?*

"Hey." The digits read six-thirty.

"Hey."

Directing his attention at what had been thrown on the bed, Cash recognized them immediately—the college and university catalogues.

Breaking the uneasy quiet that had settled within the room, Travis spoke with a broken tone in his voice. "They're yours to do with whatever." Holding out his arm, he handed Cash an envelope.

Taking it from those burly fingers, Cash looked at the return address—catching his breath as if he had been shot through the heart. The University of Oklahoma.

Knowing where Cash was taking this, Travis quickly jumped in and said, "I'm not going." He turned and walked to the window. "I'm writing them today and letting them know I won't be registering."

Cash suddenly felt the blood drain from his head. He was suddenly dizzy.

"I got a call from the U of M Friday. They need to have my decision of acceptance by the end of this week."

Now, he does this. Cash's brain continued to spin. Didn't he say they were through… washed up? And now that Lee was entering into his life… Jesus. Talk about one fucked-up mess. "You *sure* this is what you wanna do?"

He certainly didn't want him to make a decision that was based on their relationship. Cash knew Travis didn't want to stay in the Montana, as it was apparent he was above anything that could ever be offered here. And now since they were broke up, it didn't matter *what* school would be chosen. There was no doubt Travis would only come to resent it all—wishing, down the road, he would have taken the offer from Okalahoma. Christ, he needed to choose what would be *best for him*—not for anyone else.

As the awkward silence grew into a dangling participle, Cash continued to study Travis. One thing was for sure, he knew he never wanted to be blamed for coercing him into anything hasty. "Travis, I don't think you should do this." Cash could barely get the words out.

Directing his gaze back on Cash, he firmly replied, "I can't live without you." He reached up with a quivering hand and played with the hairs of an eyebrow, then looking away, his voice trailed. "My dreams are not dreams without *you* in them."

Cash couldn't budge a muscle. He was speechless. For weeks, he had been convincing himself it was done and over. Travis would go on—find a new boyfriend—and get on with his life. He had no earthly clue it would come to this. What about Lee?

The air was thick, incredibly heavy.

Travis must have sensed Cash's earnest desire for solitude as he let out a sigh and slowly retreated for the door. "I'll see you at school."

Looking up, Cash nodded. "Be careful," he called out, listening to the footsteps retreat down to the livingroom. He would have never dreamed it in a million years.

All seniors were instructed to meet at the gymnasium first thing in the morning for a dry-run of the graduation ceremony. Beforehand, they had been ordered to pick up their gowns, tassels, and caps in front of the cafeteria.

"Each of you is encouraged to try on your gown and cap in case a mistake has been made in ordering the wrong size." Mr. Ryan's voice cracked over the megaphone that he dutifully held up in front of his face.

"God, it's as if we're all deaf!" Cash complained under his breath to Cheryl McCullough, the fellow classmate who was paired-off with him for the two-by-two presentation march into the gym. The entire dry-run seemed poorly planned.

There was a lot of 'down-time' with everyone idly waiting for their next instructions. It was enough to drive the short-tempered cowboy nuts as he impatiently played with the tassel that dangled ridiculously from the rim of his cap.

After a full hour of getting everyone in proper alphabetical order and rehearsing the entire agenda through once, the less-than-jubilant principal finally released the class to their regular schedules.

"Just when I thought I was goin' into a coma..." Cash muttered under his breath to Cheryl as they made their way out of the gym.

She returned his comment with a giggle.

As Cash sauntered back to his locker, clutching his cap and gown, he felt a light tap on his shoulder.

"Can we talk?"

Without looking back, he could tell who it was. And by the sound of his voice, he could also tell there was a serious look on his face. *This outta be fun*, Cash swallowed hard—his stomach tightening. One thing about Travis, he was easy to read.

Several days had passed since their early morning chat, and Cash was still at a loss for words regarding the sudden change of mind. Deep down, he still wasn't convinced that everything would be okay between the two of them in spite of Travis' decision to go to the University of Montana.

"Sure." Without question, Cash turned on his tracks and followed the slump-shouldered boy up the stairwell to their private corner of the world.

Walking behind Travis, a gut ache gripped him. Was his eyesight playing tricks, or was this macho-man sliding down a hill with no hope of slowing down? Quiet and withdrawn, Travis dragged his feet up the stairs. Absent, was the march in his step—no strut to his stride. A sea of dark-brown curls and random waves replaced his meticulously-kept high and tight haircut. And what once was a compact waist, with abs chiseled out neatly into a defined six-pack, was now an untidy roll above the belt line—obvious *even* through a baggy shirt.

Who would guess it? Travis wasn't bouncing back. Tough and self assured... the one always in control, yet now, here he was, crumbling apart piece by piece.

They reached the landing. Travis turned face-to-face with Cash.

An awkward moment seemed to stumble between them as Cash noticed a renegade twitch playing against one side of Travis' face—making him squint, avoiding eye contact. Reaching up, Travis ran a trembling finger along his eyebrow. He seemed to be doing a lot of that lately.

Biting at Cash, that twitch was one of the little quirks he really missed about Travis—one of just a million reasons why he had fallen in love with him. Suddenly, unexpectedly, he froze. *He loved him...*

The blood rushed to his brain.

Did he? Did he love him?

Several more lingering moments passed. The two young men remained quiet.

Yes, for Christ's sake, of course he did, Cash honestly admitted to himself. Pondering on that thought, he went on to ask, why then, were they separated? Stubbornness? Bull-headedness? With a snort, he turned away—blinking back wetness in his eyes. He knew the answer to that question.

What a waste, he told himself. What a lousy, freakin' waste. All this time and energy lost because of a couple of high-and-mighty egos.

He should have seen it right from the start—that he would *never* get over this relationship. Sure enough, they were in this for life—lock, stock, and barrel. Swallowing hard, he directed his gaze back to Travis.

"You missed two buttons on your shirt." Cash ended the silence.

For a guy who was always so focused on fashion and detail, Travis was truly loosing it—his clothes didn't even match.

With arms hung by his side, Travis began. "I have only one thing to say to you."

Cash waited—braced—holding his breath.

"I'm sorry, Cash." Putting his head down, Travis continued. "I'm sorry I've hurt you… by not listening to you… blaming you for things you never did." Hesitating, he drew in air—struggling to get the words out.

"By trying to keep you from Lee, I pushed you closer to him. I know that now. As much as I try, I can't undo what's already happened. I just had to tell you how very sorry I am for everything I did, and didn't do. The only thing I can ask is if you will forgive me and give me a second chance. I know I can't live without you, Cash, because it's *you*… who makes me a better guy, and it's *you* who gives me a purpose to tackle my dreams." A gentle stillness settled over the landing. "I need you, Cash. I-I want you so badly—for the rest of my life."

Looking up, Travis wiped the tears streaking his cheeks. "No one has ever meant as much to me than you… *no one.*"

My God… Cash was taken back. That certainly was a mouthful. Was there any other human on the face of this old planet that possessed the power to dig into his soul as deep as the boy who stood quietly before him?

Stepping to the window of that dusty, little stairwell, Cash looked out over the parking lot.

For three years, it was the same sight—not many changes—except for a few more potholes. The newly green of the trees and lawns further out, past the pavement, reminded him this was all coming to a close. The world he now knew… of childhood buddies and carefree days, it would soon disappear. Yet, as the brilliant sun filled the big-blue sky, he knew it wouldn't be the end. Rather, there would be the start of another story—with events yet unknown. The question was—who would he bring on this new adventure? Who would be by his side through the thick and thin? Who would he share the rest of his life with?

Turning back to Travis, he pushed out his own words. "You know that I love you."

It took a second for it to sink in, then suddenly, Travis let out a gasp—closing his eyes. Catching himself in a near fall, he leaned against the wall.

Wasn't this where it all began? Cash asked himself. *Here at school?* An ordinary English class, a handsome boy coolly strutting through the door, purposely brushing by with a wandering finger, tossing an inviting eye, casting of a faint smile... the turning of his world upside-down.

That moment had changed his life. He knew things would never be the same—ever. What a cocky, arrogant jock from San Francisco could create within his simple, cowboy heart, only a fool would know. Cash could only give a sigh.

Truth be said, he'd never be able to leave the love of this man—*no way, no how.*

"Don't let go of me, Cash." Travis could barely see through his tears.

Stepping close to envelope slender fingers over a vacant, surrendering hand, Cash drew Travis slowly into his chest. "Our relationship isn't the easiest, but this much I know, it has the ingredients to be the best."

"Yeah?"

"Yeah."

And they stood in the stairwell, holding each other, quietly, lovingly, until the next bell rang.

Chapter 27

He dreaded it. It was the toughest, damnedest, most difficult thing to do—talk to Lee, and put on the brakes. Really, he should have seen the flags right from the start—the hand writing on the wall.

The relationship with Lee would have never worked. Not over the long haul. For one thing, they were too much alike—cut from almost the same mold. Being competition and all, this was a classic case of conflict of interest. Of course, he was infatuated with Lee, *mesmerized by him*, but he loved Travis. Period.

What's that old saying? He asked himself repeatedly while driving the empty ribbon to Great Falls. Hind sight, twenty-twenty? Christ, it was like running face front into a dust storm, shifting gears on this affair, saying it was all a mistake.

When he arrived at the disheveled apartment, Lee was once again gone. *At least he's keeping up a tradition*, Cash stewed disdainfully. Probably out rodeoing again—he figured—trying to work up some more high numbers.

Unpacking his gear, Cash wondered if he'd be able to pull it off. Thinking about the itinerary, he knew it was just plain nuts. How could he cram so much in three days? Memorial Day weekend… of course, graduation was on Monday. Sunday, he wanted to try his hand one last time at rodeoing—this time at Big Timber. Friday and Saturday, the plans were to stay at the Biruni's. Five hundred miles here, three hundred there, and umpteen hundred back home… a shitload of driving.

"Hell's forty acres and half of Texas." –was what his granddad would always say. "Nuthin' can ever be close by."

Cash was encouraged that Altiar was slowly gaining strength—finally able to get up and do a few things around the house. Heading to the kitchen, he caught her cutting up vegetables for soup. She looked cute with her apron.

"You have some when cooked." There was a sparkle in her eyes—happy to be out of bed. "Keep you well and strong."

After getting Elena settled down for sleep, he visited with Altiar at the kitchen table. She must have been in the mood to share as she told stories of the 'old country' and when she was a girl.

"Ees deeferent now," she explained, filling her face with the strange food, "than when I whas leettle."

It seemed he could have listened to her ramble on, telling her side of the stories which Lee had shared the past several months. Cash could tell where Lee got his independent, strong-willed mind. And even though she was sick, there was a lot of fight still kicking in her. Keeping the family together seemed to be her mission as she shared her concern regarding Lee and Elena—how disappointed, she was, in having to watch him spurn her. To her, family was extremely important and it boggled her mind how he could ignore it all.

"He never broot up to be that way." She spoke with hot contempt.

"Your mother…" she glared at him with her intense brown eyes, "She goot woman, no?"

Nodding with a large smile, Cash replied, "Yes, she's a wonderful lady."

"I know, you be goot to her." Reaching over with a bony hand, she tenderly clasped his rough, worn fingers into hers. "You are goot boy."

In spite of his aversions, Cash slept on the couch. Who knows, he told himself, it would be just like Lee to decide to come home early. Finding him in bed, would only make the situation that much harder to steer things back into the right direction.

Waking the next morning with a stiff back and neck, Cash realized his fears had been unfounded—Lee's room had not been disturbed. A smile came to his lips. *The fucker*, he fumed with jealousy.

Later, that afternoon, Cash learned how to cook *alanazik* and *yayla corbasi*.

"What's that?" Cash wasn't sure he liked what he saw on the cutting board.

"You call egg plant."

"Hummmm…"

"You chop and poot heer…" Pointing to the skillet. "Oil, first add."

After chopping, browning and stirring, the food was finally done. Altiar was reassuring. With a twinkle of delight in her face, she daintily tasted the simmering food. "You make fine… *afiyet olsun*—very goot!"

Would this be something he'd like? –he kept asking himself. He wasn't sure. It smelled good. Taking a tiny portion from the bowl, he risked a taste. *Holy biscuits!* It was freakin' hot! Grabbing for his glass of water, he doused the fire raging in his mouth.

Altiar laughed. "Too hot, no?"

"No," Cash choked, "I just swallowed wrong." There was no way he was going to admit he was a greenie over her spicy food.

As she filled her plate without question, there was a sparkle in her eyes revealing she knew better.

Eventually, his taste buds acclimated to the tangy flavors, and he filled his plate with a second helping.

Lee arrived late that afternoon with a bag of dirty laundry, chipped tooth, and tales as tall as the maples in the front yard. Cash was entertained; Mrs. Biruni was less than amused. Pushing back in the recliner, he watched the scene unfold with Altiar working herself into a frenzy while Lee maintained his aloofness by delicately skirting past his mother—making his way to the kitchen. .

"You go tell no one! You rood and in-con-sitter-root!"

Like an insolent cat, he gave no desired response—stoking her fire that much more.

Kicking into Turkish, her voice rose to an ear-piercing level.

"Siz Yumurcak! Birakmak!"

It was surprising to find that such a tiny lady could pack such a powerful volume. Obviously, she was regaining her strength.

Jumping in with her two cents, Elena began crying at the top of her lungs. *For God's sake,* Cash thought as he pushed himself from the recliner and went over to the little girl. He reached down, drawing her into his arms. Instantly, she quieted. With determined fingers, she embraced him—burying her face deep into his chest.

Wow, what a hell of a time to dump, Cash hopelessly told himself. Lee would not be receptive to the news pursed at his lips. He knew it. In fact, Lee would *never* be open to it.

Blasting his fist on the counter, Lee shouted at the top of his lungs, "*Beni yalnýz býrakýn!* You want a different world!"

Silence descended upon the room. With eyes of shock, everyone stood by waiting for the next move on the board. His outburst had been so unexpected.

Taking a slow, determined breath, the muscles in his jaw became set in concrete. With a penetrating tone, he spoke scarcely above a whisper, "It will never be."

Turning around, the angry boy bolted out the back door, allowing the screen door to slam against the back side of the house.

Shooting him a frantic look with her ebony eyes, Cash got the message. Handing Elena to Altiar, he went after his buddy. He knew running after Lee was like chasing a whirlwind.

Catching up with him in the alley, Cash fell into step. He didn't know what say.

Halfway down the block, Lee spoke without looking at Cash. "You are more of a son to her than I will ever be."

His words were bitter.

Hedging whether or not to allow the words to flow from his lips, Cash sent up a prayer. Instinctively, he grabbed for the rosary beads buried in his pocket. "Have you ever tried?"

"Why should I?"

"Because she's you're mother."

"She's a bitch."

"No, she's not," Cash flatly stated. "She's a good woman."

Lee let out an indignant snort.

They reached the street and proceeded to cross it. Lee's pace slowed, the lines of anger dissipating from his face. Together, they walked without speaking. The remnants of the evening shadows began to evaporate against the darkening night sky.

Thoughts raced in Cash's mind. How was he going to tell Lee about his decision with Travis?

"You're quiet." Lee broke into his friend's deep world of thoughts.

"Yeah?" Cash cocked his head, glancing at his companion.

"Well, you're not talking, that's for sure."

Ahead of them was a neighborhood park. It was now dark except for the street lights. They walked over to the playground at the opposite end—each taking on a swing.

Now was a good time as ever, thought Cash as he pushed off from the ground—breaking the silence. "We can't sleep together anymore."

Lee sat quietly staring off into the black space. Cash could only imagine the expression on his face.

After a long, obliging pause, Cash continued, "I wanna be your friend, Lee, but I don't want sex to be part of our relationship."

"Travis has sat you down."

"Whatdaya mean?" Cash tried to stall him.

"Just what I said." Lee continued to avoid looking at his face. "Travis put you up to this."

"Leave him out of this."

"Why?" Lee finally turned to him; his face lined and gaunt from the shadows. "He has everything to do with this."

Cash nervously bit at his lip. There was no way he was going to be able to pussy-foot around the matter. He knew he had to spell it out. "Lee, I'm in love with him."

An eerie hush blew in around them. Cash was chilled. Slowly, back and forth, Lee dug the heel of his boot into the sand.

This was where he wanted the discussion to go. Why then, did he have such a horrible feeling? Cash stopped the movement of the swing—gripping the chains with a tightness that sent tingles down his arms. He braced for what he sensed would follow.

"So where does that put me?"

"We can be friends… ridin' buddies, but nuthin' more." It was impossible for Cash to swallow. Anxiously, he could hear his heart beat mercilessly against his chest. It made his ears hurt.

Off in the distance, a siren from a squad car echoed throughout the park and nearby buildings. The air was laced with distinct smells of cooking and the promise of an impending rain approaching. From a nearby thoroughfare, the steady drone of traffic seemed to complete the waiting, placid scene of a typical urban evening.

Lee continued to sit stiflingly still—no response from his body.

Cash was beginning to wonder how long they were going to remain seated without talking in the small, deserted, lonely playground. His impatience was starting to surface.

Without any word or explanation, Lee rose to his feet and started to walk away. Not looking back, he made his way out of the park—continuing into the street and beyond the intersection.

Cash didn't know what to do. Remaining quietly on the swing, he watched Lee's dark form disappear around the corner without hesitation.

Did he go at this the wrong way? It was impossible for him not to second guess. He felt terrible—as if he had just shot someone in cold blood. Should he go after him, or let him be? Somehow, he couldn't shove himself into motion.

Accepting the inevitable, he slid away from the swing seat and started in the direction of the Biruni house. Perhaps it would be a good thing to leave tonight and allow Lee space and time to work through all this. Besides, it was never good to wear out a person's welcome. Hopefully, his friend would come around to understand that the decision was good for everyone.

When he got to the corner of their street, Cash instantly noticed Lee's pick-up was gone. He wasn't surprised. In fact, he had almost expected it.

"No!" Altiar's voice was emphatic. "No is goot for you to leef." She shook her head—giving him a stern stare. Elena ran to his side and began to cry.

"Lee is upset at me and I think I should go so he can feel okay to come back home." Cash's emotions raged as he grabbed for his bed roll from the couch and stuffed it in his bag. He needed to get out of here.

Insistent, Mrs. Biruni went over to the frustrated boy and slipped her hand around his slender arm. "I want you stay. Thees *your* home too."

"Altiar, it is not good that I stay." Cash was not convinced in spite of her insistence.

"Yes!" her tone raised another pitch—still clinging to his shirt sleeve. "You moos stay! Whee need you... efureewon no. You goot for us." Pausing, she looked away and quickly ran her hand across her cheek. "Whee... w-whee luf you. *Seni seviyorum.*"

Cash let go of his bag—allowing it to fall to the floor with a thud. Her words, they stopped him right in his tracks.

"You our friend too. You two disagreement—so what?" she exclaimed, swinging her arms out. "Lee moos grow up. He work ofer eet."

Leaning down, Cash scooped up the sobbing little girl and tenderly drew her in. Instantly, she calmed down—assuming her rightful place against his chest. Why, it was as if she was his. She undoubtedly had complete trust in him. "It's okay..." he softly reassured. "I'm not gonna leave."

Bouncing her gently with his arms, he leaned into her ear and whispered, *"I'll never leave you."* Did he actually say that? He couldn't believe the words that just blurted out of his mouth.

Her fingers tightly clasped his shoulders.

Not sure if it was the lumpiness of the couch, or the unsettled thoughts that stirred in his mind—sleep, however, came difficult to Cash that night. Knowing that Lee was out somewhere nursing a hurt too deep to describe gave him an uncomfortable feeling. And even though Mrs. Biruni tried to reassure him that her son would be okay, he had his doubts. With the black box missing from the apartment, one could only imagine what he was up to.

The following morning, Cash arose early and headed out for Big Timber. It would be a long day ahead of him, and he wanted some time to rest up before his event in the afternoon.

Mrs. Biruni prepared him a small lunch, thanking him profusely for staying the weekend. There was no doubt—he was adopted into *her* family.

"You call," she spoke in all seriousness. "Tell me you all right."

Cash arrived at the rodeo grounds just before noon, quickly spotting the white pick-up and stock trailer. He considered it a good sight for sore eyes. Even though Mr. McCollum had resigned his position as a stock contractor, Clayton had nobly jumped in to fill the spot saying he could use the extra bucks. Looking at it now, it was an arrangement made in Heaven—especially for Cash, now that he lost his ridin' companion. He should have known Lee was an all-or-nothing kind of guy—no middle of the road.

With a pocket full of luck and a heart heaping with hope, he pulled into a vacant spot and jumped out of the road-worn truck. Allowing a long, releasing stretch, he took in the sweet, fragrant rodeo air—gathering himself together. The day would be a bitch, but by God, his mind was set that it would be a lot of fun. This was the last rodeo before the qualifiers and long-awaited finals. What had seemed to take forever, the day he had been dreaming of—preparing for all his life—was just around the corner.

Methodically, he reached for his saddle and gear. Amid the crowd, his eyes searched for Travis and his brother. He couldn't wait to see them. As the excitement began to flow through his veins, something inside told him he was going to do well. Damn it! He knew he was hot on the trail for that coveted title. He told himself, he would win.

"Hurry up or we're gonna be late." Janice impatiently knocked on the bathroom door. It was unusual for the thoughtful, well-planned woman to be acting like that.

Even more unusual—Cash piddling in front of the vanity mirror. Why he was so concerned about his looks this particular afternoon? Fussing with a renegade strand of hair over his forehead, he gave one last inspecting look and brushed a small piece of lint off the camel-hair sport coat. *Enough!* He quietly told himself. Forcefully, he stepped away from the counter, and turned off the light.

It was strange. The day seemed so ordinary. Outside of the fact that it was Memorial Day *and* his commencement, he would have thought that it was any other normal, run-of-the-mill type of afternoon. Quickly veering into his room, he retrieved his cap and gown. He wondered if there was anything else he needed to take with him for the ceremony.

Invitations had been sent out to an elite selection of relatives and friends. He honestly wondered if any of them would actually show up. Calling earlier that morning, Clint had complained that an emergency had come up in Rachel's family. He apologized repeatedly they would be missing the ceremony. In an effort to make up for it, however, he promised they would be coming home the next weekend to celebrate with the family. Cash couldn't deny feeling disappointed, but he understood. Following his mother down the stairs, his attention was roped in on two somnolent individuals seated in the livingroom.

"About time," Clayton quipped, popping up from the sofa like a broken spring.

"Excuse me?" Mrs. McCollum instantly replied—casting him a brazen glare.

"Wondering if the two of you were ever gonna come down." Mr. McCollum muttered under his breath. Giving a sigh, he got to his feet and made his way to the front door.

"Don't blame me…" Janice said in defense of herself. "I thought Cash had passed out in the bathroom."

They all got into the white truck and drove into town. When they arrived at the school, the parking lot and neighboring streets were packed with cars.

"You'd think we'd learn by now." Eugene shifted down. "Each year we come to this damned thing by the seat of our pants. And it takes me half an hour to just find a parking space. Jiminy Crickets!"

Looking at the clock on the dashboard, Cash swallowed. "I'm gonna be late. We needed to be in the cafeteria by twelve-thirty."

"Well, you should have thought about that when you were lollygaggin' up there in front of the mirror," Cash's dad snapped. Slamming his foot on the brake, he brought the truck to a sudden stop. "Go on, git! You can't be late for this."

Cash grabbed for the door handle and jumped onto the street.

"Straighten your tie out!" Janice called from the window. Her son was already halfway across the school lawn in a dead run.

Cash got to the cafeteria just in time. Waiting for a few stragglers, everyone else was gowned and lined up—ready to go into the gym. Hastily, he slipped the cap and gown on in the hallway—nervously adjusting the tassel. Trying to be as inconspicuous as possible, he tip-toed to his assigned space. From the corner of his eye, he spotted Travis shooting him an irritated stare. With a grin of embarrassment, he glanced at his partner, Cheryl, and let out a deep sigh of relief. "Thank God."

Allowing a small chuckle to escape, she went on to whisper, "Was wondering if you were going to make it."

The class filed into the gym.

Cash scarcely remembered a thing of the ceremony except for the presentation of the diplomas and awards. Several moments stood out— especially when Travis' name was called. Each time he was recognized, there followed a series of indiscreet whistles, hoots and hollers from the spectator stands.

At one point, several players from the football team yelled out, "Way to go, Traver!!!!" Everyone in the building laughed.

Honors were given to the class valedictorian, Nathan Prosser, an offensive player with Travis on the team, and Kayla Tokarczyk, the salutatorian, who beat Tiffany Jo by a minute fraction of a point. Tiffany had been quite upset when the news had been announced over the monitors throughout the school.

"…it's because her dad's on the school board." She had complained later to Jennifer and Cash during lunch in the cafeteria. "We were tied for points, but it's because of *who* she is." Her voice had carried a sizzling contempt.

After all was said and done, Cash stood on the front-lawn sidewalk with diploma and gown in hand, looking for his family. Dozens of people milled about him. He was so glad it was finally done. It was hard to believe the *only* world knew was now ending. A totally different one lay before him—one that spelled the words: University of Montana, dormitories, and the city of Missoula. His body gave a shudder.

"Hey!" Travis approached—wearing his typical beautiful, broad grin. There was no doubt, he was pumped.

Cash broke out with a reciprocating beam. "Hey!"

"Well, we did it!"

"Yup," Cash nodded. His eyes instantly noticed the scholarship from the University clenched in his hand. That little piece of paper made him happy... so *very* happy.

"There you are!"

Cash recognized the voice coming from his side. "Jen!" For once, he was honestly pleased to see her.

"I'm glad you two are here," she said breathlessly handing him an envelope. Pushing her glasses back up on her nose, she allowed a smile to flood her face. "You both looked great getting your diplomas."

Cash's eyes drew down to the envelope and noticed her handwriting. Across the front was each of their names... Cash and Travis. He caught his breath.

Jennifer noticed his shock. "It's okay. It's for both of you." She tossed him a reassuring wink.

Suddenly, Cash wasn't exactly sure what he wanted to do. A flood of emotions seemed to swoop in on him.

Shit! Was he going to cry? He sucked in air and swallowed hard. Seeing each of their names scrawled on that card sent his mind reeling.

Travis leaned over, trying to read what she had written. "Aren't you going to open it?" He acted impatient.

Handing the card to his boyfriend, he softly said, "Go ahead."

"You sure?" His grin revealed sweet pleasure in having the honors.

"If *neither* of you open it, *I will*." Jokingly, Jennifer kicked back into her typical obnoxious self.

Travis ran his finger along the sealed flap and pulled the greeting out.

"Where's your mother?" Cash directed his question to Travis—still looking for his family.

As the big football star focused in reading the message, he automatically replied, "I dunno, she's around here somewhere."

Cash finally spotted her. Another wave of surprise swept over him. She was visiting with *his* parents.

"Look." He pointed in their direction. He couldn't believe what he was seeing.

Jennifer turned, with an effort to spy on what he was gawking at. On her tip-toes, she finally spotted what had caught her cousin's attention. She allowed a smile to cross her lips.

Travis, finished with the card, looked up, his face was flushed. "Hey, thank you." His tone was broken.

Refocusing back on the boys, she instinctively reached up with a hand and yanked on her pony tail. Today, in an odd way, she looked cute doing that mannerism. Cash wondered if she would ever out-grow it.

"What?" Cash's word had finally sunk into Travis' conscious. "What are you taking about?"

Once again, Cash pointed in the direction of his family. "Over there."

Mrs. Hunter was busily chatting with Cash's mom as Mr. McCollum and Clayton stood quietly nearby with drawn faces. The scene was funny. It was obvious that Janice was barely getting a word in worth edgewise.

Travis couldn't keep from staring. "Well, I'll be."

Handing the card back to Cash, he left the pair—walking over to his mother and the McCollums.

Jennifer's eyes met Cash's. "Aren't you gonna read it?" She was becoming impatient.

"I'm sorry," Cash apologized. "Guess I got a little sidetracked."

He opened the card and read the message…

"The last three years have gone by *too* fast. Cash and Travis, I will miss both of you very much. It has been a growing period for each of us, but here we are—still together. (smile!) Just know I'm very proud of you two, and I'm also *really* eager to see what the future will bring into each of your lives. Your cousin and cousin-to-be… Jen."

Tears welled in Cash's eyes. He was afraid to say anything as he knew it would start the water flowing.

Jennifer noticed her cousin groping to control himself. Slowly, she reached out and slipped her hand into his. "It's okay," she reassured, "I don't mind if you bawl." Through her own tears, she allowed a chuckle to escape.

"We've been through a lot," she thoughtfully added.

Cash nodded, his face still looking down at the card. This afternoon was turning out to be more difficult than he had anticipated. Without speaking, he leaned forward and gave his cousin a long, tight embrace. How someone so irregular could crawl so deeply into his heart—he'd never know.

Eventually, Cash made his way to the Hunter-McCollum circle. The sight before him was unreal. It was the *last* thing he would have ever dreamed of.

"…drop it by anytime and I'll see what I can do with it," Janice sincerely offered to Travis' mom.

"I'd greatly appreciate it because I know it's Grace's favorite one." Tina's voice was high and brisk as ever.

"Well, we better be goin," Eugene finally spoke up—pulling a set of keys from his pocket. With a jingle, he sent out the message he wanted to get going.

Later in the truck, as the McCollums were heading to the ranch, Cash asked the hundred-dollar question, "What were you all talkin' about back there?"

"Tina wanted to know if I could do some repair work on one of her aunt's quilts."

This puzzled him. "How did she find out that you work on 'em?" He knew he had never said a word about his mother's hobby to Travis.

"From the way it sounds, she found out from Dad," Janice explained.

Cash remained quiet.

Mrs. McCollum went on to explain, "Dad said something to Grace, who's Tina's aunt. I guess she moved over to the nursing home about a year ago. I gather that Grace must have said something to Travis' mother."

"Oh."

"From the way it sounds, Dad and Grace are best friends."

With that, a thought-provoking silence fell within the cab as Eugene steered the pick-up into the driveway.

In a day birthing many surprises, Cash quietly asked himself, *would wonders ever cease?*

CHAPTER 28

The call came around midnight, Cash wearily picked up the phone.

"I finally made it," Clayton's voice mumbled over the receiver. "I'm here at the fairgrounds."

"'Bout damned time," Cash muttered, glancing over at Travis lying fully extended on the bed beside him. "We're on our way."

Travis raised his arms over his head in a stretch. "Finally got here, huh?"

Cash decided not to respond—he wasn't in the mood to either explain or complain about his brother. Instead he pushed himself off the bed—pulling his boots on. "Let's go."

Despite the warmth of the summer days, the nights were still cool, so they gathered their jackets as they shambled out the motel room door. The sky was pitch black and Travis craned his neck to look about.

"No stars. Think it's gonna rain?" The Viper's keys rattled in his driving-weary hands.

Cash took in a deep breath. "You smell rain?"

"How do you smell rain?" Travis turned to look at Cash there in the darkened parking lot. "What does rain smell like?"

He had to laugh at that. "You can tell it comin' off the air, on the wind. Smells like…" then Cash stopped, not sure how to explain it. "You never smelled rain?"

Travis pushed the unlock button. "What do you think? In California, all we smelled was the ocean. I don't recall rain smelling any different."

Cash had to chuckle at that as he hopped into his seat. "Let's get goin' before Clayton passes out in the truck."

Fortunately, the drive wasn't too far, otherwise, Cash would've been tempted to tell Clayton to take care of the animals himself, or just leave them in the trailer. Since taking over stock chores from their dad, Clayton was a hit or miss proposition, but at least when it came to Cash, he eventually followed through.

They explained their mission to the security guard at the gate, who pointed them in the direction of the barns. Sure enough, when they drove up alongside, Clayton was sitting dozing in the front seat of the pickup, animals still and silent in the back.

"Clayton!" Cash commanded in a loud whisper, banging on the driver's side window. "Clayton!"

Soon his brother was awake and out of the cab, stiffly making his way around to where the boys stood.

"We can put them in the barn over there," he gestured to the building alongside them. "Shouldn't be too much trouble since they're mostly asleep."

"What took you so long?" Cash hissed, after Clayton had backed the truck into the stable. "We waited for hours in that motel, didn't even go out to eat dinner."

Clayton just shrugged. "They kept me late at work. That's all. Nothin' personal to you, little brother."

The three worked quietly as possible so as to not disturb the RV'ers. It was getting on early morning by time they finished, and everyone would be up again in just a few hours.

"You gonna stay with us at the motel?" Cash asked, as they were on their way back out. Clayton only shook his head.

"I'll probably just stay in the truck. I don't like goin' too far from the animals…"

But Cash realized it was just an excuse. Clayton still couldn't bear the idea of staying in the same room with him and Travis, a room with an extra bed, no less.

"Well, you're welcome, if you should change your mind."

"I won't change my mind."

They were headed back to Travis' car when a dark figure came up beside them.

"Cash," the security guard began, looking carefully over at Travis, "you see anything strange around here just now?"

Clayton's image immediately sprang to his mind and he had to giggle, realizing he was punch-drunk tired.

"No Marcus, why you ask?"

"One of the cowboys said he saw some strangers over around the practice area, by the rear fence. Then they disappeared and he didn't see them again. If you didn't know, there were some problems in Kalispell the other week with hoodlums letting horses loose, so we're being careful and checkin' everything out. You staying here or leaving?"

"We're leavin', but my brother Clayton is stayin' in the truck. We just settled our bulls."

"Ok," the guard glanced behind him. "Good to see you again. Good luck tomorrow."

They watched as the guard walked slowly back to the front gait.

"That's strange," Travis commented. "Ever heard of such a thing..." but the words had just come from him when they heard a commotion directly over their shoulders.

Cash heard footsteps on the grass nearby, and then some shouting farther off.

"They got out!" It was now a yell.

Cash immediately sprang towards the small back-lot corral, hearing snorting and stomping from that direction.

"Cash..." Travis called, following close behind. "What's going on?"

He didn't answer. He knew the animals had gotten loose and had to be herded quickly into the practice corral before they scattered. A few cowboys were now coming out of their RVs, half-dressed and rubbing their faces in the confusion.

"What's going on?" Travis repeated—the phrase picked-up by others now surrounding them.

Cash kept on running, hoping Travis and the others would soon figure it all out. He knew he couldn't take care of these beasts himself, but still he picked up a stray stick and swung it across his shoulder.

There they were. As he had hoped, the animals were still too sleepy to be more than just slightly disruptive, keeping themselves grouped and moving towards the open pasture they saw beyond the fences. All at once Travis overtook the lead—yelling and whooping. Clearly, his hard training with the McCollums was paying off.

"Here! Here!" A voice in the distance was trying to direct them, but Cash couldn't see anyone. Travis, however, apparently had and was managing the small herd into the pen, a shadow standing next to the open gait. Again Cash heard, "Here!" and watched as Travis quickly obeyed. Placing the stick against his side, he slowed to a walk, feeling that Travis and the other person must have things now under control. He saw Travis follow behind the bulls, entering the pen himself.

What? Cash thought, then watched horrified as the gate closed at Travis' back with a loud bang. The Brahmas' hind quarters all seemed to jump at once and Cash could see them turning and stomping in confusion, becoming more awake by the second.

"Travis…" Cash yelled, and picked up to a run. He tried to call Travis' name again, but no words came out.

Travis looked about himself, moving this way and that, unfamiliar with the small arena he was in, but unwilling to turn his back to the steadily increasing agitation before him. Cash was no sooner closing in on the pen, however, when the shadow figure that had called Travis was now moving before him, practically pushing Cash aside in his haste. The next thing Cash knew, the gate was being opened and an arm reached in for Travis.

"Christ," the person hissed in a familiar tone.

Cash stumbled to a stop, stricken where he stood.

439

Lee pulled Travis out of the corral with a forceful yank, now being joined by others who were securing the pen.

Cash only closed his mouth when he began tasting dirt. He spat and suddenly felt himself going weak. What had he just witnessed? He couldn't be sure, but soon enough a dusty Travis and panting Lee were standing in front of him, Lee's hand still gripping Travis' arm.

"Lee?" Cash began, then gathered himself. "Lee? What you doin' here?"

As if suddenly realizing his hold, Lee released Travis' and hopped aside. His smile was visible even in the blackness around them.

"Maybe engaging in a little terrorism." He continued to grin. "How you doin', Cash?"

Cash was glad it was too dark to see the expression on Travis' face. He could well imagine it, instead.

"You didn't answer me," Cash kept his gaze steady in Lee's direction, trying to conjure up the face he remembered all too well. "Why are you here?"

"Why are you?"

"Out on a mid-night stroll with the bulls." Cash was still trying to put it all together.

It was odd, Lee out here at this hour of the night. And this thing with the animals...but Cash shut the thought off. It was too much to contemplate. Lee may hate him, may want to even kill him, but Travis? No, he shook himself. Even Lee wouldn't do something like that. It had to be the pranksters, or maybe animal rights activities. They sometimes showed up at the rodeos making wild claims. That had to be it—animal activists, who actually knew nothing about rodeos or stock.

"I'm sure." Lee's voice was casual as he turned away to walk off.

"Lee," Cash went up beside him. "What was going on just now?"

For a moment Lee stood without moving, then he pivoted around.

"What do you mean, Cash?"

"Wasn't that you at the gate, calling to Travis?"

"It was indeed."

"And didn't you shut the gate behind him?" Suddenly Cash felt himself flush with anger. He began to shake, his fists balling.

"I sure did. But I didn't tell your boyfriend to get into the damned pen with the cows, now did I?"

It was too confusing, Cash told himself.

"Kind of a coincidence... you being here," Travis' voice floated out into the night, thick and menacing.

"Yes, indeed it is." Lee didn't budge.

Cash remembered that Lee had never been afraid of Travis.

"I happened to be sleeping in my truck when the commotion started. Seems I can't afford a motel room..." Lee's eyes slid toward Cash's direction, "...these days."

They stood silently, aware that they had to accept Lee's explanation. It made sense, Cash realized. It *was* actually possible he was telling the truth.

"Let's go." The tiredness in his body overcame him in a rush. "We have to get up early."

"You don't believe me, do you?" Lee came to stand in front of the both of them. "You think I set this all up, don't you?" His accusing glance moved from one boy to the other. "You really think I set it up and would be so damned stupid to try something…."

Suddenly there was a catch in his voice that caused Cash to look at the ground. A feeling of guilt replaced his weariness. At that moment he didn't know what to think.

"You're such an ass, Cash," Lee continued, bitterness and an odd sadness coating his words. "You think I would be this obvious?"

A discomfited quiet cloaked the black air—stillness and order coming back over everything.

He saw him the next morning, in his signature black shirt and black hat, standing in the practice area pulling gear out of his bag. Cash noticed his hands seemed to shake a little as he worked. Standing a moment, his wary heart went out to the lost boy. Slowly, he approached.

"Hey, Lee."

When Lee turned, Cash could see the bloodshot eyes and drooping lids.

"Hey, Cash," Lee's words slurred out.

Cash felt an immediate chill.

"Hey," Lee said again, sitting back on his heels. "You're looking good after such a late night," sarcasm dripped from his lips. "I'm a wreck myself. A night of terrorism is never easy on a body."

The overcast gray hung drearily on throughout the morning. The clouds seemed to threaten of rain, yet not a drop fell. Normally, Cash liked rain, but on rodeo days, he preferred it to be sunny and dry. To be smeared with a layer of mud after being tossed to the ground from a crazy animal on a soggy, drizzly day was never high on his list.

Something other than the clouds seemed to hang ominously over Cash's head, he could feel it. Maybe it was his apprehension of the first go-round. Perhaps it was the subtle nipping at his memory of Lee, Travis and the bulls. He couldn't tell. Whatever it was, however, chewed and nibbled at him secretly like a deer feeding on a hay pile in the middle of the night.

Quietly preparing for the first event, his thoughts shifted. He could feel his mind clearing. This was the moment of truth... what he had diligently worked for all these years. *Hell*, he told himself, only a step away from receiving the title, All-Around Cowboy, and yet it didn't seem real. Coveted and dreamed of all his life, he felt lightheaded knowing that its grasp was now within close reach.

"Are you excited?"

Travis' words floated easily into his ears. Cash turned and faced his broad-grinned boyfriend. "You bet."

"You know something'?" Travis led him away from the herd of cowboys hanging out by the chutes.

"What?"

"I'm really proud of you." His eyes sparkled.

Sensing himself being drawn in, Cash softly replied, "I know."

Travis went on to say, "Your family is too."

Cash nodded. There was no doubt about that.

"Wanna know somethin' else?"

"What?"

"I wouldn't want to be anywhere else, but here, watching you, and knowing I'm a part of your life."

It struck Cash in a way not expected. He wanted to kiss him, but this was not the time, nor the place. In spite of their differences, disagreements and fiery discussions, they always seemed to pull through. And somewhere in his soul, he knew they would be in this for the long haul. Allowing a sigh to slip from his lips, he smiled and whispered, "I love you." It felt good… no one would ever know the depth. God, it felt *damn good.*

Cash returned to the chutes. His entry was coming up. The bull he was assigned was number twelve, The Terminator. He gave a shudder as he fastened his vest and made other final adjustments. From a distance, he noticed Lee staring at him. It made him freeze. Silently, like a wildcat, the cryptic boy watched with sharp eyes. His gaze, however, was disconnected, not focused—bearing indifference that was disturbing. Cash could never recall seeing that look on Lee's face before. Something was wrong, he determined.

Heading toward that direction, Cash sensed an immediate pang as the other youth broke away from his spot and became lost in a meandering crowd. *Damn it!* Stopping fast in his tracks, it became quite apparent, Lee was not going to let go of the hurt anytime soon. In all honesty, he didn't blame him. Quickly, he scanned the area in a last-ditch effort to spot him.

His event time arrived and he reckoned he better get back to the task at hand. He'd pull Lee aside later.

From the beginning, The Terminator was nuts—as if deep inside its brain, there was a boiling batch-full of unreleased anger signaling to Cash that this ride wasn't going to be without a fight. With his heart pounding, and mind racing, he slipped his legs down along the rumbling sides of the bull—each taking on the full force blast of the hurricane exploding beneath him. No more had he settled on the animal's flanks and could feel himself becoming crushed from the raging force whipping up against the sides of the chute. This critter was hell-bent on killing. Pain shot mercilessly through his thighs.

In an eerie, strange way, Cash was thrilled of the ornery attitude. It would mean more points. On the other hand, he was scared to death.

With undaunted determination, Cash cinched up the bull rope. *He was going to stay in control,* he kept telling himself. Wrapping the rope end around his gloved hand, he weaved it dutifully between each finger—pounding his free fist against the worn leather to ensure a secure hold. Somewhere in the back of his mind, he could hear clanging of the cow bell below. Was it the last call to Mass? Before he knew it, the gate was opened and together they bounded out into the arena like a tornado tearing up the prairie.

"Once again, folks, welcome to the Montana High School Rodeo Association Finals here at the Lewis and Clark County Fairgrounds *in* the lovely city of Helena!"

Cash could barely hear the announcer.

"On The Terminator right now, we have our number one cowboy from Miles City... Mister Cash McCollum! Let's welcome him to the arena!"

From that point, Cash found himself entering the vortex. He became aware of nothing else, but himself, and the tumultuous fury churning beneath him. Coming down hard on its front hooves, and kicking out with its back ones, The Terminator began to twist and spin without reason. Frantically, he struggled to locate his center of balance, but was unable to find it. Clinging voraciously to the rope, he fought to keep himself from the well—knowing that would bury him instantly.

Oh, God... he thought. He needed to get into the damned bull's groove! As it lunged and kicked high in the rear, Cash had the sensation of horns brushing his chest and belly. The Terminator was dead-set on jabbing, hooking him in the midst of crazy spins. Backing away from the bobbing head, Cash felt his hip and lower back snap like a whip as his rump went sailing into the air. He knew he was loosing it. Two more spins and another sky-high buck—he was sent flying off the seething beast onto the unforgiving ground.

Suddenly, the bull reared and barreled at him with full force, head down and horns out. Unable to get on his feet, Cash scrambled with his knees to avoid its fury. The shoulder of his shirt became snagged—its fabric ripping as he felt himself being shoved, belly-down across the dusty surface of the arena. He could tell this beast was out to kill him. With an enraged flip of its head, The Terminator tossed him out front like a fly on a fish line. Charging at him again, it tried one more time to hook him. The crowd gasped. This time, throwing himself into a fast roll, Cash managed to narrowly escape a head-on encounter with the blunted fork-of-death. Grazing the side of his head, he could feel the breeze of pounding hooves. *Was he going to die?* Somewhere in the back of his vision, he noticed the barrel man dancing and yelling. As much as the clown tried, however, The Terminator was not interested. Like a coiled snake, it snorted and glared at Cash with red eyes of vengeance. Fortunately, that opened a window of opportunity for Cash to get up and beeline for the fence. By the time he reached the railing, he could tell he was being hotly pursued. With the help of several hands, he was quickly hoisted up and over as the bull's head slammed mercilessly into the metal, knocking several bystanders to the dirt behind the arena.

Never in all his days did he experience such a ride as this.

A mixed bag of emotions carried from the grandstands down to the chute area. As there were sighs of relief that Cash made it out alive, a definite tone of disappointment rode heavily as the crowd settled back—waiting for the next entry.

"Well, better luck next time, Cash." The announcer mustered to offer up a consolatory word. "Let's give our top boy a hand for a whole-heart effort…"

An obliging applause sounded from the bleachers.

From behind the chutes, Cash noticed Travis. No words were said. There didn't need to be.

Feeling as if he was going to pass out, Cash stopped cold in his tracks. He felt nauseous. Quickly, he reached for something to hold—his legs trembling.

Travis, along with several cowboys ran to Cash's side to give him support as he began to fall to his knees.

"Whoa, buddy!" one of the guys called out as he assisted in leading him to a quiet place. "You got knocked-up pretty bad out there, didn't you?"

"Give him some air," another suggested as they sat him on the ground away from the crowd.

"Cash…" Travis' voice was weak—his face ashen, both eyes washed with cold horror.

Cash felt his insides clench up. Instinctively, he knew what Travis' look meant—something that couldn't be dealt with at that moment. There were two more rides he still had to compete in. In no way was he going to cop out now. From a distance, he could hear the announcer's voice.

"And now for our next contestant… coming out of chute number six on Hired Hand… Lee Biruni, from Great Falls. Let's welcome him to the arena!"

Amidst applause, Cash could hear the chute gate open followed by furious stomping and snorting of an angry bull. He wanted so badly to see the action, but the others would not allow him to get up.

"Let me see." Cash murmured as he tried to push himself back to his feet.

"No, you don't," someone admonished, gently pushing him back down. "You just sit here 'n rest."

Cash's ears listened intently to the pounding of hooves as the animal struggled to free itself of his friend's control. He could picture Lee earnestly throwing himself into each frenzied buck and spin. Somehow, he knew invariably, the young turk would look good and score well.

More cheers flowed down from the stands.

Cash thought he was going to blow. He really wanted to watch.

As the thunder continued, along with repeated grunts and groans from the bull, Cash strained to hear each move from the other side of the fence.

Then, somewhere along the way, he heard a thud, followed by several muffled cries. Gasps floated down from the stands.

Immediately, a terrible sense gripped Cash. His spirit knew.

The bull was still raging in the arena when Cash jumped to his feet and broke loose from the grasps of his well-meaning caretakers.

Suddenly, the PA speakers blasted a shaken announcer's voice, "May I have your attention, we need immediate medical assistance in the arena, thank you."

"Cash!" Travis yelled out—only to be ignored.

Reaching the arena fence, Cash's eyes found Lee's form lying on the ground with a small pool of blood forming beside his head.

What? His mind went wild. *It couldn't be!* A horrible fear swept him.

The bull fighter and clown frantically tried to distract Hired Hand. All their efforts seemed useless, however. With relentless hooves, the insane beast circled and trampled over the still body. The sound of cracking bones echoed through the air. From the other end of the arena, paramedics approached the service gate.

Without thinking, Cash gripped the railing and jumped over the fence. Only one thing was before him—only one thing on his mind. He couldn't believe it. *"LEE!"* His scream echoed throughout the arena, grandstands—the entire fairgrounds.

A hushing silence overtook. No one stirred except for the emergency crew that scurried across the arena.

"Oh, my God!" Cash cried as he fell next to Lee's crumpled form. There was no response or movement—just limpness. *"Oh, my God!"*

Startled, the bull backed up, snorted, and glared at Cash.

"Get outta here!" Cash commanded—waving his arm furiously at the stunned animal. *"Go on, get the fuck outta here!"*

Cash's shouting seemed to give enough time for the barrel man and others to jump in and gain control, ushering the frenzied killer out of the arena.

Leaning forward, Cash's vision fixed on Lee's mutilated face. With eyes still open, blood oozing from his mouth, the dreaded truth sunk in. Lost thoughts spun frantically in his brain as he softly touched the young man's hand. Somewhere in his memory, he saw the dream—that dreadful, horrible premonition. For years, it had chewed at him—nibbling away, teasing at his soul. *It couldn't be!* He told himself. *No! This was not happening!* Without warning, the dam broke and all its horror engulfing him. *This was it!* This was that dream that never made sense…

He wanted to fight. *He had to fight.* Of course, this was not real.

449

Give me a pulse! Cash prayed. *Give me a goddamn pulse!* He hopefully searched for movement from Lee's chest.

"No!" His plea exploded into a sob as he drew his buddy's head tightly into his bosom—warm blood saturating through the fabric of his shirt. "Oh, God... NO!"

CHAPTER 29

No words were spoken as Travis helped Cash load Lee's saddle and gear in the big shiny, black pick-up. Cash could not allow his eyes to settle upon the bed roll—the red blanket and pillow which was neatly shoved in a back corner. He spotted the cooler on the other side—his memory shooting back to a secluded, cozy den nestled between some Missouri River bluffs and an obscure wheat field on a dreamy, starry night. He knew what was in it. The scent of Lee's body and cigarette smoke lingered heavily throughout the cab. It was odd. At any moment, he expected to hear the scuff of boots approach, followed with that familiar smart-assed voice, "Did I tell you that you could go messin' around in my truck?" Instead, the only thing he could hear was the whoops and hollers rising from the grandstands. Never again, would he hear that voice. Never again, would those words be uttered. Ironically, he waited for the pain, the drama, uncontrolled sobbing to begin. It didn't. It couldn't. He was too shocked. He was just plain numb.

Gathering their own stuff, the boys quietly pulled out of the parking lot. Cash noticed Clayton standing off in a distance—stoned faced—obviously shut down. God have mercy… everyone was at a loss for words.

There was no way Cash could have prepared himself for what he experienced as he slid into Lee's spot behind the wheel. Immediately, he could feel eyes staring, closely scrutinize, as he ignited the engine. Certainly, Lee was no longer here. He was dead. His spirit was probably long gone by now— taken to his afterlife. *Right?* He kept asking himself. But why the fuckin' feeling? Why did Lee feel so damned close? Was it wishful-thinking? Guilt? Remorse? *Jesus!* Cash fought off the trailing of his mind. Looking over, he noticed the ashtray filled with crushed-out smokes—many of those shared. There was also a half-drunk can of pop resting in the holder. On the dashboard, lay a worn pair of sun-glasses along with a wrinkled-up receipt from one of the motels they had stayed together at. Everything seemed to be waiting, anticipating, for Lee to hop back into the cab and resume his rightful rule. Slowly, Cash's insides began to fall and break down—piece by piece. He couldn't believe this loss. He couldn't fathom the pain that was beginning to swell inside. There was no way he could accept the day's finality—it wasn't real. None of it!

Lee was dead. He would never be seen, felt, or heard of ever again.

The truth of this was too bitter to believe. Cash wasn't sure he could live with this… no, he *knew* he would *never* be able to live with it. With a bloody hand, he scrambled shaking fingers across his forehead—trying to gather himself in.

He knew he looked like shit.

As Cash followed Travis and the 'Puppy'—winding through the rolling mountains, along the peaceful beauty of the great Missouri, he felt lost. What lay ahead, was completely unknown. He had no map to chart out where all this would take him—no litany on how to properly grieve and morn. From this point forward, he didn't have a clue how to prepare for—or exist through anything.

Over and over, his mind rehearsed that fateful event. Vivid like a movie, he knew he'd never forget.

Was he responsible for Lee's death? Was this all his fault? "For God's sake," he hopelessly cried out into the empty cab, "I didn't mean for you to die!"

He couldn't help asking himself several nagging questions. Would things have been different if he had pursued Lee through the crowd? And about that previous night—could it have been handled differently? He was crying out... struggling to get Cash's attention. Certainly, he had not intended to hurt Travis—right?

If Lee hadn't been so tired going into the day, there wouldn't have been the accident. Correct? Cash knew he was heading down a useless trail, but he couldn't help himself.

They could have shared a warm motel room, and he would have gotten a good night's sleep. Perhaps, if they were still together, none of this would have happened.

No! He couldn't continue with this torture.

If they were still together... it all seemed to come back to that statement— bringing him back to the break-up. Had there been something between them? If so, had he done the right thing? Would he still be alive if they were together? Obviously, Lee was depressed—yet to the point of allowing himself to be killed?

The sting in his spirit was deep—sharp and cutting.

Was this his fault? If it was, was he now a murderer? Would Lee's blood be upon his head forever? From that point on, his brain could not stop—he was in a tail spin. What happened this day to Lee, would it be something he'd carry for the rest of his life?

Cash could not stop trembling as he gripped the wheel. Tears streamed down his face. Truth be said, yes... there *had* been something between them—something extremely close *and* very personal. Now, as he looked at himself in the rearview mirror, he knew beyond the shadow of a doubt, he wanted to die as well.

Nearing the outskirts of the city, Cash's stomach knotted. With a heart aching so badly, Cash knew he was on his own with this one. No one else would ever share the grief—not as much as he. And now, what he dreaded—was only a moment's step away.

How was he going to face Altiar and Elena?

Lord, have mercy... he prayed—wetness still filling his eyes, blurring his vision. His mind could come up with no solutions, nothing that would make him feel better.

The evening air was thick and sultry as Cash left the Biruni's. Silently, he drove through town, across the river, and up to the bluffs. Looking to the west, thunderheads had pushed up off the mountains, and slowly, they were making their way toward the city.

Thinking back earlier that afternoon, it was a blessing that Travis decided to depart for Miles City. He had done his best in light of the situation—supporting Cash through all this. But taking as much as he could, it was evident he wanted to be released. Ironically, Cash wanted him on his way as well.

With a gesture of the finger to follow him into the kitchen, Travis had spoken in a lowered, broken voice, his need to go. "Cash," he struggled to get his words out, "I'm sorry. I've gotta get outta here. Will you be all right if I head back home?"

Nodding, Cash understood; he got the message. Actually, Travis had gone above and beyond—much more than average Joe.

Walking him out to the old pick-up, cradling Elena close against his heart, Cash could sense an intense awkwardness settling over them… "You'll call me when you get home?"

"Huh?" Travis had already departed.

"You'll call me?" Impatience nipped at Cash.

Nodding, Travis avoided Cash's eyes. "Yeah."

"Fine…" Instantly, Cash found himself longing to be rid of the conversation.

There was no question, he knew he had to stay on. Altiar had fallen apart. He had never seen anything like it before. Falling to her knees with sobs exploding deep within, the only English words Mrs. Biruni had been able to utter was, "Lee—my poor Lee!" Repeated countless times within a sea of Turkish, she clung to Cash—mixing her tears with stains from her son's blood on the torn shirt.

Throughout that bone-chilling afternoon, Cash had held Elena close to him. He wasn't sure who needed who more—him or her. Looking into those big, round eyes, he could see fear deeply written. *Did she realize what was going on?*

Now relieved to get out of the apartment for awhile, he hoped his memory would serve him right. He simply had to find that place—the secret hideaway in the bluffs. Recognizing landmarks, Cash's heart began to beat faster. The tiny tug that had crept into his soul seemed to intensify, swell, as he steered the truck into the wispy wheat fields. As he approached the obscure intersection, he instantly knew this was the spot. Scarcely, could he hold onto the wheel as he pulled off the highway and onto the dirt road.

This is right, he told himself. And at that moment, there was no other place on the face of this planet that mattered more to Cash, than here. Shutting down the engine, Cash sat still, quietly waiting. Only the rushing of his blood through an aching, mourning heart was audible to his ears.

This was Lee's home. Simple. Hidden. Comfortable. It was where he found freedom and a place to be at peace.

Crawling out of the cab, he could hear thunder growl from a distance—his eye catching a flash of lightening extending from a dark corner of the sky to the shadowy, veiled land below. Smells of a wet prairie began to float effortlessly into his nostrils as he reached within the canopied truckbed for the old, worn blanket and pillow.

Suddenly, he felt it—light as a feather, like a floating speck of dust against his cheek and neck. *What the hell was that?* Twirling around, Cash's eyes searched. He tingled inside. There was nothing that could have touched him. His eyes continued to scan. *Right?*

A strangest sense came over him.

Something again. The slightest touch. Was he nuts? *Something...* he had felt something brush him. *He was alone, wasn't he?* Once more, he glanced around warily.

As he carefully spread the bedroll across the ground, thunder clapped and roared. Stray drops fell to the ground and onto his weary skin. The rain would be coming soon, he reasoned. He spread himself out, anticipating the cleansing—the baptism. Silently, Cash waited.

Lying there still and silhouetted, against the deep red, a peculiar sense crept inside. Lee had lay here. Where was he now?

As if he were a sacrifice upon an altar, he remained motionless—stretching out his legs and arms. Deeply, he inhaled the strong air—defined scents of Lee, earth and rain.

I'm sorry, Lee, he thought. *I'm so sorry for what I have caused you.* If there was ever a time he wished he could rewind the past, it was now.

A vagabond breeze brushed his face and skipped onto the tall, ripening wheat—stirring waves that flowed across an anticipating field. A single raindrop was greeted with anticipation as it slapped his parched lips and slid effortlessly into his mouth. Slowly, his tongue tasted and lapped its sacred blend—the healing wine. He willed the rest to fall. Suddenly, the sky blazed from its fire shooting down—explosions that shook the ground and echoed throughout the bluffs.

Did someone call his name?

Eyes opened, he remained frozen in this holy tabernacle—earnestly praying to be forgiven.

Yesterday, as one, we rode.
I recall.
It was hardly a secret—
But so much was barely spoken, uttered.
Then, something you whispered
Chained my plans.
It caught the mighty, falling star.
Perhaps we forgot to undress from our masks.
Remember the time we laughed?
I saw you smile
As I turned to leave,
Your memory etched against my fear.

How could you go so fast, unexpectedly?
Yet I lingered to sort it out—perhaps deny
That it was you who I searched for
But couldn't find.
Remember the time we laughed?
Silently, expectantly—
With resounding quiet,
I hear the chorus;
To drink the bitter sting that tickles my tongue.
So, how can I think
Or sing the song—
When it's my mind, embalmed, that races?
Your words now squeeze my heart—
They fill my cup.
Remember the time we laughed?

The stars, I see,
Beholding no secret.
No hope is hidden from the sun.
As chill goes down upon my flesh,
And water dries and sets aflame,
It's this…
My yearn for memory,
A cloak for lost and mournful bones.
Remember the time we laughed?
If I tell you my thoughts,
To share my dream,
I'd say it's sad. Perhaps unforgiving.
That I would have considered you eternal
if not for short a day.
Zeus, or Apollo could have been conceived,
But yet, it's I who dream of vapors,
odors that drift from the pot.
Where does one go to quell the pain?

Can I find a place to hide?
Remember the time we laughed?
Oh, this is only the beginning!
The first grain on my tongue from a sea of endless, dry sand.
Here I wait silently in pain.
What is this I hear?

...Did you call my name?

Slowly, faithfully, the steady rain washed Cash—comforting his rough, tired skin... rinsing Lee's blood from the torn shirt—allowing the infinite healing to begin.

Somehow, deep in his spirit, he knew he was not alone.

For one brief second, there was no ache—no memory of what had occurred the day before. Then, as if the dam had been opened, it gushed in on him—dumping torrents and suffocating his soul.

Opening his eyes, his orientation returned. A bottle of cologne sitting on the dresser by a brush both waited to be picked up by their rightful owner. Lee's favorite baby blue tank-top randomly tossed across the arm of a chair by the bed stand lay anticipating a particular, determined hand to retrieve it—to be slipped over smooth, bronze skin. Tucked in the corner was a pair of cowboy boots—once hailed as his favorite, more comfortable than a glove. And then there was the smell—that unyielding scent which drove Cash insane. It pervaded throughout the room.

Forcing himself up—he pushed the sheets back. His body yearned for a warm shower. As the water softly brushed his flesh, he remembered the rain. "Lee," he whispered. It would be a long time.

Throughout the morning, everything he did seemed empty, thoughtless. Maybe his mind was simply on other things. Perhaps he was just going in circles in hopes he could find a beginning.

Midst a hushed apartment, Cash's first mission was set on enduring. Anything more than that and his brain would shut down. Funeral plans, the burial and things to follow, they all seemed inconceivable. The only thing he could work with, muster was the here and now. But yet, there was the past… those haunting thoughts, *his* vast and wonderful memory.

It was strange, there were things that came back to him clear as a bell, while others remained clouded. He couldn't remember what had happened after he Lee was gone. How did he get out of the arena? He had felt hands pull him away from the lifeless body. Had he said anything as the others guided him patiently out to the back fields? What had been said by the paramedics as they began working at reviving the other man he loved? *Love?* There it was… the word shot at him like a stray bullet in the night. My God, he thought. *Had he really loved Lee?* Reviewing that relationship, and recalling all the analyzing and denying, he quietly wondered. Had he only kidded himself about his true feelings? Instantly, he shook off the uncomfortable feeling.

Shuffling to the kitchen, he searched the cabinets for something to eat. Oatmeal was as good as anything, he figured—pulling the container down from the shelf, and measuring out water for a pan. While he waited for the water to come to a boil, he stood by the stove half-tranced—his eyes staring off into space. It seemed peculiar that the others were not up yet. Maybe they were having a difficult time getting up to face they day as he had.

Glancing at the phone resting at the end of the counter, his mind rehearsed the dangling conversation with Travis after he had gotten home from the bluffs. The call had come a little after midnight. Cash figured he must have trucked with the old Pup—a wonder he didn't hit a deer…

"I'm home." The voice on the line had been flat.

"Good. I'm glad you made it safely."

Then followed the silence—that damned air-sucking silence.

Cash finally broke it by saying, "Thank you for helping out." What else could he say?

"It's all right."

The phone call had been brief and distant—one more thing to gnaw at Cash's mind. It was obvious that Travis was struggling. *Of course he was.* In spite of the fact he had been willing to help pack Lee's stuff into the truck and take it back to Great Falls, he had made it apparent he did not want to get involved. Throughout the afternoon, he had purposely positioned himself in the shadows—away from everyone. Within those graying eyes, undeniable hurt radiated.

Cash couldn't blame Travis. If the shoe was on his own foot, he knew he wouldn't be as gracious. There was no tolerance for Jason, and if something ever happened that would call for Travis' to help his former boyfriend out, Cash had to admit there would be war in camp.

Arrangements were already underway when Cash, Altiar, and Elena arrived at the funeral home. A slender man dressed in dark slacks and a yellow cardigan was seated with the director and his assistant around a large table. At the sight of Altiar, the gentleman stood to his feet and proceeded to pull a chair out for her.

"I wasn't sure you would be able to make it here this morning." The man quickly began explaining himself. His words were heavy with accent.

"You heer of telephone? Goot invention, no?" Mrs. Biruni grimaced, waving her hand indignantly in his face. "What you theenk? Maybe I too invaleed to come? No for my son?" Under her breath, she hissed, "Bastard."

Looking past his estranged wife, Mr. Biruni focused on Cash who held Elena in his arms. "Who's he?" The question was directed to Altiar.

"He friend of Lee's," Altiar's tone was defensive. "He drife me heer and geef support seens you do not."

The graying haired man suspiciously eyed the three of them; and with a grunt, went back to his seat—obviously irritated over Cash's uninvited inclusion.

By the time everyone finished shuffling and getting down to business, Elena was peacefully asleep against Cash's chest. She seemed to be the only one unaffected by the stress of everything.

As they started discussing the funeral and burial, Cash's thoughts burned hot with acid. How far was Altiar's ex going to extend himself to impress everyone? What a fake! Who was he kidding? After all the shit that Lee had shared—and knowing Mr. Biruni had never once shown an interest in his son's life, Cash could feel his insides rear-up. And all his pious demands of having Lee buried in strict accordance to Muslim law seemed almost funny.

"No!" Mr. Biruni snapped—sitting straight up in his chair. "Our son must be given proper, holy burial!"

"Nonsense," quipped Altiar. "He go to afterlife regardless of hocus-pocus."

With a flame of contempt, Lee's father quickly came back by saying, "Woman of rebellion!"

In an effort to maintain some semblance of harmony, the director interjected with a plan. "Tarek, we will contact the Mosque officials requesting them to conduct the service; that will be no problem."

"And he will be buried by his formal name!" Mr. Biruni was still hot under the collar. "This 'Lee' stuff is bull-sheet!"

Well, that *was* news! Cash was stunned to discover that his friend had been going by an alias all this time… his *real* name—the name that had been given to him at birth was Abdul. *Why had he done that? To fit in?* Or was it just one more costume that hung delicately in a closet of numerous personas?

"If eet make you better to know he go weeth name *you* geef him— *not* one he choose," Altiar sighed and rolled her eyes. Looking at Cash she chuckled—a sarcastic sparkle gleamed and ricocheted throughout the room. "Islam ees *for* the man because eet ees *made* by a man."

After all was said and done, Mrs. Biruni gave Cash the low-down of what the funeral involved.

"Too much complication…" She had complained, wobbling back to her room.

Unfortunately, he had not been allowed to attend which seemed rather unfair. Altiar, however, had explained that Lee's body was washed by his father and several others according to sacred law. Afterwards, he was ceremonially wrapped with a white linen shroud and placed in a coffin. Salat had been said followed by the burial where Lee was placed in the ground without the casket—his head turned to the right—facing Makkah.

In a way, Cash was relieved he did not have to attend. It wasn't that he was afraid of facing death's reality; it was just that this particular instance would have been way over his head.

Over the next three days, women from the mosque came over to the apartment bringing food and offering any assistance for Altiar in the grieving period.

"Witches!" Altiar exclaimed under her breath as they all made their way out the front door and down the front walk to their cars on the third day. "Never see them for years—as eef I am dead and gone myself—then they appear like cock roaches!"

Ensuring that Elena and her grandmother would be okay, Cash finally decided to head back to Miles City. He had a lot of catching-up to do around the ranch. He was also looking forward in getting back to his new summer job at the State Park. He had started it the last week of the qualifiers.

Pirogue Island was an intriguing place for individuals who appreciated the wonders of nature. Set apart within the Yellowstone River, it was home to a wide variety of wildlife. Grasslands teamed with various prairie and water foul such as grouse and pheasant while other animals such as whitetail and mule deer, badger and beaver roamed along the shoreline thickets and cottonwood groves. As assistant groundskeeper, his responsibilities carried him over every stitch of the island—which seemed to keep his interest up. And since his selected major was Conservation, he considered himself fortunate landing the position. It was a glove-fit. As far as he was concerned, it was much better than sitting as a lifeguard at the municipal pool—nothing against Travis…

Out of the blue, Altiar was insistent upon Cash taking the black pick-up home. Prepared to take the bus, he questioned her as she huffed and growled with sharp disapproval. "No yoose I haf for that think. Lee haf it pait… *you* make inshooruns." And with a decisive nod of her head, she finished by stating, "Eet be okay."

Before he left, Cash promised he would come back the following weekend to check up on them.

"You no haf too." Altiar did not want to be a burden.

"No, it's all right." Cash was adamant. "I want to come back. I like being with you and Elena." It was the truth; he was beginning to enjoy his time with them. They were becoming 'family' to him.

Leaving Great Falls, he felt a portion of his heart staying behind. What was it about these people? With lives so different than his, from a culture he could barely understand, yet they were so easy to love—it boggled him. And in a strange, almost spooky way, he knew these people would never fade from his life.

As he drove the desolate landscape, wind whipping throughout the cab, he came over a hill and suddenly a memory gripped at him—one of those renegade moments shared with Lee. He could see it sharp as a movie in his mind...

"Look at this!"

Lee pulled his pickup over to the side of the road, stopping quickly.

"Look at this," he repeated.

Cash sat unmoving, looking out the window and seeing nothing but an endless mud field.

"Somethin' wrong?" He hoped the truck wasn't breaking down.

Giving a little snort, Lee threw his door open. Climbing down, he said, "Wanna look at this, or not?"

What it looked like was nothing more than a prairie dog field, with scrubs of grass and weeds scattered and possibly eaten.

"What we lookin' at, Lee?" Lee's sudden bursts of diversion were starting to wear on Cash. "Because I sure as hell don't see much of anythin'."

Lee was already moving away from the truck, walking swiftly into the field.

Cash ran to keep up since Lee was on one of his 'Brownie tears'. Before leaving the truck, however, he made sure the keys were pulled out of the ignition and the doors locked.

"Wait, Lee," he called to Lee's quickly disappearing back.

When Lee finally stopped, he had gone some distance from the road, out over a small hillside covered in ants. With the wind whipping through his hair as he stood still, his eyes seemed to be seeing something beyond Cash's vision. "Well, if you can't see it," he murmured—mostly to the air around him, "then I can't really show it to you."

Try as he might, Cash could only see the same land he had seen all of his life. He rubbed his boot in the dirt with annoyance and boredom. Best to let Lee alone at times like this, he said to himself. Best to just let him travel those twisting roads in his mind.

Suddenly Lee turned back, fixing his dark stare on Cash. His eyes were wide with excitement and anticipation. "Look hard, out there," he raised his left arm—finger pointing to the west.

Cash recalled himself squinting against the glare of the sun. Faintly, maybe almost a mile in the distance, he made out some movement that probably belonged to some animals—possibly stray cattle.

"Mustangs," Lee had whispered. "Wild ones... aren't they wonderful?" Reaching over, he grabbed Cash by the arm—pulling him to his side. "Truly free beings."

Still watching the far-away scene, Lee continued, "Wonderful..." his arm sliding around Cash's shoulder, giving him a small hug. Cash felt a little spark shoot through him, and the vague beginning of arousal.

"This is life as it should be. Life as every creature should live it."

While Cash had already taken in enough and was ready to go back to the truck, Lee stood as if transfixed. He became silent for a long while.

"I know you don't see it like I do. You don't see anything like I do, do you?"

In his mind, Cash rehearsed the silence that flowed out of him.

"You live in your little world of achievements, family and friends. And every now and then you come into my life and turn me upside down." Lee laughed at his own bluntness. "And anything more than that, I have to beg for."

Instinctively pulling away, Cash stated in a hurt tone, "I don't know what you're on, Lee, but you're not makin' a whole lotta sense. You been into something again?"

This comment made Lee laugh even harder. "Yeah," looking directly into Cash's eyes, "yeah… mostly smokin' a whole lotta you."

Giving another little hug, he then abruptly pushed Cash away. As he began to walk away, Cash stayed motionless, feet firm, unwilling to move again. He wasn't used to seeing Lee without the black hat and found his eyes traveling up and down the figure with great consternation. How could he evoke such emotion? The wind played across Lee's dark hair, blowing it up and about. His shirt sleeves rustled around on his arms in little ripples. With his hands by his side, Cash believed Lee had the potential of becoming an actual part of the land—if he ever stopped. And with that, he would root, like some tree… never to be moved again on the prairie—ever…

A great ache boiled up in Cash, as he pulled the truck off to the side of the road and got out—the prairie wind blowing into his face. Finally, it rose up and subdued him. Pain, hungry as an addict, ate his heart—licking at the longings, and gnawing at the regrets.

Each time he saw Lee like that, everything in the world stopped because there seemed to be nothing more actually in the world. Seemingly, Cash always managed to give over to feelings of wonderment and longing—all supported by a vague and peculiar sense of unease.

As his memory once again kicked-in, he could see Lee turning quickly—looking back…

"You afraid of me?"

Cash found no hesitation with his reply. "I ain't afraid of much, Lee… especially not you."

Throwing his arms up and out as though trying to touch something past the both of them, he cried out, "HA! That's what I like about you, Cash… your incredible tolerance for bullshit."

"I dunno what you're talkin' about," Cash brushed him off, although there was a suspicion lurking around at the bottom of his conscious. Slowly, he turned and began to walk away.

"Don't go back. Stay here a minute." Lee's voice was pleading. "Why don't we just stay? Why do we always have to be in a hurry?"

When he got like that, it was hard to deny him anything…

Brushing away another tear that wandered down his cheek, Cash quietly turned back toward the truck and resumed his journey down the sad, lonely road. What was it about this in-between space, the distance between his two worlds that always made him feel so alone… so completely by himself?

CHAPTER 30

It was the time for the scent of sweet clover to permeate the air. As the summer days passed—along with its hot, cloudless afternoons and the steady whispers of the wind—pain of Lee's death gradually dissipated into a quiet closet of remorse. Preparation for college started to saturate Cash's attention. What were his classes going to be like? Would Travis and he be able to share the same room in the dormitory? And what about Missoula—how was he going to survive in a city? Hell, he could barely stand it in Great Falls on the weekends. All these questions, and more, riddled his thoughts over and over.

Making his daily tours around the island park, he wondered what the mountains were going to be like. He had heard stories of how different the western side was from the eastern. Surely, it couldn't be *that* different, he reasoned. Besides, it was all still one state.

Regarding the rodeo title and scholarship, Cash had kissed it all 'bye-bye'. Historically, dropping out of the Finals was considered an unforgivable sin; so the moment he had decided to take Lee's stuff back to Great Falls, he knew he had lost his dream. Hope for reaching the life-long goal had died along with his closest rodeo companion in that quiet arena. And while driving back from the funeral, he had even wondered if he would be able to attend college.

Unbelievably, his doubts of attending the U were washed away upon the notification that he *had* received the scholarship and that he was also named All-Round Cowboy of the Year.

Thinking back, he shouldn't have been shocked about the Association's decision. The fact was, however, he had been. While he had not finished his events at the Finals, his overall scores were way more than any other player—except for Lee's. What a price that had been paid...

In light of it all, Cash made the decision to give up rodeo. He had played with the idea numerous times before, but after Lee's death, the signs were obvious, he knew he had to get out of the arena. Apart from his family, no one else knew.

"I can't believe it." Clayton had exclaimed after hearing the proclamation, "The little devil is finally hangin' up his hat and spurs."

Wanting to avoid a lot of explanation, Cash thought it would be better to publicly announce his retirement while at school.

"Personally, I'm relieved about his decision," Mrs. McCollum had stated one evening at the dinner table—drawing that particular subject to a formal close within the household.

Surprisingly, he hadn't seen much of Travis since the Finals. Trying to brush it away from his mind, even though it ate at him every day, Cash reckoned it to their separate schedules. With his boyfriend's football training and job at the pool, along with Cash's work at the park—mixed with many weekends spent up in Great Falls, their time together was rather lean. They were both very busy... or so it seemed. Cash had to ask himself if that was the *honest* reason.

"You know, Travis hasn't been coming around lately." Janice observantly stated once in passing.

"He's been busy training for the team."

Sensing the sting, Cash knew he was only kidding himself. Deep down, his insides told him why they had drifted apart.

What was he supposed to do? Act like things were all normal? How could he? For Christ's sake, a good friend had died, and how could he act like nothing had ever happened? And how could Travis ignore that fact? Of course, he knew what it all meant. There was no doubt; this entire situation had placed both of them in a very awkward position... and neither one knew how to dig out.

Several times after work, Cash had discretely made his way by the pool thinking he would confront the matter head on. Instead, he'd found himself glued to the shiny, black pick-up secretly watching his wounded lover sit quietly in the lifeguard's chair over countless swimmers playing and visiting around the water. It made his heart ache. Damn it! He knew there had to be a way to break the ice. Surely the words would come to him if only he could just muster enough courage to get off his duff.

Each passing day drove Cash more into a quandary. Travis needed reassurance and Cash needed to get the pain off his chest. He knew it was his turn to reach out, but something inside seemed to nail his foot to the floor. *God*, he prayed, *bring an angel to cross my path.*

Ironically, it was Jennifer who put on the wings...

"What's going on with you two?"

471

"What do you mean?" Cash tried to play ignorant.

"You know full-well what I mean." His short, stout cousin had cornered him at the Shop Mart in a deserted aisle after work one hot, dry afternoon. Mercilessly, she yanked at her long, brown locks.

"One more week with the two of you moping around here, wearing long faces and I swear I'll kick you both square in the ass."

"We're both busy." Instantly, he felt trapped—wanting a cigarette in the worst way.

"Look, I know about your friend's death and all… I'm really sorry." Stepping in closer, she made it clear she was not going to let him escape. "And I *know* how much he and Travis got along." –sarcasm dripping from her words, apparently alluding to the horrible scene in the high school hallway when Lee had visited unannounced. "As for those reasons, that's your-guy's business. But from what I see, Travis loves you. He misses you."

Her candidness immediately threw him back. Quickly, he scanned the area with frantic eyes—hoping that no one else was eaves-dropping.

"Jenni-" he began, but was cut off.

"No, you listen to me." Her eyes blazed with determination. "Travis loves you with his whole heart. And here you are avoiding him like he's the plague. It wrong, Cash. What you're doing to him is really wrong."

Cash could barely catch his breath.

"I wouldn't stand here and confront you if I didn't believe in you two. You're both made for each other and somehow you're gonna have to work through all this stuff." Tears began to well in her brown eyes. Hastily, she wiped them away with a brush of her hand…

Well, that was that, figured Cash, numbly walking back out to his truck. She had made no bones about it. Clearly, it was up to him to make the first move. *Dear Lord*, he prayed, crawling up into the cab and locking his door, *give me the strength.* He felt like he had just been struck down by a bulldozer.

They wandered down to the banks of the Yellowstone—Brownie and Cash. The walk was slow and deliberate, carefully stepping over the rain soaked ground, the slippery areas leading off into the water's gentle ebb and flow. Cash pulled his hat closer over his eyes, the sun was merciless now, shining with a vengeance after a soaking thunderstorm. In the east, midnight clouds rumbled and roared; their sound echoing across the river valley. As he looked over to the other side, he could imagine the Cheyenne, Blackfoot, and Crow—and who knew who before them, crossing at this very place, following the calving buffalo herds east. Lives directed by the seasons and the spirits. He couldn't help but sigh. There were memories of this place that were not just his. He felt surrounded by ghosts, and quickly, he shook off a momentary chill.

At first he wasn't sure, it just looked like the extending root of a cottonwood, spreading violently now that they had been fed by sun and fresh water. But then the more carefully Cash looked, the more he realized it wasn't a root or a branch, it was a human leg, blue jean covered in dirt. Cash gasped, but Brownie remained calm, unshaken. And as his eyes focused against the glare, Cash recognized those damned motorcycle boots. Maneuvering Brownie over to a tree, he steadied his horse, then dismounted—making his way to those boots, that leg.

"Why am I not surprised to find you here?" he asked Travis.

Travis didn't turn his head to look, instead leaned against the cottonwood trunk, hands behind his head—chewing on a piece of straw.

"I come down here sometimes," was all he said.

Cash walked past, all the way to the river's edge, boot tips playing close alongside. He stood with his back to Travis, keeping his eyes focused in one direction—away.

"Yeah, well I come down here sometimes, too." The levee would always be their home.

After that, they said nothing for awhile—adjusting to one another's presence. Cash crouched down, playing his hands lightly on the water. The river was swollen and opaque. The rapid feel of heat on the back of his neck made Cash want to plunge into that water. Perhaps when he would come back up, brown with mud himself, he would be clean—like in a newborn's baptism. He straightened.

"I figured that it was you when I heard the horse coming up." Travis sat up, brushing himself. With an unusual, rugged appeal, he allowed a grin to cross his lips. As if he should be sliding onto the worn seat of a Harley, the muscular carved boy stretched his arms out and yawned. In spite of the excess roll of weight that had now assumed its home around his once, tight waist, he looked good bare-chested, with a black leather vest, chain link belt, and obsidian wavy hair. Beside him, was what had been Clayton's old cowboy hat—all curled-up on the bills and full of grease stains. As he picked it up, ready to position it on his head, something changed his mind, and he put it back down.

Of course they both remembered the first time they had come here. It was like yesterday, or maybe the day before that. But it was forever ago as well, changed as they now were. Cash couldn't decide the exact amount of time that had passed. Or was it experience that stretched between that day to this? Recalling the sweetness of Travis' body the very first time—the day when they discovered not only each other, but their very selves, he felt a tingle shoot up his spine. Why he would ever forget those first sweet kisses, the embrace of a kind never felt before and everything that happened thereafter.

I'm only eighteen years old, he reminded himself. *Is this what the rest of my life is going to be like?*

"You remember the first time we came here?" Travis suddenly asked, breaking the spell.

"You think I'd forget?" Cash's voice choked.

"Well, there was a time when I'd have believed that. But now, with forgetting being what we tend to do…"

The air stirred gently. Funny how not long ago Cash had longed for summer, but he would have wished eternal winter in exchange for what this summer had brought him, if he realized what that wanting meant.

"I never forgot, Travis. I just got sidetracked."

At that, Travis jumped up. In a few long strides, he was beside Cash. His closeness made Cash shiver, with both desire and fear. Somehow he wanted to just close his eyes and will himself back to that first day. He knew he could take his life from there into a different direction.

"Some serious sidetracking you do there, Cash." Travis' words were hard, but his voice was gentle. "God Almighty, it's a wonder we haven't *all* died along with it."

"Yeah, well I had to work through things." There was still a hint of defense in his bones. "Besides, you know that what I did was for the sake of others. A good man can't just let people suffer." Surely Travis could see that.

The sky was the bluest Cash had seen in a long time. By now, there wasn't a cloud to be seen. For some reason, Lee came before Cash's internal eyes, clearly as if he were standing there beside the both of them. Of course he was there. It would be a long time before he would go… if ever. Cash wasn't sure that he wanted him to go, either.

Touching Cash, Travis spoke with a lowered voice, "Just remember who you're sacrificing on the altar."

"I ain't gonna ask your forgiveness, or anythin' else like that, Travis." The words came forth unhurriedly, very carefully. "I'm just gonna ask that you try to understand, try…"

"I have and I will," sighed Travis. "Every time you head to Great Falls, I remind myself to do just that."

Suddenly, a little girl floated into his inner vision—replacing the one of her father. He knew somewhere down the future her life would entwine with theirs. It would become deep… and it would be permanent. Ironically, seeing that brought him peace. It would take time for Travis to share the vision. Eventually, he would. Cash knew.

"You know, Travis," Cash started up again, hoping the words would come out right for once, "I don't expect much from people, or from life. I just do what I do, and I sometimes I make mistakes—big ones, little ones. But one mistake I never, ever made…"

He turned to the face he loved more than any other in the world. "…that was not lettin' you into my life."

Reaching deep in his pocket, his fingers clasped the cold, round object and lifted it out into the brilliant sunlight. "Been meanin' to give this to you for some time."

Travis gasped. He took a step back.

Allowing its reflection to radiate against the sapphire blue of his lover's eyes, Cash softly said, "Here…"

As if taking that final step of what he had originally planned to do all along, he tenderly reached for the big athlete's hand… and holding those 'incredible' fingers, he gently slipped the diamond ring over each knuckle to rest securely at the base of a willing and ready wedding finger. "To my husband… from this time forth and forever more. I love you, Travis. I always have… 'n I always will."

This time, the big, audacious jock was speechless, without prosecution—tears forming in his eyes.

"I lied to you, Cash." Travis allowed himself a small smile. "I come down here all the time, hoping you'll come by. I've been coming down for weeks… waiting… patiently waiting."

"Oh God, Travis." Cash replied—willing himself deep into those enormous arms. He needed to hear that.

The wind blew. Whispering something in both their ears. Or maybe it was just a thought in the cowboy's mind…

Because when I let you in my life, Travis, I let in the whirlwind…wild and all-consuming. I've opened that gate, and I'm standing aside while I let it in. And I will open the gate, again and again, if need be.

Travis sighed and looked up into the blazing, summer sun. Giving a soft chuckle, he replied, "I love you too, babe… the entire damned world can testify that I love you with all my crazy heart."

And together they kissed and embraced until the sun began to set under the stretching shadows of a great, big, starry Montana sky.

The End

* quote from Tex, S. E. Hinton, Scholastic, Inc. (1979)

or reproduction of any of the characters or scenes is prohibited by law. All images and files regarding this work are copyrighted. They can be downloaded for personal viewing only, and may not be redistributed nor posted on any other sites, new groups, interest groups or publications without written permission of Steven Bryan Gonzales. The stories, characters and situations depicted in "Under the Big Sky" and in all publications affiliated with this work are entirely fictional, and any resemblance with real life characters or incidents is purely coincidental.

About Bryan Gonzales...

Bryan is guy with a big, warm heart.

Born and raised in Montana, he grew up with a strong sense of commitment. Just as he's determined to do his best in working and studying, he strives to give 100% toward the relationships in his life. He believes we should never take people for granted.

Bryan's mission, with *Under the Big Sky*, is to tell the reader the worth of friends. Bar-none, we need each other—through thick and thin. In a day and age where people are quick to toss in the dishrag, it's his desire to challenge that attitude and encourage us to hang in there—especially with those we love.

There is NOTHING that cannot be worked through—even though it might seem impossible, *unlivable* at the moment. Even more important... violence should NEVER be an option.

Attending Northwestern College in Minneapolis—graduating with a Bachelor of Arts in Psychology of Counseling/Ministries, Bryan has come to acknowledge that we are ALL important—that we are not the 'cheap commodity' which contemporary culture continually claims.

Bryan has worked at the University of Louisville as a Program Coordinator for the 1st and 2nd year medical students. He is currently employed at Indiana State University—coordinating their distance and alternative education programs in a rural area called the Hoosier Uplands.

Printed in the United States
150877LV00001B/141/A

9 781425 965242